TWO KISSES FOR CHRISTMAS

The Snow Globe

The Nine Lives of Christmas

TWO NOVELS IN ONE

Sheila Roberts

St. Martin's Paperbacks

These are works of fiction. All of the characters, organizations, and events portrayed in these novels are either products of the author's imagination or are used fictitiously.

First published in the United States by St. Martin's Paperbacks, an imprint of St. Martin's Publishing Group.

TWO KISSES FOR CHRISTMAS

For information, address St. Martin's Publishing Group, 120 Broadway, New York, NY 10271.

www.stmartins.com

ISBN: 978-1-250-78066-9

Our books may be purchased in bulk for promotional, educational, or business use. Please contact your local bookseller or the Macmillan Corporate and Premium Sales Department at 1-800-221-7945, ext. 5442, or by email at MacmillanSpecialMarkets@macmillan.com.

Printed in the United States of America

10 9 8 7 6 5 4 3 2 1

Acclaim for the Novels of Sheila Roberts

"An absolutely wonderful holiday treat, full of warmth and charm and second chances. It's the perfect stocking stuffer."
—Kristin Hannah

"This lighthearted and charming read will appeal to fans of Kristin Hannah's magical, light romances and readers who enjoyed Roberts' previous holiday offerings." —*Library Journal* (starred review)

"Roberts' charming holiday-themed contemporary story set in the Seattle area offers hope, comfort, and a second chance for those who believe, and a nudge to change the minds of those who don't." —*Booklist*

"Roberts' witty and effervescently funny novel will warm hearts. Realistic characters populate the pages of this captivating story, which is a great escape from the hustle and bustle."
—*Romantic Times* (Top Pick)

"Hands down, this has to be the best Christmas book I have read. The characters are so meticulously developed; I had to doublecheck to see if it really was a work of fiction." —J. Kaye's Book Blog

"Roberts manages to avoid genre clichés and crafts a heartfelt novel with nuggets of life truths." —*The Press & Sun Bulletin*

"Sheila Roberts makes me laugh. I read her work and came away inspired, hopeful, and happy." —Debbie Macomber,
New York Times bestselling author

"A fast, fresh, fun, and funny story by a major new talent."
—Susan Wiggs, *New York Times* bestselling author

"Fans will relish the adventures of the three amigas as all kinds of relationships blossom." —*Midwest Book Review*

"Sheila Roberts will make you laugh and cry with her latest novel about three women facing life's trials and tribulations."
—*The National Examiner*

THE
SNOW
GLOBE

For Rosebud

ACKNOWLEDGMENTS

This was such a fun book to write! Of course it's always fun when you get to work with great people. And I want to take a moment to thank some of them right now. Thanks to my buddy Ruth, for all the great insight and encouragement. Huge thanks to Susan Wiggs, Elsa Watson, and Anjali Banerjee, for keeping an eagle eye on my work in progress. Most of all, thanks to my fabulous agent, Paige Wheeler, and my amazing editor, Rose Hilliard, and all the super people at St. Martin's Press, who worked so hard to help this story become a book. May you all see your dreams come true this Christmas!

ONE

Something drew Kiley Gray to the antique shop. It could have been the carousel horse in the window or the sight of tables and shelves beyond, crammed with cast-off treasures. Whatever was in there calling to her, she knew she had to go in. She was a big believer in that sort of thing.

Actually, Kiley was a big believer, period. She'd been sure Santa was real until she was ten and even after waking up on Christmas Eve to discover her father hanging her filled stocking on the mantel, she kept pretending for another two years. She'd believed in Prince Charming and Mr. Right clear through college. She'd even believed in happy endings until just this past October when her boyfriend Jeremy Horne dumped her at her own Halloween party (how was that for tacky?), announcing that he couldn't fight his attraction for her sister any longer.

It had been a very scary Halloween.

A bell chimed over the door as Kiley entered the shop and her nose twitched as she caught a whiff of dust.

Another shopper, a middle-aged woman in a stylish wool coat, stood at the counter, raving over the pink Depression glass pitcher she'd found. "And just in the nick of time," she added. "I'm going to have to dash to make that ferry." With hurried thanks, she took the piece the shop owner had carefully wrapped and hurried to the door, stuffing bills in her wallet as she went.

One fluttered to the floor and Kiley scooped it up. It was a fifty, maybe not a lot for this woman, who was well dressed and obviously had money to burn, but to Kiley it was a fortune. "Wait. You dropped this."

"Oh. Thanks," said the woman, barely looking at it. She stuffed it in her purse and hurried out the door.

The shopkeeper, a portly man with thinning, gray hair, smiled at Kiley. "People get in too big of a hurry."

"I can't afford to be in *that* big of a hurry," she said. She probably couldn't afford to be in here at all. But browsing didn't cost anything, she told herself as she drifted to where the carousel horse stood frozen in mid-prance. Who had owned this and how had it wound up languishing here? Kiley gave it a comforting pat then wandered past a table overflowing with nautical knickknacks toward an antique sideboard displaying tarnished silver and faded china, waiting for their glory days to return.

Then she saw something out of the corner of her eye. She turned and moved to the far side of the shop for a closer look. Tucked behind a clock with a brass horse and a chipped crystal vase sat an old snow globe. She might never have noticed it if it hadn't gotten caught by a stray sunbeam that managed to slip past the gray clouds outside and in through the window.

She picked it up, charmed by the scene inside the thick glass: a toyshop in the center of an Alpine village. She gave the globe a shake and watched the snow swirl around the little angel standing guard in front of the shop. It was simply too charming not to buy. Anyway, purchasing treasures was an integral part of any girls' getaway weekend so, in a way, she was almost obligated.

She took it to where the shop owner sat behind his cash register, now reading a book. "I didn't see a price tag on this. I'm just wondering what you want for it."

She gulped when he told her. Not exactly a wise purchase for a girl who had a steady job, let alone one who was now unemployed. Maybe purchasing treasures wasn't such an integral part of a girls' getaway weekend. At least not this treasure, not this weekend. Heck, at that price, never.

The man looked over his reading glasses at her and smiled. "But, I think, for the right buyer, I could come down in price."

Not enough, she was sure. Still, she couldn't resist asking, "What does the right buyer look like?" Hopefully, a skinny woman edging toward thirty with unruly brown hair, hazel eyes, a fashionably full mouth, and a nose she hated.

"It's not exactly about looks," the shop owner said. "It's more about where you are in life. You see, this little snow globe has quite a story to tell."

"I like stories," said Kiley, leaning her elbows on the counter.

"This one starts back when snow globes were first being made. Nobody knows the exact date, but the first one appeared at the Paris Exposition in 1878, and by 1879 at least five companies were producing snow globes and selling them throughout Europe. The woman who brought this to me claims it was one of them, so you can see it's very valuable."

"If it's that valuable I wonder why she didn't take it to *Antiques Roadshow*," Kiley mused. It seemed like the kind of thing that would go for a king's ransom at Sotheby's.

The man nodded his agreement. "She had her reasons. You see, its age isn't the only thing that makes it valuable." He removed his reading glasses and set aside his book. "Would you like to hear more?"

"I'm not in a hurry," said Kiley. "But I hope this story has a happy ending. I'm kind of in need of happy endings these days."

"Are you? Well, you be the judge."

Chicago, December 1880

It had been one year since Otto Schwartz had lost his whole world. And he was still alive, if one could call moving through each day like a ghost living. This particular day he stood at his toyshop window, watching snow carpet the street. Delivery wagons passed, people walked by with paper-wrapped parcels, happily shopping for Christmas.

Two children, a boy and a girl bundled in heavy coats, hats, and mittens, ran ahead of their mother and stopped in front of the shop window to peer at Otto's display of porcelain dolls, tin toys, and stuffed animals. They pressed their faces to the glass and pointed excitedly. One even smiled at Otto. He tried to smile back. A ghost of a smile.

The woman caught up with them, keeping her face averted. Taking the children by the hand, she led them off down the street. He could hardly blame her for not wanting to look at him. His toys called to one and all to step inside and find fun and laughter. But once inside people found Otto and they hurriedly left, recalling more pressing errands.

He watched them walk away and sighed. Children and toys were meant to go together. Men who owned toyshops should have children. And wives.

The sigh became a sob. He turned his back on the snowy Chicago street scene, then dug a handkerchief out of the pocket of his black suit and blew his nose. At least he'd tried to smile.

But the effort was coming late. People expected a man

to mourn when he lost his wife and baby—a full year in black and no social engagements (as if he had wanted any)—but they also expected a man to continue to run his business, to set aside his sorrow and take care of his customers. Otto couldn't even care for his own bleeding heart. How could he be expected to care if little Johann would like a wooden marionette or to take an interest in which porcelain doll little Ingrid would want most? At first he had been bereft. He had closed up the shop and shut himself inside his darkened house. Everyone in the city's German community had understood. But finally his sister had shoved Brötchen, sliced ham, and an egg under his nose and commanded that he eat. And that he then go and reopen his shop.

"You are not the first man to lose a wife in childbirth. You will not be the last," she'd said sternly. "Liesel and Gottlieb are in heaven."

"And I am in hell," he had growled, causing his sister to gasp.

She had recovered quickly, shaking a finger at him and retorting, "Then I suggest you crawl out. It is time. You have a business to run."

And so he had gone from bereft to morose, and his friends and neighbors tried to be patient. But when he went from morose to ill-tempered people failed to understand and he lost many a customer. Now Christmas was right around the corner and Otto was trying to remember how to smile. Except that was almost impossible with the snow coming down outside, reminding him of happier times in the village in the Bavarian alps where he had grown up, with people strolling by outside on their way to warm, happy homes.

Peter the mail carrier entered the shop, bringing with him the scent of snow. From somewhere outside the sound of a child's laugh slipped in also, grabbing at Otto's heart.

"Otto, look what I have. Something from your sister

in France," Peter called cheerfully, his grin making his moustache dance. If Peter weren't so content with delivering mail he would have made a great diplomat. He was always happy. Even on Otto's grumpiest days Peter entered the shop smiling and left the same way. "Open it and let's see what it is," he suggested. A package from France was worth a five-minute delay in his deliveries.

Otto took the package, carefully unwrapping it and prying open the wooden box. Nested inside the excelsior he found something more amazing than all the toys in his shop put together.

"What is it?" asked Peter, his voice filled with awe.

"I don't know," said Otto. He picked up the delicate item. It easily fit in the palm of his large hand. A glass globe sat on an ornate ceramic base. Inside it was a nostalgic scene of a toyshop that looked like his father's toyshop on a street in what could have been his village in the Bavarian Alps. Amazing! How had the maker managed that small wonder? The mountains, the snow-capped trees—oh yes, it could have been his village! In front of the toyshop stood a beautiful angel in a white gown with golden hair and blue eyes. She looked just like Liesel. Swallowing the lump in his throat, Otto set the work of art on his counter.

"Those Frenchmen," said Peter, shaking his head in amazement. "What will they think of next?" He motioned to the notepaper still lying in the excelsior. "Read the note and see what it's called."

Otto picked up the paper with trembling fingers and read.

> *Dear brother,*
> *I know it has been more than a year and you still grieve deeply. Henri commissioned this water globe to be made especially for you in the hope that it would bring you comfort.*

"A water globe? Is there water in there?" Peter picked up the globe to examine it.

Otto frowned at him, took the globe from his hand and set it back on the counter, then returned to the letter.

Henri has a friend who makes these in his factory. They are becoming quite popular. They are some-times called snow globes, a term I much prefer. If you shake it you will see why. Perhaps one day you would like to sell snow globes in your shop. But for now, we want you to have this special one to keep, in memory of your dear Liesel and the baby. Of course, this cannot bring them back, but per-haps it can bring you hope. I have prayed that it will.

Your loving sister, Berthe

"Shake it," urged Peter.

Otto picked up the snow globe and gave it a tentative jiggle.

"Will you look at that!" Peter exclaimed. "I've never seen such a thing in all my life."

Neither had Otto. He stared in amazement as a tiny blizzard swirled around the angel. The snow settled and he shook the globe again, starting a fresh flurry. He wanted to cry. Or laugh. Instead, he smiled.

Peter spread the news of Otto's unusual present throughout the community and soon people were ventur-ing into the store to see the amazing snow globe and ooh and ah over the little scene inside.

"It's lovely," said Mrs. Schmidt. "And the angel re-minds me of your wife."

Otto sighed. "Yes, she does." And later that day, after the customers had all left, he couldn't resist holding the thing and gazing inside at the little angel, wishing she could speak to him.

But what was this? The angel's hair, somehow, appeared darker. Was he imagining it? He shook the globe and started the tiny flakes spinning. Once more they settled at the angel's feet. Her hair still looked darker. Perhaps it had always been dark. Perhaps it had only seemed lighter because of wishful thinking on his part.

Disappointed, he set the snow globe down, wishing it would show him what he wanted to see.

Christmas was two weeks away when a man and woman entered the store. Strangers. Except with her dark hair and sweet smile the woman wasn't a stranger. Otto realized he had seen her before, inside the snow globe. He tried not to stare, but it was almost impossible.

The man spoke. "My sister and I are looking for a present for our little sister. We thought, perhaps, you could help us."

"Of course," said Otto, straightening his coat. "I will be happy to. Are you visiting?"

"No," said the woman. "Our family has moved here recently. From Garmisch-Partenkirchen."

She had the softest voice, like an angel, thought Otto, and smiled.

Fawn Island, The Pacific Northwest

Kiley smiled at the shop owner after he'd finished his story. "I take it she was the angel Otto saw in the snow globe."

He grinned. "So the story goes. Two Christmases later Otto had both a new wife and a new baby." He motioned to the lovely antique sitting on the counter. "That was passed down through Otto's family from generation to generation, always bringing hope when someone needed it most. At least that's what Mrs. Ackerman says."

"The woman you got it from," said Kiley and he nodded. "But why would she let it go?"

"She's Otto's last descendant, and she has no children. She felt it was time for it to pass on to fresh hands. But not necessarily to a collector." He gave a little shrug. "So she sent it off with a hope and a prayer that the snow globe will work a holiday miracle for someone new." He cocked an eyebrow. "Would you say you qualify?"

No boyfriend, no job? "I'd say I'm overqualified." Kiley looked at the little globe sitting on its ornate base. Costly as it was, she was sure it was underpriced. Even if it had gone for a small fortune at some fancy auction house it probably would have been underpriced. It symbolized hope, and how did you put a price tag on hope? She chewed her lip, trying to figure out how she could possibly afford it. Of course, she couldn't. But, darn, she needed it!

The shop owner smiled. "Tell you what. I'll take fifty percent off."

Fifty percent off—it was a sign. How could she refuse? She had just swallowed the last of her doubts and handed over her charge card when the bell over the shop door jingled. "We came to save you from yourself," said a familiar voice. Suz.

She turned to see her friends Suzanne Stowe and Allison Wright entering the shop. Suzanne was small; Allison was taller and about three sizes bigger. Both were blondes. A gust of wind whipped in with them, bringing the smell of Northwest rain into the stuffy little shop.

Suzanne looked at the assortment of china, knickknacks, and mysterious kitchen tools from another era, and wrinkled her perfect nose, hunching inside her North Face jacket like a turtle pulling into its shell. She didn't like the smell of anything old. Pottery Barn and Crate and Barrel were more her style.

But Allison looked eagerly around like a kid on a treasure hunt. She joined Kiley at the counter, holding out a disposable cup and sending the aroma of coffee dancing around Kiley's nose. "For energy."

"I don't need a latte, really," insisted Kiley, feeling guilty that her friends were picking up the tab for all her treats.

"Sure you do," said Suzanne. She started a fast stroll down an aisle, a petite vision in Northwest casual, her jeans showing off perfect thighs, her blond ponytail swinging.

Allison pointed to the bubble-wrapped snow globe the shop owner was slipping into a bag. "Did you get something cool?"

Kiley could feel a blush race across her face. She'd almost backed out of this weekend with her two best friends, claiming to be too broke, and now here she was spending a fortune on something her common sense insisted she didn't need. "He gave me a deal," she explained.

Allison smiled at her. "It's okay, Kiles. After all you've been through you deserve a treat."

"It's more than a treat," insisted Kiley. It was . . . well, she wasn't sure. She only knew it was somehow meant for her.

Suzanne had finished her quick tour of the store and now she joined them at the counter. "I'm hungry. Anybody ready for lunch?"

Allison nodded and followed Suzanne to the door and Kiley thanked the shop owner and hurried after them.

"I can't believe you found something in that musty old place," said Suzanne as they started for their favorite restaurant.

"Wait till you see it," said Kiley.

"Okay, I'm dying of curiosity," said Allison after they were seated inside the Chanterelle and had ordered the soup of the day and some of the restaurant's herbed bread. "Let's see your bargain."

Kiley pulled out her purchase and told them its legend.

The waiter arrived with a basket of warm bread. Allison started to reach for it, but then, true to her resolve to not get carried away with the carbs, picked up the snow globe instead and jiggled it. All three women watched the tiny snowflakes drift around the little angel. "It is lovely," Allison murmured as she set it on the table.

"But what a bunch of bull," Suzanne said. Her cell phone rang and she reached into her purse.

Allison frowned. "I thought you turned that off."

"I had to make a call," Suzanne said defensively. Suzanne always had to make a call. If not to check in on her five-year-old daughter, Bryn, then to see how things were going with her latest real estate deal.

Like Kiley, Suzanne had come close to canceling on their weekend. Money wasn't a problem for her, but her busy schedule was the sworn enemy of girlfriend time. It happened a lot lately and Allison had finally put her foot down, insisting they all go so they could recharge and reconnect.

Allison's frown grew deeper when she realized Suzanne was talking to the agent she partnered with at Dreamscape Realty.

Getting the message, Suzanne finished her business quickly. "There. Done," she announced.

"Prove it and turn off your cell," Allison commanded.

Suzanne practically paled. "I can't. What if there's an emergency?"

"At home? Guy can handle it," Allison said.

"I know. I meant at work."

"That's why you have Julie," Kiley reminded her.

Suz turned off her phone with a frown.

Allison smiled, happy to have won the battle. "We need this, and it's not a getaway if you're not getting away."

"Fine," said Suzanne, "but tonight I'm checking my messages." She picked up Kiley's snow globe and examined it. "This is kind of cool," she admitted.

"And who knows," added Allison, "maybe it will bring something great into your life this holiday season."

Kiley sighed. "I almost wish I could climb into it and stay. At least until after Thanksgiving." Then she wouldn't have to face her unfaithful boyfriend and her sister the traitor.

"I'd join you in a heartbeat," Allison said with a sigh. "I'd put my grandma in there, too. Gosh, I hate to face the holidays without her."

"You'll get through them," Suzanne assured her.

Kiley took the snow globe back and studied it. "What is it about these things that makes you wish you could live in one?"

"Escape," said Suzanne. The waiter set steaming bowls of mushroom soup in front of them and she inhaled deeply and smiled. "Everyone has times when they don't like their life."

"Like every time I have to hang out with my family," Allison said with a shake of her head.

Kiley could understand Allison wanting to escape. She had seen just enough of her friend's family to know she didn't want to see any more. Well, except for Allison's grandma. But Suz? That seemed hard to believe.

"Maybe that's why we love things like this," Allison

mused. "They give us hope that our lives can be different, better."

The little snow globe would have to work pretty hard to get Kiley to that point. But, hey, she still believed in miracles.

TWO

It would be a miracle if she didn't throttle her younger sister, Kiley decided, as she got ready to drive over to her parents' house on Thanksgiving Day. Well, she'd just avoid the traitor. And the two-timer. She had plenty of other people to focus on: Mom and Dad, her older brother, Corey, and his wife, Tara, and their four-year-old twins, Beau and Christopher, and her aunt and uncle and the cousins. She would simply pretend her sister didn't exist.

It was difficult to pretend Gwinnie didn't exist, though, when she did such a good job of grabbing the spotlight. Today she would show up in tight jeans and a sweater with a low V-neck, and she'd wear her long fake-blond hair down so she could flip it back over her shoulder on a regular basis. Kiley could do the hair flip thing, too. Only her hair wasn't blond so obviously it didn't have the same effect. Why hadn't Jeremy told her he preferred blondes? Or maybe it was that he preferred former cheerleaders to runners. Or maybe he didn't know what he wanted besides showing up and ruining her Thanksgiving.

"If you need to skip this year, everyone will understand," Mom had said. She'd phoned Kiley when Gwinnie arrived with Jeremy in tow. "I'm so sorry," Mom had added. "I never dreamed your sister would be so thoughtless. And Jeremy, I don't even know what to do with him."

Kiley could think of a couple of things, but none were anything a girl should say to her mother. "I'm coming," she'd said between gritted teeth. Those two had ruined her Halloween. She wasn't going to let them ruin her Thanksgiving, too.

She teamed her hottest sweater (red—men loved red, right?) with black pants and slipped into her sexy black heels. That would show him what he lost. She also packed her tennis shoes and sweats because she would be expected to participate in the annual post-dinner football game at the East Queen Anne playground: touch football, two hands anywhere—a rule the guys had established once they all started getting girlfriends.

The thought of seeing Jeremy putting his hands all over Gwinnie made Kiley's stomach clench. That won't happen, she told herself. Gwinnie had been opting out on football since two Thanksgivings ago when she fell and wrenched her knee. She had milked that injury for all it was worth, letting the cousins carry her to the car, taking over Dad's easy chair in the living room with an ice pack and occasionally whimpering to make sure she got waited on hand and foot the rest of the day. Not that Kiley had complained. She'd felt bad for Gwinnie and had done her share of the waiting. After all, she loved her little sister. Or had. Now she wasn't so sure.

Of course you love her, she reminded herself, as she stood in front of the bedroom mirror for one last check. Okay, so Kiley had hazel eyes, not blue. And so her nose was a little long. She still wasn't an arf-arf, and she was a good person. She was not the problem. Neither was

Gwinnie. It was Jeremy. He was the one who had done the dumping. He was the one who had chased after someone else.

But Gwinnie didn't have to let him catch her.

That was love for you. It trampled everything in its path, even sisters.

She looked to where the snow globe sat on her dresser. Nothing had changed inside it. The little angel still stood duty in the Alpine village, guarding the toyshop.

Kiley shook her head in disgust. *What had you expected to see in there, Jeremy on bended knee in front of you, begging you to take him back?*

That was not going to happen. He wouldn't beg and she wouldn't take him back even if he did. She ran a finger over the snow globe. "I know I'm not widowed like Otto, but I could sure use some help." She picked it up and gave it a shake. Snow swirled and then settled on the cobblestone street. The scene remained the same.

She returned it to the dresser with a sigh. If this were a movie the angel would pop out of its glass cage and wrap her safely in those gold-tipped wings or she would get pulled right into that idyllic scene and meet Prince Charming. But she was no Disney princess and she had Thanksgiving dinner to get to.

She climbed into her Honda and drove under a grumpy gray Seattle sky from her two-bedroom condo on Kinnear to her parents' brick Tudor on the other side of Queen Anne Hill. Halfway there Amanda Overmyer came on the radio, belting "I Hate Myself for Loving You," and Kiley shut her off with a growl.

She arrived to find an army of vehicles already lined up along the parking strip and across the street, everything from SUVs to a Prius, telling her that she was the last one to arrive.

She winced at the sight of Jeremy's secondhand BMW.

He had probably been the first one through the door. Dad would have let him in with a grunt and then left it to Gwinnie to entertain him. Dad's observation on the situation: "The dumb kid doesn't know what he wants."

Mom, ever the peacemaker, would be nice to him. After all, she had to. He was likely still going to be her son-in-law. Her take on the situation? "Obviously, he wasn't the right one for you, sweetie, and that means someone better is right around the corner. Meanwhile, keep the ring." Kiley had, and she'd sold it on eBay. So at least she wouldn't have to worry about condo payments for a couple of months. Not much of a silver lining, but it was something. As for the "someone better" waiting around the corner, sometimes Kiley wondered how far away that corner was or if it was even in the same city.

She took a deep breath. Then she gathered her purse, her football clothes, and the grocery bag with the punch makings she'd brought, and left the safe cocoon of her car.

Although her parents had done some renovating after they bought the house in the eighties, they had kept intact its best features—the old stone fireplace, the hardwood floors, and the arched doorways. Mom wasn't much of a gardener, but she'd fallen in love with the little rose garden in the corner of the front yard and had done her best to keep the roses healthy. Another one of the things she'd insisted on keeping was the enormous monkey tree that grew near the front walk. "It has character," she maintained. That it did—an evil character. The thing was the size of a small skyscraper and needed to be trimmed. Its prickly branches reached for Kiley as she made her way up the walk.

The front door was unlocked, and as Kiley let herself in the aroma of roasting turkey and the sound of a football game on TV greeted her along with raucous male laughter punctuated by the high-pitched squeals of

a child. She rounded the front hall corner in time to see
her burly cousin Mark tossing her four-year-old-nephew
Beau into the air. The child's brown curls bounced and
he let out a fresh shriek. If Beau was having this much
fun it meant his twin Christopher couldn't be far behind.
Sure enough, Beau's mirror image charged into the living
room from the other direction and latched onto Mark's
legs. Her other cousin, Zach, who was equally muscled,
pried him off and sent him in the air, too. Meanwhile,
Pansy, her parents' toy poodle, added to the confusion by
yapping at them all.

Next to her Uncle Al, her brother Corey sprawled
on the couch, a freckle-faced giant, grinning compla-
cently while his cousins tossed the boys around like Nerf
footballs. Dad was being one with his easy chair, happily tolerating the abuse of his only grandchildren. And
there, on a chair in the other corner of the room, sat
Jeremy, resplendent in holiday casual clothes and acting as
if he still belonged here. Which he did. Which made her
stomach clench again.

Kiley was wondering if she was going to cry when Corey happened to glance her way and see her standing in
the doorway. "Hey Road Runner," he called. "About time
you got here."

Road Runner. It had been her nickname since she took
up track in high school.

"Hi, Super Jock," she shot back. Her brother was
now a football coach at a small high school in eastern
Washington and she didn't get to see him nearly as often
as she'd have liked. He still looked fit enough to get on
the field and mow down a quarterback. When he first
heard about the breakup he'd called and offered to crush
Jeremy for her, adding, "Gwinnie can always find another idiot."

The sight of her made the idiot squirm in his seat. A bigger woman would have felt bad for him, Kiley supposed.

"Hey, Kiles," said Mark. He set Beau down and came to scoop her up in a bear hug. "You're lookin' good."

She couldn't resist stealing a glance in Jeremy's direction. Did he think she was looking good? Did he wonder what the heck he'd been thinking when he dumped her?

He was licking his lips, running a finger along the collar of his Polo shirt as if his neck was being squeezed by an invisible necktie. He nodded in her direction and gave her an uncertain smile. She ignored it, hugging each of her little nephews, who had started clamoring for her attention. She kissed her father on the top of his head, waved at her other cousin and her uncle, and then left to deliver the punch makings to the kitchen. There. That had been easy.

Except Jeremy was only one half of the traitor team. Gwinnie still waited in the kitchen.

Kiley took a deep breath. *You can do this.* She forced herself to walk through the dining room to the kitchen and run the next gauntlet. Grandma was still in charge of the gravy and stood at the stainless-steel stove, wearing her favorite slacks with the elastic waistband and a floral blouse, wiping her brow and stirring while Mom checked on her famous pumpkin rolls.

At Mom's state-of-the-art refrigerator, Kiley's sister-in-law, Tara, six months pregnant, paused in the middle of handing a huge bowl of fruit salad to Aunt Marion, gaping at Kiley as if uncertain where to place her family loyalties.

And, speaking of loyalties, there at the sink, whipping cream so she would have an excuse to continually dip her fingers in the bowl and sample, stood Gwinnie, dressed in jeans and the low-cut sweater Kiley had predicted she'd be wearing. Blond, blue-eyed, and beautiful—every man's dream.

Kiley narrowed her eyes and marched into the kitchen with murder in her heart.

THREE

The only thing that saved Gwinnie from annihilation was Mom looking up from the oven and beaming lovingly at Kiley, saying, "Hello, sweetie." She took out the baking sheet with the rolls and then hurried forward to kiss Kiley, cutting off access to Gwinnie the traitor. Mom was obviously psychic and knew what Kiley was contemplating.

Or maybe she's simply glad to see you, Kiley told herself, and hugged her mother. "Sorry I'm late."

"It's okay." Mom planted a kiss on her cheek. "We're just glad you're here."

Kiley wished she could say the same thing. Normally, the smell of roasting turkey set her mouth watering with anticipation, and the sight of her family filled her with joy. Today the smells and sights of the holiday were wasted on her.

She forced a smile and gave her sister-in-law a wave and a hi. Poor Tara. She was trying, like Switzerland, to remain neutral.

"You're just in time to help get food on the table," said

Kiley's aunt, stopping to kiss her before proceeding on to the dining room with the fruit salad.

. Kiley went to where Grandma stood at the stove and kissed her wrinkled cheek. Grandma studied her carefully. "How are you?"

What a loaded question! "I'm fine," she told both Grandma and herself. She'd be even finer once this day was over.

"Hi, Kiles," said a deliberately perky voice.

She turned with a frown to see Gwinnie, wearing a false smile, determined to act as if nothing was wrong.

A montage of scenes raced through Kiley's mind: she and Gwinnie wrapping a loop of elastic around chair legs and playing Chinese jump rope; Gwinnie asking Kiley to teach her how to make gum wrapper braids, and then hair braids; the two of them sprawled on the couch watching a late-night horror movie. The memories weren't enough to heal the hurt. In fact, they only inspired her to contemplate snatching the electric mixer and tangling its beaters in Gwinnie's hair.

"Hi, Gwinnie." She managed to get the words out, but she just couldn't add any warmth to them.

Gwinnie frowned and returned her attention to the whipping cream.

Kiley sighed inwardly and set her bag of goodies on the table next to where the punch bowl sat waiting. "I guess I'd better make this punch and take it out to the dining room," she muttered and got to work.

The kitchen went back to its busy buzz with the women putting finishing touches on the many dishes bound for the table and talk centered on the tasks at hand—"Do we have another serving spoon somewhere?" . . . "I think the gravy's ready." . . . "Gwinnie, stop whipping that cream before you turn it to butter."

This last comment came from Grandma, who was looking at her granddaughter with irritation.

Once upon a time—like last year, even—Gwinnie would have offered a beater to Kiley to lick. Today, she simply removed the beaters and laid them in the sink, then retreated to the fridge to put away the whipping cream for later when the pumpkin pie made its appearance.

Fine. Kiley didn't want to lick the beater anyway. She took the bowl of baby peas her mother handed her along with the mashed potatoes and went to the dining room.

"While you're at it, tell the men we're ready to eat," said Mom.

It didn't take more than one announcement to bring the men to the table. "This looks great," said Kiley's father, beaming with satisfaction at the feast laid before them, the fine china and crystal, and the cornucopia centerpiece. "You've outdone yourself this year, love," he told Mom as everyone settled in.

He said the same thing every year. And, as she did every year, Mom rolled her eyes and waved away the compliment. "Hurry up and say grace, John, before the natives get restless."

Dad complied, and the second he was finished the guys were all reaching for food. For the next few minutes, everyone concentrated on filling his or her plate and the conversational landscape was sparse.

Slowly, the time-honored topics surfaced. Which teams were going to the Super Bowl? How Grandpa would have loved to see this growing gang at the table, and, speaking of growing, had Tara and Corey settled on a name for the baby yet? Say, was this a new recipe for candied yams?

"Oh, I just haven't made it in a while," said Mom.

"Was it in the recipe book you gave me when we got married?" asked Tara.

"I think so," said Mom. "If not, let me know and I'll e-mail it to you."

"I want it, too," put in Gwinnie.

"Don't worry. You'll get it, along with all the other family recipes, when you get married," Mom said absently, and then looked like she wished she could swallow her tongue.

An awkward silence landed on the table and camped there. Eyes shot this way and that, everywhere but Kiley's direction. She was aware of Gwinnie regarding her nervously and Jeremy once again trying to loosen that invisible tie, and suddenly felt a lump in her throat the size of a golf ball, but she gamely scooped up a forkful of mashed potatoes and oh-so-calmly inserted them in her mouth.

Grandma came to the rescue. "Recipes might make a nice Christmas present for both our girls. I've been thinking it's time I parted with the one for my Christmas cake."

"I'd love to have that," Tara said eagerly, obviously happy to help steer the conversation in a safer direction.

Kiley kept her eyes on her mashed potatoes.

After dinner the men cleared the table and vanished into the kitchen to wash dishes, while the women lingered over their coffee. Kiley wished she didn't have to linger. Once the kitchen was clean the gang would be off to work up an appetite for pie by playing football. She had no appetite, for either pie or football. How soon till she could leave?

Wait a minute, she thought. *Why should you be the one to leave? The ones to go should be Gwinnie and Jeremy. They're the problem, not you.* She looked across the table to see Gwinnie gnawing her lower lip and watching her, hoping for absolution.

She turned her head.

A few moments later, Corey was leading the pack from

the kitchen. He clapped his hands together and rubbed them eagerly. "Okay, who's ready to get their ass kicked?"

"By who?" retorted Zach, who was now right behind his cousin.

Corey loomed over him. "By me, dude." He cocked his head, motioning for Kiley to follow. "Come on, Road Runner. You're on my team."

Now Kiley could see Jeremy smiling at Gwinnie. "Come on, Gwin," he said.

She shot a look in Kiley's direction. "I don't want to."

"Oh, no," said Zach, hauling her up. "Everybody plays, even sissy girls."

"I want to play," piped Beau.

"Another couple of years, bud," his father said, rumpling his hair.

"But I want to play, too," he whined.

"Me, too," put in his twin.

"Aw, let 'em," said Zach. "Like you said, everybody plays."

"Okay, then. But don't trample 'em," Corey added, pointing a warning finger at Zach.

Tara had come out in time to hear the tail end of the discussion and quickly vetoed her husband's decision. "Some games are for grown-ups and bigger boys. When you're a little bigger you can go," she told the boys firmly. "Anyway, Grandpa and Uncle Al need you two to stay here and play with them so they won't get bored."

"We're going to play some Wii bowling," added Dad, and that was all it took to change the twins' minds about football.

"Maybe I'll stay and play, too," said Kiley. Then she wouldn't have to watch Jeremy stealing kisses and hugging Gwinnie, like he used to do with her.

"Oh, no," said Corey, pulling her away from the table. "You're coming, too. Tara can't play this year, Dad's back is trashed, and Uncle Al's knee hurts. If you don't come we won't have enough people."

It was useless to protest. Kiley went to change. Unlike Gwinnie, who made a production out of everything, it didn't take her long. In comfortable sweats and with her hair caught up in a big bush of a sloppy bun, she felt more like herself. But she didn't look like much, especially when she compared herself to her sister, whose outfit was tight and pink and made her look like a cupcake. Jeremy had obviously done plenty of comparing himself, Kiley thought miserably as Corey loaded her into his car.

The cousins piled into the backseat, leaving Gwinnie and Jeremy to follow in Jeremy's car.

"Okay, what was that stunt about?" Corey demanded as soon as the door was shut.

She tried to play dumb. "What?"

"Hiding at home with Mom and Dad won't help you get past this," he continued.

"Yeah," put in Mark. "Anyway, if you ask me you had a lucky escape."

Some lucky escape. She got out with a broken heart.

"Really," added Zach in disgust. "The guy is a doof."

She turned in her seat to look at him. "What do you mean, he's a doof?"

Zach shrugged. "He just is, Kile. You can do better."

"Well, if he's such a doof why didn't any of you say something when we were first dating?"

"Like you'd have wanted to hear?" retorted Corey.

"Anyway," Mark added with a shrug, "he didn't seem like a total doof back then. But now that he's dumped you and taken up with Gwinnie . . ." Mark didn't finish the sentence, just shook his head.

"He runs like a duck," said Zach.

"Wears a Polo shirt to play football," Corey added with a snort.

He and the cousins were all in old jeans and ripped T-shirts, which they filled out with well-built pecs and abs. Compared to them Jeremy looked . . . small. And inferior.

Except he wasn't. He was sweet and thoughtful and loved to go to movies. Okay, so he'd never had any desire to run with her. They still had lots of fun together. At least they used to.

"Look, Road Runner," said Corey. "I know this is hard, but you've got to believe us when we tell you that losing this clown is really a good thing. He'd have just turned out to be a starter husband for you. He wouldn't have been enough to keep you happy all your life."

"Hell, he won't even be enough for Gwinnie," cracked Zach.

"That'll never last," Mark agreed. "This guy doesn't know what he's doing. By next Thanksgiving he'll be history."

What were they saying? "You think he'll dump Gwinnie?"

"Bank on it," said Corey with a sad shake of the head.

"If she doesn't dump him first," said Zach. "So this year we may as well have some fun," he added with an evil grin that didn't bode well for Jeremy.

Even though she was still mad at her sister, Kiley felt a moment of concern. The men in her family didn't always stay in touch with their feminine sides and if they decided to punish Jeremy it would be sure to upset Gwinnie.

"You guys . . ." she began.

"Don't worry," Corey said easily, cutting off her protest. "We won't hurt him. Much."

Sure enough. As soon as they got to the field and started playing, Jeremy became a tackling dummy. Kiley winced each time he got shoved and pelted with the football. "Sorry, man," said Zach with a smirk, after a bruising that made Kiley wince.

Finally, when Corey took Jeremy down, landing on top of him, a red-faced Gwinnie accused, "You're not supposed to tackle. You're *trying* to hurt him!"

"That was an accident," protested Mark. "Corey tripped."

Gwinnie burst into tears. "You're all being mean."

Jeremy limped over to her and put an arm around her shoulder. "It's okay, Gwin. I'm fine."

"No, it's not." She glared at the others, hands on hips. "You guys don't have any right to treat Jeremy like this."

"Oh, yeah?" retorted Mark. "Well, maybe you didn't have any right to treat Kiley the way you treated her."

The tears were streaming down Gwinnie's perfect face now. "You don't understand. We didn't plan on falling in love. We didn't mean to hurt anyone."

"You did, Gwin," Corey said quietly. "And you never thought about how hard it might be for Kiley today."

"I did so! And it's been hard for me, too." Gwinnie buried her face in her hands and began to cry in earnest.

Watching her, Kiley felt heartsick. What a mess. And maybe some of it was her fault. She should have hugged her sister when she first arrived, been friendly to Jeremy, acted like she didn't care. Then everyone would have been happy and no one would be fighting.

"It's okay," she said, and hugged Gwinnnie.

Gwinnie, ever the drama queen, threw her arms around Kiley and upped the tear production. "Please don't hate me, Kiles. I love him. I can't help it."

"Oh gawd, I'm gonna puke," drawled Zach.

"You are such a spoiled brat," Corey told Gwinnie in disgust and Jeremy, who should have jumped in to defend her, stood there with a spine like a cooked noodle.

He could have said, *Don't blame Gwinnie. This is all my fault. I'm sorry I've screwed up your Thanksgiving and your family.* Why wasn't he saying something? Maybe he didn't want Gwinnie to be upset any further. Or maybe he *was* a doof. Or maybe Kiley was just bitter.

"This is lame," said Mark. "We may as well go back and eat pie."

And so, for the first time ever, the game ended on a sour note.

Back at the house, Dad and Uncle Al were playing Wii with the twins while Pansy yapped encouragement. The women were still parked at the dining room table, visiting. Corey and the cousins went to the punch bowl to rehydrate, Jeremy went to sponge off his dirty pants, and Gwinnie plopped onto the couch to pout.

Kiley decided she'd had enough fun for one day. She gave her mother a kiss on the cheek and said, "I'm going to take off."

"Already?" protested her aunt.

"I think I'm getting a migraine," she lied. Her mother studied her with concern and she felt her face warming under the scrutiny.

Thankfully, Mom didn't ask her what was wrong. Instead, she rose and led Kiley to the kitchen, saying, "Well, then, let's get you some pumpkin pie to take home." Once it was just the two of them, Mom said, "I'm sorry this day has been so hard for you, sweetie, but I'm proud of you for being brave enough to come."

She hugged Kiley, and that broke the dam. "How am I going to get over this, Mom?" cried Kiley, tears streaming down her cheeks. "I still want him. And I hate her. I know she's my sister, but I hate her."

"I know," Mom said softly, patting her shoulder. "Right now you do. But this ugly storm will blow over, I promise."

"When?" Kiley cried. "When will I see a rainbow? It's not that I don't want Gwinnie to be happy. But why does she have to buy her happiness with my misery? My God,

Mom, it's been one thing after another this year. I wish I could catch even a glimpse of happiness."

Her mother took Kiley's tear-stained face in her hands and gave her the kind of bracing look only mothers can master. "I know you've had a double whammy, but you are a strong young woman, and a good one, and goodness never goes unrewarded." With those words of wisdom and a ton of leftovers, her mother escorted her safely to the front door.

Kiley drove away with a sore heart, the image of Jeremy sitting on the couch next to a pouting Gwinnie and looking miserable imprinted on her brain. *Good. Misery loves company.*

"You had a lucky escape," she told herself for what felt like the millionth time. A man who could swear undying love to one woman and then dump her in a heartbeat for her sister wasn't a keeper. She should feel sorry for Gwinnie. And she would, if she ever got past feeling sorry for herself.

Back home she settled in with her cat, Furina, to watch a DVD and gorge on pumpkin pie. But even though the movie was a holiday favorite it couldn't hold her attention, and the pie tasted like ashes.

She finally gave up on both, took a shower, and went to bed.

Sleep wasn't kind to her. Instead of letting Kiley sink into dark oblivion, it tortured her. She dreamed she stood in a church festooned with flowers and full of people as Gwinnie's bridesmaid, and instead of a gown, she wore a clown suit. On the other side of her sister stood Jeremy, resplendent in a ringmaster's red tuxedo and a black top hat. He leaned across Gwinnie and told Kiley, "I never wanted you."

All the wedding guests started laughing, and chanting, "He never wanted you."

"He did!" Kiley insisted, and Gwinnie reached over and grabbed her big, red clown nose, making it honk.

Her eyes popped open and she sat up with a gasp, scaring Furina off the bed. She let out a calming breath and pushed her hair out of her eyes. *Get a grip.* She scolded herself. *It was just a dream. Just a stupid, pie-induced dream.* She looked at her bedside clock. Three A.M. Good grief.

Time for a bathroom break. Then she'd go back to sleep, continue the dream, and give her sister a big kick in the butt with her clown shoe.

The little snow globe seemed to call to her as she passed her dresser. "You were a waste of money," she told it.

Waste of money or not, she couldn't resist the urge to jiggle it.

Wait a minute. What was going on here?

FOUR

Kiley blinked in disbelief. The scene in the snow globe had changed. She still saw a toyshop, but this one appeared to be in Seattle, in what looked like the Pike Place Market. A huge Christmas tree decorated with kites and dolls, and stuffed animals adorned this new toyshop window. And where was the angel? Maybe off having dinner at Ivar's.

Her eyes were playing tricks on her, that was it. She shook the globe again, stirring up a fresh snowfall, and watched the same toyshop with the toy-laden tree in the window emerge as the storm subsided. What did it mean?

Once back in bed, she snuggled under the covers and thought about the story the antique shop owner had told her about the snow globe's history. What was it trying to tell her? She suspected she wouldn't know until she found that toyshop.

Come morning, she awoke to realize something was missing. It was the heaviness that had been pressing on her heart for the last few weeks. Gone just like that. Now, there was a miracle!

She threw off the covers and padded to the dresser to

visit the snow globe. The modern toyshop she'd seen was gone and the angel and the Alpine village were back. She reached out for the snow globe, then pulled back her hand. Of course, she'd dreamed what she saw the night before. Why disappoint herself by picking it up? She'd only ruin her good mood.

She slipped into her reflective running gear and did her usual three-mile morning run. It was seven-thirty and normally Kinnear Street would be bustling with cars. Every day she saw the bus on its way downtown and other joggers out on the street. But the early-bird shoppers were already at the stores today and everyone else in the civilized world was either still off visiting relatives or sleeping in. All she had for company this nippy morning was the sound of her breathing accompanied by the rhythmic pounding of her feet. She cleared her mind of everything but the sensation of fresh morning air and the pumping of her heart. After a mile, however, her mind began to wake up, and soon two words danced in time with every footfall. *Why not?*

Of course, it was silly to shake the snow globe again looking for some fairy-tale adventure. She'd been in a dream state when she saw that vision. What was the point in looking for something that wasn't real? She might as well plan to wait up for Santa on Christmas Eve. But . . .

Why not?

As soon as she got back home, she abandoned her earlier resolve, and picked up the snow globe and jiggled it. Her breath caught when the snow settled. There it was again. Okay, she told herself, it's broad daylight and I'm wide awake so I'm not dreaming. But she could be going crazy.

There was only one way to find out. She showered and made a protein drink with a banana mixed in for good measure. Then she parked on the couch with her drink and her laptop and began an Internet search. If there was a toyshop at the Pike Place Market, she'd find it.

She was barely into her search when her cell phone rang.

"Are you at the mall with your family?" asked Allison.

"Noooo. Yesterday was enough for a while."

"Oh. How'd it go?"

"Well, it wasn't fun," Kiley said. "But you know what? I think I'm over the Jeremy flu."

"The fever broke, huh?"

"Yes, it did."

"I'm glad," said Allison. "He doesn't deserve you."

"That's pretty much what Corey and the cousins think. And you know what, I think they're right." Kiley couldn't help smiling when she remembered how they had enjoyed pummeling her ex. Sick puppy that she was, she rather enjoyed the memory of it now. "How was your Thanksgiving? Do I dare ask?"

"No big fights."

"That's an improvement over last year," said Kiley, staying positive. "How long did you last with the wicked stepmother and the crazies?"

"An hour and a half. And she's not wicked. She's just . . . clueless and self-absorbed."

It amounted to the same thing as far as Kiley was concerned.

"Anyway, that checks off family togetherness until Christmas," said Allison. "Speaking of Christmas, how about going to Northgate with me? I want to make a dent in my shopping list."

"Actually, I may be doing some shopping, but not at the mall."

"Online?" Allison guessed.

"No, closer to downtown. Actually, I'm on a quest."

"Yeah? For what?"

"Promise you won't laugh?"

"Why would I do that?"

"Because it's going to sound crazy." Actually, it was, but, crazy or not, she had to find that toyshop and see what it had for her.

"Well, now I'm dying to know, so you'd better tell me."

"I saw something in the snow globe."

"Oh, my gosh!" squeaked Allison. "What?"

Kiley told her about the mysterious toyshop. "I have no idea what it means, but I have to go find that shop."

"I'll help you," Allison said eagerly. "Hey, maybe Suz wants to come, too."

"Not Suz," Kiley said. "She'll think we're both nuts. Anyway, I'll lay you odds she's working on that holiday home tour today. Or showing a house."

"Or both," added Allison. "Okay. It'll be just us. I'll be over in a few."

Half an hour later Allison arrived, wearing jeans, boots, and a red parka that made her look a whole size bigger than she was.

"Is it that cold out?" asked Kiley. Winters were almost always mild in Seattle, and she had opted for something a little more stylish.

"It's getting there," said Allison. "And I hate being cold."

So did Kiley. Still, she was willing to pay for style with a few shivers, so she stuck with her leather jacket, the one she'd bought back when she had a job and money. But since the weatherman was predicting some unusual weather for the weekend she added gloves and a wool scarf.

It was drizzling by the time they left and Kiley's carefully straightened hair began to frizz with the moisture. Great, she thought. Soon she'd look like a forsythia bush.

Even though most people were either in the downtown department stores or the mall, Pike Place had its own loyal following. In the summer, Seattleites brought friends and relatives to the historic farmers market that overlooked Puget Sound and the stunning mountain range beyond. There they'd watch the fishmongers toss salmon back and forth, or have their pictures taken with Rachel the bronze pig. The rest of the year they came to dine in the restaurants, pick up something tasty from the bakeries, or purchase fresh vegetables from the main arcade, and many a hostess could be seen heading home from the Market on a Friday with a huge bouquet of fresh flowers. In addition, the sprawling place offered any number of quaint shops and stalls where shoppers could buy wares from local artisans. And somewhere in the lower regions affectionately referred to by regulars as "Down Under," would be a mysterious toyshop.

"So, you're sure it's here?" Allison asked as they wandered past a couple of middle-aged women.

"Pretty sure," Kiley said, pulling off her gloves. There was *a* toyshop listed on the Market's website. Whether or not it was *her* toyshop remained to be seen.

"Let's ask somebody," Allison decided, and ducked into a shop that sold Asian art and clothing.

Kiley followed her in, feeling mildly stupid. She could have asked when they first arrived. *I'm looking for this toyshop I saw in my magic snow globe.* Hmmm. Maybe not.

"Is there a toyshop down here?" Allison asked the shopkeeper.

The woman's expectant smile faded and she pointed farther down to the end of the building. "That way. Keep going. You'll see it."

Somehow, it seemed wrong to come in and ask a shopkeeper directions to a different store, especially when there were no potential customers browsing, so, ignoring the funky smell of incense, Kiley drifted over to a display of scarves under a sign that read SALE. BUY ONE, GET THE SECOND FIFTY PERCENT OFF.

The woman's smile had returned. "When you buy one you get the other half off," she said, in case there was any doubt as to the veracity of the sign.

Kiley fingered one, taking in the bold pattern and vivid colors. "Oooh, that's gorgeous," said Allison, now at her elbow.

"You like it? Good," said Kiley. "Try to act surprised when you open your present."

Allison frowned. "Actually, I was thinking maybe we shouldn't exchange presents this year. I'm broke."

Kiley narrowed her eyes. "No, you're not."

"I need to save money," Allison said.

"And I don't have any?" Kiley added, getting to the heart of the matter.

"I don't want you to buy me anything," Allison said earnestly. "You can't afford it."

That was so typical of Allison. She was always thinking of others. Between her clueless father and her self-absorbed stepmother it was a miracle she had turned out so well. If it hadn't been for her grandmother, Allison would probably have drifted off into Flake Land right along with the rest of her screwy family.

"Well, I'm going to get you something," Kiley insisted, "so it may as well be something you want."

"Second scarf is half price," chimed in the shop owner.

"I'll get one for you and one for Suz," Kiley decided. She started sorting through them. "Help me pick one out that she'll like."

Allison gave up with a sigh, and five minutes later they left the shop with Kiley carrying a bag and Allison frowning in disapproval. "I thought we were going on a quest," she said.

"We are. But we're Christmas shopping, too. At least

I am. Even unemployed people have to celebrate the holidays, you know."

Allison shook her head. Then she stopped and grabbed Kiley's arm. "Is that it?"

Kiley stopped, too, and gaped. There was the tree in the window, decorated with kites and stuffed animals. FOREVER KIDS, read the store sign. "Yes," she said breathlessly.

A tall man dressed casually in jeans and a gray T-shirt with an old beat-up bomber jacket thrown over it appeared in the doorway.

"Oh. My. Gosh," said Allison. "You saw *him* in the snow globe? I wish I'd bought it."

Kiley's mouth went dry. "All I saw was the shop."

"Well, then, he's a bonus."

He sure was. Even in the dim light of the market's lower level it was easy to see that he was fantasy-beautiful. His brown Indiana Jones hat hid his eyes but it couldn't hide a gorgeous mouth and a strong, Superman jaw. He stood for a minute in the doorway, looking at his display window like a king surveying his kingdom. Then he took a key from his pocket and inserted it in the door.

"He's locking up!" cried Allison. "Oh, no."

"Wait!" called Kiley, and they both took off at a run.

FIVE

The man looked up in surprise, then watched with a curious smile as the women dashed up to him.

"You can't be closing already," Allison protested. "It's only ten-thirty."

He pointed to a little cardboard sign with a clock hanging on the door. BE BACK BY . . . , promised the sign, and the clock was set to eleven A.M. "I was just going to Starbucks to grab a coffee. But I'm happy to open back up right now," he added, smiling at Kiley.

What a great smile. Up close Kiley could see that he had brown eyes, and dark hair fringed over his ears. And he was much taller than Jeremy. She came up only to his shoulder. She put her hand to her wild hair and tried to smooth it down.

"Or we could have coffee with you and then come back and shop," Allison boldly suggested, and Kiley felt herself blushing. *Subtle. Very subtle.*

"You probably don't want company," Kiley quickly added, overcorrecting for her friend's pushiness. "We can do some more shopping and come back."

He motioned for them to join him. "It's not every day

two beautiful women come running up and ask to have coffee with me. I'm not letting this opportunity slip away."

Beautiful? Well, Allsion, thought Kiley. Still, his flattery was balm to her wounded ego and she found herself smiling.

They fell in step with him, introducing themselves as they went. In only a matter of minutes they had learned that his name was Craig Peters, that he was a Seattle boy born and raised, that he had worked in the corporate world long enough to decide it wasn't for him and that he considered himself a thirty-three-year-old kid. Hence the name of his shop: Forever Kids. "Just because you grow old doesn't mean you have to grow up," he said.

Did Mr. Perfect have Peter Pan syndrome? Kiley sure hoped not.

"So, isn't this a big shopping day at the mall? What brings you two here?" he asked. "Superior taste?"

No way was Kiley telling him she'd seen his shop in the snow globe. Even an oversized Peter Pan would have trouble swallowing something so preposterous. Instead, she said, "The Market's got character, and you can find some unusual gifts here."

"That you can," he agreed. "Were you coming to my shop to get something for your kids?"

Kiley saw him checking out her left hand, looking for a ring, and her heart shifted from its lackluster plodding of the past month to an excited skip. "I have nephews."

Allison's cell phone rang. She pulled it from her purse and checked the screen. "It's Suz. I tell you what. You guys go ahead and get that coffee. I'll meet you back at the store." And then she slipped away, talking as she went, leaving Kiley alone with Craig.

He grinned. "Is your friend always that subtle?"

She could feel a fresh blush warming her cheeks. "Oh, yeah. It's her specialty."

At the coffee shop Craig held the door open for her, something Jeremy had never thought to do, something she had never thought to expect. The whoosh of the espresso machine as the barista steamed milk for lattes greeted her and the smell of brewing coffee embraced her. There was something so cozy about slipping into a coffee shop on a cold, misty day. She could almost forget the fact that she was unemployed. Looking at the handsome man next to her she could certainly forget the fact that she was no longer engaged.

"What'll you have?" he asked as they approached the counter.

The last thing she wanted was to come across as a coffee mooch. "Oh, you don't have to—"

"I know," he said with a smile. "I want to."

He seemed to really mean it so she requested a small eggnog latte and went to claim the last vacant table remaining in the shop, a high, small one meant for intimate conversation. She slipped onto one tall chair and occupied herself by gazing out the window. It was starting to rain in earnest and passersby were picking up their paces and putting up umbrellas. She was glad she was indoors and warm.

A couple of minutes later Craig joined her, sliding her cup in front of her.

"Thank you. I wish you hadn't."

"I had to," he said solemnly. "Now you'll feel so guilty you'll be sure to buy something at my shop."

She smiled and shook her head, then took a sip of her latte.

He removed his hat and dropped it on the table and she noticed that his hair was thinning on top. He'd probably be bald by the time he was forty but it wouldn't matter. He'd still have those warm brown eyes and that great smile.

"So, Kiley Gray, have you got a boyfriend?"

She pushed away her cup. "Not anymore. We broke up at Halloween."

Craig nodded and took a thoughtful sip of his coffee. "Scary timing. Was it serious?"

She nodded, surprised that she suddenly couldn't speak. She thought the fever had broken and she was over Jeremy. She *was* over Jeremy, but what she hadn't quite gotten over was the loss of that rosy future she had dreamed of.

"That sucks," Craig said.

"I guess it just wasn't meant to be," she said. That particular future was gone. But what was to stop her from creating a new, better future?

Craig didn't ask for details. Instead he saluted her with his cup. "Good attitude. There's plenty more fish in the sea."

And this particular one intrigued her. "Speaking of fish, why hasn't anyone caught you?" she asked, keeping her voice light.

"I'm slippery," he cracked. "Seriously, nothing's worked out. I've thought of trying one of those online dating services but I dunno. They seem so . . . planned. Where's the adventure?"

This man owned a toyshop. Of course, he'd want his search for Miss Right to be an adventure. Kiley couldn't help smiling.

He swallowed the last of his drink. "Why don't we go back to my shop? You can look around, and when you're done you can give me your phone number."

There was still no sign of Allison when they returned to the shop, but once inside Kiley forgot all about her friend as Craig gave her a tour of his kingdom. "Of course, we've got the video games. Gotta have that," he said, pointing to a corner packed with technology. "But when parents come in I usually steer them somewhere else."

Educational toys abounded, and puzzles, magic sets, marionettes, and old-fashioned tops. "I haven't seen one of these in years," Kiley said, running her finger along a fat, multicolored one.

"Those can keep a kid happy for hours," said Craig. "Heck, they keep me happy for hours," he added with a grin.

"My nephews are too old for that now."

"How old are they?"

"Five. They're twins."

"Ant farms are cool," he said.

"My sister-in-law would kill me."

"Sea monkeys? Every kid should have a chance to grow sea monkeys."

"Oh, I don't think so," she said diplomatically. Then she spotted the shelf with the kaleidoscopes. "I remember getting a kaleidoscope for Christmas when I was ten." She picked one up. It was made of wood and beautifully crafted. She put it to her eye and peered at a miniature stained-glass window. She turned the kaleidoscope, making the pattern shatter and reshape itself. "This is perfect."

"Well, okay," he said. "I was thinking kites, myself."

"Not for them. For me." She gave the end another twist and marveled at the new mosaic of color. One more turn, one more look. "Another time," she added, and reluctantly set it aside. "I'll take two kites. Not too expensive," she added.

"Got ya," he said, and led her to the window with the Christmas display and they spent several minutes discussing the merits of the kites hanging on the tree. Of course, he had more in another corner, set up over a tiny seaside scene, complete with sand and a beach umbrella.

She finally decided on two octopus-shaped kites in two different colors.

"Good choice," he approved. "Those are just right for little kids. Anything else?"

Not until she got a job. "That will do it," said Kiley. But just because she was done didn't mean she couldn't look. And there was much to take in. Every corner of the shop had been arranged to look like a child's fantasy. Stuffed animals stalked each other in a jungle of plastic plants, bats and sports balls of every variety hung in a net over a mannequin dressed up in athletic shorts and a basketball jersey. Dolls had tea at a small table. How had he managed to fit so much merchandise in the small space and make it not feel crowded? "I could easily spend a fortune in here," she said, following him to the counter.

"Tell me about it. I have. So, do you work around here?"

"Farther uptown," said Kiley. "Or at least I used to."

"Used to?"

"I'm exploring new opportunities," Kiley said, trying to put a good spin on her present unemployed condition.

He gave a grunt and a sympathetic nod. "Been there, done that." He studied her a moment. "I don't suppose you design Web sites."

"I have." She remembered that she hadn't found one for his place. He was listed only under the market's Web site. "You don't have a site?"

"Haven't gotten around to it yet," he confessed. "I only bought the business last month." He shook his head. "The previous owner had pretty much run it into the ground. I got it for a song." He rang up her purchases and she handed over her trusty charge card. "I think I can make a go of it," he continued. "I'm already talking with some people about sponsoring a couple of kids' fairs in the spring. And I've got a Christmas ad campaign planned. But I need to get a Web site up ASAP." He handed back her charge card and she signed the receipt. "So, how about that phone number? I'm thinking we should have dinner and talk."

By the time Allison returned Kiley and Craig had a dinner date for that night and were already discussing ways he could promote the shop.

"Are you ready for lunch?" Allison asked.

Lunch? Kiley looked at her watch. It was almost twelve-thirty. Where had the time gone? "I guess so."

"Enjoy the rest of the your shopping," Craig said as they left.

"So, tell," Allison commanded as soon as the shop door shut behind them. "Is he as wonderful as he looks?"

"He could be," Kiley said. "Although I keep thinking this all seems too good to be true."

Allison frowned and shook her head. "That's what Suz says. But she's a cynic."

Kiley felt a sinking in her stomach. "You didn't tell her about what I saw in the snow globe, did you?"

Allison's guilty expression gave Kiley her answer.

"Great," said Kiley. "Just what I need, Suzanne telling me I'm hallucinating." Although maybe she was. Or maybe this was all a dream and she'd wake up any minute.

But that night, as she and Craig sat at a window table eating pasta in a cozy Italian restaurant on lower Queen Anne, she couldn't help hoping that if she *was* dreaming she wouldn't wake up.

It wasn't hard, listening to him talk, to see what a good heart he had. His mother had raised him and his brother single-handedly. He admired her greatly and helped her when he could, doing small repairs and keeping her lawn mowed. Most of his time was taken up with the toyshop. He'd left his corporate job to take a gamble on it and was hoping his savings would last until he turned the shop around. "I know I'm competing with the big chains and the Internet," he admitted, "but I think I can make a go of this. Plus, once I get the site up and running, I'll sell stuff on the Internet, too."

It was risky, but she couldn't help admiring his determination. "At least you only have yourself to worry about," she said.

"Pretty much."

"Pretty much? What does that mean?"

It meant that even though he had a business to launch he was still helping his little brother through college. Saint Peters.

"That's really sweet of you," said Kiley.

He shrugged. "Nah. I don't have to kick in that much. He's got some scholarship money and he's working part time."

"For you?" asked Kiley.

"Nope. He works weekends as a waiter. He can make more in tips than I can afford to pay him. Anyway, even though he thinks the shop is cool, it's not his dream. Well, will you look at that?" Craig said, pointing out the window. "I guess for once the weatherman was right. It hasn't snowed in Seattle on Thanksgiving weekend since I was a kid," he added in awe.

Kiley had noticed earlier that the temperature had dropped drastically. Still, in spite of the weatherman's predictions, she was surprised to see soft flakes drifting to the ground, dancing in and out of the beam of the streetlights. People hurried down the street, hunched inside their coats, their collars held tightly together. Here inside the restaurant it was warm and pleasant, a haven fragrant with the scent of Italian spices and simmering sauces.

They finished off their dinner with tiramisu and coffee, and then walked out into the frosty night. The snow was sticking now and a white carpet of flakes crunched beneath their feet as they walked. A winter wonderland, she thought.

Craig drove her home, letting his car radio serenade them. Then, at the door of her condo, he ran his fingers through her hair and kissed her good night. As her whole body warmed in his embrace she thought, If I could freeze one moment in a snow globe, I'd pick this one.

SIX

Saturday she half expected Craig to call, but he didn't. Well, he was trying to start a business. He'd probably call on Sunday. That night, before she went to bed, Kiley couldn't help visiting her magical snow globe one more time, and giving it a shake. As before, the snowstorm she started cleared, and again showed Craig's toyshop, but now there he was, too, standing in the doorway. It looked as if he was smiling at her. She gave the decoration a loving pat, and went to bed to dream.

Sunday was glorious. The snow fell all night, forcing busy city dwellers to slow down and enjoy life. Kiley was all for that. She dug out a pair of boots she hadn't used in years and donned her parka, hat, and gloves. Then she went out to put her mark on the pristine blanket that covered the sidewalk in front of her condo.

How different the city looked. The Space Needle reigned over a kingdom of white with snow-topped houses that made her think of the gingerbread artwork she loved to see on display at the downtown Sheraton Hotel every Christmas. Cement disappeared under a white carpet, and trees and shrubs sported lacy shawls. Laughter echoed to her on the crisp air.

She hadn't walked far before she saw a group of children building a snowman. They had given him a smile made of small rocks and popped two larger ones above it for eyes. Someone's mother had seen fit to donate a carrot for the cause, which they had used for a nose, and they'd found branches for his arms. But he was sadly lacking in wardrobe.

Inspired, Kiley stopped and offered them her knitted hat. Now her hair would go crazy, but oh, well.

"Wow, thanks!" said one of the girls. She took Kiley's offering and settled it on the snowman's head.

"That's a girl's hat," protested one of the older boys, eyeing the pink pompom at the tip of it in disgust.

"So?" retorted the girl.

"So boys don't wear hats like that," said the dissenter.

Neither did girls with any fashion sense, thought Kiley. It was a stocking cap that looked like the world's ugliest rainbow Popsicle. In short, it was the kind of hat that would have inspired the *What Not to Wear* duo to great heights of sarcasm. The only reason Kiley had donned the thing was because it was warm. Allison had made it for her a couple of Christmases ago, when her grandma was teaching her to knit combining different colored yarns, and Kiley had kept it out of a sense of girlfriend duty. Getting rid of it to support budding artists was, if Kiley did say so herself, brilliant.

Meanwhile, the battle over whether a wild colored chick hat was acceptable snowman attire raged on. Finally the girl who had accepted it wadded a couple of handfuls of snow into a giant snowball.

Uh-oh, thought Kiley with a smile.

But instead of throwing it the girl pushed her lump of

snow onto one side of the snowman's chest, saying, "Then we'll make it a girl."

The other children giggled and the dissenter pitched in to help give the snowman a sex change.

Oh, that all disagreements could so easily be solved, thought Kiley, and walked on. If that had been her and Corey and Gwinnie they'd have been pelting each other with snowballs until someone gave in—usually her or Gwinnie.

Gwinnie. Would she wind up at Jeremy's place today, curled up on his couch, watching movies? Would he make cocoa for her?

Did Kiley really care anymore? She smiled. No.

Her ears were starting to burn from the cold. Time to go home and pull a packet of hot cocoa mix out of the cupboard. She didn't need a man to make it for her.

Although she wouldn't object if a certain toyshop owner offered.

Back home she checked her cell for messages. Nothing from Craig Peters. He probably had to go shovel snow for his mother. Or something.

She did have one message, though. "Okay, what is going on?" Suzanne demanded. "Call me and fill me in. I'm snowed in so I'll be here."

To smother Kiley's good mood under an avalanche of skepticism. She looked out her condo window at the wintry scene and sighed. It wouldn't last long. The fat, white drops lazily floating down would soon turn silver as temperatures rose, and rain would turn the pretty snow to slush. Then the fluke snowstorm would be gone as quickly as it had come and everything would be back to normal. Meanwhile, though, the view outside her window was storybook wonderful.

She decided she'd deal with Suzanne later. After she'd heard from Craig. He had all day.

She pulled out her favorite Starbucks mug and made herself some cocoa, then moved to her couch, where her cat Furina was already lounging. She and Jeremy had picked out this couch together—sage-colored microfiber, and on sale. It had been one of their first purchases for their new life.

Try not to think of it as losing a boyfriend but as gaining a couch, she'd told herself after they broke up. Now she told herself that maybe soon she'd have a new boyfriend to share her couch.

Furina let Kiley settle in with her cocoa before lazily stretching and relocating to Kiley's lap. Like all well-trained owners, Kiley knew what to do. She started petting the longhaired calico. "Yeah, I know. You just happened to be in the neighborhood and thought you'd drop in. Right?"

Furina purred as if to say, *Talk all you want but keep petting. My wish is your command.*

Furina had never warmed to Jeremy. She had mostly kept her distance and the few times he tried to pet her, she'd hissed at him.

"Maybe you were smarter than me," Kiley mused.

Furina purred on. *Yes, I am, but I love you anyway.*

"Well, it's a new day," Kiley murmured.

And, as if to prove it, her cell rang again.

Kiley's heartbeat picked up in anticipation and she snatched the phone from her coffee table. She looked at the screen and felt her spirits deflate. Suzanne again. "May as well get this over with, huh?" she said to Furina.

Suzanne barely gave her time to say hello. "Okay, what's this I hear about that snow globe helping you find the perfect man? Was Allison high on scented candles or something?"

"No," said Kiley with a frown.

"Look, I know you've had a rough month and—"

Kiley cut her off. "Friday wasn't just wishful thinking. It really happened and Allison is my eyewitness."

"She saw the toyshop in the snow globe?"

"No, but—"

"So, the only person who saw it was you? Maybe you just imagined you saw it," Suz suggested.

"If I only imagined I saw it, how did I find it?" demanded Kiley.

"I don't know," Suz admitted. "That part is weird."

"And what about the man I met?"

"Coincidence," Suzanne countered.

"Well, that's some coincidence," said Kiley.

"It's the only rational explanation."

When were miracles ever rational?

"Look, I just don't want you to rush into anything," Suzanne said, her voice softening. "After everything with Jeremy, well, you're vulnerable."

Jeremy. Her friends hadn't liked him any more than her cat. What vibes had they picked up on that she hadn't? Had she been so anxious to find someone that she'd dulled her senses? Was she doing the same thing now with Craig?

Kiley relocated Furina from her lap to the couch. Insulted, the cat jumped down and stalked off, asserting her independence. Kiley ignored her and went to the bedroom to where her snow globe occupied prime real estate on her dresser. The Alpine village was back once more. Suzanne was still talking, but Kiley tuned her out. Instead, she listened to the voice somewhere at the back of her mind that whispered, *Shake me.*

So she did. The little curtain of snow fell away and again she saw the Seattle toyshop and Craig Peters standing in the doorway. And . . . what was this? Someone new had joined him: a woman with long, curly brown hair who looked suspiciously like her. "Oh, my gosh," she gasped. "It's changed again."

"What?" Suz demanded. "What do you mean?"

"I'm in it. I'm in the snow globe with Craig."

"I don't like this," Suzanne said in a low voice. "I'm coming over."

"You don't drive in the snow," Kiley reminded her. *Thank God*.

"I just heard the weather report. It will be slush by afternoon. I'll be there."

"Goody," muttered Kiley as she ended the call. She wandered back out into the great room area and saw that Furina was now prowling the kitchen counter. "You know better," Kiley scolded, and lifted Her Majesty off it.

Offended yet again, Furina jumped from her arms and returned to the couch, curling up on the afghan Allison had made Kiley as a housewarming present. Of course, she would leave as much fur on the cream-colored blanket as possible. Kitty revenge.

Kiley had barely reheated her cocoa when the phone rang. This time—big surprise—it was Allison.

"I got tired of waiting for you to call. How was dinner?"

"Fabulous."

"And what about the snow globe? Did you see anything new?"

"I did." Happiness settled over Kiley like a cloak. She closed her eyes and savored the feeling. It was one she'd almost convinced herself she'd never have again. How wonderful it was to be wrong!

"What did you see?"

"Well, I saw the toyshop again. And Craig."

"And?" prompted Allison.

"And a woman."

"Was it you?"

"Yep."

"Oh, my God. That is sooo romantic. I wish I'd bought the thing."

"You already have a boyfriend," Kiley reminded her.

Allison gave a little grunt. "Lamar, God's gift to woman-kind. Let me tell you, I'm not sure how much longer I'm going to have him."

So, Lamar was in the doghouse again. It happened on a regular basis, but he always charmed his way back out. Sometimes Kiley wondered if Allison kept the studly Lamar simply because she didn't want to part with his mother and grandmother, who were more like a family to her than the dysfunctional one she was stuck with.

"Anyway, never mind about him," Allison said briskly. "Tell me more about Mr. Wonderful. What did you guys talk about at dinner?"

"Everything and anything. You know he grew up here in Seattle. Went to Ballard High. And he was on the track team."

"A runner," Allison crowed. "Perfect. Did he say he'd call you?"

"As a matter of fact, he did. I'm going to design a Web site for him, and I'll probably help him with his online store, too."

"I'm so glad for you, Kiles," said Allison. "And what an amazing way to find your perfect man. Except no one will ever believe it when they hear how you found him."

"Suzanne sure doesn't," Kiley said. She guessed she couldn't blame Suzanne. It did all sound pretty far-fetched. "She's coming over later to see for herself, thanks to a certain big mouth."

"I know, I know," said Allison. "I probably shouldn't have told her. But it's just so awesome. Maybe I'll have to come, too. I'm dying to see the snow globe in action."

"Sure. Why not," said Kiley, resigned to her fate. She'd nursed the hope of having company before the day was over. Only she'd envisioned someone with a lower voice and slightly different body parts. She looked out the window to see that the white flakes had already morphed into silver slivers. Seattle's famous rain was back and soon the snow would be nothing but a pleasant memory, a weather anomaly to be discussed around water coolers and on morning walks around Green Lake. He could still call, still come.

"I'll bring brownies," Allison offered. "I'm making a ton for Suz's holiday home tour."

Allison was a physical therapist by day, but in her off hours she channeled Julia Childs, and she picked up extra money catering Suzanne's events.

Kiley's taste buds suddenly took an active interest in the conversation. "Those mint ones?"

"Those would be the ones. I'll see you later."

All right. Chocolate mint brownies weren't on a par with spending the evening with Craig Peters, but she'd make do.

Suzanne was the first to arrive. "Thank God the snow is going away," she said as she blew into the condo in a mist of perfume and style. Her red scarf was cashmere, the coat was a black wool number from Nordstrom's—not from the Rack, where Kiley occasionally prowled for bargains. The boots were from Nordy's, too. Suzanne had bragged about getting them on sale, although even on sale they'd been too rich for Kiley's blood. But Suzanne settled for only the best. She once said she'd walk barefoot before she'd buy bargain chain-store shoes.

"I kind of hate to see it melt so quickly," Kiley said.

Suzanne frowned. "That's because you are currently unemployed and don't have to be anywhere." She pulled off the scarf, shaking her blond hair free, then hung her coat in the closet where Furina couldn't reach it.

"You're self-employed," Kiley reminded her. "You could take a day off."

Suzanne shook her head and looked regretful. "Not if I want to pay my mortgage."

She and Guy had bought and refurbished an old house on Magnolia. It had been about to go into foreclosure, and thanks to her real estate connections Suzanne had gotten it for a song. But the more she talked to the architect and interior designer the grander the song had gotten. Now she had a gorgeous house with refinished hardwood floors, crown molding, and expensive furniture that she enjoyed on the rare occasions she wasn't working. She also had huge payments, which gave her the perfect excuse to remain a workaholic.

"Anyway, I did take time off." She whipped out her digital camera from her purse and displayed the evidence. "See?"

Yes, sure enough. There she was, rosy-cheeked and beautiful in jeans and a white parka, black mittens on her hands, a black cashmere scarf around her neck and a matching black tam on her head. Next to her, holding her hand, her daughter, Bryn, looked like a miniature Suzanne, bundled into a pink snowsuit, her golden curls poking out from under a pink hat.

They stood beside a snowman wearing a very ugly scarf. Kiley recognized those colors. Obviously, when it came to figuring out how best to use Allison's early craftwork, great minds thought alike. The snowman's wardrobe didn't catch Kiley's eye as much as the expression on Bryn's face. She looked up at her mother as though Suzanne was the Madonna.

And Suzanne's expression? It was one Kiley recognized. It said: *Okay. Snowman completed? Check. Now, let's get on to the next thing on the list—pronto.* And there was always a next thing on the list. Suzanne liked to live in the moment, the moment that belonged to the future. She was constantly looking ahead: to the next decorating project, the next listing, or the next sale, busy building an empire in which her home was the crown jewel. Kiley admired her friend's efficiency, but she sometimes worried that Suz didn't really appreciate how much she already had.

"So, let's see the snow globe," said Suz, cutting to the chase.

"How about a cup of tea first? Allison's coming over with chocolate mint brownies."

"Her Christmas ones?" Suzanne asked hopefully. Kiley nodded and she said, "Okay, I'll wait."

"What do you mean wait?"

"Well, I can't stay too long. I have to run over to the office and do a couple of things."

"You know, rest is not a four-letter word," said Kiley.

Suzanne made a face. "I'll rest in January, but right now I have a million things to do for the holiday home tour." She checked her watch, reminding Kiley of the White Rabbit in *Alice in Wonderland*.

"You don't have to stay, you know," Kiley said, miffed. "No one forced you to come over and check my grip on reality."

Suzanne's expression turned penitent and she let her hand fall to her side. "Sorry. But cut me some slack, okay? I wouldn't be here if I didn't care." She went to the couch and perched on one end. "Tea sounds great." As Kiley moved to the stove to heat water for brewing she saw Furina stalking toward Suzanne's lap. Suz held up a hand, stopping the cat in her tracks. "Don't even think about it."

Furina jumped off the couch and walked away, tail held high. Poor Furina. Suzanne had never allowed her within lap range after the night Furina yakked up a fur ball on the cream-colored sweater Suz had left laying on a chair.

The doorbell rang and then the door flew open. "I'm here," announced Allison. "Let the brownie binging begin."

That brought Suz off the couch.

Kiley started herbal tea steeping in her Fiestaware pot, then joined her two friends at the kitchen counter, where Allison had set down a small decorative Fitz and Floyd Christmas plate laden with brownies thickly topped with green frosting and sprinkles.

"Oh my gosh, I think I just gained two pounds from simply looking at those," said Suzanne, awe in her voice.

That was a joke. Suzanne managed her weight as efficiently as she did her calendar. Her body wouldn't dare harbor any fat.

Kiley never worried about her weight. Running burned up enough calories that she could splurge when she wanted. Which was just what she intended to do now. She picked one up and bit into it. Heaven.

Suzanne took a delicate nibble of one, then closed her eyes and savored. "Better than sex," she murmured.

"Nothing is better than sex," Allison informed her.

She merely shrugged. "This takes less energy." Both friends looked at her in disgust. "What?" she protested.

"If we have to explain, you're beyond help," Allison said sternly.

Any minute Suz was going to demand to check out the snow globe. "So, what does Bryn want from Santa this year?" asked Kiley, trying to postpone the inevitable.

Suz rolled her eyes. "A puppy."

"Aw, that's sweet," said Allison.

"Oh, yeah. It's especially sweet when the thing is whining to go out at two in the morning or when it pees on the carpet. No, thanks."

"You have hardwood," Kiley said dismissively.

"Excuse me? Are you forgetting my new Persian rug

in the living room? Anyway, having a puppy would be just like having a baby and I don't have time," Suzanne added. She leaned on the counter and started in on another brownie.

"Even Martha Stewart has a dog," protested Allison.

"And a staff to train it," countered Suzanne. "Anyway, why are we talking about me? We're here to hear about Mr. Wonderful and gaze into the snow globe."

Allison took a brownie from the plate, looked at it longingly, and then returned it. "Has he called yet?"

Kiley picked it up, broke it in two, and handed Allison half. "No. But we only met Friday," she said as much to herself as to her friend. And talked for hours and shared a good-night kiss that had curled her toes. Why hadn't he called?

"But he's perfect," said Allison. She took a bite of the brownie then threw the rest in the garbage. "And the snow globe led her to him."

Suzanne took a quick sip of her tea, then said, "Okay, I want to see this for myself."

"Doubting Thomas," muttered Kiley, but she took them to her bedroom. Furina was now stretched out on her bed, happily getting little black cat hairs all over her comforter.

Suzanne walked to where the snow globe sat on the dresser. "It is beautiful, I'll say that. I have to admit, if I'd seen it before you I'd have bought it. It would have looked great on my mantel." She picked it up and handed it to Kiley. "It's show time. Let's see it do its stuff."

Kiley made a face at her and took it. There was the Alpine village and the toyshop and the angel. Her heart sped up. What if, all of a sudden, it decided not to work?

"Come on," urged Allison. "I'm dying to see."

Kiley took a deep breath and gave it a jiggle. The snow swirled. And then settled. And there it was: Craig's toyshop. He still stood in the doorway. And she was there, too, right next to him, smiling up at him. A thrill ran through her and she grinned.

"Do it again," suggested Allison. "Maybe it needs to, you know, get warmed up."

Kiley blinked. "What do you mean? Don't you see it? There's the toyshop, there's Craig, there's . . ."

Both her friends were exchanging worried looks.

Her heart sank. "You don't see it?"

SEVEN

An uncomfortable silence settled over the room. Kiley gave the snow globe another shake and all three women stared at it.

"Sorry, Kiles," said Suzanne. "I'm still not seeing it."

Kiley looked hopefully to Allison, who shook her head slowly and said, "Maybe you're the only one who can."

"Or you dreamed what you saw," said Suzanne. "Didn't you say it was the middle of the night?"

"I saw it this morning, too, the same thing that's there now," Kiley insisted. "And I'm not imagining it." She set the snow globe back on the dresser and left the room. "Maybe it doesn't show itself to skeptics."

"I'm not a skeptic," Allison protested, following her out.

Suzanne fell in line behind them. "Okay, maybe it is there and I'm blind. And maybe you've found the perfect man and your future will be great. I mean, I hope you have. I just don't want you to get hurt, that's all. So don't be mad at me."

Kiley sighed. How could she be mad at a friend who

cared enough to worry about her? Suzanne was looking at her, defensive, hopeful, sympathetic. "I wish I could be."

Suzanne smiled and hugged Kiley. "Keep me posted on what happens with Toy Boy. If that snow globe works I may have to borrow it and ask it to show me where the buyers for the house on Eleventh Avenue are."

Leave it to Suz to want to turn the snow globe into an Aladdin's lamp.

Their friendship restored to an even keel, Suzanne pulled her coat from the closet. "I've gotta go. Allison, I'll talk to you more next week about the food for the home tour," she added. Then she was gone.

Allison shook her head. "How did we ever wind up becoming friends with such an overachiever?"

"You're a bit of an overachiever yourself, you know. Working full time and catering on the side."

"Yeah, but the catering is fun," Allison said with a grin. "Sometimes, when I'm in the kitchen, I can almost feel my grandma there with me." It had been almost a year since her grandmother died, but Allison's eyes still glistened with tears.

"She'd be proud of you," said Kiley.

"I hope so," said Allison, and wiped at a corner of her eye.

Kiley helped herself to another brownie. "So, do you think I'm nuts?" she asked, careful not to look at her friend.

"Absolutely not," Allison said firmly. "Of course, I'm probably the wrong person to ask. I still put out cookies for Santa."

Kiley regarded her skeptically. "You don't."

"Of course, I do." She grinned. "Then on Christmas morning I eat 'em. Seriously," she added, "I believe in miracles. After all, isn't that what this time of year is all about?" She hugged Kiley. "And I believe you. If you say you see the toyshop and Craig in that snow globe then you do. And that's that."

Allison's support should have been enough, but Kiley found herself doubting her own eyesight. After Allison left she settled on the couch with the snow globe and started a blizzard. Even before the snow finished falling she could see the Pike Place toyshop. She was not imagining this. Couldn't be. But how could she prove it?

Inspiration hit. She jumped off the couch and ran for her digital camera. Allison hadn't been looking carefully enough. Suzanne had been deliberately blind. The light had been bad. As with many live shows, something had gone wrong. But this time she'd capture that image and then Suzanne would have to believe her. Camera in hand, she shook the snow globe and then set it on the coffee table and snapped the picture. Ha!

Smiling, she looked at the camera screen. There was the snow globe, but the Pike Place Market toyshop was nowhere to be seen. Instead, the angel in its Alpine village seemed to mock her. Icy fingers of fear ran over her skin and she dropped the camera. She *was* hallucinating. "I *am* going crazy," she said to herself in shock.

But crazy people didn't find a shop, let alone a man, that was an exact match to what they had seen in a snow globe, did they?

Kiley suddenly remembered Otto Schwartz, its original owner. He probably thought he was crazy when he first saw his future wife inside that glass ball, but a miracle happened anyway. Miracles had a way of happening when people needed them most. Kings were born in mangers; angels serenaded shepherds. Not everyone saw miracles when they happened, but that didn't make them any less real.

She erased the false picture from her camera's memory card and returned the snow globe to her dresser. Then she settled in with her new issue of *Runner's World,* keeping the phone handy. Craig would call. They'd be together. It was her turn for a holiday miracle.

She got three more calls that night. One from Mom, asking how she was doing, another from Gwinnie, calling to reassure herself that Kiley hadn't yet disowned her, and another from a telemarketer. But nothing from Craig Peters. To distract herself from her disappointment and the possibility that she might be going insane, she watched her favorite TV shows until, finally, there was nothing left to do but to go to bed and feel let down.

She avoided even looking at the snow globe as she turned off the bathroom light and padded to her sleigh bed (the second purchase she'd made with Jeremy for their new life together).

Craig would call. Tomorrow.

Kiley began her next day with a morning run, splashing through puddles, enjoying air still fresh from the weekend's snowfall, breathing in, breathing out, welcoming the endorphins racing through her body as she jogged her way along the sidewalk. She returned home feeling energized. Until she checked her cell and found she had no messages.

He'll call, she told herself. Meanwhile, you have things to do. And to prove it, she spent the rest of the morning on the Internet, catching up on her social networking, searching job sites and sending off e-mails to let friends and former coworkers know that her services were now available if anyone needed a Web site designed or a mailing list managed or . . . anything. Just a couple of clients would keep her boat afloat until she found full-time employment again.

Having done all she could on the job front, she put on her favorite Carrie Underwood CD and went into a cleaning fever, singing along with "Before He Cheats" at the top of her lungs. Okay, all better now, she told herself. So what if Jeremy had dumped her, if Craig Peters hadn't called. Her life was still good. She had . . . she had . . . What *did* she have?

Furina. She picked up the cat, who was twining around her legs as she cleaned off her kitchen countertops, reminding Kiley that her cat food bowl was empty. "Who needs men, anyway, right?" she told the cat, running her hands through Furina's soft fur. Of course, employment was another matter. "I am not going to get depressed," she informed the cat, setting her back down on the floor. "And you are not getting anything more until tonight. You're on a diet. Remember?"

Furina rubbed against her leg again. *Pleeease? You think you've got it bad? I haven't had a man in years. The least you can do is let me enjoy a little extra tuna.*

Kiley gave in. "Okay, okay. But you're not getting the whole can. You have to have a little self-control." Like Kiley had exerted over the last of the brownies? Good thing she'd gotten that run in.

The job hunting was done, the condo was clean—what next? She plopped on her couch and frowned at her library book. Then she frowned at the TV. Finally, she glared at the phone. This was ridiculous. Pathetic. She was not going to sit around and wait for a man to call. She needed groceries. She'd go see what she could get for twenty dollars.

She bought the makings for soup, which would get her through the week (and give her something to do when she got home), and all the while her cell phone sat silent and useless in her purse. That night as she readied herself for bed, she averted her eyes whenever she passed the snow globe. It wasn't that she'd lost faith, she told herself. But there was no sense getting her hopes up.

Who was she kidding? She *had* lost faith.

The next day fell into the same familiar pattern. Go for a run. Feel great. Come home and check messages. Lose some of the great feeling. Job hunt, send out résumés, check e-mail, do the tweet 'n' meet thing. Clean some more. Listen for the phone.

Maybe she should call him. They had talked about her designing his Web site. Time was money. Every day he went without a Web site he went without business. She picked up her cell, started to thumb in the number, and then set it down again. She didn't want to look pushy. Or desperate.

She heaved a sigh. What else needed to get done? She'd clean out her closet and take some things to the Goodwill. Perfect. They could always use donations before Christmas.

She not only found items in her closet to donate, she added several paperbacks she'd finished and knew she'd never read again. That was two bags' full now. It felt good to get rid of the clutter, made her feel efficient and organized, like she was clearing the deck for new opportunties. Now, what else could go?

Her eyes fell on the snow globe.

EIGHT

Kiley picked the thing up and frowned at the little angel inside. "You made a fool of me, you know. I should give you away. Or sell you to some other sucker." Of course, the angel had nothing to say for herself. Since she was holding the snow globe, Kiley had to shake it. After the blizzard subsided she saw, once again, Craig Peters and his toyshop. And herself.

Okay, was she delusional? Why hadn't he called?

Who knew? One thing she knew for certain. She couldn't get rid of her treasure, even though she suspected she'd make back at least some of her money if she put it up for auction on eBay. She set it down and resigned herself to hanging in limbo, just like the people inside that glass ball.

Except hanging in limbo wasn't acceptable. She had a life. To prove it she marched to the kitchen and baked some gingerbread cookies. And the next afternoon she went to the food bank and did data entry at the office. If a certain man called and wanted to do something he could just wait his turn. And if he didn't call, oh well. She still had Furina.

She was just walking in the door when her cell phone rang. "Hi," said a male voice. "Remember me, Craig Peters?"

How could she forget?

"I've been thinking about you," he said.

Now her heart started racing like a sprinter in the Olympics. "You have?"

"I had a great time the other night with you at dinner."

"You did?" *Sparkling conversation, Kiley.* She tried again. "I did, too. I've been doing a lot of thinking about your Web site design since then." Okay, she'd been thinking more about him than the Web site, but it wouldn't look cool to say that.

"Want to talk about it while we watch the Christmas boat parade tonight?" he asked.

The popular Northwest tradition had been going on for sixty years. A local cruise line decked one of their boats with Christmas lights, and then with local choirs aboard, visited various waterfront communities, broadcasting concerts to those on shore while passengers enjoyed the live entertainment. Other boats followed, also decorated for the holidays. Greater Seattle residents loved catching the boat parade. Local beaches blazed with bonfires and people hung out to await the floating show.

Kiley had never had a date take her to the boat parade and, yet again, Craig Peters scored points, this time for creativity. "That sounds like fun," she said.

"Dress warm and I'll pick you up about six. By the way, I meant to call you Sunday, but my mom slipped on an icy patch Sunday morning and broke her arm. I had to take her to the emergency room. The last couple of days I've been helping her out."

So there was the explanation as to why Kiley hadn't heard from him. She hadn't been delusional, and the snow globe was magic. She'd known it all along! Never doubted for a minute. As soon as she was off the phone, she went into hyper-drive, working on Web site ideas and working on herself.

The work paid off. When Craig arrived he took in her Christmas red sweater and her snug jeans and smiled approvingly as she grabbed her coat and hat and mittens. Her hair she'd corralled in a ponytail. Between that and her hat maybe she'd be able to contain it. Maybe.

Richmond Beach, one of the parade's scheduled stops, was alight with an uncountable number of bonfires and people milling around them, drinking cocoa and cider and roasting hot dogs. Kids and dogs darted everywhere along the rocky beach. "This is amazing," Kiley said as they made their way down the hill to the beach.

"Yeah, and somewhere in all this mess is my bro and his friends. If we find them we've got eats waiting."

Amazingly, they did find his brother Jed and a group of his college buddies and girlfriends, who were more than happy to welcome them with steaming cups of hot cider.

Jed, a slightly younger, shorter version of Craig, eyed Kiley appreciatively. "Any time you've had enough of this dweeb, let me know."

Craig pointed a gloved finger at his brother. "Hey, just 'cause you can't find a woman doesn't mean you have to go hitting on my date."

Judging from the way a curvy brunette was watching from the other side of the bonfire, Jed didn't have any problem finding women.

He grinned. "We got hot dogs. You guys hungry?"

"That's why we're here," said Craig. "Free food."

A few minutes later Kiley and Craig had settled on a log with freshly roasted hot dogs and refills of hot cider and were sharing more about their interests.

Their conversation was revealing, showing her more than common interests. As they talked she couldn't help realize how few interests she and Jeremy had really shared.

"So, tell me about your ideas for the Web site," Craig finally said.

She started tentatively, but the excitement on his face encouraged her.

"Awesome," he said when she finished. "Total yes to making the site interactive. I like being able to click on the different toys to go somewhere. And the Kidz Korner with stuff just for kids, that is a really great idea. You know, you are one smart woman."

Kiley tried to look humble. Yes, she was. Well, except for when she'd thought she was in love with Jeremy. What had she been thinking?

"When do you think you can have it up and running?" Craig asked.

"How about by the end of the week?"

"That fast?" He looked impressed.

It wasn't like she had a ton of other work, but she didn't tell him that. Instead she simply smiled and nodded. "I'll send you the link."

"Great. I can send you a check first thing tomorrow."

It was all she could do not to say, "For you, I'd work for free." But she managed to stay professional. "Let's wait to make sure you like it first," she suggested.

"Okay then. Here's to the new Web site," he said, touching his cup of cider to hers.

"To the site," she echoed.

"And to getting to spend more time together," he added. The look in his eyes now had nothing to do with business, and it sent heat rushing through her. "You know, since we're both runners we should run together sometime."

"I'd like that," she said, and felt her heart already taking off at a gallop.

"How about Saturday? No rain or snow predicted. It should be perfect."

"Your store," she protested.

"Doesn't open till ten. I've got time for a run. Eight?"

"Perfect." On so many levels.

They wandered back toward the fire and mingled with the others. Another ten minutes and people began cheering.

"Here they come," Craig said, pointing toward the water. A parade of boats, gaily lit, came into sight. "It doesn't get any better than this," he said, and put an arm around her.

"It sure doesn't," Kiley agreed. But then, later, when he pulled her to him and kissed her, she added, *Oh, yes it does*.

T he Web site was finished, approved, and up and running on Friday. It involved few changes, but several conversations. With each one, Kiley fell further and further in love. Craig was enthusiastic and encouraging. And Saturday, after their run, he had a final check for her.

She looked at it. "This is more than we agreed."

"You did more than I ever imagined," he replied. "Hey, we should celebrate."

"Yes, we should," she agreed, smiling. "And I know how."

That evening she made him dinner, serving meat loaf and her mother's fabulous macaroni and cheese because he said he loved comfort food. She also made pie from the blackberries she'd swiped from her mother's freezer.

"This must be a special dinner," her mother had probed.

Kiley had smiled and kissed Mom on the cheek. "I think it is. And when I'm sure, I'll tell you all about it."

"Just take your time," Mom had cautioned.

Kiley had assured her mother that she would, but as she sat across from Craig, watching him tuck into his second helping of pie and ice cream, listening to him talk about his life growing up and his dreams for the future, it was hard to come up with any reason for dragging her feet. He wasn't merely perfect; he was perfect for her.

She fingered the kaleidoscope he'd brought her as a hostess gift and found herself blurting, "Do you want to have kids?" *Oh, geez, way to scare the man off.*

He set down his fork and looked at her seriously. "Of course. Family is important." He grinned. "Besides, what's the point of having a toy store if you don't have kids to play with? How about you?"

She could feel her cheeks suddenly warming. "Oh, yes," she said with a nod. "But I'm not in any hurry," she added, remembering her mother's cautionary words. "I'm not in a hurry for anything."

He cocked his head to the side and studied her. "What does that mean exactly?"

Then it came out, all the details of her whirlwind romance with Jeremy and his betrayal. "So, I'm taking my time this time around."

Craig nodded slowly. "I can see why. Been there, almost done that. You ever been to Amsterdam?"

She shook her head. She hadn't traveled much. She'd been too busy building a career that had toppled, falling in love with the wrong man, important things like that.

"It's a cool city," said Craig. "Lots of museums, diamond cutters," he added, waggling his eyebrows. "The canals at night are something else. The houses are interesting, too. Not much really, and all close together, but they have these great façades that make 'em look cool." He paused a minute to see if Kiley was following. "A lot of people do that. They build a façade, hoping the other person won't see there isn't much there."

Kiley ran her finger along the rim of her coffee cup. "So you think that's what Jeremy did?"

"Well, it sure doesn't sound like there was much there. Except a lot of bullshit." Craig leaned back in his chair and smiled at her. "But hey, I'm all for taking the long way home. I'm gonna tell you right now, though, Kiley. I'm hooked on you and I can see what we've started going somewhere good."

She smiled. "Me, too."

After a while they moved from the table to the couch, and then from conversation to a kiss. And another and another. She had thought Jeremy was a good kisser, but he was a rank amateur compared to this man. Her lips were buzzing when Craig finally pulled away and looked at her as though she was the most beautiful woman in the world. He picked up a length of unruly curls and twisted them around his finger. "Man, I love your hair."

That was when she decided it was time for show-and-tell. She fetched the snow globe from her bedroom.

"Whoa," he said, sitting up straighter. "That is awesome. Where'd you get it? I've never seen one like it."

"I got it in an antique store." She handed it to him and sat back down on the couch.

He shook it, watching as the snowflakes flew. When they settled, his easy smile changed to an expression of amazement. "That's my shop!"

"You see it?" Was it possible?

"And there's . . . me?" He looked up at her as if to ask if he was crazy. "And you. What the hell?" He began examining the globe. "Is this like those digital photo frames? Did you program it somehow?"

She shook her head. "I didn't do anything."

He frowned. "Okay, I don't get it."

But he'd seen what the snow globe could do. So she told him its story.

When she was finished he simply sat, staring at it. "That's amazing." He looked up at her, his eyes full of wonder.

"If it hadn't been for the snow globe I never would have found you."

"Well, then God bless it," he said heartily. He continued to gaze at it. "What a story to tell our kids." As if realizing what he'd just said, he looked up, his cheeks russet. "Someday," he added. "We don't want to rush into anything."

"No," she said, staring at his lips. "No rushing." But would Valentine's Day be too soon to get engaged?

NINE

Suzanne scowled as she dashed through the freezing rain from the day care to her car, cell phone pressed to her ear. "You just met this man," she scolded Kiley. "You can't know he's the one."

"But I do. I know it sounds crazy," Kiley continued, "but he's perfect. He really, truly is."

She sounded so happy Suzanne wanted to smack her. Kiley lived in la-la land. Did she really think she was going to find Mr. Perfect just like that? As if there was such a thing. Guy came close, but even he had his faults. Like always messing up her house on fight nights, when he and his buddies used watching boxing matches as an excuse to spill beer and pretzel crumbs everywhere. Thank God she could relegate them to the bonus room.

"I'm not saying we're rushing into anything," Kiley continued, "but I know we'll be together for the rest of our lives. I can tell."

"So now you're psychic," Suzanne said with a sneer.

"No. And neither is he, but he saw us in the snow globe, too."

Suzanne rolled her eyes. "He probably just said that to

get in your pants. You haven't slept with him, have you?"
Sleeping with some man she barely knew was the last
thing Kiles needed. She was way too vulnerable.

"Of course not," Kiley said, sounding insulted. "I told
you we're taking things slow."

"Just remember you said that," Suzanne cautioned. She
plopped her soggy self inside her Lexus and started the engine. She had less than ten minutes to get to the office,
where she was meeting a couple looking to find a house
on Upper Queen Anne. "I want to meet this guy."

"I didn't say we wanted to take it that slow. I have to
make an appointment six months in advance to do anything with you."

"That's not true," said Suzanne, wheeling out onto the
street. Oh, great. There was a garbage truck right ahead.
Why did these guys have to hog so much of the road? "I've
gotta go. Keep me posted on what's going on, okay?"

She hardly gave Kiley time to say goodbye before ending the call and tossing the phone on the front passenger
seat. Then she pulled out around the truck and passed
him, barely squeaking past a man in a compact tin can
heading in the other direction. He commented on her reck-
less driving with an angry honk.

"Sorry," she muttered. But he'd have done the same.
Anyway, she'd had plenty of room to pass, really. The clock
on her car dash told her to hurry, hurry, hurry, and she
pressed down just a little harder on the gas. Oh, except
there was a patrol car farther up the street. She lifted her
foot and ground her teeth. Why was she always running
late?

Of course, the answer to that was easy. She had way
too much on her plate. Today was no exception. Between
showing four houses, following up on a listing lead, picking up the signs for the holiday open house, and checking on two deals that were in escrow, her workday was

full. Then Bryn had her ballet lesson at five. After that it would be time to go home and make dinner. Or maybe she'd pick up a pizza on the way, even though she'd done that three days ago.

But that couldn't be helped. She'd planned to make a nice meal until a couple called dying to see a condo that had just come on the market. They both worked during the day and had wanted to see it that evening. She'd barely had time to grab a slice before running back out the door.

Tonight the calendar was clear after ballet, but the thought of slaving away in the kitchen made her shudder. Guy usually cooked on Friday nights. Maybe he'd trade.

She parked in front of the office and put in a quick call to suggest it.

"Wait a minute," he protested. "You pulled that one on me last week and then on Friday you were too tired to cook." He politely refrained from mentioning that she had also been too tired for sex.

"I promise I won't back out this Friday," she said. "I'll make Indian," she added to sweeten the pot.

He heaved a long-suffering sigh. "All right. Deal. But it's going to be spaghetti. You're not the only one who comes home pooped, you know."

"But I'm the only one who comes home pooped and has to take Bryn to ballet." Oh, yeah, he'd done that for her last week, too. Bad argument.

"Yeah?"

"Okay, never mind. I forgot about last week. Come on, Guy, don't give me a hard time here."

"All right, all right."

"I love you," she cooed. It always helped to remind him why he so often went the extra mile.

"I love you, too," he said, "even though you're working both of us into an early grave."

She let the comment go but she hung up with a frown.

What did he expect? They had a big home improvement loan to pay off.

Loan or no loan, though, they'd probably work just as hard. Guy loved his job as a systems analyst and would have worked at his company for free. And she felt the same about what she did. Beautiful houses—she breathed, ate, and dreamed them. She always felt like she'd done something good when she helped a family find their dream home, the place where they could build happy lives in a lovely setting. A nice house was the most important gift a person could give herself, and the nicest gift she could give her family. Sometimes Suzanne suspected Guy didn't get that.

She climbed out of the car just as Melanie and James Cox pulled up behind her.

"Hi," she called, hurrying up to them. "I think I've found the perfect place for you." It came with a view and a high price tag, but it was worth every penny.

Melanie and James loved the house and agreed. So did another couple who were looking with her archrival Sasha Hearst over at Windermere, which meant Suzanne had a bidding war on her hands. She hated bidding wars. Except when her people won.

Melanie and James didn't win. They dropped out after offering a measly thousand dollars over asking price, even though Suzanne tried her best to convince them that they could well afford to go up yet another five. But James was conservative and Melanie was a wimp. Suzanne pasted a smile on her face and assured them that she'd find something else for them that would be equally wonderful, even though she knew she wouldn't. That had been the perfect house and they'd let it get away.

To top off her day she learned that one of her deals wasn't going to make it through escrow. Ugh.

But that was the real estate business, she reminded herself as she left the office. Tomorrow would be better.

Still, she felt grumpy as she sat on a cold metal chair at the Happy Feet dance studio, watching her daughter and a dozen other five- and six-year-old ballerinas do their *battement tendus*. The dance recital was right around the corner and the person Suzanne had paid to make Bryn's costume hadn't even started it yet. Frustrating as she found this, Suzanne understood. Everyone was overextended, especially with the holidays looming. Holidays. Shopping. She hadn't even begun.

Simply thinking about all she had to do started a headache blooming. She reached into her purse, pulled out her little bottle of Excedrin, and popped one. She used to need water to wash them down. Now she swallowed them dry.

The girls began to work on their dance number for the recital. They were all going to be sugar plum fairies and Bryn was so excited it was almost all she talked about. The only subject that took precedence over fairyhood was the hope that Santa would bring her a puppy for Christmas.

Suzanne had already informed her daughter that Santa didn't carry puppies in his sleigh. They might fall out and get hurt. Bryn had assured her mother that Santa's sleigh came equipped with seat belts. Who had told her that? Probably Guy. He was the moving force behind this, sure that every kid needed a dog. Well, every mom didn't need a dog, and this mom needed one like she needed to take up mud wrestling. Bryn would get a pretty stuffed puppy to put on her bed. That kind of dog never peed in the house.

The dance lesson was over and Bryn hopped up to her. "Did you see me, Mommy?"

"Yes," Suzanne lied. Actually, she'd gotten so preoccupied that she hadn't seen a thing. But she knew she was safe in adding, "You were great."

Bryn beamed and jumped up and down. "Can we get ice cream?"

On the days when Guy took their daughter to ballet they always stopped on the way home for ice cream, thus succeeding in spoiling Bryn's appetite for dinner.

"Not tonight, sweetie. We have to get home. Daddy's making dinner."

By the time they got home the aroma of Italian spices filled the house.

"Daddy, we're home!" Bryn called. She started to race across the entryway.

"Ah-ah! Shoes," Suzanne reminded her.

Bryn fell down and quickly pulled off her shoes, tossing them in the general direction of the wicker shoe basket Suzanne kept by the door, then raced off down the hallway toward the kitchen.

Suzanne followed at a slower pace. She was suddenly so tired she barely had enough energy to admire the antique table in the entryway or the shine of her highly polished hardwood floors and how well they set off the new rug as she walked past her living room. It looked exactly like something out of *Better Homes and Gardens*. In fact, the whole house looked that way and good looks didn't just happen. She had worked hard making the house into something beautiful, a real step up from her childhood home.

Step? This wasn't a mere step up; it was an entire staircase. The rickety mess of a house Suzanne had grown up in had been nothing to bring friends home to. Not so here. Suzanne could entertain Martha Stewart herself.

"Hi, babe," Guy greeted her. He had shed his suit and was standing at the stove in jeans and his old University of Washington sweatshirt, stirring his favorite brand of bottled spaghetti sauce. He'd rumpled his dark hair in the process of changing and hadn't bothered to unrumple it. Because he was so darned handsome, the look fit him well. Two glasses of red wine sat next to him on the counter and he held one out to her. "You look pooped. Not a good day in the real estate biz?"

He leaned down and kissed her and she took the wine. "You could say that. I found the perfect house for the Coxes and they wimped out." She shook her head sadly at the memory of the couple's foolishness.

"Bidding war, huh?"

"It's hard to have a war when one side surrenders after the first shot's been fired."

"Well, maybe they're on a budget."

"They could afford it," Suzanne scoffed.

"Maybe they don't want to sink everything they own into a house. Maybe they have other priorities."

Was that some kind of hidden message? She studied her husband, but he didn't give her much to study.

She watched as he shoved a handful of angel hair pasta into a pot of boiling water. "What could be more important than having a nice home for your family?"

He shrugged. "Everyone has a different definition of nice, babe."

"I guess," she conceded. "But they were fools. That was the ideal house for them and they let it get away. The Turner deal is going south on me, too." She started pulling plates out of the cupboard. "What a day."

"I know all my steps, Daddy," piped Bryn, and demonstrated.

Guy smiled fondly at her. "Good for you, princess." He ruffled her hair and then set to work draining pasta.

"Grammy is going to be so proud when she comes up to visit," added Suzanne. Now, why had she mentioned her mother's upcoming Christmas visit? Just the thought of the mess that would come with her was enough to destroy all the good work of the Excedrin: Popsicle sticks and glue everywhere, chaos in the kitchen 24-7, tacky popcorn strings—ugh. Her mother was like Martha Stewart's trashy cousin and, of course, she'd want to spread the love. Well, she wasn't touching the tree. Suzanne would make that clear. Hopefully, since she wasn't coming up until the day before Christmas she couldn't cause too much of a problem. Please, God, let that be true.

"If I dance nice maybe Santa will bring me a puppy," said Bryn.

"Oh, sweetie, Santa doesn't have any puppies scheduled for this neighborhood," Suzanne said. Somehow the puppy message wasn't getting through.

"But I asked," Bryn said, determined as ever to win this argument.

"Yes, but there are only so many puppies to go around. And I think the last delivery will be in . . . Virginia."

"What's Virginia?" asked Bryn.

"Someplace that's not here," replied Suzanne. She could feel Guy's gaze on her and turned to see him looking at her with disappointment. "What?" she said defensively. He shook his head and turned back to the spaghetti, a sure sign that they would be discussing this later. Goody.

TEN

Sure enough, later that evening, after Bryn was in bed and Suzanne and Guy were settled on the couch with a fire in the gas fireplace and another glass of wine, he said, "I think we should reconsider the dog thing. You know the Lovgrins are trying to find homes for those foster puppies."

How could she not know? Every time she came to the day care provider's house to pick up Bryn she had to see the smelly beasts.

"Golden labs are great dogs for kids," said Guy.

She set down her wineglass and sat up and frowned at him. "Who are you kidding? I saw the trailer for *Marley and Me*. Anyway, just because Bryn wants a dog it doesn't mean she has to have one. My God, I'd like a Jag for Christmas. Are you going to run out and get one for me?"

"Not after all the money we've spent on this place," he teased.

"We don't have time in our life for a dog," she reminded him. Sometimes it seemed like they barely had time in their life for each other. That thought bothered her so she shied away from it. "Who'd housebreak it?"

"We both could," he said, pulling her back to him.

"Nice of you to volunteer me."

He grinned, unrepentant.

"Guy, we're never around. It wouldn't be fair to the animal."

Now his grin got bigger. "That's changing."

A sick feeling settled over her. What horrible news was he about to announce? Was he quitting to run a home business? "What?"

"Remember I told you I was going to talk to Jameson about working from home a couple days a week? Well, I did. Starting in January I'll be home on Mondays and Fridays."

"And what about the other days?" she argued.

"You're around in the mornings sometimes."

"And sometimes I'm not. And on the days I'm not, a dog will chew up shoes, rip sofa cushions, and gnaw my new rug to bits."

"Not if we get a baby gate and a crate."

Which the thing would turn into a doggie bathroom.

"Let's at least think about it," Guy urged.

"I'll think," she said, "but not very hard and not very long. Bryn's too young for a pet anyway. We should wait until she's older and more responsible."

"I had a dog by the time I was her age," he argued, and kissed her ear.

And he'd had dogs ever since. He'd grown up with the sloppy, smelly things. In fact, he'd had a dog before he met her. It was an ugly mutt. She'd seen pictures of Guy and Morris the Mutt posed on hiking trails, in boats, on his front porch. They were just dating when Morris finally expired of old age, and Guy had mourned the dog as if it were a child. He'd always said he'd never get another and that had been fine with her, but now, with Bryn asking, he was teetering on the edge of dog ownership again, ready to take her over with him.

"Can we please not talk about this anymore tonight?" she pleaded. "I am so tired."

"Tired? There's a surprise." He started to move away.

She stopped him. "But I'm not that tired," she murmured, setting aside her wine. Actually, all she wanted to do was fall into bed and sleep for a hundred years, but she could put off sleep long enough to show her husband some love. And distract him from talking about dogs.

It was harder to distract herself. Her guilty mother's conscience continued to prod her. She didn't spend enough time with her daughter. The least she could do was let the child have a pet. She told her conscience to shut up. Several times. Yes, Bryn wanted a dog, but once the novelty wore off it would be Suzanne taking care of it. A stuffed puppy would be perfect. She and Bryn could play with it together. Maybe they'd name it Morris and Guy could play with it, too. Ha.

Wednesday was a great day. A miracle occurred and Suzanne found another perfect house for the Coxes, and it was a steal. They had learned their lesson, and this time they didn't dither on price and won the prize. Later, when Kiley called, Suzanne was in a great mood.

"I have a prezzie for you," said Kiley.

"I thought we weren't going to do presents this year," Suzanne protested as she sorted through the pile of papers on her desk. Not that she minded exchanging presents, but she hadn't had time to shop.

"I know," said Kiley, "but this is something I really want you to have."

It was sweet of Kiles, but dang, now Suzanne had one more thing on her to-do list. She'd race to Nordstrom's on the way to pick up Bryn and get something. Maybe she'd give Kiley a gift certificate. She could use some new clothes. While she was at it she'd get one for Allison, too.

Problem solved, deep breath. "Okay, why don't you come over for dinner Friday? I'm making Indian."

"Can't. I've got a date."

Suzanne cringed. "With the snow globe dude?"

"That would be the one. We're taking his mom to the living Christmas tree concert."

Suzanne could hear the smile in her friend's voice. Oh, boy. Kiles was sliding right over the edge of the romantic cliff. Suzanne just knew it.

"I thought I'd swing by tonight on my way to Allison's."

"Oh. What are you guys doing?"

"We're making fudge."

Suzanne liked fudge. How come she wasn't invited?

"We'd have told you except you've been so busy lately," Kiley added.

"I'd have made time."

"Well, then, want to come?"

She watched the fingers of rain slithering down her office window and shivered. This would be a perfect evening to hang out in Allison's kitchen, surrounded by the aroma of melting chocolate. But . . . "I can't," she admitted. "I have to show a house at seven-thirty."

"I'll stop by at six," Kiley said, her tone of voice adding, *See? That's why you didn't get invited to make fudge.*

Suzanne hung up and drummed her fingers on her desktop. What else had she heard in Kiley's voice, a little bit of judgment? As if it was a bad thing that she worked for a living?

Her conversation with Kiley left Suzanne feeling out of sorts, but she pasted on a polite smile for April Lovgrin when she picked up Bryn. The Lovgrins' home was kid heaven, full of toys and pets. The Lovgrins also took in foster puppies, keeping them until they got adopted. This had seemed like a plus when Suzanne first put Bryn in day care there. Now it was a thorn in her side. Every day, just like today, Bryn greeted her, holding a roly-poly puppy. Was April putting her up to this?

"Look, Mommy," said Bryn, holding up the pup. "His name is Happy."

Wasn't that the name of one of the seven dwarves? Messy would have been more accurate.

April stood behind Bryn in jeans and a green sweat-shirt, a Santa hat shoved over her auburn hair. "We only have two left. This one and his sister," she said, giving Suzanne yet another chance to stake a claim.

"I'm sure you'll find a nice home for him," said Suzanne.

"Guy was pretty interested in this little fella," said April.

Guy and April were in cahoots. "We're not quite ready for a dog yet." The puppy wriggled in Bryn's arms and lapped her cheek with a sloppy dog tongue. *Eeew.* "Don't let him lick you like that," said Suzanne. "He probably just finished licking his bottom. Here, honey, put him down. We have to go."

Bryn set the puppy down with reluctance. Of course, it tried to follow them, bounding after Suzanne like she was a giant dog toy.

"No, no, doggie, get away," said Suzanne, giving it a nudge with the toe of her high heel.

April made a face and snatched the stupid thing up as if she'd just rescued it from Cruella De Vil.

Okay, so Suzanne's shoe had a bit of a pointed toe. She hadn't hurt the dog. Still, she felt her cheeks warming. "Don't want him to get out and get hit by a car," she explained.

April just nodded.

Suzanne felt like a dog-beating monster now. "Well,

thanks for watching Bryn," she said, injecting extra appreciation in her voice. "You're the best."

April's smile didn't thaw, so Suzanne got the heck out of there.

"Can we write a letter to Santa tonight?" asked Bryn as they drove away.

"Another letter?" Oh, geez. She already knew what was going to be in it.

Bryn nodded. "I want to ask him for Happy."

"I think Santa already has a home in mind for Happy."

Bryn's lower lip jutted out and a tear slipped down her cheek.

Great, thought Suzanne miserably. First she'd kicked a dog. Now she'd made her daughter cry.

But she hadn't kicked the dog. She'd just nudged it away. And it was really Guy's fault that her daughter was crying. He was the one who put the idea of a puppy into Bryn's head in the first place. *Maybe Santa will bring you a puppy.* What was that about? Maybe Santa would bring Guy a lump of coal. He sure deserved it.

Kiley arrived promptly at six, just as Suzanne was serving the frozen pizza she'd picked up at QFC on the way home.

"Want some?" Guy offered. "There's plenty."

Kiley shook her head. "Thanks, but I already ate. I can't stay long, anyway."

Because she was off to make fudge while Suzanne was off to try and make a sale. Kiley looked so happy, so relaxed, like life was wonderful. For one delusional moment, Suzanne found herself feeling a tiny bit jealous. A nice, fat commission would buy an entire house full of fudge, she reminded herself.

Kiley set a green foil gift bag bursting with gold tissue paper on the kitchen table. "Open it."

"This is pretty," said Suzanne. She loved presents, loved pretty wrapping paper almost more than what lay under it, and she always coordinated her present wrapping with her Christmas tree decorations. This year she intended to dress her tree, her house, and her family to the nines.

"Come on, open it," urged Kiley.

Suzanne fished inside the bag. She knew what it was the minute her fingers closed around it. *Oh, no.* Sure enough.

"Hey, a snow globe," said Guy. "That's a great one."

And it would look gorgeous on her mantel. The only catch was, Kiley would expect her to see something in it. "I can't take this," Suzanne protested. And not just because of the woo-woo factor. "You paid a small fortune for it."

"Yes, but what I got from it was priceless. I think I'm supposed to pass it on."

"But I don't need anything," said Suzanne.

Bryn held out her hands. "I want to see it."

Suzanne moved her daughter's dish out of the way. "Okay, hold it very carefully," she said, and hovered.

"It's so pretty," whispered Bryn in awe.

"Shake it," said Guy. He leaned over and helped her.

Suzanne held her breath, fearing her daughter would drop the snow globe. Or, worse, Kiley would start seeing things.

The snow settled, revealing the same little village and the angel. Good. Safe.

Bryn gave a gasp of delight. "A puppy!"

A what?

ELEVEN

ook, Daddy!" cried Bryn.

Guy grinned. "Well, whaddya know."

Suzanne looked, too. There was nothing in the snow globe but an angel window-shopping outside a toyshop.

"It looks just like Happy," Bryn said, exercising her imagination to the max.

"Oh, look. He's found a home in Virginia," said Suzanne.

"No, he hasn't, Mommy," insisted Bryn. "That's our house."

"It sure is," agreed Guy, smiling. "There's our red front door and the Christmas wreath Mommy just got."

Okay, enough encouraging false hope, Suzanne thought irritably. "What do you know! A house in Virginia that's just like ours," she said, giving her husband a look that warned retribution if he didn't cease his naughty behavior.

Meanwhile, Kiley the Typhoid Mary of Christmas was beaming cluelessly.

Bryn shook the thing again, watching it in delight.

"What else do you see? I think I see a new doll," said
Suzanne.

Bryn was focused on the snow globe. "I just see
Happy," she said matter-of-factly.

"Well," said Suzanne briskly, "I bet the puppy in there is
tired." She took the snow globe from Bryn's reluctant hands.
"We'll put him on the mantel so he can go to sleep, okay?"

"Can't he sleep with me?" begged Bryn.

"No, baby," said Suzanne. "This is very old. It might
break. We'll put it on the mantel where it will be safe."

"Can I see Happy in it again tomorrow?" asked Bryn.

I hope not. "Maybe," said Suzanne. "Or you might see
something else. You never know."

Kiley stood, saying, "I'd better get going."

Yeah, fine. Run now that the damage is done.

"It looks like you guys are getting Bryn a dog for
Christmas after all," Kiley as she took her coat from the
hall closet.

"Uh, no."

Kiley's brows knit. "But Bryn saw—"

"What she wanted to see," finished Suzanne. "The dog
thing is not happening."

"Oh." Kiley looked nonplussed for a moment. "But
Guy saw it."

"Guy was playing along. He wants a dog almost as
much as Bryn. Sorry to burst your bubble."

"I can tell," said Kiley with a scowl.

Now she'd offended Kiles. The part of Suzanne that
felt bad was quickly devoured by its sensible twin, which
said, *The sooner Kiles learns that grown-ups do not live
in la-la land the better.*

Still, she only wanted to be the voice of reason, not
the Grinch. "I'm sorry I can't make fudge with you guys.
Save me some?"

"Sure." Kiley's voice was frosty.

Suzanne laid a hand on her arm and added, "I do love the snow globe. It's beautiful and it will look lovely on my fireplace mantel."

"It's not just a decoration, Suz," Kiley said, looking at her earnestly. "I hope you give it a chance to do something for you."

"I don't know what it's going to do," said Suzanne. "There's nothing I need." Well, money. That always came in handy. Now Kiley was looking so disappointed Suzanne added, "Except my friends. Don't be mad. Okay?"

Kiley sighed and nodded. "Okay."

After she left Suzanne found herself feeling like she had failed some secret test. She was a hard-working realist; therefore she didn't qualify for the fudge reward. *We'd have told you except you've been so busy lately.* The implication: You're too busy for your friends. Then there was Guy's crack the night before. *Tired? There's a surprise.* As if she got worn out on purpose. What was wrong with everyone these days? This was a crazy time of year. What was so shocking about the fact that she was busy? And tired?

She'd make a superhuman effort to go by Kiley's place after she'd shown that house. She could have her clients through in under an hour.

Or not. Her clients loved the house and wanted to make an offer immediately. A good real estate broker didn't say, "Tell you what. I have to go make fudge with my girl-friends, but I'll be on that first thing tomorrow." So she drew up their offer. Of course, the seller counteroffered. So by the time Suzanne and the listing agent were done it was after nine and she was pooped. But very satisfied. She'd closed the deal. She'd found her clients the perfect house and she'd made a perfectly respectable chunk of change. That trumped making fudge any day, even at Christmas.

Still, hanging out with Kiley and Allison would have been fun.

She came home to find Guy up in the bonus room, flopped on the leather couch, watching a remake of *A Christmas Carol*. He looked up at her and said, "Congratulations," robbing her of the opportunity to announce her success.

"How'd you know I made the sale?"

"The smug smile."

She lifted his feet and plopped down on the end of the couch, letting him use her lap as a footstool. "Well, then, since you were smart enough to figure out that I made the sale you should also be smart enough to be praising me for my brilliance."

He smiled. "You're brilliant, babe. Are we rich yet?"

Not with the bills they had.

"Your daughter asked for a puppy when she said her prayers tonight," Guy informed her.

First Santa, now God—Bryn was really bringing in the heavy artillery. Suzanne had found it easy enough to explain why Santa couldn't come through. God was another matter. And Kiley hadn't helped with that darned snow globe. Which reminded Suzanne: "Did you have to say you saw a puppy in the snow globe?"

"I call it as I see it," he said with a shrug.

Suzanne pointed a finger at him. "No way did you see anything. You just said that to encourage Bryn and to back me into a corner."

Guy dropped his smile and studied her intently. "Suz, what's happened to you?"

"What is that supposed to mean?" she bristled. Nothing had happened to her. She was the same person she'd always been.

"What happened to just working part-time? That was all you were going to do. Remember?"

"I can't help it if my business has grown," she said. She shoved his feet off her lap and stood up. "I'm working really hard to give us a nice home, Guy, and you don't seem to appreciate it."

"No," he corrected her. "You're working hard to give us a nice house, and I never said I wanted that."

"I can't believe what I'm hearing," she said, throwing up her hands.

He heaved a long-suffering sigh. "I understand that you want things nice, babe, but come on. You've turned into friggin' Martha Stewart on steroids."

She was working her fingers to the bone and this was the thanks she got. "Well, thank you for your appreciation," she snapped. "I guess next time I want to celebrate making a sale I'll do it with someone at work," she added, and left. *There, chew on that.*

She took a bubble bath, and then went to bed with the latest issue of *Better Homes and Gardens*. She didn't find out whether Guy had given any thought to what she said because she fell asleep before he came to bed, and by the time she woke up the next morning he had already left for work.

That was just as well, she decided. There really was no sense in picking up the potentially explosive discussion. Better to let sleeping puppies lie.

But as she got ready for her day a new concern niggled at her. She'd thought that Guy was as happy with their life as she was. Surely their happiness didn't depend on whether or not they got a dog. And surely he didn't really want her to scale back when she was doing so well with her career.

Every marriage has issues, she reminded herself as she dropped Bryn off at day care.

And every mother has parenting challenges, she added

later, when Bryn pouted all the way home after Suzanne told her they couldn't bring Happy with them.

"We don't have a bed for him," Suzanne had pointed out. "He'd have nowhere to sleep."

Of course, Bryn had a solution for that. "He can sleep with me."

Now, there was a disgusting thought. "We don't have a dog dish or dog food or a flea collar," added Suzanne.

"Let's get them now," Bryn suggested.

"Bryn, we are not bringing Happy home," Suzanne had finally said.

Bryn had crossed her arms and scowled just the way Suzanne used to when she was a little girl. Then she'd added tears, and they were still rolling down her cheeks when they walked through the front door.

"Whoa, what's this?" Guy greeted them.

He was already out of his suit and in his stocking feet, wearing his favorite ratty sweats in honor of fight night. Another hour and the bonus room would be a rocking place, with men shouting at the TV screen, punching the air with their fists, and spilling beer everywhere. The perfect ending to a perfect day.

"Mommy won't let me have Happy," sobbed Bryn. "And now Santa won't bring him."

Not if he doesn't want to come down the chimney and get barbecued by a roaring fire.

Guy frowned at Suzanne. It wasn't your normal, garden-variety frown. It was something worse, tinged with an emotion Suzanne had rarely seen, at least not when he was looking at her: disgust.

She realized she'd taken a step backward. She stopped and put up her chin. "There is more than one person living here, you know."

"Yes," said Guy. "There is." He picked up Bryn and

carried her out to the kitchen. "Don't worry, Brynnie, Santa will have something cool for you. Hey, how about some leftover spaghetti?"

Suzanne slammed down her briefcase. Fine. Make her the bad guy just because she was trying to be practical. And, speaking of practical, Guy hadn't even removed Bryn's shoes, Suzanne fumed as she slipped off her heels. He'd done that deliberately, to irritate her, she was sure. She followed them to the kitchen where Guy was already heating spaghetti in the microwave—a small bowl for Bryn, nothing for his wife, the puppy hater. No wineglass sat on the counter, either.

Fine. She could pour her own wine. She pulled a glass from the cupboard and a bottle of white wine from the fridge.

"There you go, kidlet," Guy said, setting the bowl in front of Bryn. "How about some milk?"

Bryn was still sniffling. "I want Happy."

"Yeah, well, sometimes Mrs. Claus makes it hard for Santa to come through," Guy muttered.

"Maybe that's because Mrs. Claus knows who will wind up doing most of the work," said Suzanne.

"Mrs. Claus doesn't know squat," Guy said flatly. The doorbell rang. "That's probably Clay. Looks like you're on duty now," he added, and left her alone with her sniffling daughter and a traitorous conscience that was turning guilty.

Oh, this is ridiculous, she thought. Sometimes kids need to learn to take no for an answer and now is one of those times.

"I saw Happy in the snow globe," Bryn said, and gave the table leg an angry kick.

Suzanne removed her daughter's shoes. "Finish your spaghetti, sweetie."

She went to the front hall and deposited the shoes in

the basket. Guy had vanished upstairs with his buddy for a night of testosterone overload. That was fine with her. She hoped he knocked himself out shadowboxing. Frowning, she straightened the mess of keys and receipts Guy had dumped on the entryway table. Dogs. Bah, humbug. It would have been nice if the snow globe had produced something worthwhile, like her and Guy and Bryn all strolling along a downtown street window-shopping, or at the Sheraton enjoying the gingerbread village display. Or a glimpse of the living room all done up for Christmas as proof that the decorator would get to her before New Year's Day.

With everything in place once more she turned and started back for the kitchen. She'd give Bryn a bubble bath and then they'd read a story. That would distract her from her dog fixation.

But Bryn was no longer in the kitchen. As Suzanne passed the living room door she spotted her daughter balancing on tiptoe on the arm of the wingback chair Suzanne had positioned by the fireplace, one hand on the mantel, the other on the snow globe. And the chair was just about to tip.

"Bryn!"

Of course, startling her daughter was the equivalent of trying to make one final addition to a teetering tower of blocks. Bryn gave a guilty start and the chair began to go.

A shot of adrenaline gave Suzanne superhuman speed and strength and she leaped the rest of the way across the room. She managed to catch her daughter but she also caught the side of the glass-topped coffee table, lost her balance, and came down on a very twisted ankle before winding up splayed on the floor, Bryn on top of her. As all this happened she heard glass shatter and she felt a lightning bolt of pain flash up her leg. She saw stars, she saw the chair tumble away, saw the upended coffee table and her daughter's startled expression, and the snow globe in Bryn's hands churning up a white cloud.

Hitting the floor knocked the breath out of Suzanne. Pain made it difficult to regain it. Good God, she'd thought labor pains were bad, but this—there were no waves to peak and subside. This pain kept relentlessly pounding up her ankle.

"Get Daddy," she finally gasped.

With a wail of terror, Bryn set down the snow globe and ran off.

Suzanne closed her eyes against both the pain and the scene emerging as the snow settled inside the glass globe. *Nooooo.*

TWELVE

Bryn ran from the room, crying, "Daddy, Daddy!"

Suzanne gritted her teeth and sat up. The sight of her ankle was enough to make her light-headed and sick and she lay back down with a cry. No human ankle was meant to look like that.

Bryn had barely left before Suzanne heard the pounding of feet. Guy's friend Clay stopped at the door and gawked.

Guy rushed past him and knelt by her. "Suz, my God. What happened?"

"Bryn was climbing on the chair and fell. I think I'm going to be sick." *On the carpet. Noooo.* Suzanne clutched her stomach and willed the nausea back.

Bryn hovered in the doorway next to Clay. "I just wanted to see Happy," she said, and burst into fresh tears.

"It's okay, Brynnie," said Guy. "Suz, baby, we'd better get you to the emergency room."

"Yeah, that looks bad," Clay said as he picked up the crying Bryn.

"That damned snow globe," Suzanne growled, brushing tears from her cheek. "I wish Kiley had never brought it." The thing had been like Pandora's box, loosing all kinds of troubles on them. If they'd never seen it Bryn would have dropped her puppy fixation, Guy wouldn't have been mad, and Suzanne wouldn't have wound up with a foot that looked like it belonged on an elephant. And her coffee table would be in one piece.

"Let's get you to the car," Guy said to her.

"Bryn needs to go to bed," she protested.

"I can handle it, huh?" said Clay, giving Bryn a toss and making her smile for the first time since the accident. "Want Uncle Clay to put you to bed?"

Bryn sniffled and nodded. "Is my mommy going to be okay?"

"Of course, she is," said Guy. "Okay, babe. Up we go."

Suzanne tried not to groan as Guy carried her out and settled her in the car, but the pain was excruciating. No one ever died of a sprained ankle, she told herself, though it just felt like her injury was going to kill her. If she didn't get something for the pain soon she was going to gnaw off her leg.

The ride to Group Health Ballard took only minutes but it felt like hours, and the examination and X-rays were nearly unbearable. She had obviously angered the patron saint of dogs.

The final verdict was worse than anticipated. She hadn't simply sprained her ankle; she'd managed to break it. As soon as the swelling went down she'd be in a big, ugly cast. How was she supposed to drive with a broken ankle? How could she show houses? How could she do *anything*? Why the heck, if something had to get broken, couldn't it have been the snow globe?

When she finally came home it was with crutches and a splint. And, thank God, pain pills. Those not only took away the pain, they made it feel like not such a big deal that she suddenly had no life. Who cared, she decided as she floated away on clouds of drug-induced comfort and joy.

The next morning Suzanne awoke to the smell of coffee and an urgent message from her ankle that it was time for more painkillers. She spotted the bottle on her nightstand and raided it, then lay back against the pillows with a groan. While waiting for the meds to take effect she occupied her time listing the many ways she would destroy the snow globe once she was up and moving again: throw it off the Aurora Bridge, donate it to some gun club to use for target practice, beat it to smithereens with her crutches. That last one appealed the most. The enjoyment would last longer.

The pills kicked in and she decided it was safe to try and get up. A glance at the clock told her it was almost nine. Sheesh. She should be on her way to the office. Instead she was only on her way to the bathroom. It wasn't an easy trip with one working leg and, once there, she managed to drop one of her crutches and knock her fancy soap bottle off the counter. Of course it broke, sending a puddle of soap across the floor. Great. The way her luck had been going she'd slip on it and break her other ankle.

She managed to escape slipping on the soap and had just gotten back in bed when Guy arrived, bearing a mug of coffee. "I thought I heard you."

She frowned. "It was probably hard not to. I'm sure I sounded like a rhino."

"But a small one," he assured her, handing over the mug.

"Thanks," she murmured, then nodded to the clock on her nightstand. "You didn't go to work?"

"I took the day off."

Both of them missing work. Great. "Sorry. By the way, I managed to knock over the soap."

He shrugged. "Not a problem. I'll take care of it."

"What a mess everything is," she said miserably.

"It could be worse," he said. "Bryn could have been hurt. That was some rescue you managed, Supermom, leaping over the coffee table in a single bound."

"Not much of a leap considering the fact that I knocked it over," she said with a frown. "How on earth am I going to do anything?" Right before Christmas—could she have picked a worse time for this?

"Don't worry. Help is on the way," Guy said from the bathroom.

She could hear the sounds of glass scraping on the floor. What was he using to clean that up? One of her good towels, of course.

"You hired someone?" she called. Where had he found somebody so quickly?

He reappeared in the doorway bearing a towel full of mess. "This help is free."

She got a sudden uneasy feeling in the pit of her stomach. "Free? Who?"

"Your mother. She's already on her way up from Portland."

"My . . . ? Oh, no."

Suzanne knew what that meant. Corny movies on TV every night, including a command screening of *It's a Wonderful Life,* the dreaded tacky home-crafted decorations, and, of course, a lecture on what a great blessing in disguise Suzanne's broken ankle was. Now she could take time to savor the joys of the season. As if Suzanne didn't already.

But she didn't savor the season the way her mother did, which meant she didn't do it right. Like all daughters since the dawn of time, she didn't measure up to her mother's expectations.

She could hear her mother now. "You don't need a decorator, dear, not when we can cut out snowflakes and paint Santas on the windows." Just the thought of what the house would look like under her mother's reign was enough to make Suzanne shudder.

"Why did you have to call her?" Suzanne groaned.

"I didn't," Guy said. "She happened to call last night and Clay told her what happened. She called again after you were in bed and insisted on coming. What could I do?"

"You could have told her we're fine," Suzanne said irritably.

"Yeah? You're on pain pills and crutches. Just how fine are we?"

"Perfectly," Suzanne insisted, even though she knew it was a lie.

"You'll be better if you get some help and some rest," Guy said. He leaned over and gave her a kiss on the forehead. "The more you rest the faster you'll heal."

"What's Bryn doing?" she asked.

"Watching a Disney princess movie. So I'm going to check on my e-mail and make some calls," he said, heading for the door. "Do you want breakfast before I start?"

The last thing she wanted was food. She shook her head.

"Okay. Call or bang on the floor with your crutch if you need something," he said, and left.

What she needed he couldn't bring her. She glared at her useless foot. This was grossly unfair.

The phone rang. She snapped it open and said a pissy, "Hello."

"It's nine-thirty. Are you on your way?" asked Julie, her partner. Julie was the office's other top seller. She and Suzanne had dreamed up the holiday home tour the year before, and with their combined flair and drive it had been a huge success. This year they anticipated twice the turnout and twice the business.

Of course Suzanne was supposed to have been in the office by now and they should have been working on the home tour. "I broke my ankle," she said bitterly. But the cursed snow globe was just fine.

"Oh, no."

"Oh, yes. Right now I'm in bed getting high on pain-killers," said Suzanne, smoothing the comforter over her legs.

"Gosh, I'm sorry. Do you need anything?"

"Only a new foot."

There was a moment's silence on the other end of the line, followed by a tentative, "Um, how long are you going to be in bed?"

"Just a couple of days," Suzanne promised. "I'll be up and around by the tour. Don't worry."

"Well, okay," said Julie, sounding doubtful. "But if you're not I can pull in Maria. We can handle it."

And the sales that went along with it. "I'll be fine," Suzanne assured both Julie and herself.

Or not. It seemed all she was good for was sleeping, and when the painkillers started to wear off she wanted to scream. The crutches were instruments of torture and the thought of going downstairs made her shudder. She could just see herself falling and breaking her neck. Ugh.

Bryn was restless and alternated between wanting to play Candy Land and wanting to know why Happy couldn't come live with them. "Because that's how it is," Suzanne finally said wearily.

Her mother arrived early that afternoon. She floated into the bedroom in a cloud of cheap gardenia perfume, wearing her latest discount store bargains. She was still living on a teacher's salary, but she was an empty-nester now and could afford better clothes. Still, she insisted on dressing like she hadn't a penny to her name no matter how many gift cards her daughter sent her.

"Who do I need to impress?" she always said.

No one, obviously. Certainly not a man. Mary Madison had been a widow way too long to ever think about adding a new man to her life. Although maybe she should. Then she'd have someone besides her children to drive crazy.

She took one look at Suzanne and her face filled with pity. "Oh, my poor girl." She perched on the edge of the bed and laid a gentle hand on Suzanne's brow as if Suzanne were dying of a fever.

All right. Maybe it hadn't been such a bad idea to call her.

"How do you feel?" she asked.

"Rotten," said Suzanne. Frustrated. Grumpy.

"Well, I'm going to make you some good, old-fashioned vegetable soup. You used to love that when you were sick."

Her mother's vegetable soup—the finest restaurant in Seattle couldn't touch it. "That would be great," said Suzanne.

Now Bryn was in the room, squealing, "Grammy!" and running pell-mell toward her grandmother.

Mom intercepted her just before she could crash onto the bed. "Hello, my littlest angel," she cooed, and gave Bryn a big kiss. "Would you like to come help Grammy make soup for your mommy?"

Bryn jumped up and down and clapped her hands. "Yes!"

Suzanne searched her memory for a time Bryn had been that excited over doing something with her and came up empty. That was because her brain was fuddled with pain pills. Later she'd remember something. Wouldn't she?

THIRTEEN

The second time Suzanne awoke it was to the aroma of tomato and spices and the yeasty fragrance of home-baked bread. Those were the smells of her childhood and as comforting as the blankets she was nestled under. Her mother's taste in clothes and décor were abysmal, but when it came to cooking, Mary Madison could have had her own show on the Food Network.

Suzanne stretched and then reached for her cell phone only to find it was no longer on her nightstand. She checked to see if it had fallen on the floor. No cell phone there, either. She frowned. If Bryn had sneaked it away to play with she was going to be in big trouble.

Suzanne pushed herself off the bed and grabbed the instruments of torture known as crutches, and made her clumsy way to the upstairs hall. "Guy!"

Guy didn't come. Instead her mother appeared at the foot of the stairs. She had donned an apron over her polyester pants and Bryn appeared at her side like a living accessory. "Oh, you're awake," she said.

Bryn detached herself and ran up the stairs, bearing a

miniature marshmallow tower covered in pink sprinkles. "Look, Mommy. We made marshmallow snowmen."

Goody. The craft marathon had begun.

Bryn held it out for Suzanne to take.

Suzanne kissed her daughter and gave her a hug. "That's very nice, Brynnie."

"This one's for you. Try it, Mommy," urged Bryn, shoving it in front of her nose.

"I can't right now, baby," said Suzanne. *Thank God.* "Mommy needs to take her pain pills first. You keep it for me in the kitchen. Okay?" Her daughter's hands were a sticky mess. "And then go wash your hands before you touch anything."

Bryn made a face and trudged back down the stairs and Mom's brows took a disapproving dip.

Ah, how well Suzanne knew that expression. "Where's Guy?"

"I told him there was no need to hang around here when he had things to do," said Mom, "not when I can take over."

Take over was right. And Guy had been happy to let her. What was with that? Her husband just ran off and left her the minute the next shift arrived?

He has to work, her rational self reminded her, but she told it to shut up. "Do you know where my cell phone is?"

"Oh, I took it downstairs," said her mother as if it were perfectly acceptable to take someone's cell phone. "I figured you need your rest."

Suzanne could feel her blood pressure rising. "I've had my rest. Now I need my cell phone."

Her mother's easy smile stiffened. "Fine. I'll get it. Would you like some soup?"

"That would be great," said Suzanne, equally stiff. "Thanks."

There was nothing else to say after that, and besides, Suzanne's ankle was not happy. Scowling, she maneuvered herself back to her bedroom. By the time she got back to bed she was exhausted. This was so not fun. She grabbed her bottle of happy pills and popped one. At the rate things were going, by the time her mother left she'd be a drug addict.

Mom appeared a few minutes later, carrying a tray with a steaming bowl of soup and a plate with a slice of fresh-baked bread smothered in Suzanne's healthful butter-substitute spread. The aroma of tomato, garlic, and onions spread through the bedroom. Suzanne sniffed and closed her eyes. Just the smell made her feel better.

She opened her eyes as Mom set the tray on her lap. There, next to the bread, lay her cell phone. Good. She was connected to the outside world once more.

Mom perched on the foot of the bed. "How are you feeling?" Her tone of voice said, *Let's make up.*

Sick in bed with her mommy bringing soup; suddenly, Suzanne felt twelve years old again, and in need of understanding. "Crummy. Frustrated." She tested a spoonful of soup. "This is great," she said, and dipped the spoon back in, dredging up a pile of finely cut carrot, celery, and parsnip. Mom had given her this recipe last winter but she'd never gotten around to making it.

"You always did love that soup. Your daughter likes it, too," Mom added with a smile.

Suzanne bit into the bread. Wait a minute. This wasn't her spread. This was real butter. "You bought butter?"

"Real butter is better for you than that awful imitation stuff," said Mom.

"You went out and bought butter?" When had she found time for that?

"I brought a few things up with me," said Mom. "I

figured if I was going to come up early for Christmas I might as well bring some ingredients for baking. I think Bryn will enjoy that."

"She'd like anything her grammy made," said Suzanne in an effort to be gracious. "I suppose she's been talking your ear off."

"A little." Mom smoothed the bedspread. "Mostly about a dog named Happy."

Suzanne shook her head. "That dog."

"She appears to have her heart set on it."

"Well, I have my heart set on a diamond necklace," Suzanne retorted. "That doesn't mean I'm going to get it."

"You're not a little girl," said her mother, with that same superior smile she always used when handing out unrequested advice. Before Suzanne could think of anything to say, she stood and moved away. "I'd better get downstairs and see what she's up to."

Suzanne let out her breath in an irritated hiss as her mother bustled her busybody self out of the room. Shouldn't she be at school still, bossing around helpless children? Two weeks of this. Suzanne would go crazy.

"I'm losing my mind," she told Allison when her friend called to check on her Saturday morning. "Julie is having to take my clients around, Bryn is making an army of marshmallow snowmen and expecting me to eat every one, and my mother is, well, my mother."

"Any time you want to trade moms let me know," said Allison, her voice taking on a scolding tone.

"How about now? I'll send her right over. She can help you make some more fudge."

"Deal," said Allison.

Suzanne could see Allison and Mom in Allison's state-of-the-art kitchen, whipping up exotic confections in Allison's designer pots. Those two had a mutual admiration society going. "Why don't you come over here for dinner tonight instead?" What the heck? Let Allison have a dose of Mom. It would give Suzanne a break.

"That sounds good to me."

"Great," said Suzanne. "I'll call Kiles, too." Like Allison was always reminding her, girlfriend time was important.

"Don't bother," said Allison. "She already got a better offer. She and Craig are going skating at the Lynnwood Ice Center and then out for pizza."

Kiley was going into this new relationship at a gallop, racing for another heartbreak. "Have you met this guy?" asked Suzanne.

"Actually, he came by when we were making fudge. He's funny and kind, perfect for her. It looks like that snow globe was the best investment Kiles ever made."

"Yeah, well, it sure paid off for me," Suzanne grumbled.

"If you don't want it, I'll take it."

"You can have it with my blessing." Right along with her mother. "Just don't sue me when it ruins your life."

They chatted a little longer. Then Allison went back to her baking for the holiday home tour and Suzanne returned to being bored.

Until she remembered that the decorators were finally coming. Yes! She threw off the bed covers. She was going downstairs no matter what.

Since it was Saturday Guy was on hand to help her clean up and get downstairs. But on hearing about the pending invasion, he took off for the gym. She had coffee and a piece of toast for breakfast and averted her eyes from the ratty snowman and snow lady Mom and Bryn were constructing from cotton batting.

"We thought they would look nice on the fireplace mantel, right next to the snow globe," said Mom. "Didn't

we, Brynnie?" She smiled at Bryn who was happily glu-
ing a lopsided eye on her snow lady.

"We'll see," said Suzanne noncommittally. "I've got
the decorators coming today."

"Ah." Mom nodded, her politeness poorly masking her
disapproval.

Too bad, thought Suzanne. This was her house, not her
mother's.

To prove it she set up court in the living room and
watched while the place became a thing of beauty. When
the Holiday Creations crew left a nine-foot tree graced
the bay window, simply yet tastefully decked with gold
balls and wine-colored ribbon and tiny white lights. The
same theme was carried up the stair banister and along the
mantel.

Suzanne made the circuit with her crutches, pleased
with all she saw. Everything was perfect, from the front
hall to the powder room. "It looks like we're ready for the
holidays," she said happily as she swung her way back
into the living room.

Bryn, who had been following the workers from room
to room, looked at the mantel and frowned. "Where can
we put our snowman and snow lady, Grammy?"

Suzanne's mother cocked an eyebrow at her. That
eyebrow. Her mother always could say so much with it.
Right now Suzanne didn't particularly like what she was
saying.

"How about we put them on your dresser?" Suzanne
suggested.

Bryn's lower lip stuck out. "But then nobody can see
them."

That was the general idea.

"How about here?" Mom suggested, plopping the tacky
things on the new coffee table, right next to the pillar candle

arrangement. The perfect tacky finishing touch, and a fire hazard to boot.

"They might catch fire there," said Suzanne. Had her mother thought of that? Nooo. "I think your room would be better."

"But I want Aunt Kiley and Aunt Allison to see them," protested Bryn, frowning.

"They will," Suzanne assured her. "They'll come up to your room and look. And just think, you'll have your very own special Christmas room," she added. "You can put them right next to your pink Christmas tree, and you'll be able to look at them every night when you go to sleep."

Bryn gave up. "Okay." She hugged the ugly things to her and left the room, frowning.

Suzanne kept her gaze focused on her daughter, successfully avoiding visual contact with The Eyebrow. But she didn't escape The Sigh, which was almost as bad.

She turned to her mother and demanded, "What?"

"The house looks beautiful, dear. It really does. Certainly more lovely than anything you had growing up." Her mother stopped and bit her lip.

She was on a roll. Why stop now?

"But," prompted Suzanne. As if she didn't know what was coming next.

"I just think what makes a home truly beautiful is the happiness shared by the people who live in it."

"We're happy," Suzanne protested. How could they not be? "Our life is perfect."

"It certainly looks that way," said her mother. The sneaky little dig wasn't lost on Suzanne, but before she could respond, Mom said, "I think I'll get busy in the kitchen. If Allison's coming over she'll want Spritz Christmas tree cookies," then made her exit, leaving her daughter smarting.

The sting continued all day and into the evening, making it hard for Suzanne to appreciate her friend's visit. Guy had insisted on moving their daughter's craft project back down to the living room and the snow couple was now on the coffee table in place of the candles, sitting in judgment on Suzanne, and pronouncing her the world's worst mother. To top it all, Mom fussed over Allison as though she was the daughter Mom never had.

Finally, Suzanne had enough. "My ankle is hurting. I think I'm going to go to bed."

"Do you want help up the stairs?" Mom offered.

"You've helped enough for one day," Suzanne assured her.

"I'll help her," said Guy, getting up.

She would have appreciated his offer if his tone of voice hadn't added, *Pain in the butt that she is*. "I can manage," she said stiffly.

"Let your husband help you," said Mom. "That's what he's here for."

More unrequested advice. "Mom," Suzanne said sternly.

"You can pretend you're Scarlett O'Hara and he's Rhett Butler," quipped Allison in an attempt to lighten the moment.

"I can do it myself," Suzanne snapped.

Guy shrugged and said, "Okay then. Knock yourself out, babe."

Suzanne turned around in a huff and hobbled off.

By the time she got to her bedroom she had a thin film of sweat on her forehead and tears on her cheeks. No one understood her.

She managed in the bathroom, then popped a pain pill and fell into bed.

She had just gotten settled when her mother arrived with a cup of cocoa. She handed it over with an empathetic look. "I thought you could use this."

Mom always did think cocoa was the solution to all of life's problems. It had made Suzanne feel better when she was a child, but she wasn't a child now, even if she was acting like one.

"I know this isn't fun," her mother said gently, "but maybe there's a silver lining here. Maybe this is God's way of slowing you down a little."

Oh, that was helpful. "I don't need to slow down. I need to make money. This place doesn't maintain itself. It takes two salaries."

"I understand," said her mother.

What a joke. Their house growing up had been a hodgepodge of garage sale furniture and ugly, home-made decorations. Always a mess. Mom had never cared. She'd never even tried to improve the house. Instead she'd bumped along as if life was just fine as it was. Maybe for her, but not for her daughter. Suzanne still remembered having to make excuses for why she couldn't go on trips with her friends or to school dances when the truth was that there was no money in the budget for those extras. Was it so wrong for her to want to spare Bryn the same disappointments?

"No, you don't," Suzanne snapped. "I don't want to live like you."

She regretted the words the minute they were out of her mouth. They were true but they were also cruel. It was the pain pills; they were scrambling her brain.

Her mother turned to stone. "I know I couldn't provide you with the kind of elegant lifestyle some of your friends had, but really, was your life so bad, Suzanne? Our home wasn't full of expensive knickknacks but it was full of love. Which would you rather have had?"

Love, of course. Suzanne bit her lip.

"There's more to life than selling houses," her mother continued. "And there's certainly more to life than living in one that looks like something from a magazine layout. You're becoming so consumed with this place that you're starting to forget about the people who live in it. This isn't a dollhouse. Your husband and daughter are real people with real needs. And let me tell you, life is short. You can lose the people you love in a heartbeat. Now, drink your cocoa."

Suzanne scowled and set the cocoa on the nightstand as her mother left the room. She didn't want cocoa and she didn't want a lecture and she didn't want a broken ankle!

Even in sleep the torture continued. She dreamed that the angel flitted out of the snow globe and stood before her, an eight-foot tower in a glowing robe and a halo that looked suspiciously like Christmas lights. "You're a mess," she observed in disgust.

"Gee, thanks," Suzanne retorted. "It's your fault I'm like this, you know."

The angel rolled her eyes. "Oh, please."

"Is there a reason you're here?" Suzanne demanded.

"Yes, as a matter of fact, there is. I've come to show you your future. Look."

At first all Suzanne could see was mist. Then, slowly, it cleared and she made out a middle-aged, slightly over-weight woman sitting in a living room decorated for the holidays. The décor could have been lifted from the pages of *Better Homes and Gardens*.

"Well, the house looks great," Suzanne said.

"It should. There's no one in it to mess it up," said the angel.

"What happened to me?" wondered Suzanne, regarding her plumper, older self in disgust. "When did I gain all that weight?"

"Menopause," said the angel. "And you were de-pressed."

"Why was I depressed? What happened?" Suzanne asked, and braced herself.

"Your husband left you. He remarried. She's a total slob."

The blow to both her heart and ego made Suzanne gasp. "You're kidding, right?"

The angel cocked an eyebrow. "Do you think angels kid about things like this?"

"Why did he leave? I don't understand."

"Oh, don't play dumb," snapped the angel, adjusting her halo. "Why do you think he left?"

Suzanne decided to plead the Fifth. "What about my daughter?" she asked in a small voice. "Where is she?"

"Look," the angel said with a sweep of her hand.

"Oh, good Lord," gasped Suzanne as the angel showed her a garish house laden with multicolored lights, its yard a dump for every plastic holiday decoration ever invented.

"Don't worry," said the angel. "You don't have to deal with it. She never invites you over. She never comes to see you, either. You're a pain in the butt."

Suzanne blinked in shock. "What kind of a way is that for an angel to talk?"

"The truth hurts," said the angel. "By the way, I brought you a present." She turned around and picked up something hiding behind her robe and Suzanne saw it was a dog, a grown version of Happy.

The dog jumped out of the angel's arms and ran over to Suzanne and chomped into her ankle with huge fangs.

Suzanne woke up with a strangled scream to a dark room. She was sitting up in her bed and Guy was next to her.

He sat up, too. "You all right, babe?"

Suzanne pushed her damp hair out of her eyes with a

trembling hand. "It was awful. Bryn hated me and I was alone. And fat."

"You just had a nightmare. Everything's all right," he assured her, his voice heavy with sleep. He kissed the top of her head and then flopped back down and turned over on his side.

"Guy, am I a pain in the butt?"

"Sometimes," he mumbled, burying his head deeper in his pillow.

She leaned over him. "Would you leave me for a slob?"

"I wouldn't leave you for anything. Come on, babe, it's three in the morning. Let's go back to sleep," he added, easing her back down next to him.

"Guy, do you love me?"

"Of course I love you. Do you need another pain pill? Are you hurting?"

She was hurting, but it was nothing the pills on her nightstand could combat. "I'm fine," she lied. "Sorry I woke you."

"No problem," he said, and a moment later he was snoring.

But Suzanne lay in bed, wide awake, fearing that if she shut her eyes she'd fall back asleep and the angel would get her.

It gave her a lot of time to think.

By the time the first light of morning slipped past the bedroom curtains Suzanne had found a new attitude. Changes of heart were wonderful, she decided. She felt like a whole new woman, swathed in holiday warmth. This was going to be a truly perfect Christmas. She was going to make sure of it!

As soon as Guy went downstairs to help her mother

with breakfast she grabbed her cell phone and called the
Lovgrins, her heart racing with excitement. She barely
gave April time to say hello. "We'd like to get Happy for
Bryn for Christmas."

"Suzanne, I'm sorry," said April. "Happy was adopted
yesterday.

FOURTEEN

Suzanne stared at her phone in disbelief. "Yesterday?" How could this be? What kind of sick angel appeared to someone in a dream a day late?

"You said you didn't want him," April reminded her.

"I know, but I changed my mind." Here she was, turning over a new leaf, and the Spirit of Christmas was rewarding her by dropping a Christmas tree on her head. That wasn't how it worked for Scrooge. Something was terribly, terribly wrong here. "Don't you have any dogs left?"

There was a moment of silence on the other end of the line. "Maybe it was just my imagination," said April at last, "but you didn't seem interested in a dog. In fact, I got the distinct impression you don't much like dogs."

"Man's best friend? What's not to like?" lied Suzanne. "Guy has had dogs all his life and you know Bryn is dying for one."

Another pregnant pause.

Suzanne rushed to fill it. "April, I've had a dog epiphany. Really. If you have any puppies left it would mean so much to all of us to be able to adopt one."

"We still have Hildy."

Hildy, Happy, who cared? As long as it was a dog. "Great," said Suzanne. "We'll take her."

"All right," April said, her tone of voice adding, *I hope I won't regret this.* "We'll get things rolling for you. By the way, how's the ankle?"

"It's getting better," said Suzanne. It had to, she thought, since after Christmas she was going to have a new baby to care for.

She'd barely hung up the phone when her mother entered the room, carrying a mug of coffee and a plate with freshly baked cinnamon rolls. Her smile looked a little forced and Suzanne felt the weight of all the mean things she'd said the night before. "You didn't have to bring me anything. I was going to come down."

"That's okay," said her mother, handing over the goodies. "I wanted a minute to talk alone."

That meant another lecture was coming for sure, but this one was well deserved. "I'm sorry I've been such a brat," Suzanne said earnestly. "And I'm sorry about what I said last night."

Her mother shook her head and laid a hand on Suzanne's arm. "No, I'm the one who needs to apologize. There's no shame in working to have nice things. God knows I gave you few enough."

Suzanne saw the glisten of tears in her mother's eyes and felt fresh guilt. When had she become so shallow? Surely she hadn't been born that way. She hugged her mother fiercely. "You gave us love and that was plenty." Why had she thought she needed more? Why had she felt such a burning desire to be just like her rich friends?

"Thank you, darling," Mom said, and kissed her cheek. "Now, about this holiday home tour. How can I help you?"

* * *

The holiday home tour was a smashing success. Suzanne parked herself, cast and all, at the house that served as the reception home, plying visitors with Allison's brownies and brochures while Mom helped Julie and two other agents from the office squire visitors from house to house. By the end of the day three of the agency's listings had offers on them. Suzanne's mother had cinched one of the deals by informing a pair of expectant parents that their child would thank them someday for giving her such a lovely home to grow up in. Of course, being Mom, she had also thrown in as a bonus a little lecture on how to have a happy home.

"Do you really believe what you told them about having a nice house?" Suzanne asked as her mother tooled them home in Suzanne's Lexus.

"Beauty is a subjective thing," she said with a shrug. "I could tell they were in love with the house. They simply needed someone to give them permission to buy it."

Mom was a natural. "Maybe you should forget teaching and go into real estate," said Suzanne.

Her mother shook her head. "No. I'm exactly where I want to be. I like helping children learn and grow. And I like having time off at the holidays to be with my family," she added with a smile.

Actually, so did Suzanne.

When Christmas Eve came, Mom was in her element. Suzanne's brother, Loren, and his family ferried over from nearby Vashon Island and her mother stuffed them all to the gills with her famous Swedish meatballs. After the presents had been exchanged and Loren's family had left, she cleaned up the mess, restoring order to chaos, then led Bryn off for a bedtime story so Guy could steal away to fetch home the new puppy.

"I'd ask if you're going to be okay while I'm gone, but with your mom here that would be a dumb question," he said after he'd helped Suzanne upstairs. "Looks like her coming up early turned out not to be such a bad thing after all."

"It's worked out," Suzanne admitted.

"I'll say," agreed Guy, giving his stomach a satisfied pat. "Well, I'd better get going."

He gave her a quick kiss and started to leave but she caught his arm. "Remember when Bryn saw the puppy in the snow globe and you said you saw our house?"

"Yeah," he said slowly.

"Did you?"

Guy made a face. "Of course not. I was just playing along. I'll be back in half an hour."

Suzanne gave her lip a thoughtful chew as he left the room. Had she imagined what she saw? She supposed it didn't really matter at this point.

She was settled in bed by the time Guy returned with the female version of Happy. He plopped the new baby on the bed.

"My spread!" protested Suzanne as the puppy bumbled its way to her.

"It'll be okay," Guy assured her.

Happy the Second clambered up Suzanne's chest to lick her face, nearly bowling her over with a strong dose of puppy breath.

"Someone needs an Altoid," Suzanne said, picking up the pup and holding her at arm's length.

The puppy wriggled in her hands, anxious to display affection.

"Yes, you're a good dog," Suzanne assured her. "Now go see Guy," she added, holding the dog out to him.

"Come here, you," Guy said. "Time to be in your

crate." He cuddled the puppy to him much the way had cuddled Bryn when she was a baby.

The sight made Suzanne's heart catch. She had definitely done the right thing. But if the dog peed on her carpet . . .

Fortunately for Hildy-Happy, she didn't. And Bryn's ecstasy when she saw her father sitting at the foot of the tree on Christmas morning, the puppy in his arms, was worth more than a thousand ruined carpets.

"What a perfect present!" Allison exclaimed when she and Kiley stopped by on their way to their family celebrations. She picked the puppy up and it immediately went to work covering her neck and face in puppy kisses.

"No," said Suzanne, holding out a box wrapped in burgundy paper and tied with an elaborate gold ribbon. "This is a perfect present. Open it."

Allison set the dog down and reached for the present. "Is this what I think it is?" she asked with an eager smile.

"It's your turn," said Kiley.

Allison ripped into the paper, making Suzanne wince. She lifted the lid and fished out the snow globe.

"Shake it," urged Kiley.

Allison hesitated a moment. Then she shook her head and nested it back in its tissue paper bed. "No. Not before I have to go to my parents. It would be bad luck."

"Oh, come on," urged Kiley. "It'll help you get through the day."

Allison pulled out the snow globe, and gave it a jiggle.

"Well?" prompted Kiley. "See anything?"

Allison looked like she was going to cry. Uh-oh, thought Suzanne, and exchanged a worried look with Kiley.

"It looks like my grandma," Allison said. "Not exactly, but close enough."

"What's she doing?" asked Suzanne.

"She's drinking tea with me." Allison closed her eyes and hugged the snow globe.

"Maybe the snow globe is giving you courage," Kiley suggested.

Allison opened her eyes and nodded. "Probably. God knows, with my family I'll need it."

"Speaking of family"—Kiley checked her watch—"I've got to get going. Craig and I have to be at my parents' by one."

The three friends exchanged their other presents and then Kiley and Allison left Suzanne and her family to enjoy their holiday meal and their new baby.

"Happy looks different," Bryn observed later as she and the dog settled on the couch with Suzanne while Guy and Mom did K.P.

Uh-oh. "How?" asked Suzanne, hoping her tired brain would be able to come up with a quick explanation, appropriate for a seven-year-old, to account for for Happy's missing body part.

"He looks happier," said Bryn, petting the puppy's head.

"That's because he's found a happy home," said Suzanne.

"I'm glad Santa didn't take him to Virginia," Bryn said in a tired voice as Suzanne stroked her hair.

"Me, too," murmured Suzanne.

A few moments later both Bryn and the new puppy were asleep, Bryn snuggled next to Suzanne and the exhausted dog curled up on Suzanne's lap.

It was the best Christmas she'd had in a long time, she decided as she gazed at the flame in the gas fireplace.

"Now, that's a perfect picture."

She looked up to see Guy leaning in the doorway and smiled back at him. "Merry Christmas. Have I told you lately that you're a great husband?"

He grinned. "You're just saying that because it's true." He grabbed his digital camera from the coffee table and recorded the moment, then turned the camera so Suzanne could see.

She didn't need to look, really. She'd already seen this scene, in the snow globe.

FIFTEEN

Allison carefully set the snow globe on the front seat of her car to ride shotgun as she drove to her parents' house.

"You came on the scene just in time," she muttered. "I could use some moral support."

If she hadn't broken up with Lamar the week before she could have been with his family, enjoying the holiday with sane people. But she'd finally realized she loved his mother and sister more than him—not the right reason to keep a man. So today all she had to look forward to was Christmas dinner at her father and stepmother's house. With no Grandma to ease the torture.

It's only two hours, she reminded herself, two hours out of your day, out of your life.

Except what usually happened during those two hours was enough to give her nightmares for the following eleven months. In the past she'd had her grandmother to balance out the chaos but this year she was on her own.

She pulled up in front of the modest brick rambler in Ballard and parked in back of a black Hummer. So her stepbrother, Joey, and his wife were already here. How long had everyone been whooping it up? More to the point, how much eggnog had been consumed?

She took a deep breath to steel herself, then got out of the car and took her red velvet cake and the shopping bag full of gifts from the backseat. Maybe she was worrying for nothing. Maybe it would be okay.

Oh, who was she kidding? The day was bound to be a disaster. Grandma had always held the reins of what was left of her daughter's family, keeping an eye on things in the kitchen, frowning and gently shaking her head when the partying started to get out of hand, discreetly monitoring the punch consumption. No one was holding the reins now.

The neighborhood was an old one, consisting mostly of smaller homes, many renovated, all worth a small fortune. Several houses were festooned with Christmas lights. Her stepmother had gotten right into the spirit of things. The house dripped icicle lights, and a fat wreath sporting candy canes and red bows hung on the front door. To look at the place you'd have thought June and Ward Cleaver lived inside. Looks could be deceiving.

Allison heard the noise even before she opened the front door. Joey was playing one of his favorite tacky Christmas songs at full blast, and over that she could hear raucous male laughter and the barking of a dog—Boozle, her father's bloodhound.

She took a deep breath and forced herself to open the door. Just in time to hear the crash of something breaking in the living room. She walked in to find her father, her stepbrother, and another man, obviously a friend of Joey's, staring at a broken floor lamp, which now lay in pieces on the wood floor along with a few dust bunnies. With their rock concert souvenir T-shirts and droopy, faded jeans, Joey and his friend looked like redneck twins.

Dad had dressed up for the day and was resplendent in

slacks and a sweater so brightly red Allison almost needed sunglasses to look at him. "You've done it now, sport," he said to Joey with a shake of his head.

"It wasn't me," protested Joey. He gave his friend a shove. "Way to go, bigfoot."

Here was a case of the pot calling the kettle black. Joey was the size of a small nation, easily dwarfing his buddy, a thirty-something man with a receding hairline.

Now Allison's stepmother Sandi, Aunt Connie, and Joey's wife, Carissa, were in the living room. Sandi's dyed blond hair was already going limp and her face was flushed—hopefully from working in the kitchen and not from having sampled too much eggnog. She wore tight jeans to show off the fact that she'd recently lost five pounds and a sweater as insistently red as her husband's and trimmed with rhinestone-studded snowflakes.

"My lamp!" she cried, throwing up her hands. "What were you boys doing?"

"Just a little wrestling," said Joey.

Meanwhile, Boozle had spotted Allison and trotted over to greet her, jumping up on her with an excited bark.

"Down, Boozle," she commanded, struggling to push him away and keep a hold on her presents and the cake.

Joey's face lit up at the sight of Allison. "Hey, Sis. Long time no see." He walked over to her and gave her a playful punch in the shoulder, then checked out her leather jacket, jeans, and black turtleneck sweater, nodding appreciatively. "You look good. Lost weight?"

Yes, but she wasn't going to admit that in front of some stranger. She ignored the question, kissing her father, who swept her into a big bear hug with a "Merry Christmas, Allie."

Sandi pointed a finger at Joey. "Clean up that mess and no more wrestling." She broke off to welcome Allison with a kiss on the cheek. Yep, Sandi had already been in the eggnog.

Carissa fetched the broom and dustpan. She was a pretty woman, with auburn hair and big green eyes and a perfect figure, not to mention a great job. What she was doing with Joey, the king of the unemployment check, was a mystery to Allison. They'd gotten married right after high school, so maybe she just didn't know any better.

Meanwhile, Joey was already saying to his friend, "This is Allison. Didn't I tell you she's hot?"

The friend smiled sheepishly at Allison. "Hi. I'm Ed. I didn't break the lamp," he added.

Allison sighed inwardly. Two hours. Just two hours. She said a quick hi to Ed, then set her bag of gifts by the tree and kissed her Aunt Connie. When Allison was little she had thought Aunt Connie was a movie star—an easy mistake to make considering the fact that Aunt Connie had looked like Audrey Hepburn, slim, lovely, and well dressed. She'd lost her svelte figure when she gave up smoking, but never her taste in clothes. Today her curves were concealed under an ensemble in classic lines and fashionable colors, and her dark hair, now shot with gray, was cut short and stylish. She wished Allison a merry Christmas and managed a sour smile.

Allison supposed she'd be sour too if she'd gone through two husbands and was reduced to spending Christmas with the flake who'd married her brother.

"I'll take the cake into the kitchen," Aunt Connie volunteered. She lifted the plastic container from Allison's hand and marched back to the kitchen, past a table made festive with Spode Christmas dishes that had belonged to Allison's mother. Someday they were supposed to go to Allison, but every year another piece got chipped or broken and she wasn't holding out much hope that there would be many pieces left by the time her stepmother got around to giving them to her. Sandi had cleaned off the dining room table for the occasion. It was usually piled high with the flotsam and jetsam of her life: department store coupons, magazines, plants that never quite made it to the garden, flavored Vodka from the liquor store—anything and everything. A good amount of the junk was now piled on top of the buffet, pretty much burying Mom's old silver service.

"Can I help?" asked Allison, following her aunt.

"You sure can. You can take the damned turkey out of the oven. It's been in there so long it looks like it belongs in Death Valley," snapped Aunt Connie. A pot on the stove started boiling over and she yanked it off the burner. "I told Sandi an hour ago it should come out, but would she listen? No."

Oh, it was going to be a long day. It was almost enough to make Allison want to reach for the eggnog. Almost. Instead, she poured herself a glass of water and took a fortifying sip.

Sandi was in the kitchen now. "I'm just keeping it in there to stay warm, Connie. I told you that." Sandi shook her head. "She takes one cooking class at Shoreline and thinks she's Julia Child."

"Is that so?"

"Yes, it is. Now quit acting like you've got PMS. We all know you're too old," Sandi added with a wink at Allison. "We're going to open presents before dinner." She turned and led the way back to the living room where Carissa was sweeping the last bit of broken lamp into a dustpan. "Thank God we pulled up the carpet," Sandi said. "Hardwood makes cleanup so much easier."

Given the way things happened in their household, stainless-steel floors that could be hosed down would have been the best bet, if you asked Allison. What would their family have been like if her mother had lived? Surely not this.

All the furniture had been arranged to face the artificial fiber optics tree, a vision in changing colors and Hallmark collectible ornaments. Everyone settled in with a cup of eggnog or beer bottle in hand. Boozle settled on Allison's feet.

Allison wrinkled her nose. The room smelled of pine-scented candle, male sweat, and . . . oh, yuck, what had they fed Boozle? Allison removed her feet from under the dog's hindquarters and relocated to the sofa. Sitting next to Aunt Connie beat the heck out of smelling Boozle.

Dad played Santa, passing around presents. "Here's a big one for you, Sis," he said to Aunt Connie, handing her a shirt box. Wonder what it is."

"An inflatable man," said Sandi, and snickered at her cleverness.

"I don't need a man to feel good about myself," Aunt Connie informed her. "Unlike *some* people."

Meanwhile, in the background the radio station Sandi had found was playing "We Need a Little Christmas."

"Hey," said Dad, distracting Sandi by jiggling one of Allison's presents at her. "I'll bet there's something good to eat in here."

"Oh my God, my hips," protested Sandi, rolling her eyes.

Aunt Connie removed the lid from her box and pulled out a hideous, multicolored sweater. "This is a 2X. I don't wear a 2X."

"Oh, I thought I had the right size," Sandi said, opening her present. "You can return it." To Allison she said, "Thanks, Allie, but I'm on a strict holiday diet." She handed Allison back the tin of fudge.

Allison looked down at the sad little tin she'd carefully

put together. What kind of person gave back a Christmas present because they didn't like it? Sandi could at least pretend to like it and then regift it later. That was proper Christmas etiquette, wasn't it?

"Well, I'll take it if she doesn't want it," said Joey, snatching it out of Allison's hands. He pulled off the lid and dove in.

Now Sandi was pulling the wrapping off a large box, joking, "This is one big bottle of perfume." As the wrapping fell away it became plain to see that it didn't hold another box that might eventually lead to a small perfume box. Instead, it was . . .

"A Thigh Master!" Sandi cried in disgust. If looks could kill, Dad would have been as dead as the Death Valley turkey waiting in the oven. "You got me a Thigh Master?"

Dad's round face lost its anticipatory smile. "You said you were unhappy with your thighs."

Sandi looked at him like he was insane. "So?"

"Well, I saw this on eBay and I thought you'd like it."

"It's used?" Sandi said in disgust. "You bought me a *used* Thigh Master for Christmas? I wanted perfume and you bought me a used Thigh Master!"

"Okay, fine," Dad said with a scowl. "I'll put it back up on eBay and get you some perfume."

"And you'd better not go looking for it on eBay," Sandi snarled.

Dad snatched a box out from under the tree with so much force the tree did a frantic hula. "Here, Allie, this is for you."

"From your dad and me," added Sandi.

"Thanks," Allison said. She knew she didn't exactly sound excited, but so what? Sandi hadn't been excited about the fudge. *Well, what did you expect*, she scolded herself, *that your stepmother would suddenly become your best friend*?

She opened the box and pulled out a stack of books: *How to Succeed with Men*; *If I'm So Wonderful, Why Am I Still Single?*; *Dating for Dummies*."

"*Dating for Dummies*. Ha! That's a good one," said Joey, reading over her shoulder.

She picked up the last book. *Stop Getting Dumped!* "I didn't get dumped," she protested.

But Sandi was too busy pouring herself another cup of eggnog to notice. Allison ground her teeth.

They should have been close. Sandi had wanted a daughter, or so she'd said, and Allison had needed a mother. What they'd each gotten instead was a rival, and the disconnect was complete when Sandi realized that the child she'd inherited would rather be a spectator and a homebody than a cheerleader, a caterer instead of a party girl. And now, apparently, someone who was destined to be a love reject.

"A secondhand Thigh Master," Sandi was muttering. "Who on earth gets his wife a used Thigh Master for Christmas?"

Dad was now looking distinctly uncomfortable. Tomorrow they'd be in the mall and he'd be making amends.

Allison watched as Sandi took a healthy slug of eggnog and then slammed it down on the coffee table with an angry slosh. *Are we having fun yet?*

SIXTEEN

The opening of presents turned more rowdy as the afternoon wore on. The men laughed uproariously over such treasures as a beer-toting reindeer that sang "Grandma Got Run Over by a Reindeer." Dad, the outdoorsman, was given slippers shaped like a trout, complete with glass eyes.

Aunt Connie gave Sandi a kitchen timer, starting fresh hostilities.

"I have a timer on my stove, Connie," Sandi said, her jaw tight and her eyes narrowed.

"You might have an easier time working this one," Connie said with artificial sweetness.

"Oh, that's funny," Sandi snapped as a chorus crooned "Silent Night" over the radio. *All is calm; all is bright.*

Not for long, thought Allison nervously. Aunt Connie's tongue and Sandi's temper—they mixed as well as oil and water.

"We've got to get going," said Carissa, standing. Carissa always knew when to scram.

Allison looked at her watch. Okay. It had been long enough. She could scram, too. "Actually . . ." she began.

"Aw, no." Dad protested. "We've got to have dinner. Sandi went to a lot of trouble."

"We have to get to my parents'," Carissa said firmly.

"Come on, Rissa," said Joey. "We've got time for some turkey."

"We're having turkey with my family," Carissa said.

"Well, we can have some here, too," Joey decided. "Can't leave old Ed here by himself." He gave his friend a playful shove that almost sent Ed off the couch and toppling into the tree.

Carissa didn't seem to care about Ed. She was already giving Sandi a goodbye kiss on the cheek.

"Oh, stay a little longer, honey," begged Sandi. "We hate to see you run off."

"They'll probably be the only ones who don't get poisoned," Aunt Connie predicted under her breath.

She was drowned out by Joey booming, "I'm not ready to go anywhere. I told you I want to eat here at my parents' first. Now, we had this all decided."

Or at least Joey had.

"Sorry," Carissa said to Sandi, "we really do have to go. I thought we'd be eating sooner."

"Well, I'm not going," said Joey, crossing his arms in a show of manly independence. It might have been easier to take him seriously if he hadn't hiccupped.

"Suit yourself," said Carissa. "I'll see you back at the apartment."

"Now, wait just a damned minute." Joey jumped up, listing a little in the process. He reached out to steady himself, catching a handful of Christmas tree and tipping the thing into the wall.

"Joey!" cried Sandi. "Be careful."

He righted himself after trampling two shirt boxes, and gingerly put the tree back in place. Meanwhile, Carissa was already putting on her coat. "You can't leave!" he hollered at her.

"Yes, I can," she yelled back. "I've got the car keys."

"How the hell am I supposed to get home?" he demanded.

"Ed can drive you. You're too drunk to drive anyway." Carissa glared at him. "And you promised you'd only have two beers."

"Looks like someone's sleeping on the couch tonight," predicted Dad in a pathetic attempt to cut the tension.

"Right along with you," snapped Sandi, making him scowl.

"Ha!" bellowed Joey. "Lately I've slept on the damned couch more than in my own bed."

"Thank you for sharing," said Aunt Connie sarcastically while Ed sat hunched on the couch, staring at his feet, probably wishing he were elsewhere.

Allison sure wished she was.

"I may as well become a monk for all the love you show me these days," Joey yelled at Carissa.

Carissa's face turned Christmas-stocking red. "Maybe I'd show you some love if you weren't a sweaty, unshaved, beer-breath slob. Ever think about that?"

Joey burped in response.

"I'm this close to filing for divorce, Joey." She held up two fingers an inch apart. "Go ahead and push me."

"Kids," shouted Dad. "Come on, now. It's Christmas."

Joey crossed his arms. "She called me a sweaty slob."

Carissa had resumed her march to the front door. "Go ahead. Stay here and drink yourself senseless. I have a real party to go to."

Joey gave her the old one-finger salute. "I didn't want to hang out with her family anyway," he announced as the front door slammed shut. "They're all boring. Boring!" he added at the top of his voice as if Carissa could hear him all the way out on the street. Maybe she could.

Right now boring sounded wonderful to Allison.

For a moment an awkward silence hung over the room. Dad broke it, rubbing his hands together and proclaiming heartily, "Well, I'm hungry. When's dinner, hon?"

"About two hours ago," said Aunt Connie.

"Oh, for God's sake," grumbled Sandi. She left her chair and started for the kitchen.

"I'll help you," said Aunt Connie grimly.

This meant World War Three was right around the corner. Allison longed to stay rooted to her chair, or, better yet, follow Carissa to safety, but it seemed wrong to let hostilities erupt without doing anything to try and stop them. "I'll help, too," she decided, and reluctantly followed her stepmother and aunt to the kitchen.

She left Joey on his cell phone yelling at Carissa for ruining Christmas.

"Son, watch the tree," Dad cautioned. "Boozle, no! Don't eat that! Joey, grab the fudge. Why'd you put it on the floor anyway? Watch the tree!"

From the dining room Allison heard a whoosh of branches scraping against the wall and the soft crunch of breaking ornaments but decided not to look. She knew she'd already have enough to deal with in the kitchen.

She arrived in time to see that the turkey was now out of the oven. Aunt Connie had been right. It should have come out hours ago.

"I told you," Aunt Connie was saying.

"It will be fine," Sandi insisted. "Just take the rolls out of the package and put them in the bowl."

So much for Grandma's biscuit recipe.

Aunt Connie looked shocked. "You don't want to heat them up first?"

"Okay, heat them up. I don't care." Sandi threw up her hands. "Why do we always have to do the holidays here?" she wailed. "I wish my mother-in-law was alive," she added, and began to cry.

Connie's hard exterior crumbled at that and she actually came over and put an arm around Sandi's shoulder. "It'll be okay. We'll get through it."

There was hope for world peace. Allison smiled.

"Now," Aunt Connie said briskly, "Allison, why don't you put the peas in the microwave and I'll mash the potatoes."

"I'll make the gravy," Sandi said with a sniff.

"Do you want me to do that?" asked Connie.

"No. I can handle it."

Allison wasn't so sure as she watched her stepmother slosh drippings from the turkey pan into a large skillet. Some of the drippings made it in, but more landed on the burner. Oh, that didn't look good.

"Um, Sandi, I can do that," Allison offered.

"I've got it," Sandi snapped, and cranked up the burner. This started a cozy grease fire on the stovetop.

Sandi let out a surprised squeal and grabbed the half-consumed glass of water Allison had left behind on the counter. Allison and Aunt Connie both cried, "No!" just as she threw the water on the fire.

With a spatter and a demonic hiss, the flame spread like some special effect in a magic show, making Sandi jump back with a howl. "Fire!" she shrieked. "Oh, my God, we're on fire!"

"Where's the baking soda?" Aunt Connie demanded, diving for a cupboard.

Dad was in the kitchen now with Joey right behind him. "What's going . . . oh, my God!"

Now the flames were licking at the wall behind the stove and one of the side counters. The radio was blasting "There's No Place Like Home for the Holidays."

"Joe, get the fire extinguisher," barked Dad. "Girls, get out of the kitchen!"

He didn't have to ask Sandi twice. She was already on her way, screaming like her hair was on fire. It was a wonder it wasn't.

Allison would have followed her but now Ed was blocking the doorway, gawking, and Joey was running back in with the fire extinguisher. Meanwhile, Aunt Connie was pulling things out of the cupboards like a cop with a search warrant, muttering, "We just need baking soda."

Dad swept her aside with a mighty arm. "Get out of the way, Connie." He turned off the burner, then grabbed the fire extinguisher from his son and aimed, spewing a white stream at the stove.

A moment later everything was covered with gook and the kitchen smelled like a toxic dump. As for the turkey, it lay buried under a drift of chemicals. For a moment, everyone stood in silent awe, while from the living room a holiday chorus crooned, "Let it snow, let it snow, let it snow."

"Well," said Joey, "there went dinner."

SEVENTEEN

Allison had been so young when her mother died she barely remembered her. Dad, Grandma always said, was a bad boy with a good heart. He gave up his bad-boy ways when he married Allison's mother, and their life was like a storybook romance up until the day her mother died. Then her father returned to being a bad boy.

But Allison's grandmother had been a constant: the resident babysitter when Dad came out of mourning and decided to date (his euphemism for hitting bars and chasing bimbos). She'd also been the chauffeur, the sharer of Nancy Drew and Babysitter Club adventures, the keeper of secrets, and the queen of the kitchen. Allison's favorite after-school haunt had been her grandmother's house, located a convenient four blocks from home. In its sunny kitchen she had learned the art of making pie crust ("Don't handle it too much, dear. It makes the crust tough"), and the secret to fluffy biscuits ("Always use half cake flour, and add an egg"). With her grandmother so close by it hadn't felt strange to live in a home with only echoes of femininity left behind from her mother. Before Sandi came on the scene her father often took Allison fishing, but she never complained when he went hunting with his buddies and left her at her grandmother's, a bastion of doilies, pretty knickknacks, and kitchen gadgets. When she was older and found herself overwhelmed by Joey's teasing and Sandi's lack of interest, she could always run to her grandmother. And when she decided to try catering for Suzanne's events her grandmother had given her a gift certificate to their favorite kitchen shop by the Pike Place Market so she'd have the best possible tools. She was an ace baker and confectioner and the fudge she had made this year was her best ever. Now Grandma, the one person who really understood and cared, wasn't around to share it. Except you still have your memories of her, Allison reminded herself as she drove away from the scene of Christmas carnage.

It was a relief to return to the little house that had been her grandmother's. It was hers now, free and clear. She'd updated the kitchen, making it state of the art, but the rest of the house she'd kept pretty much the way it had been when Grandma was alive, taking comfort in the antiques and vintage decorations. Her pretty Christmas tree sat in the bay window, decked out with fat, colored bulbs and blown-glass ornaments. The scene was set for a perfect holiday.

She turned up the heat, hung up her coat, and then settled on the couch with a cup of peppermint tea and the snow globe. "You weren't much help today," she told it. She idly shook it, watching the flakes swirl. When it settled to reveal the same scene it had showed her earlier, Allison sighed and set it aside. Maybe it was broken. Maybe it would like to go home to Mrs. Ackerman.

She looked out the window. This had been one of the worst Christmases ever. Where were the grandma and the tea service that the snow globe had promised her?

She could almost hear her grandmother whispering in her ear, "Life is what you make it, dear. Sometimes you have to go find your happiness."

She tapped her cup thoughtfully. What could she make the rest of this day into?

She left the couch and wandered toward the one room where she'd always found happiness: the kitchen. Moving on autopilot she pulled out measuring cups and spoons, one of Grandma's old Pyrex nesting bowls, and her favorite mixing spoon. And smiled. Happiness wasn't that hard to find when you looked in the right place.

Half an hour later the kitchen smelled of melted chocolate, and the scent of almond extract danced in her nostrils. Another hour and she had a platter filled with cookies. She covered it loosely with foil, then went to fetch her coat and car keys.

The Grace Olsen House was dressed up for the holidays with swags in the windows and an artificial tree in the reception area, but these festive efforts couldn't overcome the pungent smell of urine and cleaning solution that crept along its vinyl floors. A few visitors strolled the halls, pushing old ladies in wheelchairs, but for the most part, residents lay on beds in their rooms alone or sat slumped in chairs here and there like vacant-eyed sentinels guarding the past.

One woman with wispy white hair and faded blue eyes to match her faded dress held out a clawed hand to Allison as she passed and croaked, "Help me."

Mrs. Manning. She'd been calling for help ever since Allison started visiting here.

Allison stopped and took a cookie from the platter. "Merry Christmas, Mrs. Manning," she said, and slipped the cookie into the woman's hand.

Mrs. Manning took a bite of the cookie and looked past Allison, possibly at the Ghost of Christmas Past. "You can't leave yet. The bird's not done."

Allison gave her arm a pat and kept going. She turned down the hall and went to a different wing. There was still vinyl on the floor here, and the same pungent smell followed her, but the rooms were bigger. They all looked out on the lawn and held a bed, a dresser, and a chair.

She ducked into room number 112, knocking on the door as she entered. A plump, little woman in a pink bathrobe sat in a chair by the bed, a book in her lap. She looked up curiously at the sight of Allison. Someone had brushed her hair today. Maybe her daughter had been in.

"Hi, Mrs. Baker," said Allison, coming into the room.

Her grandmother's old friend smiled at her tentatively. "Hello. Are you my daughter?"

Okay, not one of Mrs. Baker's good days. "No, I'm Allison. You and my grandma were best friends."

Mrs. Baker smiled. "Oh, were we? Who was your grandmother?"

Allison blinked back tears. This had been a stupid idea. "How about a cookie?"

"I love cookies," said Mrs. Baker, helping herself to one with a trembling hand. "You know, I won a baking contest once. I won a pink Sunbeam Mixmaster." She suddenly looked confused. "Do you still have it, Babs?"

"Yes," lied Allison. "I still do, and I love it."

Mrs. Baker smiled and took a bite of her cookie. "These are delicious." She stared at Allison, her brows knit. "What did you say your name was?"

"Babs."

Mrs. Baker smiled and shut her eyes. "It's nice to have company."

"Yes, it is," agreed Allison.

Some church group was caroling their way down the hall now, singing "We Wish You a Merry Christmas."

It was a little too late for that, but who knew? Maybe the new year would be happy. One could always hope.

EIGHTEEN

The new year brought new adventures. Kiley got engaged and Suzanne got pregnant. The year started well for Allison, too, who received a good review at work and a small raise. She never got what she saw in the snow globe, though.

"You know what I want to do," Kiley said as the three friends sat in Allison's kitchen, sipping tea and sampling Allison's new scone recipe. "I want to go see Mrs. Ackerman."

"Mrs. who?" asked Suzanne.

"Mrs. Ackerman, the woman who owned the snow globe before I bought it at the antique shop. I want to thank her and tell her everything that's happened. I think she'd like to hear that her family heirloom helped us."

Most of us, thought Allison, being careful to keep her expression neutral. She'd voiced her doubts once to Suzanne and had immediately regretted it. Suzanne now had all the zeal of a reformed cynic and she'd been quick to defend the powers of the snow globe. "You have to give it time," she'd insisted.

January was over now. As far as Allison was concerned, time had run out.

"Not a bad idea," Suzanne was saying. "If you want, I'll go with you."

They both looked at Allison.

That was what she wanted, to spend an afternoon listening to her two friends gush about the powers of the snow globe while she sat there like a holiday dud with no story to tell. "I don't think I can get away," she began.

"Oh, come on," pleaded Kiley. "We'll go on a weekend."

"It'll be fun," added Suzanne. She turned to Kiley. "See if you can track Mrs. Ackerman down and ask her if we can come this Saturday."

And just like that they were off and planning, assuming that Allison would come along. She frowned into her teacup. No way was she going.

Saturday was gray and blowy, and Allison looked like a thundercloud as the little ferry to Fawn Island dipped and rolled its way across a choppy Puget Sound. "I'm going to be sick," she predicted, crossing her arms over her down vest and scowling out the window at the sea of whitecaps.

"Stop pouting," Suzanne scolded. "I'm surviving and I feel like crap."

You could have fooled Allison. Suzanne looked totally put together in trouser jeans and a great jacket with a faux fur collar. And she was positively glowing. If that was what morning sickness looked like, where did a girl sign up?

"Anyway, you know you didn't want to be left behind," Suz added.

"Yes, I did," snapped Allison. She had no Christmas miracle to report, no good news. All she had was the snow globe, which had obviously run out of steam. Maybe Mrs. Ackerman would like it back.

"It'll be fun," Kiley promised. She crossed her booted legs and admired the engagement bling on her left hand.

"For you two," Allison said bitterly. All she was bringing into the new year was five extra pounds she'd gained after a post-Christmas cookie binge.

Suzanne shook her head. "You're becoming a real Scrooge."

"Who knows?" Kiley quickly put in. "This woman may have some great antiques. And you love antiques."

Allison loved her grandmother's antiques. There was a difference.

"Arriving Fawn Island," a voice announced over the loudspeaker. "All passengers must disembark. All car passengers please return to the car deck at this time."

"That's us," said Kiley cheerfully. "Let's go."

Suzanne hobbled off toward the exit, Kiley falling in next to her and allowing Allison to follow. This was a dumb idea. She wished she hadn't come. What was she going to say to Mrs. Ackerman, anyway? *Hi. I'm Allison and your snow globe hates me.*

She settled in the backseat of Kiley's car, thinking how appropriate it was that she was there like a third wheel. The two blessed ones sat up front, casually chatting, a road of promise stretching out before them. All she had back here in the loser's section was a good case of grumpiness.

They drove off the boat and through the quaint downtown, then, following the directions Kiley had written, turned onto a residential street, passing Cape Cod and Craftsman-style homes snugged in among fir trees and well-tended gardens with picket fences. Toward the edge of town, they came to a large, gray Victorian set high on the bluff overlooking the water.

"This is it," said Suzanne, and Allison's stomach clenched.

The paint was faded, but the yard was well tended, the flower beds weeded, and the rosebushes trimmed and waiting for spring. "This place would fetch a pretty penny," Suzanne mused as they went up the front walk.

They weren't even to the door yet when it opened, framing an elderly woman in a black dress and a European-style red wool jacket with gold braiding and buttons. She was short and stout, and wore glasses, and her white hair was elegantly styled.

"Welcome, ladies!" she called. "I'm Rosamunde Ackerman."

Allison hung back during the flurry of greetings, tongue-tied, clutching the snow globe for dear life.

"And this is Allison," Kiley added.

Mrs. Ackerman held out a hand. "Welcome, dear."

"Thanks," Allison managed. She took Mrs. Ackerman's extended hand. It was plump and dotted with age spots like Grandma's had been. Allison swallowed down a bittersweet lump in her throat.

"I'm so delighted to have a chance to meet you all," said Mrs. Ackerman, ushering them into a living room thick with old furniture decked out in antimacassars. Everything smelled faintly of mothballs and lavender. In one corner of the room, an old brass birdcage housed a blue parakeet that hopped from perch to perch in excitement. Allison had seen that birdcage before. She'd seen this all. Her heart began to beat in time with the flitting bird.

"You just make yourselves at home," said Mrs. Ackerman. "I'll bring the tea."

"Let me help you," offered Allison.

The woman smiled at her. "Why, thank you."

In the kitchen, Allison took in the old Formica table like the one she owned now, the one that had been her grandmother's, the white shelf displaying Quimper plates and an antique brass teapot, the vintage mixer on the counter, and felt contentment settle in her chest. "This is lovely."

"Oh, I'm afraid it's all out of date," said Mrs. Ackerman with a sad smile. "Just like me."

"You don't have a daughter who's into antiques?" asked Allison.

"I don't have a daughter," said Mrs. Ackerman. "And I'm sad to say I lost my son in Vietnam." Her eyes took on a faraway look and Allison suspected she was envisioning happier times when her son was alive. She returned to the present with a little shake of her head and motioned to a china pot sitting on the counter next to the old stove. "I put the kettle on already. Perhaps you wouldn't mind pouring the water into the teapot."

"Not at all," Allison said with a smile.

They worked companionably, assembling cookies on a plate, fixing the teapot and teacups on a serving tray. Soon all was ready. Mrs. Ackerman took the plate of cookies out to the living room and Allison followed with the tray.

"Your house is lovely," said Suzanne.

"Yes, but it's a lot of house for one woman to rattle around in."

Suzanne perked up. "Have you ever thought of selling?"

"Maybe someday, but I'm not ready to leave behind my memories just yet," the old woman said with a smile that tugged at Allison's heartstrings. "Not that I'm complaining, mind you. I have my church and my wonderful neighbors." Her voice trailed off.

And no husband and no children, thought Allison sadly.

"But let's not talk about me," Mrs. Ackerman said

briskly. "Tell me about the snow globe." She reached for the teapot with a shaky hand.

"Let me," said Allison.

She picked it up and poured tea while Kiley launched into her story. Mrs. Ackerman sat enthralled, never touching her cup.

Suzanne went next. "Who knew breaking my ankle would turn out to be good for my health?" she joked in conclusion, and Mrs. Ackerman chuckled.

Then the old woman turned to Allison. "And what about you, my dear?"

"She saw something in it at my house," said Suzanne, "but so far . . ."

"I saw you," Allison blurted. I saw this room and this teapot, and we were drinking tea, just like we are now. It almost looked like Grandma, but it was you. It was definitely you."

"I knew it would come through for you," Suzanne crowed, pointing a finger at her.

Then all three friends were talking at once, explaining how much Allison's grandmother had meant to her and how she'd served as a counterbalance to Allison's flaky family.

Mrs. Ackerman stirred cream into her tea. "Well," she said thoughtfully, "I've always said there are two kinds of family. There's the family of your flesh, and the one of your heart. One builds character, the other rewards it." She smiled at Allison.

Allison felt tears prickling her eyes. "If you're my reward, Mrs. Ackerman, I'll take it."

"Why, thank you, my dear," said the old woman.

They stayed another half hour, until it became clear that their hostess was getting tired. "We'd better go," said Kiley.

"First, we'll clean up, though," said Allison.

"Oh, that's not necessary," protested Mrs. Ackerman,

but she didn't put up too much resistance when Kiley and Allison scooped up the tea things and took them to the kitchen to wash.

They were about to leave when Allison held out the snow globe to the old woman. "Would you like to have this back? It's obviously served its purpose for us."

Mrs. Ackerman smiled and shook her head. "As it has for me. No, you take it with you. I'm sure you'll find something to do with it." She hugged Allison. "And do come see me again."

As if she had to ask.

An hour later the three friends were back on the ferryboat, sailing home over waters much less troubled than when they came. A sliver of sunlight slipped through the gray skies and seagulls soared alongside the ferry, providing a feathered escort.

Allison studied the snow globe in her lap. "So, do you think this thing is like Aladdin's lamp?"

Suzanne shrugged. "I don't know about that. I sure never would have wished to break my ankle."

"Yes, but look at what you got," said Kiley with a smile.

Suzanne shrugged. "So maybe it's more a window meant to show you possibilities."

"I don't know," said Allison, running a hand over the treasure. "One thing I do know. We can't keep it."

"You're right, of course," Kiley said.

"Are you two insane?" Suzanne protested. "We need to hang on to it, pass it on to our kids. It's an heirloom."

"I'd say it's more than that," said Kiley.

"You can't just give it away," Suzanne said sternly. "Mrs. Ackerman would never approve."

"Actually, I think she would," said Allison. "After all, she told us to put it to good use."

"So, what should we do with it?" asked Kiley.

"You decide, Kiles," said Allison. "You're the one who found it."

Kiley chewed her lip thoughtfully for a moment, then said, "Leave it here."

Suzanne stared at her in disbelief. "Here? For just anyone?"

The three women looked around, taking in their fellow passengers. Over by the vending machines a harried mother was trying to corral a rambunctious preschooler and a toddler simultaneously. An elderly couple sat a few benches down, side by side in silence, staring out the window at the seagulls swooping over the waves. A sad-faced ferry worker slowly collected leftover newspapers for the recycling bin. A middle-aged woman hurried past, towing a beat-up carry-on suitcase.

"No," said Kiley. "For the right someone."

"Arriving Seattle," said the voice over the loudspeaker. "All passengers must disembark. Car passengers please return to the car deck at this time."

Kiley stood. "The snow globe found us. I think we can trust that it will find its way to the next person who needs it." She started for the car deck without so much as a backward glance.

Suzanne heaved a long-suffering sigh and followed her.

Allison took one last look around and then set the snow globe on the bench. Then, inspired, she fished a pad from her purse, tore off a piece of paper, and scrawled a note.

This is for someone who needs a miracle.
If that's you, please take it.

She smiled as she read what she'd written. Then she set the paper under the snow globe and hurried after her friends. It was going to be a great new year for someone.

THE
NINE LIVES
OF CHRISTMAS

For Ruth

ACKNOWLEDGMENTS

As always, I have lots of people to thank for helping me tell Ambrose's tale. Thanks to Daniel Olson, fire chief for Poulsbo, Washington, for taking time to explain the workings of the fire department. Keeping the citizens of Poulsbo safe and keeping Sheila on track—I don't know which was more challenging! Anyway, both Ambrose and I thank you. Thanks also to my writing pals Susan Wiggs, Elsa Watson, Anjali Banerjee, and Kate Breslin for all their great input as I worked on telling Ambrose's tail . . . er, tale. Last but not least, a huge thanks to my awesome editor, Rose Hilliard, and my amazing agent, Paige Wheeler. You two make work fun!

ONE

When a guy is in trouble he starts making deals with his Creator, and Ambrose was dealing like crazy. Vicious teeth snapped at him, and his whole life (actually, all nine of them) flashed before his eyes. If this dog got him it was all over.

Becoming dog food looked like a distinct possibility, as the tree Ambrose had chosen was small and the particular branch he was perched on was a flimsy twig barely capable of holding a kitten, let alone a mature cat. And the big, black beast below seemed to have springs on his paws.

I'll do anything, Ambrose yowled. *Anything! Please, let me live a little longer.*

This was life number nine. He knew he wouldn't get any more but he'd settle for a longer one in which he could finish his days in comfort. Under the circumstances, it would be a miracle if he survived to see that happen. But he'd seen people stringing up colored lights on their houses just the other day, which meant Christmas season was about to begin, and wasn't Christmas supposed to be the season of miracles? Not that Christmas had ever been good to Ambrose. That was when he usually managed to meet his end.

So he wasn't surprised at what was happening to him now. That didn't mean he had to like it, though. What a horrible way to go! Pulled from a tree and brutally murdered by a bloodthirsty mongrel. All these houses and there was not a single human around to help him on this cold, gray morning. No surprise, really. Humans bought houses and then rarely stayed in them . . . until they got old, and by then, like Ambrose, their days were numbered.

Below him the dog showed his fangs again and growled. *Needing a miracle here. Soon!*

Not that he deserved one. He thought of little Robbie, who he'd scratched many a time in his seventh life, and poor Snoopy the beagle, who he had tortured in his eighth life. He shouldn't have made the dog's life so miserable but he'd been getting bitter by then. How he had enjoyed driving old Snoopy crazy by jumping on him and riding him around the house with his claws dug into the dog's back. Hee-hee. That had been . . .

Bad, very bad. He would never do anything like that again.

Why oh why hadn't he picked a tall, sturdy tree to climb instead of this immature maple? What had he been thinking? The answer to that was easy enough. He'd been thinking, *Run!*

It started to rain—fat, freezing pellets that dug under his fur, and an angry winter wind pushed the tree, making its branches sway. *Noooo.* Ambrose dug his claws deeper into the bark. *I'll be a good cat and earn my keep here on Earth. Just send me some help and I'll prove it.*

Now the dog was up on his hind legs, pushing against the tree and reaching for Ambrose like he was some kind of doggy chew toy. Determined not to go down without a fight, Ambrose hissed at him and took a swipe with claws unsheathed. That only made the beast more berserk.

Where was a dogcatcher when you needed one? *Help! Is anybody listening?*

Out of nowhere, appearing as suddenly as the rain had come, Ambrose saw a man wearing what humans called jogging clothes. He ran up to the dog and yelled, "Go on, get out of here."

Between the man's aggressive clap and that big, canine-like growl of his, he not only scared away the dog, he almost gave Ambrose a heart attack.

The beast loped off down the street and the man said, "Okay, guy, looks like you're safe."

Safe, the best word in the world. Ambrose peered down at his rescuer. The fur on top of the man's head was what humans called blond—not as handsome as Ambrose's orange coat, but a shade that humans admired greatly, and his eyes were as blue as a Siamese kitten's. He was large, which meant he probably had a spacious, comfy lap. The friendly smile he wore showed the man was a kind person. Something about that face looked familiar. Where had he seen this man before?

"You're on your own now," he said to Ambrose, who was still clinging to his branch. "I know you can get down anyway. You aren't going to want to stay out in this weather any longer than me," he added, and then jogged off down the street.

Ambrose could hardly believe he was safe. Wet, uncomfortable, and hungry, but safe. The freezing rain was letting up now and the angry clouds began to drift away, ashamed of all the misery they'd caused. It was going to be a good day after all. He settled down to give his racing heart a chance to calm.

One last gust of wind wooshed past him with a whisper: *Remember what you promised.*

Of course Ambrose remembered. And he would be a better cat. When the opportunity presented itself. There was no hurry, really.

He made his way down the tree and was halfway across the lawn when he caught sight of the same dog loitering on the corner. The dog saw him, too.

Yikes! Time to scat. Ambrose darted into the street.

A screech of brakes, a spray of water, and an angry honk of a horn made his lives flash before his eyes once again as Ambrose barely dodged the huge metal monster. Once more the wind whispered. This time it said: *Last chance.*

Okay, okay, he got it. The time to atone for his wicked past was now. But how, exactly, was he supposed to do that? Where to start, and with whom? The storm had pretty much scrubbed the street of living creatures. Except for the murderous dog and that big man.

Helping the dog with anything was out of the question. That left the man, which made sense. A life for a life.

He set off at a run. His rescuer had a head start but Ambrose had four legs, which evened things considerably. He caught up with the man in time to see him enter a house on a quiet street. It was a large house, much the same as Ambrose's old home, freshly painted and blue as a robin's egg, and it had a chimney. That meant a warm fire on a cold day. Not a bad place to land.

It took patient camping under the bushes by the porch but finally Ambrose was rewarded and the door opened to reveal the same man, this time wearing different clothes. He stepped out of the door and Ambrose rushed in. *Oh, delicious warmth.*

"Whoa," said the man, "what's this?"

What? He couldn't tell? Ambrose refused to dignify such a silly question with a response. Instead he began to prowl the front hall of his new home. Interesting. Wood floors, a stairway on one side, and off to the other an arch opening onto what humans referred to as a living room. The house felt old and it hummed with memories, like the one his last owner, Adelaide, had lived in. That had been such a cozy home. Her horrible offspring hadn't cared about the memories, though. All they'd cared about was putting the place up for sale.

Put it up for sale, indeed! Just where had they thought Ambrose would live if they sold the house? Of course, he'd soon found out and that was why he'd run away.

"Whoa there, Tom," said the man, scooping Ambrose off his feet.

Tom? What an insult! Did he look like a common cat? His name had never been Tom. Never! He was Cupcake-Tiger-Morris-Muffin-Macavity-Blackie-Toby-Claus-Ambrose—Ambrose, of course, being his latest moniker.

"This isn't a hotel for cats," the man informed Ambrose as he opened the door. He stepped back outside and shut the door behind him, then plopped Ambrose on the porch. Back out in the cold. Of all the nerve!

Ambrose watched, tail twitching as the man strode down his front walk, got in a shiny, black car, and drove away. *If this inhospitable human is the key to keeping my ninth life I am in the doghouse.*

He could almost hear Adelaide saying, "Be patient, Ambrose dear." (Something she always told him when he was half starving and rubbing against her legs while she poked around opening his cat food can.) Good advice now, though. He could be patient.

The man would be back. Humans went away to work, whatever that was, but they eventually returned, and when this one did he and Ambrose would settle this misunderstanding. Ambrose crawled back under the bushes and settled in to wait.

* * *

Zachary Stone returned home from working his forty-eight-hour shift with his eyes feeling gritty and his head muzzy. People thought firefighters just sat around and watched TV or slept when they weren't putting out fires or helping with medical emergencies, but they were always busy at the station. This shift had proved to be no exception. On Wednesday, Zach, Ray, and Julio had spent the day cleaning equipment and swapping out batteries on two-way radios and heart monitors. They'd gone out on two emergency calls during the wee hours of the night and then Zach had to be bright eyed and bushy tailed for a school visit the next morning. When he'd returned to the station he'd had to clean the kitchen. The oven was a disaster thanks to Stevens, who couldn't cook anything without making a mess and who never seemed to be on the schedule when kitchen day rolled around.

But Zach had preferred stove patrol to the 911 call that involved an old lady who had managed to fall out of her recliner. He frowned at the memory of his new nickname: Little Old Lady Killer. It would be a couple of weeks before he didn't have to endure a million jabs from the paramedics about how the old woman had kept patting his arm and offering to make him cookies after he'd gotten her back into her chair (no small feat since the "little" old lady had weighed almost as much as Zach). On top of those adventures he had done his mandatory daily workouts, three home safety visits, and the crew had been called out to help with a bad accident on the highway at one A.M. That one had almost been enough to make him question why he did what he did for a living.

The answer was simple, really. He liked helping people. Doing what he did gave him a feeling of purpose. He also appreciated having so much time off during the rest of the week. It allowed him to work on big projects like flipping this old Victorian.

"Oh, you should keep it," his mother had said when she and his stepsisters stopped by uninvited to check it out shortly after he bought it. (Yet another attempt to insert herself into his life.) "I can already see it with a Christmas tree in the bay window."

And a wife and kids running around. She hadn't said that, but Zach knew she'd thought it. "It's not me," he'd said.

"It could be," she'd said right back.

That was when he'd looked at his watch and announced, "I'd better get going. I've got an appointment to look at flooring."

Mom had eyed him suspiciously. "Since when do you need an appointment to look at flooring?"

"Special order," he'd improvised, and escaped to the safety of the hardware store.

Mom wanted grandkids, who knew why. Maybe she thought she could do better as a grandmother. Whatever. It didn't look like his younger brother David was going to give her any—he was too busy taking pictures for *National Geographic* and surfing in Australia—but it was useless to pin her hopes on Zach. He wasn't signing up for eHarmony anytime soon. Or going on *The Bachelor*.

His stepsister Natalie had nominated him for the show and someone had actually contacted him. He'd thought the guys at the station were playing a joke on him and had managed to get in some pretty insulting cracks before he realized the call was for real. Then he'd gone from amused to pissed.

Both Natalie and Kendra (whom he referred to collectively as the Steps) had been indignant that he'd passed up the opportunity to let the whole world watch while a bunch of ring-hungry chicks closed in on him. Yeah, there was a lost opportunity all right. You'd think a college freshman and a high school sophomore would have more to do than butt into their stepbrother's love life. You'd also think all three women would have figured out by now that he wasn't a get-serious kind of guy.

At least not anymore. Zach was done being a masochist.

Anyway, marriage was for . . . who was it for? His friends were all either single or divorced. Mom hadn't exactly been a shining example of wedded bliss, either, at least not with Dad. She'd stuck it out the second time around but Dad was still a mess.

No, Zach liked his life as a single dude just fine. No worries, no stress, just good times.

He had reached his front porch when the orange tomcat that had followed him home emerged from the bushes. The animal joined him at the front door and wound around Zach's legs meowing, playing the cat sympathy card.

"Hey, Tom, what the heck are you still doing hanging around? Go home, bud," said Zach.

The cat repeated his meow and rubbed Zach's leg.

Zach wasn't really into cats. He was more of a dog man. At least he had been back in high school, but when Dexter died Zach swore off dogs.

Just as well. Pets required care, and with his job Zach couldn't give an animal the kind of attention it needed. Still, he felt kind of sorry for this mangy, orange tomcat. The poor guy looked pretty skinny. Judging from his chewed-off ear he'd taken a few knocks.

But he had a flea collar and a tag. He obviously belonged to somebody. "So, are you lost, dude, is that it?"

Well, it was December—peace on earth, goodwill toward men. And cats. It wouldn't hurt to bring this one in and hang on to him until his owner could come pick him up. Zach could do that much.

He picked the little guy up and brought him inside.

Then he checked the tag on the cat's collar. "Ambrose, huh? Kind of a wussy name, isn't it?"

The cat yowled at him.

"I don't blame you. I wouldn't want to be called Ambrose, either. Well, don't worry. I'll get you back where you belong."

But when he called the number on the cat's tag, the woman on the other end of the line wasn't thrilled to hear from him. "He was my mother's cat. We were getting ready to take him to the animal shelter when he ran away."

"The animal shelter, huh?" Zach looked over at the cat only to see him dash under the leather couch.

"I just lost my mother and we're a little stressed over here," the woman added brusquely. "I only have a few days left to take care of things before I fly back to Florida and I don't have time to worry about that stupid cat. He's on his own."

Whoa, somebody was going to get the Good Samaritan seal of approval, but it wasn't this woman.

"Thanks for calling," she added before hanging up.

Zach stared at his cell phone in disbelief. "Geez, lady." How could somebody be so callous about an animal?

The cat came back out and started rubbing against Zach's legs. Zach picked him up and tried to explain to the little guy that this wouldn't be much of a home for him. "I know you got a tough break, guy, and I'd like to help you out, but I'm a firefighter. I'm gone at the station a lot and there's no woman here to look after you." At least there never was on a permanent basis.

Now the cat was purring. *Aw, geez.*

Cats pretty much took care of themselves, right? At least that was what Zach had always heard. Still, he had his hands full remodeling this place. The last thing he needed was an animal.

"Okay, tell you what. I'll give you something to eat and then you're on your own."

He put the cat down and went to the fridge. The cat trotted after him.

The animal shelter found homes for animals. He should take the cat there right now and be done with it. Except this little dude was no cute kitten. Who would want him? He'd end up in the kitty gas chamber for sure.

Zach looked down at him and frowned. "Why did you have to show up on my doorstep?"

The animal meowed and snaked around his legs.

With a long-suffering sigh, Zach opened the refrigerator and pulled out a carton of milk. "Tell you what. You can stay until we find a real home for you. How's that?" He poured milk into an empty sour cream container and then set it on the floor. "Drink up, dude."

The animal sniffed at it, then turned and walked away.

"What?" Zach called after him. "You're a cat. You're supposed to like milk."

Old Tom kept walking.

"Oh, yeah," Zach called after him. "Way to be a good guest."

This animal was going to be a pain in the butt, he could already tell.

TWO

If the cat thought this was some frickin' restaurant he was in for a rude awakening. Zach had stuff to do and he didn't have time to make a cat food run.

He was going to catch some Z's and then, in the afternoon, start demolishing the kitchen. All the cheap cabinets were coming out to be replaced with new ones Zach had found at Mike's Home Center in downtown Angel Falls. The floor was coming up, too. Mike had given him a deal.

After a couple hours of shut-eye Zach threw on his rattiest T-shirt and ripped jeans and got to work. His new roommate sat in the doorway and watched him set out his tools, but once Zach started making a racket, he was gone.

"Get used to it, Tom," Zach called after him. "We're doing a remodel here."

Hopefully he'd be finished come spring. Then he'd sell the house, and take the money and run. There was no point in a single guy keeping a big house like this. He'd buy himself one of those slick new condos they were putting in over on Falls Ridge, where he could have a view of the town and the Cascade Mountain range beyond.

Thinking about how he would invest his profits gave Zach plenty of energy, and by the time his firefighting buddy Ray arrived he had taken up half of the old vinyl. He'd also managed to mangle the subfloor pretty good, too. Tim the Tool Man, the next generation.

"Whoa, dude," said Ray, taking in the pile of vinyl pieces. "You didn't waste any time."

Ray was a big guy like Zach, but unlike Zach, he actually knew one end of a hammer from the other. He was divorced and his only child was a Chihuahua named Taquito (Tacky for short) that went everywhere with him. Ray had been more than happy to help remodel the kitchen in exchange for pizza and beer.

He frowned at the dents and craters in the subfloor and said, "We're gonna have to do some major patching before we can put down new vinyl." He started into the kitchen, the quivering Tacky in his arms. The toe of his boot made contact with the container of milk Zach had put out earlier and tipped it, starting a white stream running across the pocked floor. "Whoa, what's with the milk?"

"Forgot to pick that up." Zach tossed the container in the sink and dropped a paper towel on the milk.

"Why was it down there in the first place?" asked Ray, setting Tacky down. The animal tucked his tail between his legs and trembled.

"I took in a stray cat," said Zach, and tossed the towel.

Ray made a face. "Cats."

Zach handed him a hammer. "What have you got against cats?"

"They're chick pets. Women love 'em cause they're cute. Me, I want an animal that does something, like play fetch, guard your house." Tacky was jumping up on his pant leg now and Ray gave him a pat on the head.

Zach crossed his arms and leaned against the counter. "Like Killer there?"

Ray frowned. "Hey, he knows how to sound the alarm. Dontcha, boy?" he added, his voice softening.

"You have to take care of a dog," Zach argued. "Look at you. You've got to leave Tacky with your mom when you're at the station. Cats are different. They take care of themselves."

"Yeah? I guess the cat got the milk out of the fridge all by himself," Ray said with a smirk.

Zach pointed a crowbar at him. "Okay, smart ass. How about putting something besides your mouth to work?"

Ray grinned and got busy.

"Anyway," Zach said to both Ray and himself, "I'm just keeping him till I can find a nice home for him." Where that would be he wasn't quite sure. But it wouldn't be here. The cat needed someone who would love him the way Ray did that dumb rat-dog of his. And besides, the little guy wouldn't be happy here. All the banging and noise scared him.

It didn't do much for Tacky, either, who went running when his master tossed his first chunk of vinyl on the pile with a thud.

By the end of the afternoon the kitchen looked like it had been hit by a hurricane and the two men were sweaty and starving and ready to order pizza.

"Hey, thanks, man," Zach said as Ray popped the top off a bottle of Hale's Ale. "Get out a beer for me, too, will ya?"

"Uh," Ray said, looking guilty. "This is the last one."

Zach gave Ray's gut a slap. "At this rate you're going to have to start running with me."

Ray made a face. "I'm in shape. This is just insulation for winter. And the only run I'm doing today is a beer run. Come on, Tacky." He bent to pick up the Chihuahua, which was back and climbing his pant leg.

"Naw, I've got it," said Zach. "You and Tacky stay here

and chill. If old Tom comes out of hiding you can introduce them."

Ray picked up the little dog. "We better hope your cat stays hidden. Tacky would eat him alive."

Zach was still laughing when he hit the shower to clean up.

Fifteen minutes later, the pizza order had been called in to Little Lola's and Zach was on his way to Safeway for more beer. Most residents of Angel Falls really got into holiday decorating, so he had a scenic drive, past neighborhoods with a mix of old and new houses snuggled in among fir trees and shrubs, and decked out in holiday lights. Inflatable Santas and snowmen waved from lawns, and it seemed every home had a wreath hanging on its front door.

Zach supposed his house, which sat unadorned, looked like he was harboring the Grinch. But hey, he was busy with important projects. He didn't have time to screw around turning his place into a Christmas clone of every other house on the block. And he didn't have to. There was another advantage to being single: no honey-do list. Anyway, this wasn't his favorite time of year, so why be a hypocrite and deck the halls?

It was the first Friday in December and the parking lot was full of cars. Outside the grocery store a Salvation Army volunteer dressed up as Santa was braving a drizzle of sloshy snowflakes, ringing his bell and wishing people a merry Christmas. Zach dropped a dollar in the bucket and went inside. The store was crowded with people on their way home from work and picking up last-minute dinner supplies. He caught a whiff of deli chicken. It made his stomach rumble and he hurried toward the beer aisle dodging shoppers as he went. A woman passed him coming the other way, looking hot in black heels and a red party dress. *Yow, Mama!* At the end of another aisle he came upon a vignette of what always happened after the party was over. A harried mother snapped at her little boy: "I said we weren't buying that. Put it back!" *Now, there's another shining testimonial for family life,* Zach thought with a silent sigh.

His mom may have split up the family but she'd never snapped at him. That was one thing he'd say for her. It was about the only thing he could say for her.

En route to the beer he caught sight of the pet food aisle and remembered the spilled milk. Since he was there he might as well look for some food for Tom.

Half the aisle was cat food, and he stood for a moment in front of the mountains of bags. *Good grief. How many brands of this stuff do people need, anyway?*

He didn't realize he'd spoken out loud until a soft voice at his elbow said, "It's hard to know what to get, isn't it?"

He turned to see a redhead with big green eyes smiling timidly at him. She only came up to his chest and with her short curly hair and turned-up nose she reminded him of an elf. Elfette? Whatever the chick version was. She was lost in a down coat that looked way too big for her and her calves were swallowed up inside some ugly rubber galoshes, but judging by what he could see of her thighs he was sure she was hiding a nice little bod under that coat. Out of nowhere the chorus from Dr. Hook's "You Make My Pants Want to Get Up and Dance" popped into his mind.

He kicked it out right away. This woman also looked like the girl next door, the kind you settled down with, had kids with, the kind of girl a man didn't want to hurt. Not that Zach made a habit of hurting anyone. He didn't have to worry about that with the women he hung out with, women who were content with just having some fun and keeping things casual.

He reached for something generic and the elfette gave

a little gasp. He looked over his shoulder. "Not good?" The price was right.

"Well, not the best. Do you have a cat?"

"I just took one in."

Her eyes lit up and she looked at Zach like he'd told her he rescued a child from a burning building. "Oh, you adopted him?"

Zach squirmed inside his jacket. "More like foster care. His owner died. The kids were going to take him to the shelter." Like he probably should have done.

"It's great you took him," said the elfette.

Just for a while. You should remind her of that, thought Zach. But he didn't.

"The shelter always has a surplus of cats and not all of them find homes. Some of them . . ." The corners of her mouth fell and she didn't finish the sentence.

She didn't have to. Now Zach could hear the theme music from *Psycho* running through his head.

"Anyway, it's wonderful that you've saved one."

Yeah, that was him, Mr. Wonderful. He could have fessed up that cat adoption hadn't exactly been his idea, that old Tom hadn't taken no for an answer. Instead he asked, "So, what's wrong with this food?" putting the conversation back on track before he could be tempted to do something dumb, like suggest she come over and meet his cat.

"The cheap dry food can be hard on their kidneys. And if you have a boy cat, well, they have a tendency toward prostate problems," she added, and her cheeks grew pink.

Cute. Zach couldn't remember the last time he'd seen a woman blush. That probably had a lot to do with the kind of women he hung out with.

"I always buy the top of the line and alternate it with canned cat food."

"Top of the line, huh?" Well, he supposed he could do that for old Tom. "Which brand do you buy?"

She showed him, and then she led him straight to what she said was her favorite (and, naturally, most expensive) brand of canned food.

"Thanks," he said. "You're a real expert. Are you a vet or something?"

The blush returned. She shook her head, making the curls bounce. "No. I work at Pet Palace."

His girlfriend's family owned Pet Palace. Zach almost shared this information. Almost.

"Cats are my specialty," the elfette added.

"I'll remember that if I need some expert advice," Zach said. They were starting to get pretty friendly here in the pet food aisle. It was time for him to get back to Ray and pizza and the safety of his own home. "Uh, thanks."

"My pleasure," she said.

Pleasure. The word conjured some naughty images of himself and the elfette that were bound to earn Zach a lump of coal in his stocking. *If you're going to think pleasure, dickhead, think about Blair.* Good old Blair, who always preferred being naughty to being nice. She'd done the marriage thing and gotten it out of her system, which made her and Zach a perfect match.

With his thoughts properly realigned, he gave the girl next door a pleasant nod and then got out of there. Nice girls were a heartbreak waiting to happen. He knew from personal experience.

Hey, about time you got back," Ray greeted him as he walked in the door with a giant sized sack of cat food slung over his shoulder. "The pizza got here five minutes ago. Let's break open the beer."

Beer? Shit. "Oh, man, I forgot the beer."

"Well, if that don't beat all. We come over and bust our chops all afternoon and who does he remember?" Ray asked Tacky, who was camped out on his lap. "The damned cat. Never send a boy to do a man's job." He stuffed the last of a pizza slice in his mouth, set Tacky aside and started to get up.

Zach propped the bag by the door, along with the plastic sack full of canned cat food. "I'm on it. Don't get your Jockeys in a knot. And don't eat all the pizza before I get back," he added before shutting the door.

He'd run over to the Gas 'N Go and pick up some overpriced cheap beer. No way was he going back to the grocery store. If he saw the elfette again he might just suffer a moment of insanity and get her name and number.

M erilee White stood in line at the checkout flipping through a copy of *People* and trying to find her holiday spirit. Darn. For a moment there she thought she'd connected with that gorgeous man on the pet food aisle. He'd looked like a modern-day Viking, blond and big. His face had been almost perfect, the only flaw a slightly crooked nose that looked like it might have gotten broken at some point. And those eyes! Blue as a fjord. He'd seemed so nice, and he was an animal lover, too, which, as far as Merilee was concerned, made him a perfect man.

From the way he'd looked at her she could have sworn he was interested. But then he'd gotten skittish and bolted. What the heck had she said? What had gone wrong?

She sighed. So much for the grocery store being a great place to meet men. Where had she heard that, anyway?

Oh, yes, her sisters. It seemed they were always meeting men in the grocery store. They also met men at the gym, at the mall, the coffee shop, business conventions, the women's lingerie department. Sheesh. Why couldn't she have been a sexy fashion diva like her successful older sister or a bubbly blonde like her baby sister?

She sighed. Her sisters always told her she didn't send out the right vibes.

What did they expect? Her pheromone broadcast tower was broken. She frowned at her down coat, which was now way too big for her, and could almost hear her older sister's scolding voice.

"Advertise," said Gloria (nickname Glorious). "Who can even find you buried under those ugly clothes? Men are lazy. You have to make it easy for them."

Gloria's idea of advertising was wearing low-cut tops and butt-hugging jeans, but outfits like that weren't for Merilee. She'd never worn clothes like that. Of course, she'd never had the figure for clothes like that. Maybe now she did, but she sure didn't have the confidence for them.

"What exactly would I be advertising?" she'd muttered. "In those kind of clothes men are going to ask me how much I charge." Even as she'd said it she'd thought, *You should be so lucky.*

She'd turned down Gloria's offer to take her shopping and Gloria had given up in disgust.

"Guys don't like to take risks," said Merliee's younger sister, Liz. "You've got to send out a clear signal that you're interested so they know they've got a green light."

So far very few men had seen the green light. (It worked about as well as the old pheromone broadcast tower.) She was now twenty-six and she'd had only a handful of relationships—a very small handful at that. Okay, it was more like two fingers' worth, and neither had been a keeper. Of course, the prime time for finding keepers was in college. In college, just as in high school, she hadn't been the kind of girl who keepers looked at. Even now, although she'd lost fifty-two pounds in the last three years, the insecurity that had ridden her since middle school, right along with the extra weight, refused to budge.

"You've just got to put yourself out there a little more," Liz insisted.

Easier said than done. Merilee had always been quiet. Her embarrassment over her weight had made her painfully shy around guys. On top of that she'd gotten lost in the giant shadow of her overachieving siblings. Not only were her sisters magnificent, her younger brother was a star. Literally, on a television soap. Then there was her older brother who had his successful business, his perfect wife, and his two gorgeous children. Well, so what? She had . . .

She slapped the magazine shut and put it back in the rack. The last thing she needed was to read about beautiful people.

You are not a failure, she told herself firmly. Dropping out of veterinary college didn't make a girl a failure. It simply made her broke. She'd go back and finish when she got more money. And meanwhile there was nothing wrong with working in a pet supply store and volunteering at the local animal shelter. Animals needed love, too. And animals appreciated a girl no matter what she looked like. Animals saw into a person's soul.

Merilee paid for her groceries—cottage cheese, salad makings, and a candy cane (a girl needed to live it up once in a while)—and left the store with a stoical smile. But as soon as she was in her car she let out a sigh.

"Oh, stop already," she scolded herself. "Your life is not so bad." And to prove it she flipped on the radio to a station that was playing Christmas music and began to sing along. *'Tis the season to be jolly. Fa-la-la-la-la, la-la-la-LA!*

There. She felt better already. Life was good. She had food and shelter and people in her life who loved her.

Christmas was right around the corner, which meant lots of family fun and time-honored traditions. So what if she didn't have a man. Did a woman need a man to be happy?

Some little voice at the back of her mind whispered: *No, but it sure helps.*

THREE

The cat stayed hidden the entire time Ray and Taquito were over. "Just as well," said Ray.

"Oh, that's right," sneered Zach. "Killer there would have hurt him."

"Dogs hurt cats," said Ray, scowling.

"Big dogs, yeah, but I've seen rats bigger than that mutt of yours," Zach teased, making Ray frown. "And, judging from the looks of him, old Tom's survived a few fights."

"A real beauty, huh?" Ray shook his head and took a swig of beer as the action movie they were watching boomed its way across Zach's TV screen. "That seals the deal. You won't be finding anyone who wants him. Looks like you've got yourself a cat."

"Oh, no. I'll find a home for him." *Somewhere, some-place, somehow.*

There had to be someone he knew who'd want a mangy orange tomcat with a torn ear. "Anyway, what was I supposed to do, let the little guy get the needle?"

Ray shook his head. "Man, you are a pushover."

"I am not," Zach retorted. "I'm just not a cat killer."

"You don't know that they'd have killed him," Ray observed.

"Trust me," said Zach. "They would have. They have too many cats at the pound already."

"How do you know that?"

"Someone told me," Zach hedged.

"Someone? Who?"

"Just someone I met in the store," Zach said, keeping his eyes trained on the TV. But he could feel his friend studying him. He turned to see a grin growing on Ray's face.

"Like a chick someone?"

Zach shifted on the couch.

Ray nodded knowingly and pointed a finger at him. "So that's why you forgot the beer." He gave a snort. "Well, well. My man is going domestic. Got himself a cat and next he's gonna get a woman and find the old husband collar slipped on his neck same as what happens to all the rest of us."

"No, not going there," Zach assured both Ray and himself. "She wasn't my type."

"Had her act together, huh?" Ray teased.

"Hey, are we going to watch this movie or not?" Zach snapped.

"Yeah. Sure," said Ray, and he sat there on the couch the rest of the night with a smirk on his face.

Crab-in-the-pot syndrome, Zach thought irritably. There was nothing a guy who'd been burned liked better than to know his buddies were suffering right along with him. Just let a man try to climb out of the pot, or, in Zach's case, not fall in, and they were reaching out to pull him down into the hot water with the rest of them. But Zach wasn't going to end up like Ray, led around by his zipper, taken for a ride, and then tossed and left living in a ratty apartment, using garage sale pots and pans because he'd lost his shirt somewhere in divorce court. Oh, no. Not him. And having a cat didn't make a man domestic.

Zach's new furry friend came out of hiding once Ray was gone and the television was off. Zach suddenly realized it had been hours since the animal had been outside. Cats went outside at night, right? That gave them a chance to do their business, hunt, cat around.

"It's time to do your thing, dude," he announced and walked to the front door.

The cat followed tentatively.

Zach swung the door wide, an invitation to freedom. A cold gust whooshed in. It was sleeting now and he suddenly felt like a Scrooge.

Well, it couldn't be helped. He didn't want to have to deal with getting the smell of cat pee out of his wood floors or the carpet. "Probably lots of mice out there for you to chase," he said, trying to put a good spin on the situation. "Come on."

The cat slinked to the door, stuck his head out and sniffed. He raised one tentative paw.

"Out you go," said Zach, using the door to nudge him onto the porch.

Instead of getting the message and going out, the cat whirled and started in the other direction.

Zach couldn't say he blamed the little guy, but he was sure Tom had to take a whiz after all this time. He grabbed the animal, saying, "Come on now, dude, you've got to go do your business."

He gave the cat a gentle toss and shut the door firmly.

And then felt like King Rat as he headed for his nice, warm bed.

He felt even worse in the morning when he opened the front door and Tom darted back into the house, his fur wet.

Zach put some canned cat food in a cottage cheese container and set it on the floor. The animal settled in front of it and started chowing down like it was his last meal.

"Sorry about sending you out in the cold last night, guy. That was a shitty thing to do."

The cat ignored him, tossing back a mouthful of Tuna Surprise and giving it a vicious chew with his sharp little teeth. No leg-rubbing today.

Zach couldn't blame him. He heaved a sigh of resignation. The last thing he wanted to mess with was a litter box, but if he was going to do a good deed he might as well do it right. "I'll make it up to you, bud. No more cold nights stuck outside."

True to his promise, he hightailed it over to Pet Palace as soon as the place opened.

A huge warehouse of a store, it had everything for every kind of pet imaginable. Shoppers stood mesmerized in front of tropical fish tanks, compared prices on gerbil cages, and strolled up and down the aisles with their dogs on a leash, checking out chew toys and doggy sweaters.

Funny he'd never been in here before considering the fact that he was hanging out with the owner's daughter. And it hadn't occurred to him before now to wonder why Blair didn't have a pet when her family owned a pet supply store. What was that about? Probably, like him, she'd lost an animal she loved and decided she didn't want to go through such misery again.

Zach found the cat section and picked up the first litter box he saw. Then he snagged a couple of bags of litter and, what the heck, a cat toy, and started for the one open checkout stand.

There she was, standing at her cash register, ready for business, the little elf from the night before.

For a moment, his steps stalled. He should put the stuff back and go somewhere else. She'd think he was stalking her.

No she won't, he argued to himself. *Why would she? Just be cool and casual.*

Today she wore a brown polo shirt tucked into khaki slacks. The company logo, a mutt sitting in front of a castle, was emblazoned over her left boob. The uniform was ugly, but it confirmed what Zach had suspected the night before. She did, indeed, have a nice body.

Her name tag (right boob) showed that she had a nice name, too. *Happily serving our pets: Merilee.* It was the kind of name that made a guy think laughter and good times and a good life.

Zach quickly reminded himself that he already had all that.

At the sight of him she stared wide-eyed and blinked. Then she blushed. Then she stammered, "Good morning. Welcome to Pet Palace."

So, he flustered her. She thought he was hot. The ego stroke made him smile. Until he remembered he didn't want anything stroked by this kind of woman. "Hi Merilee. I forgot something important," he said, setting down Tom's toilet supplies.

The simple statement put her at ease and she smiled. "So, your new cat is an inside kitty."

"He wants to be. He wasn't real happy when I put him outside last night."

This bit of sharing produced a disapproving little frown. "They do like to go outside, but not in the cold and rain."

"Hey, who does?" Zach cracked, trying to make light of his heartless behavior of the night before.

"I do," she said brightly, then looked like she was reconsidering her confession. "I like to hike," she explained.

"Yeah?" He liked to hike. Most women he dated didn't, though. They were always worried about their hair or their clothes getting dirty.

"I think walking in the rain is romantic," she confessed. This brought another deeper blush, and she kept her gaze riveted on her cash register.

"You're the first woman I've met who actually thinks that," Zach said. "You don't worry about your hair?"

She gave a handful of curls a self-conscious tug. "It's hopeless."

"Naw, it's cute." It was. He wasn't flirting, just making an honest observation. *Dude. What are you thinking? No more "honest observations."*

She cleared her throat and got busy ringing up his purchases. "You're smart to keep your cat inside."

Zach almost reminded her, *He's not really my cat. He's just staying with me for a while.* Instead, he said, "Oh? Why?"

"It's safer for them," she said, her voice taking on authority. "They can contract diseases like feline leukemia or get hit by cars. So inside is best. Credit or debit?" she added after telling him his total.

That much just so the animal could shit indoors? "Uh, debit," Zach said, fishing out his card. The cost of being a Good Samaritan was starting to climb.

"Thanks for coming in," she said when they'd finished the transaction. "If you need any help with your cat, I'm here."

She may as well have said, 'Call me.' With those big green eyes and that hot little bod he could have been tempted. If she'd given him any sign she wasn't looking for something that led to the church altar and then divorce court, if he wasn't already with someone who had no dreams of white wedding gowns.

I'm here.

Which meant that from now on, he would have to make sure he was . . . there.

* * *

Merilee poked her head outside her second-floor apartment door. Good. The coast was clear. She slipped outside, her garbage bag in tow, and hurried for the Dumpsters out back. When she got to the ground floor she did a quick bolt past Mrs. Winnamucker's unit, her heart beating an anxious tattoo. Fortunately, no curler-clad head poked out the door to ask where she was going.

Thank God. That had been known to happen. Mrs. Winnamucker, manager of the Angel Arms Apartments, took her job seriously and kept a careful eye on all the residents. (Which was why most of them were over fifty and sedately settled. No one with a girl-gone-wild kind of social life stayed for long.)

Mrs. Winnamucker especially kept an eye on Merilee, even though she was a quiet renter—never a wild party or a TV turned up too loud. But Merilee worked in a pet store, and in Mrs. Winnamucker's mind that made her suspect. She was a resident who might just fraternize with the enemy: animals. The Angel Arms Apartments didn't allow pets (a new policy they adopted right after Merilee moved in) and Mrs. Winnamucker took her job as a guardian of the complex's carpets seriously. Living on the ground floor just two apartments away from her was, well, dangerous. At least it was dangerous these days because Merilee was harboring a cat.

But what could she do? Queenie had been one of several kitties the animal shelter had brought to Pet Palace, hoping to find families for them. All had gotten homes but poor Queenie. For some reason she had gone beyond her expiration date. The thought of the little white cat being destroyed had been more than Merilee could bear, so she'd done something very un-Merilee. She'd broken the rules and smuggled Queenie into her apartment. And she wasn't sorry. Not one bit!

She was, however, nervous. If Mrs. Winnamucker got

wind of this, if someone heard Queenie meowing, they'd both be cast out of the Angel Arms and into the cold sans damage deposit. She could always go home to her parents but because Merilee's mother was allergic to cat dander Queenie would be homeless. Merilee couldn't do that to the poor cat. If only she could afford a nice, snug rental house with pet-friendly landlords. Sigh.

The best way out of this was to find a home for her furry houseguest soon, before she got caught. Queenie was such a sweet cat. Surely someone would want her. Merilee had put a picture up on the bulletin board at the library and placed an ad on Petfinder.com but no response so far. She'd tried to convince both of her sisters that they needed an animal, but they'd turned her down with flimsy excuses like allergies and busy schedules. Her younger sister, Liz, had even quipped that she was already engaged to an animal and one was enough. Ha, ha.

What was wrong with people, anyway? Didn't they get how dependent animals were on them? It was too bad there weren't more people out there like the man she'd met in the grocery store.

Envisioning his smile heated Merilee to the point that it made her coat unnecessary. If only she could have said something clever to him when he came into Pet Palace maybe she'd have had a date with him instead of her TV tonight. If only she'd thought to toss her hair, or run her tongue across her teeth or do any number of things that worked for women in the movies. Except she didn't have enough hair to toss. (*You should never have cut it. Fool!*) And doing the tongue-tooth thing when talking about feline leukemia would have made her look demented. Anyway, it was too late now, so there was no point in even thinking about it.

Merilee made it to the Dumpster and threw away the bag with the damning litter box contents. Mrs. Winnamucker had been known to poke around the Dumpster for tell-tale signs of excessive partying or drug use but luckily for Merilee it was winter. Even Mrs. Winnamucker had her limits. Anyway, who here did she think was going to go wild?

Merilee, of course. If only.

The evidence of her criminal behavior ditched, she pulled her jacket close and hurried back toward her apartment. She was ten feet from Mrs. Winnamucker's door when the manager stepped out, her plump body encased in a long, red quilted coat, her gray curls hidden under a jaunty red hat.

With her round face, wire-rimmed glasses perched on a button nose, and sweet granny smile, one could almost mistake the woman for Mrs. Claus. Looks were deceiving. Mrs. Winnamucker could sprout fangs at a moment's notice. Merilee knew. She'd seen it happen.

"Hello, Miss White," she greeted Merilee in the deceptively sweet voice she favored.

Merilee's steps faltered, but she pulled herself together and smiled at the manager like a woman who had nothing to hide. "Hi, Mrs. Winnamucker. Nasty night, isn't it?"

"It certainly is," said the woman. "I'm surprised you're out in it, my dear." She added a cocked eyebrow to the smile. Every time Mrs. Winnamucker cocked an eyebrow Merilee felt as if she was in one of those police interrogation rooms you saw on TV shows, getting the old good cop–bad cop routine. Except in Mrs. Winnamucker's case there would never be a good cop. Him she'd have devoured for breakfast right along with a box of donuts.

"I'm just dumping some garbage," Merilee stammered. "I've been cleaning my refrigerator."

Mrs. Winnamucker nodded but now her mouth had turned down. "Velma Tuttle thought she heard a cat the other day."

Velma Tuttle, the old bat on the other side of Merilee, couldn't hear a Rottweiler barking in her ear even with her hearing aid turned up.

"Have you heard anything, Miss White?" asked Mrs. Winnamucker.

"No, but we are surrounded by houses and there are several cats in the neighborhood."

"Yes, well, I suppose. Have a nice night." Mrs. Winnamucker heaved her bag over her shoulder, locked her door, and marched toward the parking lot.

Merilee watched her go with a frown. The woman didn't need to bother with a car. She could probably manage fine with a broom.

Ambrose was still vague on the specifics of what he had to do to keep his ninth life, but the reason he was here with this particular human came to him in a blinding flash of clarity when the man was dishing up his food.

"Hang in there, guy," he had said while Ambrose brushed against his legs to remind his new human that he was starving to death.

Hang in there, guy. Hang in there!

The words hurled Ambrose into the past. It was the Christmas of his second life. Big white trucks with the letters FedEx printed on their side were rushing everywhere. He'd been minding his own business, just getting ready to cross the street when one of them rushed right into him, adding a new word to his vocabulary: *splat*.

Out of nowhere a stranger had appeared, picked Ambrose up, laid him on a car seat, and rushed off to the animal hospital. *Hang in there, guy. Hang in there!*

So that was where he'd seen this man before. No wonder his face had seemed familiar. It was the same face that had looked at him with such concern in that car all those lives ago. The man had grown older—bigger, too—but he and that noble youth were one in the same. Once upon a life, back when Ambrose was still innocent and trusting, this man had tried to save him.

Surely it was no coincidence that their paths had crossed. Twice now. It was payback time.

So how could Ambrose repay him? The man had to need rescuing, but what, exactly, did he need rescuing from? He seemed to be doing fine.

Ambrose carefully observed his new human, checking him out from many different vantage points: the top of the dresser, the foot of the bed, the fireplace mantel, the floor, and, of course, the man's lap. Like all the other humans Ambrose had known in his past lives, this one dedicated a great deal of time to sleeping, grooming, and playing with his food—all good uses of one's time, as any cat could attest. But he also wasted much time and energy ripping out and replacing parts of his house. And talking on his cell phone.

Ambrose didn't care for those objects. A female human using one had robbed him of a life.

She'd been in a car, talking into it and looking the other way, and before Ambrose could scat out of the way it was *Thump, thump, good-bye Life Number Six*. Those things were dangerous toys, if you asked Ambrose. Didn't humans talk to each other enough as it was? Why did they have to carry their phones with them everywhere?

Still, much as he hated them, Ambrose understood that he could learn a lot listening when a human played with one. So he hung around and eavesdropped while the man talked into his, mostly to females.

One was Mom. Ambrose knew what a mom was. In all his dealings with families he had found that she was most often the person who fed him. She prepared food for the other humans, too, and kept their house clean. (Sometimes the males helped, but usually the females did most of the work.) Moms fussed over the small ones and mated with the large male frequently. In spite of all that mating, moms rarely produced a litter. The few who did wound up appearing on television or in magazines. The rest managed to occasionally produce one small human called a baby, and when that happened, oh, the fussing that went on. Human babies took forever to grow into children. And children . . . ugh. They could be torture. They did everything from pulling a guy's tail to stuffing him into doll clothes. Very humiliating. Moms still loved their children in spite of what the little monsters did to their cats, and children all gravitated to their moms. Whatever their age, they would often seek out those moms for long conversations about things like school projects and boys or work or how to cook a turkey.

For some unknown reason, this man didn't call his, but she called him and he didn't seem very happy about it. He said things to her like "Yeah, the remodel is going fine."

Remodel. Was that what you called the mess the guy was making?

He also said things like "I don't think I can come" and "Sorry, Mom. I've got plans."

Tonight's plans appeared to be with someone called Baby, obviously not the small, diapered version since this particular baby knew how to operate a phone. When the man talked with her he said things like "I can hardly wait to see you in it, Baby" and "Come on over. I'll get takeout."

Baby was obviously someone important, Ambrose decided, as he and the man sat on the big leather couch, the man petting Ambrose as he talked.

It didn't sound like Ambrose was going to meet Mom anytime soon, but he would see Baby tonight. Ambrose licked his paw and began to slick back the fur on his head.

A guy wanted to look his best when he met someone important in his human's life.

Ambrose stared in horror as Baby stepped through the door. He knew this woman, this taker of lives, this callous creature who talked on her cell phone when she drove and ran over helpless cats who had so much to live for. His tail quivered at the memory of her standing over him, still talking on her cell phone.

"What do I do? Pick it up? Are you crazy? It might bite me. Oooh, I think I'm going to be sick."

Her? What about him? He was the one who was dying.

She hadn't cared. It had been all about her. Still crying and babbling, she'd returned to her fancy car and roared off, leaving Ambrose alone and in pain. Heartless creature. For all she knew he could have been on his last life.

And now, here she was again, back like a bad dream. She still had the same long, yellow fur on her head and her mouth was painted bloodred. She was wearing shoes designed to make her look almost as tall as the man and pants that stuck to her skinny legs. Over them she wore a long coat trimmed with . . . fur! If there'd been any doubt before there couldn't be now. The woman was an animal hater.

Why would this kind-hearted guy want to be around such a person? Was she even young enough to produce offspring? Like Ambrose, she'd seen a few lives since their last encounter. Ambrose could tell by the small cracks around her eyes.

Well, this was simply further proof that the man wasn't too bright and needed help from someone wiser, someone who had the kind of wisdom that could only come from having several lives under your collar.

"I told James he doesn't have to be home till midnight," she said. "Which means I don't have to be, either." She slipped off her coat to reveal something black and shiny on her top half that barely covered her skin. "You like?" she purred.

Oh, gag me with a hairball. What was there to like?

Something, since the fool was eyeing her the same way Ambrose once watched the tempting canary that cost him his fourth life. "Oh, yeah," the man said, and his voice, too, was a purr.

Ambrose watched in disgust from his spot in front of the fire as they fit themselves together and kissed (a popular human custom connected with mating that seemed a complete waste of time). This was the first fire his new human had lit since Ambrose had moved in and now he realized that it hadn't been lit for him. The man had built that fire for this unworthy female. Ambrose and Adelaide, his old woman, had watched plenty of TV, and Ambrose knew exactly what this Baby person was. She was a cougar, just like in the show *Cougars in Connecticut*. The rude and naughty behavior Ambrose had seen on that show—it had been enough to make him glad he was a cat. The last thing this poor fool needed was to be mating with that type of female.

They finally broke apart and the cougar moved into the living room. She got halfway to the couch and stopped short at the sight of Ambrose. *Yeah. Remember me? I'm back.*

"Zach, what's this? You got a cat?" Her tone of voice made it sound like the guy had contracted some fatal disease.

A cat? How about the cat you flattened? Obviously, humans didn't remember things they'd done in past lives.

"You didn't tell me," she said.

Ambrose had heard this enough over his lifetimes.

Human females expected their men to tell them every little thing. What a pain. He was glad he was cat.

"More like he got me," said the man called Zach. "I rescued old Tom and he followed me home. I'm keeping him until I can find a place for him."

Tom. Ambrose cringed at the mention of his pathetic new name. And what did Zach mean by that? This was Ambrose's place. It was where he was supposed to be, where he was supposed to earn his nice, long, ninth life.

The female looked down her nose at Ambrose. "Good luck with that. He's not the best-looking cat on the block, is he?"

What? Was she serious? What did she know about what made for a handsome cat? The ladies liked him just fine. So what if he was missing the tip of his right ear? Battle scars . . . Baby.

"Hey, Blair, you'll hurt his feelings," said Zach.

Ambrose narrowed his eyes. He knew a teasing tone of voice when he heard one. Suddenly Zach didn't seem to care very much about his feelings. Blair Baby sure didn't bring out the best in Zach. Hardly surprising, considering her past.

"Well, I'm sure he's really sweet. Aren't you?" she cooed to Ambrose.

"Tom, come say hi to Blair," said Zach.

Ambrose was no dummy. He knew she was only fussing over him to impress Zach. Well, he was having none of it. Instead of coming to the cat killer, he walked away and brushed against the leg of an old chair, marking it. *I'd rather identify with this chair than get anywhere near you.*

"He makes my nose itch," said the cougar, rubbing a finger underneath her nose. "I hope you're not going to have him for long."

Ambrose narrowed his eyes. *We'll see who stays around the longest . . . Baby.*

Brave talk, indeed, considering how much Zach seemed to like Blair Baby. It wasn't long before he and Blair were entwined on Zach's leather couch, talking, touching, laughing. Ambrose left for the kitchen before his appetite got completely ruined. At least the cougar didn't live there. She'd soon be gone.

Maybe not. Blair Baby hung around like a giant burr, clinging to Zach and stealing his attention. They ate. They went upstairs to Zach's bedroom and shut the door in Ambrose's face. Finally they came back downstairs, turned on the TV, and cuddled up on the couch. She put a bowl of popcorn in Zach's lap—right where Ambrose would normally be sitting.

Humph. Ambrose settled by the fire and turned his back on them. Out of sight, out of mind.

But he could still hear just fine. And he heard a voice in the TV, reminding Zach and Blair to come to Pet Palace and get their pet's picture taken with Santa.

Santa! He was big and sadistic. He grabbed little children and made them sit on his lap, terrifying them and making them cry. Ambrose knew. He'd seen the pictures. Humans obviously used Santa at this time of year to punish their offspring. But who would do that to a defenseless animal?

Pet Palace, of course. The place was evil. He shuddered, remembering that day in his fifth life when his owner had taken advantage of Pet Palace's discount coupon for neutering. Emasculation! He had been so terrified that first time. No wonder he'd had a heart attack and died on the operating table.

"You should take Tom to get his picture taken with Santa," said Blair.

Nooo, he shouldn't.

"I don't know," Zach said. "That's right up there with putting reindeer antlers on your dog."

Wearing reindeer antlers? That sounded like something a dog would do.

"I'm just thinking that if you put a cute picture of your lost cat all dolled up in a Santa hat on Craigslist or Pet Finder you'll get a home for him."

Cute! Ambrose didn't do cute, and he certainly didn't do cute with the big mean Santa monster. He'd rather throw himself into that fire than fall into the clutches of the man in red. And what did she mean by lost? He wasn't lost. He knew exactly where he was.

Ambrose used the need for a stretch as an excuse to turn back around and observe. Zach was frowning slightly.

"James will be with his father next weekend, so I can help you," said the cougar. "The poor cat should have a home. In fact, the sooner the better," she added, and rubbed her nose again.

Now Zach was looking thoughtful. And that didn't look good for Ambrose.

FOUR

The next time Blair came by the house she barely gave Zach a chance to kiss her before she wrinkled her pretty nose and said, "Ugh. What is that smell?"

"What smell?" He'd showered.

"Cat box," she said in disgust. "When was the last time you changed the cat box?"

"Tuesday, before I left for the station," said Zach.

She made a face and shook her head. "Your whole house smells."

He sniffed. Okay, it did stink a little. "I guess I'd better change it."

"I guess you'd better do something about the cat. Coming in here to that nasty odor is a definite buzz kill." She dug a small bottle of perfume out of her purse and spritzed it around the front hallway, shuddering the whole time. "I'll wait for you in the car," she said, leaving him alone with his stinky house and his stinky cat.

He started a new topic of conversation as they drove to Captain Crab for lunch, but later, when they sat in a corner booth, hemmed in by red tinsel garlands and looking over the menus, she brought up the subject again. "So, how are you coming with finding a home for the cat?"

"I'm working on it," Zach hedged. He set down his menu. "You know, Blair, I'm kind of surprised you don't like him. I thought you'd be more of an animal lover. I mean, your dad owns Pet Palace, for Pete's sake."

"Don't be silly," she said, making him feel both stupid and irritated. "That's like expecting someone who owns a Japanese restaurant to like sushi."

"Yeah? Why would you want to own a Japanese restaurant if you didn't like Japanese food?" he argued.

"To make money," she replied. "Look, I have nothing against cats, and I have nothing against the one you found except that he makes me sneeze. And now he's making your house smell. Really, Zach, I get one whiff and I have no desire to hang around there."

He knew what that meant. It meant, well, no desire. Blair's house was pretty much off-limits due to the presence of her teenage son. And the neighbors, who she was sure would tell the teenage son that she wasn't just cleaning house when he was gone. Dumb, if you asked Zach. The kid had to know she had a life. Still, that was the way she wanted it, so he had no objections. Except if hanging out at Zach's place stopped being an option . . . This didn't bode well for their love life.

"Don't worry. I'll take care of it," he promised.

"I hope you do," she said. And to prove she meant business she went straight home after lunch.

"No problem," said Ray, when a very frustrated Zach called him. "I can come over this afternoon and we can put in a cat door. Then he can come and go when he wants. No more cat box, no more smell."

It was a perfect solution, and when the guys were done Zach had a dent in his charge card and a dent in his thumb from where he'd hit himself with the hammer. But Tom had a cat door. Zach smiled as Tacky demonstrated how easy it was to use. Perfect.

But that evening, when Zach tried to introduce Tom to the wonders of having his very own door, the little guy balked. He not only balked, he ran away.

"Hey, come on, now," Zach called after him. "I'm trying to work things out so you can stay." He fetched the cat and tried again, and Tom dug in with all fours. When Zach flipped the door and tried to nudge him through he hissed and took a swipe at Zach and bolted a second time.

"Okay, guy. You had your chance," growled Zach, his feeling of goodwill toward cats evaporating.

The following morning Zach was back at Pet Palace, this time for a cat carrier. *Somebody* was going to get hauled here tomorrow to have his picture taken with Santa because *somebody* was getting a new home for Christmas.

He stood looking at the vast array of carriers and suddenly felt mildly guilty about stuffing Tom into one. The little guy had made up the night before and sat in Zach's lap while Zach read the December issue of *Do It Yourself*.

But if a man had to choose between having a cat or a woman on his lap . . . Blair was absolutely right. Tom needed a real home, and posting a picture of him all dressed up for Christmas was a good way to ensure he got one. Zach grabbed a cat carrier and then went in search of cat treats, figuring bribery would make both him and the cat feel better about the whole thing.

Wouldn't you know? There on the kitty treat aisle stood the elfette, stocking shelves. Her cheeks turned rose pink at the sight of Zach and she managed a tentative smile.

He held up the carrier. "Had to get a cat carrier." *Well, duh.* "I'm bringing my cat in for a Santa picture tomorrow."

Her eyes lit up and her smile got big.

"With my girlfriend," he added. The pink in her cheeks turned to red and the smile faltered, a sure sign that he had, in just a couple of encounters, managed to lead her on. He felt like a heel.

She nodded gamely. "I guess I'll see you then. I'm taking the pictures."

"Oh," said Zach. *Too bad you'll have Blair with you.* Whoa, where had that come from? He wanted Blair with him, didn't he? Of course, he did. Blair came with no strings attached. "Well then, see you Saturday," he said, and got out of there.

He was back on the road when he remembered he never did snag any cat treats for Tom. He'd get the little guy some after they were done with the pictures as a reward for good behavior. And maybe, if he was lucky, Blair would give *him* a reward for good behavior.

Ho, ho, ho. He grinned as he pictured . . .

Oh, no. Not a redhead with green eyes. Where was the blue-eyed blonde? *Blair. You're with Blair. You're happy with Blair.* He booted out the image of Merilee posing for him in a skimpy outfit of red velvet and brought Blair back on stage wearing nothing but a Santa hat.

But she was looking stage right and scowling.

A second later there was Merilee again, tap-dancing her way to center stage, and suddenly Blair was nowhere to be seen.

Zach gave his head a vigorous shake in an effort to dislodge the image. *What is the matter with you?*

It was a question he found he couldn't answer, at least not comfortably.

A woman looking slick in designer jeans and an expensive jacket reached past Merilee to snag a couple of cans of cat food, the diamond ring on her left hand taunting Merilee. Everything about the woman, from her stylish coat and jeans to her makeup, said, "I'm perfect and I know it."

Merilee gave her a feral smile and pulled fresh cans out of the carton she was emptying, slamming them on the shelf. *Jealousy is not attractive,* she scolded herself. If only she was better looking she wouldn't have to fight the green-eyed monster.

But even if she transformed herself on the outside, she'd still probably find it impossible to untie her tongue and manage the art of flirting. Why, whenever she was around hunky men, did her confidence fade like the Cheshire cat?

Ha! Years of practice, that was why. The cool guys had never seen her, either in high school or college. They still didn't.

These days just being nice wasn't enough for a girl. You had to have pizzazz. You had to connect.

Sadly, Merilee connected better with animals than she did with men. Animals loved you whether or not you wore makeup. Animals didn't need you to be sexy or witty and clever and entertaining. All they wanted was love and acceptance, and Merilee was good at that. She cared about helpless beings. She cared about anyone in need of help or a shoulder to cry on, which was why she had never lacked for girlfriends. In high school all her friends came to her with their boy problems. Looking back it was easy to see why. They knew they'd get plenty of empathy and no competition.

She slammed down another can of cat food. Men didn't want nice, they wanted hot, and she was never going to be hot. She wasn't sure she could even achieve lukewarm. Why were people (especially male people) so shallow? It was what was inside that counted.

The last time she'd said something like that around

her sisters Liz had informed her that most people would rather look inside a nicely wrapped gift box with a pretty bow than take a chance on a dirty paper sack.

She frowned at the memory. "I am not a dirty paper sack."

"Thanks for the update," said Dennis the floor manager as he walked by, proving that a girl could, indeed, get noticed no matter how she dressed.

Cat carriers were nothing more than portable cages, humiliating modes of transport for an animal. And in all Ambrose's lives not one of those contraptions had ever carried him someplace he wanted to go.

He watched through slitted eyes as Zach stowed the ugly gray thing in the downstairs closet. So Zach and the cat-killing cougar thought they were going to stuff him in that thing to go see the Santa monster, did they? Well, they could try.

Zach disappeared upstairs but Ambrose remained in the living room under the couch, ever vigilant. Today must not have been the day for the visit to the Santa monster because a few minutes later Zach appeared in his tattered clothes. That meant . . . sure enough, soon he was in the eating room, pounding and banging.

Ambrose bolted up the stairs and hid under the bed. All that noise! It was enough to shatter a guy's nerves. Why oh why did he have to end up here? Why couldn't his mission have involved bringing comfort to another nice old lady like Adelaide? Of course, he knew the answer and it was the only reason he was still hanging around. He owed Zach. And Zach definitely needed help.

Later that evening, when they were settled in on the couch with the TV on, Ambrose decided this mission wasn't so bad after all. Zach was a nice enough human.

Easily led, though, which obviously was why he needed to be with someone other than the cougar, someone who would be a good influence on him and teach him how to consider the feelings of others, like his cat.

They had a cozy sleep that night—Zach under the bed-covers, Ambrose curled up on top of them. Beds were wonderful things, soft and warm, and lying on one next to a human (even if he wasn't the brightest one on the block) gave a guy a sense of security—a sense of community, too. Contrary to popular belief, cats weren't snobs. They liked to belong. And Ambrose could see himself with Zach for a long time. Once he got the boy whipped into shape.

He was still on the bed in the morning, dreaming he was feasting on a nice, fat mouse, when Zach picked him up. "Hey, guy, it's showtime."

Showtime? That had to mean they were going to watch something on Zach's TV. Zach would make a home for Ambrose on his lap and pet him. What a good idea! Ambrose allowed himself to be carried downstairs.

But as they reached the foot of the stairs Ambrose spied the pet carrier and . . . the cougar. Oh, no! They were not putting him in that thing.

Zach had anticipated Ambrose's reaction, though, and even as he tried to propel himself to freedom, Zach held him tighter. "Sorry, buddy," he said, and the next thing Ambrose knew he was caged.

Zach should feel sorry, Ambrose thought indignantly. This was betrayal of trust, plain and simple. He watched from behind his prison bars as Blair Baby showed Zach the hat she'd brought for Ambrose, a small version of the silly red hats with the white pom-pom that some humans wore this time of year in honor of the Santa monster.

"This will cover his torn ear," she said. "It's got an elastic strap so it will stay on."

She had to get it on first, and if she thought Ambrose was going to let her anywhere near him with the ridiculous thing she could just think again. A dog would go along with such nonsense and think it a great joke, but no self-respecting cat would lower himself to that level.

"That may be pushing it," Zach said doubtfully.

There was an understatement.

"Oh, he'll be fine," said the cougar.

He would not!

The next thing Ambrose knew, he was airborne and swinging like a bird in a cage. *Eeew.* He was going to be sick. He watched bushes and lawn and trees pass dizzily by and then he was in the back of the shiny black car. Zach and the cougar climbed in front and the engine roared to life. Once again Ambrose was moving . . . and getting more nervous by the second. Why was Zach torturing him like this?

The cougar, of course. It had probably been her idea to install that horrible pet door.

Oh, the terror he had felt at the mere sight of the thing. It had brought back vivid memories of his most humiliating death. Granted, if he hadn't dug his claws into poor Snoopy and ridden the crazed beagle all over the house he wouldn't have met his end in the first place. Those pet doors weren't meant for piggy-backing pets. Snoopy had ducked through theirs at the last minute and, like some silly cartoon character, Ambrose had crashed into the actual door. The impact had broken his neck. So, yes, his bad. He'd gotten what he deserved, but still, those things should be outlawed. And women who convinced impressionable men to install them should be put down.

It felt like an eternity before the car stopped. Zach took the cat carrier from the backseat and Ambrose got a view of an endless field of cars. In front of them loomed a big,

big building. Ambrose huddled in the corner of his cage. This wasn't going to be good.

Inside, the building was larger than all the houses Ambrose had lived in put together. And scary, with humans milling around and . . . dogs!

Ambrose backed farther into the corner of his cage. This was worse than the animal shelter. At least there the horrible beasts were behind bars where they belonged. Here they strolled around on thin leashes attended by distracted humans. Ambrose's fur began to stand on end. This was awful. And they hadn't even gotten to the Santa monster yet. At this rate Ambrose would probably never live to complete his assignment and save Zach. He'd die of fright right here. Good-bye life number nine.

He bobbed and swayed as Zach carried him across the huge place. Somewhere a chorus of cats was meowing "Silent Night," a Christmas carol Ambrose remembered from past lives. But he didn't see any of his fellow felines. Where were they, and how could they be so calmly singing in such a dangerous place? Were they brain damaged?

Finally Zach set the cage down and Ambrose got a close up glimpse of human feet and legs, and more dogs—a little dachshund, a sloppy old basset, and, oh, no, there was a German shepherd, sitting with his tongue hanging out. Nasty things, German shepherds. Horrible. Unpredictable. Mean. He knew this from personal experience. He'd had a horrible encounter with one in the life he'd lived as an alley cat, right around the holidays, naturally. Talk about your blue Christmas. At the sight of Ambrose, this one stood and barked, almost giving Ambrose a heart attack.

Never let them see you sweat. (A man in Adelaide's TV had said that once.) Ambrose arched his back, puffed out his fur, and hissed.

Zach's voice drifted down to him. "It's okay, Tom. He can't get you."

So you say.

As if to prove it, Zach picked up Ambrose's carrier and moved him out of range.

"Hi," said a disembodied female voice.

"Uh, hi," said Zach.

"We're almost done with the dogs," said the voice. "If you'd like to browse and come back in five minutes that will give your cat a chance to calm down."

The only thing that would help Ambrose calm down was getting out of here. When would the torture end?

Never. Zach and the cougar wandered around the store, giving Ambrose glimpses of birds he couldn't hunt and fish swimming out of reach. The ways people could find to torture a cat in this place were endless.

The carrier finally came to rest once more and this time Ambrose saw no dogs, only a few sets of human legs and feet. Still, he couldn't relax. He may have escaped the dogs, but the Santa monster was still waiting.

The cage door opened and even though Ambrose tried to resist, Zach managed to haul him out.

"It's okay," cooed Blair Baby, the animal hater.

No fur today. Instead she was wearing a sweater with snowflakes. It was too late for camouflage. Ambrose already knew she was the enemy. She came at him with that ridiculous hat and he pushed up against Zach with his ears flat to warn her she'd better back off.

Here was another reason not to like her. (As if he needed another!) She was stupid. She kept right on coming. Ambrose averted his head, but her bloodred claws continued reaching for him. So he did what any self-respecting cat would do. He defended himself. With a hiss, he unsheathed his claws and shot out a paw. *Ha! Got her.*

His attacker backed away with a bleeding scratch and let out a screech followed by a word that Ambrose learned way back in his third life. It was not a nice word. She held out her hand. "Look what that animal did to me!"

So it was bleeding. So what? She started the fight.

"Damn it, Tom," snapped Zach, and shut Ambrose back in the cage.

Imprisoned unjustly, and in trouble with Zach—this was not good.

Meanwhile, outside the carrier, Blair Baby was still carrying on. "That animal should be put down. He's dangerous."

"No, he's not," scolded the same female voice Ambrose had heard earlier. "He's just scared."

"Excuse me?" snapped Blair Baby.

"I said he's scared," the voice snapped back.

"And what are you, a cat shrink?"

"Come on now, Blair," said Zach. "That's uncalled for." You could say that again.

"I know a few things about cats," said the other female.

"Naturally. You have to be highly qualified to work here," said Blair Baby.

Probably, so why was she using that sneering tone of voice?

"The biggest qualification is a heart," the other female retorted. "So you shouldn't bother applying."

"Do I look like I need to work here?" snapped Blair Baby.

"I have no idea what you need," said the voice sweetly, "but you might consider therapy."

"Ho, boy," said Zach under his breath.

Blair emitted the human equivalent of a growl, then announced she was going to go wash the cut before it became infected, and stomped away on her skinny legs, her haunches jiggling.

Zach said to the other female, "Sorry, Merilee. She's, uh . . ."

"Yes, she is," said the Merilee person. "Really, you can't blame your cat for being upset. Most cats don't like to travel. It unnerves them. You have to kind of ease cats into a situation like this. After all, this is a strange place. That can be scary."

A human who understood? What a treasure!

"I can see that," said Zach.

Yeah, finally.

"I guess the hat wasn't such a good idea, either," said Zach.

"Right up there with me telling your girlfriend what I thought of her. I'm sorry."

"She'll get over it," said Zach. "Blair's a sport."

Here was a new word for Ambrose to add to his vocabulary. *Sport: horrible human female.*

Merilee squatted down and looked into the carrier. He regarded her with an air of wounded dignity befitting someone unjustly incarcerated.

He could tell right away that this woman understood his plight. She had kind eyes. And . . . wait a minute. Was it possible?

"I'm sorry you're scared, sweetie," she said.

He looked closer. Yes, this was indeed the volunteer from the animal shelter. They had met in another life. She'd tried to save him when his owners banished him to the nasty place for scaring that stupid canary to death. Sentenced simply for behaving like a cat—grossly unfair! Merilee had gotten him featured as a pet of the week in the *Angel Falls Bugle,* but all to no avail. "Someone will want you," she'd assured him.

No one had, though. Was it any wonder Ambrose had turned bitter in his later lives and taken to torturing unfortunate beagles? A guy couldn't trust anyone, not even Merilee, who had failed to save him from destruction.

She opened the door and Ambrose braced for betrayal. Now she would pull him out and feed him to the Santa monster.

Much to his surprise, however, she merely dropped a couple of kitty treats in his carrier and then shut it again, saying, "There you go. You just relax and enjoy those."

Relax? Here on the floor right in the middle of a store that allowed people to bring in dogs? Right.

But the door to his carrier remained shut and the cougar stayed gone. When no one was looking Ambrose moved forward and sampled the cat treats. Delicious.

So Merilee was still a nice woman, trying to bring some goodness into dark places like this. Ambrose peered up to see Zach smiling at her. Obviously, he liked her. Surely these two good people should mate. They were bound to produce more good people.

Here came the cougar again, a paper towel pressed to her hand. Who invited her back? She grabbed Zach by the arm and said, "Let's go, Zach."

"Uh, thanks, Merilee," said Zach.

Then the cat carrier was airborne once more and they were leaving the store, and that was the end of pictures with Santa. Good.

Even better, Zach and the cougar were fighting.

"What were you thanking that clerk for? Did you hear how she talked to me?" Blair Baby ranted as they pulled away from Pet Palace.

"Did you hear yourself?" Zach retorted.

"That animal is feral."

"No, he's not. He was just pissed," Zach snapped. "I told you putting the hat on him was a dumb idea."

You've got that right.

"Well, excuse me for trying to help," huffed Blair Baby. Zach said nothing.

At last she let out a long sigh. "I'm sorry. You're right; it was a bad idea. Let's not fight over a silly cat."

Silly? This woman who just made a public fool of herself is calling me silly? I've seen birds with bigger brains.

"I'm not the one doing the fighting," said Zach.

She said nothing to that. Instead she came back with, "I guess you'll just have to snap a picture of him when he's sleeping. If you can get a shot that doesn't show his ragged ear you might find a home for him by Christmas."

By Christmas? So now the cougar had set a deadline for getting rid of him. How soon till Christmas? Zach's mother had stopped by the other day to remind Zach that Christmas was right around the corner. But which corner? How much time did Ambrose have to get back in Zach's good graces before the cougar found a way to make him disappear?

"It might not be so easy," said Zach.

"I'm beginning to suspect that you don't want to get rid of this cat," said Blair Baby.

Good. He shouldn't want to.

"I didn't say that."

Well then, say it now. What are you thinking?

"Look," said Zach, not sounding happy. "Can we forget about the cat?"

Forget about the cat? What a bad idea!

"Fine," she said, her brittle voice reminding Ambrose of a small, yappy dog.

Now there was fresh silence in the shiny black car, and it wasn't the cozy kind of silence Ambrose and Zach enjoyed when they were lounging on the couch in the evening.

At last the cougar spoke again. "I guess I'll just go home."

Good idea. Go home and stay there.

This time it was Zach who sighed. "No, don't do that. We'll drop off Tom, then we can go do something fun."

"All right. But I am not coming back to your stinky house," said the cougar.

Fine by me, thought Ambrose.

"Not unless we stop by Hallmark and pick up some scented candles," she added. Now her voice was a purr. "Cinnamon, perhaps. Something . . . spicy?" She reached a red-tipped hand across the seat toward Zach and started slithering it up his leg.

"Hey, now, I'm trying to drive," he protested, but Ambrose could tell it was halfhearted. Zach and the cougar were back on friendly terms.

This turn of events robbed Ambrose of the satisfaction he'd felt over his small victory in Pet Palace. Zach hadn't figured out what to do with him but the cougar had. She wanted him gone by Christmas. Gone where, he had no idea, but he did know one thing: the way his luck had been running it wouldn't be any place good. This did not bode well for his ninth life. It didn't bode well for Zach, either, who clearly needed Ambrose to save him from a fate worse than death by a cat door.

Ambrose shifted his paws under him and settled down to think. He was going to have to do something to fix this problem.

FIVE

Back at the house Zach turned Tom loose with a stern reminder to use his cat door. "Litter boxes are like diapers, dude, and you're too old for diapers. Don't let me down."

If he and Blair came home and Tom had whizzed inside the house it wouldn't be pretty. Blair would be mad. Actually, so would Zach, and Tom would be a dead cat.

"Are you sure he knows to use his cat door?" asked Blair.

"He'd better," said Zach. The cat was becoming a problem.

That wasn't fair, he concluded as he trailed Blair around the Hallmark store, past rows of holiday wrapping paper, ribbons, and cards. For the most part the little guy was pretty easy to get along with as long as Zach remembered to feed him. And Tom didn't make scenes.

Which was more than Zach could say for Blair. He'd seen a whole side of her he'd never witnessed before, and it hadn't been pretty. The way she'd carried on at Pet Palace when Tom scratched her had made shoppers gawk and had set a three-alarm fire racing across Zach's cheeks.

Worst of all, though, had been the disgusted expression he'd seen on Merilee's face. He couldn't blame her. He'd been pretty disgusted, too, not just with the way Blair had treated Merilee but also with himself. He'd known the poor cat was scared the second he looked in the carrier. He should have left the store right then.

He sniffed the candle Blair held under his nose. "Yeah, that's nice."

She smiled. "Good. I'm getting it for you."

A candle, just what he'd always wanted. "I can get it myself," he said, reaching for it.

"Huh-uh. I want to." She danced out of range. "Think of it as a peace offering," she added, looking penitent.

She wanted to make up for the scene in Pet Palace. Now, that was sweet. It was times like this, when Blair was being cute and fun that he liked hanging out with her. Okay, so she'd been a bit of a drama queen back at the store, but maybe she had a right to be a little dramatic. After all, the cat did scratch her.

The candle purchased and bagged, she propelled him toward the door. Outside, though, she stopped to put her change in the Salvation Army bell-ringer's bucket.

"Thank you," said the man. "Merry Christmas."

"Merry Christmas to you, too," she said. "I never pass one of those buckets without putting in something," she informed Zach.

How could a guy stay mad at a woman when she did things like that?

"Now," she said briskly, "let's go get some dinner. And when we get back to the house I've got a surprise for you."

New lingerie? He grinned. "Okay."

But the surprise was nothing pleasant.

"A tree?" he said, staring at the gigantic cardboard box in the back of her SUV.

She nodded eagerly. "I found it on sale, fifty percent off. Merry Christmas early!"

"A tree," he repeated. And a fake one at that.

"And I've got the most gorgeous ornaments for it," she continued, grabbing a smaller box. "We can put it up tonight." She smiled at him. "Are you surprised?"

"Speechless." She was looking so pleased with herself, so ready to please him. How to tell her he didn't want the thing?

There was no way, of course, not without hurting her feelings. *A tree in the bay window, and a wife and kids.* He suddenly felt like all the air had been sucked from his lungs. In a desperate search for oxygen, he took a deep breath.

"You don't like it?"

He knew that expression. She was staring at him in disbelief, like he'd somehow betrayed her.

"No, no. It's just, well, I hadn't planned on a tree. I mean, what does a single guy need with a tree?"

"It'll give you Christmas spirit," said Blair.

"I don't know." Zach had pretty much lost his Christmas spirit. Watching your dad move out over Christmas break, getting dumped by your fiancée on Christmas Eve—little things like that tended to make a man lose his zest for the holidays.

"Trust me," Blair said. "It'll be gorgeous, and we'll have fun putting it up together, just you and me."

He swallowed his reluctance and nodded.

"Anyway, this is our first Christmas together and I wanted to give you something special, something significant."

Something significant? What was she expecting to get from him? He forced a smile and tried to breathe.

"Come on," she said eagerly. "Let's get it in the house and get started."

More like get it over with. Tom sat watching from a far corner, tail flicking back and forth, as they set up the lighted tree. Zach was feeling a little twitchy himself. "Now, before we start, let's set the mood," said Blair. Next thing he knew she'd set up his iPod to give them some background Christmas music, the scented candle she'd bought was burning, and they were trimming the tree with silver garlands. Okay, this wasn't bad, kind of nice, actually.

"Our first Christmas together," Blair observed as she pulled out a box of blue ornaments. "I wonder what my sweetie got for me." She gave him a playful look. "Something from Tiffany's maybe? I love Tiffany's. Or maybe a vacation? It's been forever since I've been to Cabo."

Zach turned to hang an ornament and hide his dismay. He thought of the chocolates he'd ordered on line. He'd been pretty pleased with himself at the time. Now the words "not going to cut it" echoed through his mind.

It was no secret that Blair had never lacked for the finer things in life. Her parents and her ex-husband had made sure she was well provided for—and then some. The last time he'd gone shopping with her she'd dropped more money on a single handbag than he'd spent on his entire wardrobe . . . for the past three years.

Still, she knew he was a firefighter so she couldn't really be expecting anything that lavish. Could she? She'd been teasing. Hadn't she?

Ho, boy.

They finished with the tree and she slipped her arms around his waist and leaned her head on his shoulder. Had she put on more perfume? Maybe that scented candle was getting to him. Maybe he was allergic to cinnamon. His throat started to close and he coughed.

She looked up at him in concern. "Are you getting sick?"

"No, just a tickle in the throat. I must be allergic to decorating," he cracked. "Or cinnamon." Or . . . something.

"It's probably cat dander. Good thing he'll be relocated by Christmas," said Blair. She blew out the candle, then caught Zach by the hand and led him to the couch. "There. Now let's take a break."

And what a break it was. Blair decided to spend the night.

So, once more, all was calm, all was bright . . . until he drifted off to sleep and found himself in bed, tied down with more chains than Marley's ghost. A figure stood at his bedside: Merilee from Pet Palace, and she was holding Tom and looking at Zach with disappointment. "That woman . . . I thought you had better taste."

"She's not so bad," Zach protested.

"You can say that, after the way she acted today? She showed her true colors and there you are, pretending to be colorblind. Shame on you," Dream Merilee scolded. "Choosing that woman over this poor helpless kitty. I thought you were more noble."

"I am noble," he protested. "I took the little guy in."

"And then threw him away just so you could get laid."

"I haven't thrown him away," Zach protested. "He's still here somewhere. Anyway, I never said I'd keep the cat."

"You don't keep anything or anyone, do you?" taunted this new and unimproved Merilee.

"Hey, I wasn't the one who gave back the ring on Christmas Eve," he protested. "And she dumped me for my best friend!"

"Nice try," sneered Merilee. "Blame your problems on your ex-girlfriend. But it won't work. She knew you were getting cold feet. Cold feet to match that cold heart."

Zach was about to protest that he didn't have a cold heart when, out of nowhere, a dump truck backed up to his bed and started unloading a ton of iron chains on top of him. The weight was crushing him, suffocating him. "Help! Somebody help me!"

He woke up with a strangled cry to find the room awash in predawn shadows. Blair had thrown an arm across his chest. He gently removed it and she gave a snort and rolled over onto her side. He stayed on his back, staring at the cciling and willing his heartbeat to settle.

It was just a dumb dream, he said to himself and forced his eyes shut.

He never got back to sleep though. Instead, he lay there and dredged up memories of the good times he'd had with Blair over the last few months. She'd been the perfect woman, a few ycars older than him, happily single, and just out to enjoy life. They'd had some fun times: played a lot of tennis before the weather turned, spent some rainy autumn afternoons enjoying matinees at the Falls Cinema. But right along with those pleasant memories came less pleasant ones: her temper tantrum in Pet Palace, how she'd pouted when he took her to Angelina's on her birthday and then later admitted that she'd been hoping he'd surprise her with a weekend jaunt to San Diego instead. When she'd told him she was craving Mexican from her favorite restaurant in San Diego she'd been giving him a hint—which he hadn't quite gotten.

Now he thought of her hints while they had been putting up the tree. What, exactly, did she want from Tiffany's? He started to sweat. While he'd spent the last three months thinking they were inner tubing down the river of life, having a good old time, she'd had them in a speedboat headed for the falls. Did he want to go over the falls with a woman he couldn't afford? Did he want to go over the falls at all? Nooooo.

He squeezed his eyes shut tighter but it didn't help. Next to him, Blair murmured something in her sleep and gave a little giggle. What was so funny?

Ambrose knew he had to do something to redeem himself for his behavior when Zach and the cat-killer took him to see the Santa monster. But how?

Of course! He'd bring Zach a present. The early morning was frigid and there was frost on the ground, but Ambrose was a hunter. He could endure cold if it meant finding some juicy prey. And he had to find something this morning. It would be a bad idea to delay offering a sacrifice to Zach to prove his penitence.

He spent a good, long time huddled beneath a bush by the back door before his patience was finally rewarded. A fat robin landed on a bush and began foraging for berries. Ambrose crept forward inch by careful inch, his eyes never leaving the bird. *Get the prey, get the prey. You must succeed.*

Succeed he did. He took down the bird with a giant leap and in no time the thing was dead and mostly gone. After all, Ambrose had worked up an appetite with all that hunting. But he saved the very best delicacy for Zach, his family: the feet.

He picked them up and carried them in his mouth as carefully as if he were a mother with her kitten, forcing himself back through the dreaded cat door—using that thing still made his fur crawl—and into the eating room. He padded through the room and then trotted down the hall and up the stairs to the sleeping room where Zach and the cougar had disappeared the night before.

The door was slightly ajar and Ambrose slipped through, quiet as a shadow. Ah, he was in luck. Zach was in the room with the big drinking bowl, cleaning himself with water. (*Ugh.*) Ambrose could leave his present as a surprise on Zach's pillow. He only hoped Zach wouldn't share it with the undeserving cougar.

He jumped onto the bed and carefully deposited his gift. Then he hopped off and positioned himself by the door where he could see Zach's delighted reaction to his big surprise. This would be great.

A moment later the cougar rolled over, stretched, and then looked for Zach. Then she looked at his pillow. Puzzled, she picked up one of the bird feet Ambrose had laid out so carefully.

No, that is not for you!

Suddenly the cougar let out a shriek and dropped the foot like it was dog feces. She dove from the bed, tangling herself in the blankets in the process and losing her balance. That sent her flying like a giant plucked bird into the nearby dresser. She bounced off of it and stumbled toward the middle of the room, stubbing a foot in the process and howling in pain.

Now Zach was in the room, staring at her in confusion. "What's wrong?"

"Bird feet!" she wailed, pointing at the bed.

Zach looked confused. "What?"

"Bird feet, bird feet, BIRD FEET!" She started running toward the door, probably with murder in her heart.

Ambrose didn't wait to see what happened next. He dashed out of the room and down the stairs.

And, oh no! Here came the cougar thumping along right behind him, still howling, feathers flying from the scanty bit of black cloth she was wearing. It was like being chased by that huge black dog all over again. Driven by terror, Ambrose did what any good cat in need of safety would do. He scaled the nearest tree.

What had he been thinking, climbing a Christmas tree! Did he have a death wish? Christmas trees were death traps. It had been a sizzling jolt from something on a Christmas tree that cost him his first life. Oh, not good. Not good at all. The thing tottered and swayed, its decorations jingling. He couldn't stay here.

He took what humans called a leap of faith, launching himself from the dangerous tree before it could fall. The tree went one way and Ambrose sailed another. He landed right on the cougar, who let out a screech and sent him flying again even as the tree toppled with a crunch of ornaments.

Ambrose managed to land on his feet and bolted for the safety of the couch. Even as he squeezed under it the cougar was screaming all kinds of words he knew weren't nice. And Zach was next to her now, trying to make himself heard over the racket she was making.

"Either that cat goes or I go," she roared, pointing to where Ambrose cowered under the couch.

"Babe, just calm down, okay? Did he get you with his claws?"

She put her hands on her hips and glared at him. "What do you mean calm down! Your stupid cat just tried to attack me. If I hadn't reacted so fast I'd be covered in scratches!"

"I think you're just shaken up. Let's just calm down and—"

"Never mind calming down," she roared. "I want an answer."

Ambrose held his breath.

"Blair, I can't just turn the little guy out."

She pointed a finger at him. "You *are* choosing the cat over me! Zachary Stone, you are insane. And I must have been insane to get involved with you. You're nothing but a selfish, immature—"

"Now, wait a minute," Zach protested. "I get that you're upset but there's no need to start throwing around insults."

"I am not staying here another second with you and

that . . . beast!" She opened a door to the closet where Zach kept coats and yanked hers out. "You two deserve each other," she snarled as she wrapped it around herself.

"If that's the way you want it, fine," Zach snapped. "I'll bring your tree back this afternoon."

Ambrose blinked as she told Zach to put the tree in a part of his anatomy where Ambrose knew it surely wouldn't fit.

"Keep the tree and the damned cat. I hope you'll be very happy together," she snapped. She grabbed some keys from the hall table and then exited, slamming the door after herself.

Zach glared at the door as if Blair Baby were still standing there. Then he muttered a very bad word and marched into the living room and grabbed the tree. He hauled it to the front door, sending little blue balls bouncing every which way.

Ambrose was strongly tempted to chase one as it bobbled past, but considering Zach's mood, decided it was wiser to remain under the couch.

Zach opened the door and hurled the tree out into the cold, then slammed the door shut. "I never wanted a friggin' tree anyway," he growled.

Well, well. It looked like Ambrose had succeeded in saving Zach. This was an even better gift than the bird feet.

He watched as Zach cleaned up after the cougar. The first thing Zach did was gather the stray ornaments into a plastic bag. Then the bag followed the tree out the front door. Next he tossed Ambrose's present in the can in the eating room where humans threw food that was still perfectly good. If Ambrose had the muscles for it he would have frowned. What ingratitude! Finally, Blair Baby's clothes went into another plastic bag. Zach put them into the shiny black car along with the ruined tree and the ornaments. Then he drove off. Where he took everything

Ambrose had no idea, but the cougar didn't return and that was all Ambrose cared about.

Except Zach seemed restless. When he returned home he banged things with his hammer and growled bad words. At night he flipped from program to program on the TV, always changing channels just when Ambrose was getting interested. Did he miss the cougar?

"Nah," he said as he talked on his cell phone to his friend Ray. "It's just as well. Things were getting, I don't know, weird. It was only a matter of time before she left for good anyway. I should probably keep away from women."

His friend laughed so hard Ambrose could hear it all the way up where he sat on the back of the couch, watching Zach pace while he talked.

"No, I mean it," said Zach. "I'm fine on my own."

Fine? He wasn't acting like it. Ambrose knew what was wrong with Zach. He knew the symptoms well. He'd experienced them himself when he was an alley cat. He understood the crazy, driving itch that made a guy restless, made him want to sit on a fence and yowl, made him fight anything and anyone to get to a female cat. Zach was getting the itch. People, like cats, needed to connect with another living being. In fact, people needed that a lot more than cats. Most of them didn't seem designed to function well alone. Zach could say all he wanted to the contrary, but he was no exception. He needed a female in his life.

Not the cougar, obviously. But Merilee would be perfect, for Zach (and Ambrose). If he could bring Merilee and Zach together it would more than pay them back for their kindness to him in past lives. It would also guarantee all three of them a wonderful life now. Yes, that was the answer, which meant Ambrose needed to get Zach back to the Pet Palace.

But how? He hunkered down to think.

SIX

How to get two humans together? It wasn't as if Ambrose could sit Zach down for a talk, tell him, "Look, pal, you need this female. She'd be good to you." And he couldn't exactly hop in a car and drive over to Pet Palace, wherever that was, and fetch Merilee back home to Zach.

Ambrose spent the time Zach was away at work giving this problem some serious thought (in between naps, of course). He finally concluded some naughty kitty behavior might send Zach running to her for advice. Then it would just be a simple matter of letting nature take its course. After careful assessment of the situation he decided that clawing a piece of furniture was his best bet. Anyway, he needed to sharpen his claws and Zach hadn't provided him with any other tool. Well, other than the upstairs carpet, but it would take too long for Zach to discover that spot.

Ambrose chose an old chair Zach kept on one side of the fireplace. He knew better than to attack the leather couch.

It was morning, and Zach was on the couch, putting on what he called his running shoes when Ambrose made his move. He stood on his hind legs and went at it with both claws. Aaah, that felt good.

"Hey!"

The sharpness in Zach's voice about startled the fur off Ambrose and he sprang away from the chair and ran to the far end of the room.

"Yeah, you'd better cut it out," growled Zach. "That was Gram's and it's lucky for you I hadn't gotten around to getting it re-covered." He bent over to assess the damage and frowned.

Oh, come on. It's not that bad. I barely got started.

He straightened and pointed a finger to where Ambrose crouched, peeking around the corner of the couch. "Touch my leather couch and you're dead."

Well, duh.

Zach had many things to consider as he did his morning run, like what to work on next now that the kitchen was done, when would be the right time to put the house on the market, and . . . what he'd been smoking when he decided to exchange a hot woman for a mangy orange cat.

Saying good-bye to Blair had been a good thing, he reminded himself. The woman was hot, all right, but hot things burned. Anyway, he couldn't really afford her. He was better off on his own.

But the cat? Zach shook his head as he jogged across Spruce on his way back to Lavender Lane where his Victorian sat, a plain cousin in the midst of houses dressed to the nines for the holidays. Why *had* he taken in the cat? More to the point, why was he keeping him? He hadn't intended to, that was for sure. But somehow, in spite of this morning's assault on his grandmother's chair, Zach liked having the little guy around. He was good company.

Good company. There was the bottom line. Zach liked

the company. Something about living in that Victorian made him aware of the downside of his choice to live alone. Oh, he had people in his life: his fellow firefighters, his pals, the Steps. But they swirled around him, much like twigs and leaves moving down a river past a stone stuck deep in the riverbed. Old Tom was different. He had settled in and exercised squatter's rights, and that was okay by Zach. Blair had known instinctively what he was just realizing. He had no intention of getting rid of the cat.

Which meant they had to find some way for Tom to get his kicks other than by scratching the furniture. It looked as though Zach was going to have to make another trip to Pet Palace. He smiled and picked up his pace.

Later that morning he drove through downtown Angel Falls to the strip mall at the edge of town that housed Pet Palace. Downtown was already buzzing with residents ducking into the Bon Croissant for their morning latte and a slice of eggnog cake or stopping by the bank to make a deposit. Lampposts were adorned with fat red ribbons and cedar swags, proof that Christmas was right around the corner. A Mini Cooper buried under a giant fir tree drove past him. Funny. No matter how dysfunctional their families, people always marched into this time of year determined to enjoy the holidays.

Compared to the downtown area the strip mall looked like a dinner guest who never got the message that everyone was dressing up. The warehouse stores sat side by side, big plain boxes, adorned only by their big name signs. No need for fancy dress out here. People came for the low prices.

Zach parked in the gigantic parking lot and wandered into the store. He was greeted by Christmas music: dogs barking to "Rudolph, the Red-Nosed Reindeer." He looked over toward the checkout stands. No sign of Merilee there. Maybe she wasn't at work today.

Not that he'd come to see Merilee, he told himself. He'd come looking for a scratching post. But she'd be able to help him. Where was she? He wandered around the store, all the while convincing himself he couldn't possibly get a scratching post without her expert advice.

He finally found her in the pet food aisle, setting out cans of cat food. He offered a friendly hello and startled her, making her drop a can. It rolled his direction and he snagged it and handed it back.

"How's your cat doing?" she asked as she put the can on the shelf.

She was concentrating on that can like it would jump off the minute she turned her back and Zach suddenly realized he was standing smack-dab in the middle of an awkward situation. Last time he'd seen Merilee he'd been with Blair.

How to proceed? He cleared his throat. "Well, I think he's upset."

That got her attention. "Oh, no. Why?"

He shrugged. "We've had a lot of changes lately. My girlfriend and I broke up."

Merilee became suddenly busy pulling cans out of the cardboard carton at her feet. "Oh?"

"I think Tom's acting out." Did cats act out? Who knew? It sounded good, anyway.

She set a couple more cans carefully on the shelf and then turned to look at Zach. "What's he doing?"

"Scratching the furniture."

"Hmmm. Does he have a scratching post?"

"No. I thought maybe you could help me pick one out."

"I know the perfect one," she said with a decisive nod, and started down the aisle, leaving Zach to fall in step beside her. "I'm sorry about your girlfriend."

"Well, I don't think we were much of a match. She didn't like my cat."

"A person's attitude toward animals says a lot about them," Merilee commented and left it at that.

"I guess you've got a ton of pets," said Zach. She seemed like someone who would be good with animals. And kids. Not that Zach needed to know.

Her mouth turned down at the corners and she shook her head. "No pets allowed where I live."

She had a great mouth. *Never mind her mouth!* "Where do you live?" he asked. It would have been rude not to.

"The Angel Arms Apartments. I'm afraid I'm breaking the rules, though."

Funny. Merilee didn't look like a rule breaker. But then Blair hadn't looked like a cat hater. Sometimes people weren't what they seemed.

"I rescued a kitty and I haven't been able to find a home for her. I just couldn't take her to the shelter," Merliee added with a little shrug.

"I know the feeling," said Zach. Speaking of feelings, one was stealing over him that wasn't safe, so he shoved it away. They were in front of a vast array of scratching posts now. "Which one of these do I want?"

She surprised him by reaching for a long, thin, cardboard box. "This is the best. Just flip the lid and you're good to go."

She handed it to him and he stared at it. "It's cardboard."

She nodded. "Embedded with catnip. You'll have to replace it every so often, but believe me it's well worth the price. Your cat will never scratch the furniture again."

"Sold," Zach decided. And then there didn't seem to be anything left to say, at least about cats. So he thanked her and left. But as he walked out the door he was accompanied by the nagging thought that he hadn't come away with everything he needed.

He was halfway to his car when he saw Blair approaching from the other direction. She was wearing her favorite long, fur-trimmed coat and black boots with heels that made her legs look a million miles long. There was a time when he would have looked at her and thought, *sexy*. Now he just thought, *scary*.

She'd seen him, too. He could tell from the way she was bristling, with every step an angry fashion model stomp that sent the slush underfoot spraying in all directions.

Shit.

Well, they were bound to run into each other sooner or later. He'd been hoping for later, though. It was easier to face a three-alarm fire than a pissed ex-girlfriend any day. He stopped and mentally braced himself. When she got closer he said a civilized, "Hello, Blair."

She returned his greeting with a scowl. "Still have the cat?"

"Uh, yeah." That was his excuse for being here. What was hers? He nodded toward the store. "Did you decide to get a pet?" he joked in an attempt to lighten an awkward moment as heavy as a fire hose.

"Actually, I'm meeting with my father. Business," she added, her voice snippy.

Zach couldn't think of anything to say to that. He couldn't think of anything to say, period. He was too busy thanking his lucky stars they were no longer together.

Blair obviously couldn't think of anything more to say, either, so she simply marched on into the store like a general riding into battle.

Zach got in his Land Rover and got out of Dodge.

Sometimes getting called to the boss's office means something good, like a raise, but when Merilee got her summons she knew there was no raise waiting in her future.

She'd been manning the checkout stand when the reincarnation of Cruella De Vil whom she'd done battle with on Saturday entered Pet Palace. The woman had shot her a vengeful glare right before flying up the stairs to the second level where Mr. Carlyle's office was located.

Kate Hendrix, who was at the stand next to Merilee's, said, "Uh-oh. The boss's daughter looks mad. Somebody's head's gonna roll."

It wasn't hard to figure out whose. Merilee swallowed hard but it didn't help push down the panic rising up her throat.

If there had been any doubt her head was about to roll, walking into the inner sanctum—a huge room that was quickly closing in on her—she could have no doubt now. Mr. Carlyle, a normally pleasant little man was sitting at his desk, frowning. Merilee had always thought he looked a little like Santa with his round belly and his equally round face, his nose like a berry or cherry or whatever it was, and his snowy white hair. Today his stern expression made her think of Scrooge.

Next to him stood Daughter of Scrooge, wearing a fur-trimmed coat, unbuttoned to reveal a black knit dress that clung to a perfect body. Her hair was perfect, too—perfectly highlighted, perfectly blond. And her makeup, perfect, of course. And underneath all that perfection was a heart rotten to the core.

It wasn't nice to hate people. Merilee hated her anyway.

"It's come to my attention," said Mr. Carlyle, "that you have not been putting the customer first, Merilee."

Not hard to figure out who told him. "I value all our customers who love their animals," she said. Could she help it if this creature was an animal hater? How could Mr. Carlyle have such an awful daughter?

"Well, you didn't value me," snapped the woman. "She

was simply awful, Father. A woman like that makes a poor ambassador for the store."

And a woman like you makes a poor ambassador for women. Merilee kept her lips pressed tightly together.

"Is what I'm hearing true?" asked Mr. Carlyle.

There was no point pretending she didn't know what he was talking about. She knew. They all knew.

"I'm afraid we had a misunderstanding," said Merilee, opting for diplomacy even though she was wishing she had claws and could give the woman another scratch to match the one she'd gotten from the poor, scared cat.

"Is that what you call it?" sniped the woman.

Mr. Carlyle's frown dipped further south. "Merilee, you know the customer is always right. Sometimes we encounter people when they're not having the best of days, but it's not our job to judge them."

Merilee could feel her cheeks sizzling. "Yes, Mr. Carlyle," she murmured.

"I'm afraid you should have been more understanding," he chided.

"It won't happen again," she said, almost choking on the words.

"No, it won't because I'm afraid we're going to have to let you go. We simply can't have our employees insulting our customers."

Or our daughter. This was wrong and unfair. "Mr. Carlyle," Merilee began.

"We will give you two weeks' severance," Mr. Carlyle said, his voice hard. "I'll have Mrs. Olsen send you a check. Please clean out your locker."

Next to him, Daughter of Scrooge looked on, her self-righteous expression adding, "That'll teach you."

"Yes sir," said Merilee. Face flaming she turned and managed, somehow, to find her way to the door—not an easy task considering the grim image she was envisioning:

herself standing on a snowy corner, begging for money.
What oh what was she going to do?

"What will you do?" asked Kate, who was now taking
her break in the employees' lunchroom where the lockers
were located.

Merilee swiped a tear from the corner of her eye. "I
don't know. I'll think of something."

"Gosh, right before Christmas. What a rotten thing to
do!"

Yes, it was rotten. But when a girl decided on a ver-
bal smackdown with the boss's daughter, rotten was all
she could expect to get for Christmas. *You brought it on
yourself.*

Still, it had been so wrong to blame that poor cat for
simply acting like a cat. Of all the nerve!

What business had it been of hers? Really?

Anytime an animal suffered it was somebody's business, and the way that woman had been carrying on the
poor animal's future hadn't looked good.

Sigh. She was the Superwoman of cats. It would be
nice if she could develop some super powers on her own
behalf.

"I wish I knew of something," said Kate.

"I'll be okay," Merilee said. "I've been volunteering at
the shelter and I know they've got a part-time opening. I'm
sure they'll hire me."

"Part-time anywhere probably pays as good as full-
time here."

It beat starving anyway, and since there was no Prince
Charming rushing to the rescue it would have to do until
the new year.

Kate came over and laid a hand on her arm. "When
I said what I said down there, about somebody's head rolling, I never thought it would be yours. It's because of
what happened Saturday, isn't it?"

Too miserable to speak, Merilee nodded.

Kate frowned. "She'll get hers someday. Meanwhile, if you need anything, call me. Okay?"

What she needed was a job and Kate couldn't help her there. She murmured her thanks, then topped her small pile of belongings with her lunch sack, said her good-byes, and left Pet Palace.

A leaden sky pelted her with sleeting rain as she crossed the parking lot, a final cosmic "Neener, neener" sending her on her way.

She got into her car and cranked up the music as high as possible, determined to stave off self-pity and tears. An unknown choir was singing "God rest ye merry gentlemen, let nothing you dismay."

No dismay, she vowed. This wasn't the end of the world. It was the beginning of a new chapter. *Life has more in store for you than working at Pet Palace.*

Somehow, somewhere, she would find it.

Tom was obviously happy with his magic scratching box. It seemed as though every time Zach turned around the cat was at the thing, clawing up a storm. Better that than the couch.

"Looks like our problems are solved, dude," he said, scratching Tom behind his ears. "Now maybe I can stay out of Pet Palace for a while."

And that was a good thing. Really. He had other stuff to spend his money on, like new flooring and a shower unit for the downstairs bathroom. He didn't need to be always running into Merilee.

Or any other woman. Women complicated things and Zach didn't need complications.

Speaking of complications. "Have you talked to your

chief yet about getting Christmas Eve off?" asked his mother.

He knew he shouldn't have answered his cell. "Mom, I really don't think that's going to happen."

Mom had cancelled the family togetherness card when she and Al, husband number two, had taken the Steps and moved to the East Coast to start a new life that hadn't included Zach and David. That had been fine with Zach. He'd been thirteen at the time and what Al so lovingly termed a pain in the butt, so he'd been shunted off to live with Dad, who was slowly sliding into the bottle, while Mom and Al had skipped off to live the good life.

At first she'd made the right sounds about missing Zach and wanting him to come out for the summer. (Like Al was anxious for that!) But their conversations were never good and soon the phone calls dried up, maybe scorched by the heat of teen boy anger. Or maybe because she just hadn't given a damn. Either way, what did it matter? By the time Zach was sixteen they were down to a yearly check enclosed in a birthday card. He never cashed the checks. They always felt like bribes. She finally gave up on checks and switched to gift cards like that was, somehow, more personal. He'd tossed those, too.

Mom and the gang had moved back to town in June and she was ready to be one big happy family again. Zach had no problem being a family with the Steps. Both girls had friended him on Facebook a couple of years back and now they were constantly messaging him, stopping by the station, or calling him on the phone . . . or siccing producers from *The Bachelor* on him. But Mom, he wasn't ready for her or her plans for a cozy family Christmas.

He could already see how that would play out. David would conveniently forget to call from Australia, and that would leave Mom all teary. Al would feel honor bound to comfort her and mutter that the kid was just like his dad. Not a compliment. When Mom was finished mourning the fact that her baby was so far away she would tell Zach how happy she was that they all were able to be together again. Of course, one of the Steps would be sure to have her laptop handy, primed to sign him up for eHarmony. He'd balk. Then his stepdad, the PC king, would teasingly suggest he was gay. Otherwise, why wouldn't a man want to settle down with a wonderful woman like Zach's mother? Aw, sweet. And a good way to assure Al got his for Christmas. Later, to top off the evening, Dad would call Zach on his cell, drunk and maudlin—his favorite way to celebrate the holidays.

Yeah, Mom's party would be as fun as a toothache, not to mention hypocritical since he and Al had never gotten along. It would also feel wrong to be with a family that shouldn't have been his family. And they wouldn't have been if Mom hadn't dumped Dad.

When he was little he didn't get it, but as he grew older he had pieced things together pretty easily. Somehow, Dad hadn't been enough so Mom had dumped him and splintered their family unit. Then she upgraded to Al and got a bigger house and the daughters she'd probably always wanted.

The fallout had been major. Now brother David was living Down Under and poor Dad was trying to make a life in another state with his third wife. The last time Zach had talked to Dad, that relationship was looking shaky. No surprise. Getting too close was a recipe for disaster. At least it was for the Stone men.

"I was so hoping we could have Christmas dinner together and then go to the Christmas Eve service," Mom said wistfully.

Thank God he'd be working.

"You could bring someone," she added to sweeten the pot. "Didn't you tell Natalie you were seeing someone?"

Probably he had, at some point, in an effort to keep Nat from suggesting friends for him on Facebook (all female, single, and too young). "Uh."

"She'd be more than welcome."

"I'm not with anyone right now."

A long-suffering sigh drifted over the phone. "It seems a shame you can't find a nice girl to commit to."

Was she joking? "Yeah? How'd that work for Dad?" he retorted.

The huge silence on the other end of the line made him wish the words back. If anyone deserved such a slam it was her. Still, he felt like a Scrooge for saying it. "Sorry," he muttered.

"No, I'm sorry," she said softly. "I have a lot to make up for."

That was the understatement of the century.

"The girls adore you," she said, moving to more comfortable conversational territory. "They'll be so disappointed if you don't show."

"I can't help it," he said. He was no dummy. He'd traded days with Julio, effectively making himself unavailable on both big family disaster days. "Lots of fires over the holidays. People burning candles where they shouldn't, starting grease fires in the kitchen. You wouldn't want all of Angel Falls to go up in smoke because your son wasn't doing his duty."

"I'm just thinking someone else's son could do his duty this year so I can spend Christmas with mine."

"Sorry," was all he could think to say. At least all he could think to say that was civilized.

"Could you at least stop by the day before you start your shift? I have something for you."

Probably a gift card. "I'll try."

"Great," she said, as if he'd just given her a firm confirmation.

Zach ended the call with a sigh and tossed his cell phone on the couch. "Be glad you're a cat," he told Tom, who was perched on the back of the couch. "You've got it good."

The cat blinked and flicked his tail.

Zach decided to make dinner easy: Chinese takeout. "Food of the gods," he told Tom as he dished up some canned cat food. "And I've got your fav, here, too, dude."

But Tom didn't trot up to his food bowl and start chowing down. Instead, he turned and walked away.

"Hey, since when aren't you hungry?" Zach called after him.

Tom kept walking.

"Fine. Suit yourself," Zach muttered, and grabbed his carton of General Tso's chicken.

He didn't give another thought to Tom's lack of appetite until the next morning when he went to set out some more food for the little guy before heading out the door to the station and found the bowl still full. The canned cat food had dried out to a smelly, crusty, unappetizing lump. What was wrong with Tom? He always snarfed down his meals the minute Zach put them in the bowl. Zach dumped out the food and dished up a fresh helping. He also put out some dried food. Something there should tempt Tom while he was gone.

He had just finished when, Tom wandered out into the kitchen. "Breakfast, bud," said Zach.

Tom walked over to the dish, sniffed at it, and then walked away again.

"This isn't a freakin' restaurant," Zach called after him. "You eat this or you starve."

Of course Tom didn't pay any attention to Zach's

threat. Zach watched him go and frowned. How many days could a cat go without food? Would old Tom be okay while he was gone?

Ambrose sat in the window and watched Zach drive away. He hoped Zach was going to Pet Palace to get advice from Merilee. Maybe he'd even bring her home. Then Tom could end this hunger strike.

But what if Zach was going to work? Ambrose would be on his own for a long time. This place didn't have a problem with rats or mice like some houses he had lived in, which meant he'd be reduced to living off the occasional bird landing in the yard to forage for berries. And he'd have to use that horrible cat door even more. Ugh. The mere thought made his tail twitch.

Hunger. Ambrose still remembered the miserable gnawing he felt in his gut on a regular basis when he lived his third life as an alley cat. He didn't relish the prospect of experiencing it again. But feigning disinterest in his food was the only thing he could think to do to drive Zach back to Merilee.

He jumped down and trotted to the kitchen, the aroma of Tuna Surprise beckoning him. He crouched in front of the bowl and sniffed. *Ah, just one lick. What would it hurt?*

No, no. If he so much as took a lick he'd devour the entire bowl. *Willpower, Ambrose. You have survived on little before. You can do it again.*

At least he hoped he could. He'd grown accustomed to eating on a regular basis.

He eyed the cat door with reluctance. Oh, the things a guy had to do to help his human.

SEVEN

Zach returned home from the station to find Tom's food bowl untouched. Okay, what was that about? He dumped the untouched food and tried again but Tom just sniffed at the fresh serving and then opted for winding around Zach's legs instead.

"What's wrong, guy?" he asked, picking up the cat. Had he lost weight since Zach was gone or was Zach imagining it? "You know, tuna's your favorite." The little guy just sat docilely in his arms. This wasn't good. "Okay, bud, something's not right. We'd better go see the vet."

At the word *vet*, Tom leaped out of his arms and left the kitchen at a fast trot. Okay, that was obviously not the magic word.

"I don't care," Zach called after him. "You're going. You should probably have a checkup anyway."

Informing a cat he's going to the vet and getting him to the vet are two different things, as Zach discovered once he'd made an appointment. First he had to find the cat. Tom wasn't under the couch or the bed, or any other chair. He was getting sneaky.

And Zach was getting irritated. "I know you're in here somewhere." Unless he'd run outside.

Except he still hated his cat door and used it as little as possible. Besides, there was a light snowfall on the ground and Tom was not fond of snow. Zach kept searching.

He finally found his quarry crouched in the far corner of the bedroom closet, his head barely visible behind Zach's bowling ball.

Zach shoved aside his shoes and a pile of dirty underwear and crawled in. "Okay, now you're just being a wuss. We have to find out what's wrong with you."

Tom backed up and growled. Who knew cats could growl?

"I'm bigger than you," Zach informed him. "That means I will win this fight, so you might as well surrender now." He leaned in and reached out and Tom hissed and took a swipe at him, scratching the side of his hand. Zach pulled it back in shock and Tom bolted. "Oh, not cool."

He wiped off the blood with the closest T-shirt and ran down the stairs after the cat. This time old Tom wasn't so smart and Zach found him under the couch and hauled him out, getting another scratch in the process.

"You really are pissing me off," he snapped, stuffing Tom in his cat carrier. "You'd better have something wrong with you."

However, after listening to the animal's pitiful yowls all the way to Dr. Burnside, Zach's anger dissipated, and by the time he took the cat carrier out of the back of his Land Rover he was feeling sorry for Tom. "The doc will make you all better," he promised.

But then they entered the clinic and Zach saw the Great Dane. *Oh, boy.*

Tom hissed.

"He can't get you, I promise," said Zach.

The Great Dane barked and Tom pressed himself into the far corner of the cat carrier, arching his back and puffing out his fur. Zach kept himself between the two animals as he made his way to the reception desk, which lay across the vinyl floor and past the row of chairs where the dog sat at the feet of his owner (a senior woman half the animal's size).

"Hi," he said to the receptionist. "We've got an appointment with Dr. Burnside."

The doc was obviously a popular guy, judging from the long row of Christmas cards strung across the front of the reception desk. If people liked him this much he had to be good with animals.

The receptionist was a hot blonde with a nice rack. Normally she would have gotten Zach's attention, but he was too worried about Tom to care. "Name?" she asked.

"Zach Stone."

"No, I mean your pet."

"Oh, yeah. Uh, Tom."

The receptionist smiled at Tom and cooed a hello. "The doctor will have you feeling better in no time," she promised Tom, and Zach almost added, "See? I told you."

With Tom checked in there was nothing to do but sit and wait, and try to ignore the animal smells floating around the room. They took a seat as far as possible from the dog, which was straining at his leash to come over for a visit. The walls were painted hospital green, supposedly a calming color. Maybe that only worked for humans. The dog barked again and pawed at the vinyl, making Tom hiss.

"No, Tiny," said his owner firmly, and the dog sat back on its haunches, tongue lolling.

The nurse came out and called Tiny in. "There. He's gone now," Zach said to Tom.

Tom just growled.

Yeah, we're both having fun now.

Another ten minutes and Tiny and his owner trotted out the door and it was Tom's turn. He yowled as they went into the exam room.

"I know," said Zach, "I don't like going to the doctor either." In some ways it didn't look all that different from a regular doctor's exam room. Well, except for the fact that there were animal charts on the walls and the exam table was stainless steel.

Dr. Burnside entered shortly after them. He was about the age of Zach's father, with salt-and-pepper hair and a short muscular body, but with soft hands, an odd contradiction that made Zach vaguely uncomfortable. "So, what seems to be the problem with our boy," he asked, removing a now limp Tom from his cat carrier and setting him on the table.

"He's not eating," said Zach.

"Well, that's not good, is it?" the vet said to Tom, and petted him. "My, my. You're a dead ringer for another cat I've seen." The doctor opened Tom's mouth and checked his teeth. "And how long has this been going on?"

"A couple of days," said Zach, watching nervously.

"Has he been lethargic?"

Zach thought of their chase around the house and the fresh scratches on his hand. "No."

The doctor grabbed a rectal thermometer and lifted Tom's tail.

"Whoa, he's not going to like that," Zach predicted.

Sure enough. Tom let out the cat equivalent of a yelp and looked over his shoulder at Zach. Accusingly.

"Sorry, dude," Zach said. "It's for your own good." Geez. Now he sounded like his mom. How many times had she said that to him when he was a kid?

"Is our boy on any medication?" asked the vet.

"None that I know of."

One of the doctor's graying eyebrows rose. "You would know, wouldn't you? You are his owner?"

"Yeah, but only recently. I took him in. His owner died."

Out came the thermometer for inspection. "No fever. The owner died, you say?" Now the doctor was poking and prodding. Amazingly, Tom was tolerating the abuse quite well. "What was the owner's name?"

"I'm not sure," said Zach. "I talked to her daughter."

The doctor checked the tag. "Ambrose. Well, well. I saw that torn ear and wondered. So Adelaide is gone. She was a nice old lady. Good for you for taking in her cat."

Like he'd had a choice?

Dr. Burnside kept on with his examination. At last he said, "I see no broken bones, no evidence of injury. His heart is fine."

"Then what's wrong with him?"

"We'll do some blood work," said the vet, "but I suspect he's just anxious. Changes in environment can upset cats. He lost his owner recently, he's in a new home. It's understandable."

"Except he'd settled in okay and there was nothing wrong with his appetite until a couple of days ago," Zach protested.

"Have you had any changes in your home?"

Breaking up with Blair probably didn't count since she and Tom hadn't exactly bonded. Other than that, Zach couldn't think of anything. He shook his head.

"Change in routine? Travel?"

Zach thought of their failed excursion to see Santa. "We went to Pet Palace. He didn't like it." Neither had Zach. "But that was Saturday."

"Well," said Dr. Burnside. "I suspect he's simply upset. We don't want to let this go on too long but I'd like to wait another day before prescribing anti-anxiety medication. It's highly effective but it can have detrimental effects on your cat's personality and disposition."

After their tussle in the closet anything would be an improvement on Tom's disposition, if you asked Zach.

"You'll pull it together, old boy. Won't you?" The doctor slipped Tom in his carrier. "If he doesn't improve in the next twenty-four hours bring him back."

Yeah, that would be fun. Zach drove home wishing the vet had prescribed some anti-anxiety meds for him. "You know, you're stressing me out," he told Tom.

There was no reply from the carrier.

Zach frowned. He needed a cat whisperer.

And he knew just where to find one.

They did a detour by Pet Palace. "Don't worry, I'm not going to make you go in," Zach assured Tom.

He cracked the window for fresh air and then made his way across the slushy parking lot.

Not many people were inside shopping today. Hardly surprising, since the weatherman had predicted more snow and the sky was a sheet of bloated gray clouds, just waiting to dump. Zach looked toward the checkout stands. No sign of Merilee. He went to the cat section. No one. He walked around the whole store but saw no sign of her. It was a weekday. She should have been there somewhere.

At last he snagged a couple of cans of cat food and wandered up to a checkout where a plump girl with short black hair and a nose ring was busy gossiping with the woman at the stand behind her.

"It was so unfair to fire her for standing up to that beeatch," said Miss Nose Ring. "Just because her family owns the store. Poor Merilee. She left in tears."

So that explained why Merilee was nowhere in sight. And it sure wasn't hard to figure out who the *beeatch* was. Zach ground his teeth.

"She did get hired part-time at the animal shelter. God knows how she'll make her rent working part-time, though."

Behind her the other woman caught sight of Zach and tried to tip off her coworker, nodding his direction.

"It just goes to show, you shouldn't get involved," finished the cashier. The other woman cleared her throat and nodded again. Miss Nose Ring followed her gaze and saw Zach. Her face turned fire engine red and she cleared her throat. "Uh, hi. Welcome to Pet Palace. Can I help you?"

"You already have," he said.

He stormed out of the store and marched to his car, pulling out his cell phone as he went. He barely gave Blair time to answer before snarling, "You got that girl fired. And right before Christmas. Nice, Blair. Way to go."

"Excuse me?" Her voice was huffy.

"There is no excuse for you," he snapped, and ended the call.

Good God. He sure could pick 'em. Here he thought he'd been hanging out with a fun-loving, hot-blooded American girl and he'd really been with Scrooge in drag. That was it. He was done with women.

Except Merilee. He needed to find a way to set things right for her. How, exactly, he was going to do that he had no idea.

Tom was getting restless in the backseat so Zach took him to the house and set him free. "Try to eat something, and don't whiz in the house," he told Tom, and then drove off.

Halfway to the animal shelter the snow started falling, big fluffy flakes that looked like they meant to stick. That was sure to result in traffic accidents and trouble. It didn't snow a lot in the Northwest, but when it did people freaked out. He passed very few cars on the way to the shelter and once there he found only two in the parking lot, probably belonging to the employees. Was one of them Merilee's?

He was halfway to the door when she came out, all bundled up in that ugly coat and galoshes she'd been wearing when he first met her. She looked small and lost and he felt an overpowering urge to hug her.

"Merilee," he called.

She turned and her eyes opened wide at the sight of him. "Hi," she stammered. "I'm afraid we're just closing. Snow," she added.

Behind her a middle-aged man slipped out the door and locked it. "Better hurry, Merilee. This stuff looks like it means business."

She nodded, pulled her coat collar more tightly together, and looked up at Zach.

Suddenly he felt at a loss for words. "I was just at Pet Palace looking for you."

Her face flamed and her gaze dropped. "I'm not working there anymore."

"I know. I'm sorry. It's because of what happened Saturday, isn't it?"

She shrugged. "It's not your fault. I should have been . . . more understanding."

Her reply sounded like it that had been programmed into her. "It was an abuse of power and we both know it." She didn't have anything to say to that and they stood there for a moment, snow swirling around them. "Are they paying you enough here?" Dumb question. Of course, they weren't. Working at an animal shelter was the kind of thing people did because they wanted to try to make a difference in the world, not because they wanted to make money. Now she looked embarrassed. "Sorry," said Zach. "That's none of my business." Except it was partly his fault, so didn't that make it his business? Sort of?

"I can pay my rent. Thanks for asking."

But what about food? Utilities? "Look, could I pay you to help me with my cat?"

She shook her head. "Really, you don't need to do that. It's not your fault."

"Yes . . . I do. Anyway, the fire department pays me more than I can spend." Slight exaggeration but anything to convince her. Still she hesitated.

"This is a legit job," he insisted. "Tom won't eat. I just came from the vet's."

Her eyes filled with concern. "Oh, no."

"I think he needs a cat whisperer, and you're the closest thing I know. You'd really be helping us. So see? It would be a win-win."

She smiled. Then she looked uncertainly at the snow quickly carpeting the parking lot. "My car."

Was now the only one left in the lot and it was a beater—an ancient Chevy with tires that were going bald. "Tell you what," offered Zach. "I'll follow you home and then we can take my SUV. If you don't mind making a house call," he added. "I'll pay you whatever the vet would have charged."

"You don't have to do that, really," she repeated.

"I want to." It was the least he could do. And maybe it would help Tom.

She came to a sudden decision and nodded. "All right then. I'll just check on my cat and then we can go look in on yours."

She hurried to her car and Zach climbed in behind the wheel of his Land Rover. This was great. For Tom, he amended.

EIGHT

As usual, Queenie was waiting for Merilee by the door. Not because Queenie was dying to see her, but because Queenie was dying to see what lay beyond the door. Merilee had informed her secret houseguest on many occasions that this was exactly the kind of curiosity that killed the cat, but Queenie paid no heed.

"Oh, no, you don't," Merilee said, putting her foot between Queenie and the dangerous freedom she coveted. "We have dogs around here and last week someone saw a coyote. You'd be dinner in no time."

Queenie wheeled around and trotted toward the kitchen—always her second destination when the great escape failed.

Merilee hurried in after her and dished up some canned kitty food, all the while trying to decide if she should invite Zach in for some eggnog when he brought her back home. It was light eggnog. Hmmm. What else could she give him? She didn't have any Christmas cookies sitting around. She had cheese, though, and Rye Crisp. Cheese and Rye Crisp and light eggnog. He'd take one look at that holiday snack and ho-ho-ho. The apartment looked festive enough. She'd hung red tinsel garlands across the top of the windows and put up a tree with all the ornaments out of reach of little white paws.

Really, she didn't know why she was even entertaining the idea of entertaining. A handsome fireman like Zach wasn't going to be interested in hanging out with her. She probably couldn't even lure him into her apartment with the promise of a Christmas goose and a red velvet cake. All he wanted her for was to whisper to his cat.

Still, she wasn't about to whisper with day-old breath. She dashed to her bathroom to give her teeth a quick brushing.

The girl in the mirror had flushed cheeks and bright eyes. But they were plain, like the rest of her face. Why hadn't she bothered with mascara today? Or any day, for that matter?

She spat out toothpaste and then scrounged around in the vanity drawer for mascara. She'd had this for . . . how many months? Years? Millennia? Oh, good grief. It was all dried out. Still, she poked the wand around, mining for what she could find, and applied it. Not much, and not much of an improvement. She added pink lip gloss, which Liz had convinced her to get last time they were at the mall. Okay, better.

Who was she kidding? She was never going to look in the mirror and see a pretty girl. Old high school wounds had produced scars that had left Merilee blind to her good features. Even now, though her family assured her she was indeed pretty, she groped unsuccessfully for a positive self-image.

She shoved the makeup back in the drawer, and then grabbed cat treats from her kitchen cupboard. Then she hurried back outside to meet Zach. Okay, so she wasn't the most beautiful girl on the block, and maybe cat whispering wasn't on a par with looking like Heidi Klum, but right now it was what Zach needed. And having something he needed . . . well, it was a beginning.

"Sorry to keep you waiting," she said, as she climbed into his SUV.

Unlike hers, this vehicle was in mint condition and still had its new-car smell. She'd once bought an air freshener that produced the same fragrance, but the contrast between the smell and the appearance of her car had been enough to confirm what she already knew: new-car air freshener scent does not a new car make. Next time around she bought a vanilla air freshener.

"No problem," he said. "Thanks for dropping everything to help me."

Like she'd had anything to drop. She wisely kept this information to herself. "I'm happy to help. I love cats." Woman who lived alone and loved cats—did she sound like some sort of cliché? Well, if she did, too bad. There was nothing wrong with loving cats. And there was certainly nothing wrong with living alone. It showed independence. So there.

Zach shook his head. "I can't figure out what his problem is."

"We'll figure it out," Merilee assured him. *Together.* There was nothing wrong with togetherness, either. Just this small dose of it, sitting within reaching distance of this hunky man was sending a buzz running through her.

They turned onto Lavender Lane. Merilee took in all the cozy houses, most with their holiday lights already on, and was seized with a sudden wanting. These so reminded her of her parents' house one town over—cozy and inviting, places where people could love and laugh and grow a family. Oh, that Tudor was cute. She could easily picture herself in it. And look at the pretty blue Victorian up ahead.

She was surprised when they turned into the driveway.

"This is yours?" A gorgeous man paired with a blue Victorian? Talk about perfect.

"For a while," he said. "I'm rehabbing it. Keeps me busy when I'm not at the station. I'm going to put it up for sale come spring."

"It's lovely," she said wistfully. "I don't know how you could stand to part with it."

"Well, it's not much of a guy house. It'll be great for a family, though."

Yes, it would.

The inside was as charming as the outside. Merilee took in the staircase and its railing with the newel posts, the hardwood floors, and the etched glass window over the front door and experienced instant house lust. "This is so cool." And how lovely it would look all dressed up for the holidays!

"It's getting there. I just finished the kitchen. Come on, I'll show you. Maybe Tom's food dish will be empty," Zach added as he led the way down the hall.

The kitchen was gorgeous—buttercream wood cabinets with glass fronts, granite countertops, a hardwood floor, and an overhead light fixture made out of some sort of old-fashioned glass. "It's lovely," she said.

"Oh, man, it's still there," muttered Zach from behind her.

She turned and saw him frowning at a dish full of untouched food.

"He's going to starve to death."

A big man worried over his small cat—Merilee's heart was going to melt into a puddle right there on the kitchen floor. "We'll make sure he doesn't," she said, determined to make everything right.

He dumped the contents of the dish in the garbage. "Tom, where are you? Damn it, come on out."

He was about to stalk out of the kitchen when Merilee

caught his arm. "Let's try something else." She gave the box of cat treats she was holding a shake.

"He's probably hiding upstairs. He won't hear that," Zach predicted.

"Maybe," said Merilee, and shook the box again.

A moment later the orange cat trotted into the kitchen. Without hesitation he walked over to Merilee and rubbed against her leg.

"I guess he wasn't so far away after all," Zach said, and scratched his head, obviously puzzled.

Merilee bent and petted the cat, and in return he rubbed his head against her palm. "What do you mean by worrying poor Zach like this, you naughty boy?" She shook out a treat and offered it to him. He snapped it up and snarfed it down. Then he gave her hand a head butt. "Oh, no," she said, standing up. "No more treats until you eat your food." She turned to Zach. "Let's get a fresh bowl and try again. Only this time, just give him half the can."

"Okay," Zach said dubiously. "But I doubt he'll eat it. I've wasted two cans on him so far."

"We'll see," said Merilee. Whatever had been bothering the cat, he was fine now and purring as she petted him. She'd purr too if she lived in this lovely house with this kindhearted man.

He set a fresh bowl with half a serving of food on the floor and Tom hurried to it as if it were his last meal, then hunkered down and dug in.

Zach shook his head and let out a snort of disgust. "What is your problem, dude?"

"Cats can be sensitive to changes in their environments," Merilee said. "Have you had any changes recently?"

"Nothing other than breaking up with Blair, but since she didn't like old Tom I don't think he was too upset. And neither was I," he added.

Merilee bit back a smile. She may have lost her job but

the Pet Palace princess lost her man. Now Merilee was here with him instead. There was justice in the world. "Well, he seems to be fine now," she said, keeping her ungracious thoughts to herself.

"Thanks to you," said Zach. "You know, you've really got the touch with animals. Have you ever thought of becoming a vet?"

Only since she was ten. "I'm working in that direction. I had to stop school for a while until I could save up more money." Did that make her sound like a loser? Lots of people talked about going back to school, writing a book, becoming a doctor, whatever, and then never followed through. But surely she wouldn't become one of those people.

Zach leaned against the kitchen counter. "I bet you could get a student loan."

"I did get a small one. Then I tried to pay as I went. I guess the money went faster than I did," she added with a fatalistic shrug. Now she did sound like a loser. She could feel her cheeks heating up.

"No family to help?" he asked. Then he added, "Sorry, more stuff that's none of my business."

And yet he was asking. Men didn't want to know those kinds of things unless they were interested in a girl, did they? "I don't feel right asking my family. They're great but they all have their own bills to pay. Anyway, my parents paid for college. I figured that was enough."

He nodded slowly, taking in the information. "Pretty noble."

"Hardly. Risking your life to put out fires, that's noble."

"We don't have that many fires around here," he said, shrugging off her compliment. "Hey, I owe you some money. Let me grab my checkbook."

"You really don't need to," she said.

"I'm paying," he insisted, "and that's that. And then

we're celebrating Tom's recovery. I'll send out for pizza before Little Lola's wimps out and closes," he added, and strode out of the room before she could protest. As if she would object to spending more time with him.

The cat was finished eating now and sat licking a paw. "I don't know what your problem was," she whispered to him, "but thanks."

He stopped his grooming and regarded her for a moment, almost as if he understood. Then he trotted over to her.

She got the message and picked him up. "Funny, isn't it, how we always think you know what we're saying?"

Zach returned a moment later with his checkbook. He wrote her a check, then ignored her protests that he'd paid her way too much and got busy calling Little Lola's. It was a short-lived call. "They're closed due to the snow," he announced with a frown. "People around here are such wusses."

"That's okay," Merilee said, hiding her disappointment behind her perkiest voice. "You can just take me home."

"Oh, no. Not until I've fed you." He opened the fridge and leaned in to investigate.

She peeked over his shoulder and saw a couple of bottles of beer, eggs, a carton of Chinese takeout, several jars of condiments in the door, and cheese and some bologna in a drawer—not much.

"Hmmmm," he said.

"Well, I do see eggs and cheese," said Merilee. "I can make omelets."

"So can I," he said, and pulled out the carton of eggs. "You sit down and relax and I'll cook."

That sounded good to Merilee. She sat petting the cat and watched as Zach worked. He seemed at home in the kitchen. Heck, he seemed at home in his own skin. With a body like that, no wonder.

"Here you go. We can pretend it's pizza," he said, setting a plate in front of her.

It wasn't a fancy omelet—just eggs and cheese and some onion he'd found and chopped and sautéed. Still, sitting at Zach's cozy kitchen table, enjoying it and sipping instant hot cocoa was as satisfying as dining at a fine restaurant.

"You're pretty good in the kitchen," she said.

He shrugged off her compliment. "We take turns cooking at the station," he said. "I can make all kinds of stuff."

"You'll make some lucky woman a great wife," she teased. Now why had she said that? Fresh warmth crept into her cheeks.

His looked a little sunburned, too. "I'm not much of a commitment guy."

Now her face was on fire. "I didn't mean . . ." she began.

"Oh, I know," he said quickly. "I didn't mean—that is, uh, it's a gamble," he finished lamely.

She nodded. "You're right."

An uncomfortable silence drifted into the cozy kitchen and spread big black wings over them as they finished their omelets. At last Merilee managed a chipper, "That was great. Thanks."

"No problem," he said, taking her plate.

She studied him as he put their plates in the dishwasher. The sinews in his arms, the wide shoulders, the long legs that looked like they could leap buildings in a single bound—everything about him said strength and confidence. Only at the mere mention of marriage he'd reacted like an elephant in a room full of mice. Merilee had once read that elephants feared mice for a very real reason: if one ran up its trunk the elephant wouldn't be able to breathe. Hmmm.

"You know, I'd love to see the rest of the house," she

said. Now, that was bold. Her sisters would have been proud.

"Sure," he said, and she could hear in his voice that he was relieved she had turned them away from the dangerous topic of marriage.

He started by leading her upstairs. The cat accompanied them, as if equally interested in inspecting the improvements Zach had made.

The house was all charm—interesting slopes, cubbyholes, and balconies, crown molding and bead board. "I finished the master suite in August," he said, leading her into what was obviously his bedroom. She took in the king-sized bed with its rumpled, brown comforter and felt a fresh sizzle on her cheeks.

"Uh, it's kind of a mess," he said, kicking a pair of blue boxers under the bed.

As he threw the comforter up over the rumpled sheets Merilee flashed on an image of two bodies happily putting them in that condition. The female one looked suspiciously like her. "It's very big. Your bed." *Oh, Lord.*

"It gets the job done," he said with a grin, and led the way down the hall.

They stopped by a second room, which was doubling as an office, and then checked out the guest room. This one appeared to be freshly painted. Robin's egg blue, lovely. It held an antique dresser with an oval mirror and a brass bed covered with a quilt done in fabrics predominantly blue.

"The furniture was my grandma's," he said.

Merilee stepped over to the bed for a closer inspection of the quilt. A star pattern, hand stitched. "Did your grandma make this?"

"Yeah. She made one for both of us kids."

"I bet she loves this house."

"She would've," he said. "She died three years ago."

"Oh, I'm sorry." She always hated hearing that people had lost loved ones.

"I miss her," Zach said simply. "She was a big part of my life when I was a kid. We visited her and my granddad every summer. I never saw her just sitting, you know. She always had something going on and she was always making something for someone."

"Sounds like she was a wonderful person," said Merilee. And it sounded like Zach had the perfect family growing up. Wouldn't he want to replicate it?

"She was great," he said. "Live life to the fullest, that was her motto."

"Good advice," said Merilee. Advice she should take.

"Gram practiced what she preached, too. She was taking an Alaskan cruise when she died. Stroked out at the sight of the Mendenhall Glacier. Not a bad way to go," Zach finished as they went back downstairs. "So, here's the dining room. Living room over here."

Merilee walked past him into the living room. "This is great. It would look really awesome if you painted one wall a dusty rose."

He nodded thoughtfully.

"And I could see a Christmas tree in the bay window."

For some reason the suggestion made him squirm. He twisted his neck like he had a sudden crick in it.

Maybe he wasn't catching the vision. Merilee continued, "Not a fake tree; a big, fat one you go out and cut yourself and then load up with lots of old-fashioned ornaments. You know, like the Griswold family tree in *National Lampoon's Christmas Vacation*."

He smiled. "That movie rocks."

"I love it, too," said Merilee. "Especially the part where the squirrel jumps out of the tree."

He gave a snort. "Oh, yeah, and the gift box with the

cat in it. Sorry, Tom. Nothing personal," he added, and picked up the cat, stopping it from circling his legs.

This man proudly displayed his grandmother's quilt, took in stray cats, tried to help women who had been unjustly fired. With such a big heart, why was he so afraid of sharing his life with someone? Of course, she barely knew him so it would be rude to ask. She wished she could, though.

Instead, she said, "I love the window seat. My grandma in Oregon has an old house with a window seat. When we were little she stored all kinds of games in it for us to play when we visited: Monopoly, Aggravation, Clue."

"Oh, man, I remember playing Clue with my brother and the neighbors' kid," said Zach, shaking his head and smiling. "I always won."

"Me, too."

"Yeah? Nobody beats me," he teased.

"Guess you've never met your match. Until now," she retorted. *Merilee White, are you flirting? Who knew you had it in you!*

"Yeah, well, we may have to see about that. I bet my mom still has the game somewhere."

"Let me know if you find it. If you're brave enough."

That made him chuckle.

Flirting was fun. And empowering. Merilee grinned, pleased with herself.

Until she realized she had run out of things to say.

Actually, she had a lot to say. *Why are you afraid of commitment? Want company in that big bed? Let's go get a Griswold Christmas tree and see how it looks in your bay window.* None of those were appropriate. There was nothing more to say about Tom the cat, either, since he appeared to be over his eating disorder.

It was probably time to go home. Had Cinderella

gotten hit with this same wave of disappointment when the clock struck midnight?

"I guess my work here is done," Merilee said, keeping her voice light. Maybe Zach would suggest she stay a little longer. Maybe he'd say he had a copy of *National Lampoon's Christmas Vacation*.

He didn't. Instead, he nodded and set the cat down. "Okay. I'll run you home."

Would he have been so quick to run either of her sisters home? Of course not, and maybe Zach would be asking her to hang around if she'd tried harder to be more like them. Why hadn't she gotten to the mall and bought some hot new clothes and makeup?

Why did she think that would make a difference? Sigh.

Back outside the snow was still at work, laying an ever-thickening carpet on the ground. The falling flakes made the festive lights on the surrounding houses look blurry and soft, like a Thomas Kinkade painting. Merilee stopped a moment to take it all in. "This is such a lovely season," she murmured. "Sometimes I wish it could be Christmas all year long."

"Once a year is more than enough," said Zach, crunching past her.

What a sad thing to say! "I don't think I've ever met anyone who didn't like Christmas," she mused as they drove home. Oh, no. Had she just said that out loud? *Way to go, stupid*.

"It's just the family thing gets a little too much, you know."

No, she didn't know. She loved spending the holidays with her family. Her brothers always made a special trip out to join the others, and they all packed the house from floor to attic. On Christmas Eve her mother made a huge turkey with all the trimmings, which they washed down with fruit punch. Later they'd consume copious amounts of Christmas cookies (never good for the diet, but Merilee intended to splurge this year anyway) and after dinner her sister Gloria would play the piano and they'd sing carols. Then they'd all go to the candlelight service and sing more carols. On Christmas morning they ate cranberry pancakes and opened presents. Someone always slipped a game of some sort under the tree, which they then spent the afternoon playing while stuffing themselves with turkey sandwiches and leftover dressing. What was not to like about Christmas?

"I guess it depends on the family," she said.

He looked at her in surprise. "Don't tell me, your family is perfect."

"Oh, we're not perfect," she admitted. "But we're close to it. And we have fun together."

He responded to that remark with a grunt. Very telling. His grandmother may have been great, but obviously the rest of his family didn't measure up.

They would have ridden the rest of the way in silence if Merilee hadn't thanked him for taking her home.

"That's the least I could do since you got my cat to eat."

She suspected the cat had gotten himself to eat but decided to leave Zach to his delusion. "I was happy to help."

They were in the parking lot of the Angel Arms Apartments now and Zach slid the vehicle to a stop. "I'll walk you up to your apartment."

"Oh, you don't need to," she protested. Surely he'd had enough of her by now.

But he was already out of the car and coming over to open her door. There was nothing to do but be gracious and let him be noble. And wonder if she should invite him in for eggnog.

She was still debating when they reached her door. "I loved seeing your house," she said as she fumbled for her key.

"Thanks for the paint suggestion," he said.

Would you like to come in for a minute and warm up? No, that was stupid. He hadn't gotten that cold walking from the SUV to her front door. *How about some eggnog?* He probably liked it spiked. Heck, he probably preferred beer. *I have a quilt on my bed, too. Want to see it?* Gag.

She was so busy trying to think of what to say that she didn't pay close attention as she opened the door. A streak of white slipped out and bolted down the open walkway for the stairs and freedom. "Oh, no! Queenie!"

"I'll get her," Zach offered and took off after the cat.

And Merilee took off after Zach.

Just as she'd feared, Queenie had quickly disappeared. "She's an inside kitty. She can't be out here. Oh, and if Mrs. Winnamucker sees her or something gets her . . ." It was all too gruesome to contemplate.

"Don't worry, we'll find her," Zach said, bending over and peering under the rhododendron bushes.

In spite of her concern for Queenie, she couldn't help noticing what a fine butt he had. Did that make her a bad cat mommy?

"There she is." A moment later he was on his hands and knees in the snow, reaching under the bushes. "Come on, cat. I know you've got a fur coat but you don't really want to be out here."

It appeared Queenie did because she retreated further. "You got any more of those kitty treats?"

Merilee had left the box at Zach's house. But wait. "I've got something that will work just as well." She rushed back to the apartment and grabbed a can of Salmon Supper, then hurried back to where Zach was crouched by the rhodies. "This should bring her," she said, and opened the lid with a pop.

Sure enough, a moment later a little white head poked

out from under the bushes. Slowly Queenie edged forward, sniffing the air.

Zach snatched her up. "Gotcha."

"What's going on out here?" called a high, tremulous voice.

"It's the apartment manager," hissed Merilee. "I'm not supposed to have a cat. I'm screwed."

Sure enough, a moment later, Mrs. Winnamucker appeared, her red coat thrown over a bathrobe, her feet slipped into boots and her favorite red hat pulled down over her curls. "Miss White?" Her eyes got big. And then they narrowed and her mouth turned down at the corners. She took a deep breath, causing her ample chest to puff out and making Merilee think of the big bad wolf about to blow down a house. "That cat—"

Oh, this was so not good.

"It's mine," said Zach, thinking fast. "He, uh, ran away. I was out looking for him."

Mrs. Winnamucker's eyes narrowed suspiciously.

"And I was helping him," added Merilee, trying desperately not to look guilty as she shoved the can of cat food at Zach.

Mrs. Winnamucker still looked suspicious, but since all she had was her suspicion she had to content herself with simply saying "I see" in a tone of voice that added, *what you're up to.*

"Well, thanks for your help," Zach said to Merilee. "Guess I'd better let you get in out of the cold."

"You're welcome. Any time," Merilee said. Then, with a nervous smile for Mrs. Winnamucker, she scurried back to her apartment, leaving Zach stuck with her kitty.

By the time she shut the apartment door her heart was pounding. She felt like a criminal who had managed a lucky escape. She also felt badly that poor Zach the fireman had been left holding the bag. Or, rather, the cat.

What to do? She wished she had his cell phone number. She remembered his last name from when he'd made his purchases at Pet Palace. She could look him up in the phone book, call and leave a message on his home phone apologizing for the silly mess she'd dragged him into. But when she searched her phonebook she found no Zach Stone listed. He probably kept his number unlisted so besotted women couldn't harass him.

She perched on the edge of her couch and gnawed a fingernail, trying to decide what to do. It didn't take much gnawing for her to realize there wasn't anything to do except wait.

Half an hour went by, and then another fifteen minutes before she heard a soft knock at her apartment door. She opened it to find Zach standing there with Queenie in his arms. He slipped inside the apartment and shut the door behind him. "Sorry it took me so long to come back. I wanted to wait until I was sure the prison guard wouldn't be watching from her window or out patrolling the grounds."

"She takes the no-pet rule very seriously," said Merilee. "I guess I can't blame her. It's her job, after all. But it's a stupid rule."

"Rules were meant to be broken, huh?" Zach teased as he handed Queenie over. "You know, there's a lot more to you than meets the eye."

There used to be a lot more to her that did meet the eye, but she wasn't sharing that information. The old Merilee who used to run to the cupboard for comfort was, hopefully, long gone, never to return. "Thanks for helping me find Queenie."

No problem. "Looks like we've got a lot in common."

They did?

"Cats with issues." He stroked Queenie's head and she purred and pressed into his large palm.

Oh, that.

For a moment they stood there, looking at each other. Something flashed in his eyes, something male and elemental that hot-wired Merilee's heart and sent a sizzle racing through her. It suddenly felt very warm in the apartment.

He cleared his throat. "I better get going. See you around."

Then, before she could say, "Wait, I've got some light eggnog," he slipped back out the door.

Merilee stood there, staring at the closed door and gnawing her lip. Maybe his cat would have more issues. Maybe he'd need a cat whisperer again.

Or maybe she should make an attitude adjustment, go shopping for some new clothes, makeup, and a Clue game.

NINE

"Shopping tomorrow? Absolutely. I'll take an extended lunch break and we'll power shop," said Merilee's older sister, Gloria, when Merilee called her. "It's about time you started listening to me."

"I've got the week off. I'm there," said her little sister, Liz. "And right before Christmas, we are for sure going to find bargains. This will be *sooo* much fun."

Merilee wasn't sure how much fun it would be staring at herself in the dressing room mirror. But it sure wasn't fun living in the shadows. It was time to take a lesson from Zach's grandma and start living life to the fullest.

Just remember you can't afford to live too fully, she reminded herself. Not with her current job situation. Still, a few new clothes would be an investment in her future. She couldn't live indefinitely on what she was making at the shelter. She'd need a new outfit for job hunting. And . . . other things.

She'd take a whopping fifty dollars out of savings and see what she could get with that. Probably not much, but you never knew. She could stumble on some fabulous holiday sales. 'Tis the season, after all.

Her sisters were already waiting at a table in the Angel Falls Mall food court, indulging in hot chocolate from Chocolate Heaven, when Merilee arrived. Gloria was tall and willowy, with long chestnut-colored hair and perfect features. She was wearing a crisply tailored white blouse with a black skirt that showed off her legs. She'd topped them with a red leather jacket accessorized with silver jewelry, proving that she deserved her nickname Glorious. Everything she wore demanded *Pay attention to me,* unlike Merilee's wardrobe, which said *Maybe you'd rather not look.* Liz was just as big an attention grabber as Gloria. She was petite and blond—eye candy in a small package. She wore jeans coupled with a pale pink sweater, her winter jacket draped over a nearby chair. Gold bangles dangled from her wrist and the fat diamond in her engagement ring winked hello as Merilee walked over.

As often happened in the presence of her glamorous sisters, the Ghost of Ugly Past hovered over Merilee, whispering in her ear that she would never be as pretty as her siblings. *Why are you bothering?* it taunted.

Good question. Because she wanted to be better, to become more than what she'd been. On fifty dollars. Oh, boy.

At the sight of Merilee, Liz jumped up to hug her. "All right! She's here. Let the games begin. Have you lost more weight? You look great."

"Correction," said Gloria, waiting her turn to hug Merilee. "She *will* look great when we're done with her."

Liz grinned and relinquished her hold on Merilee. "We've already been making a list of what you need."

"Which is practically everything," added Gloria.

Uneasiness crept over Merilee. She had a vision of her fifty dollars sprouting wings and flying away within the first five minutes of their shopping expedition. "I can't go too crazy now that my paycheck has shrunk to next to nothing."

Gloria linked an arm through hers and began to stroll her toward Macy's. "Not to worry. We've got it covered."

Merilee stopped. "What do you mean?"

Liz was on her other side now, moving her forward again, past a forest of artificial trees and giant candy canes. "We are taking care of your makeover. Merry Christmas from your sisters."

"Oh, you guys, you can't," Merilee protested.

"Of course, we can," said Gloria. "I made an obscene amount of money this year. I have to spend it on something."

"Me, too," said Liz. "Well, not as much as Glorious. No one makes as much as her."

"So sue me for climbing the corporate ladder," said Gloria with a shrug.

"You guys, I didn't call to bum money off you," Merilee insisted. "I've got money."

Gloria cocked an eyebrow. "How much?"

Merilee raised her chin to its haughtiest level. "Fifty dollars."

Liz let out a guffaw that made two women and a clerk turn and stare. "My God, how long has it been since you've been shopping?"

Merilee felt her cheeks burning. "Not that long."

"Well, fifty will buy you a bra and some panties and that's about it," Gloria informed her.

"Panties are good," said Liz, her eyes dancing. "A leopard thong, I'm thinkin'. *Rrrrr,*" she added with a giggle and gave Merilee's arm a squeeze.

They were in the cosmetics department now. "I say we stop here first," said Gloria. "If I have to spend the next two hours looking at that great face of yours neglected and naked I'll wind up strangling myself with a scarf."

"Oh, yeah," agreed Liz. "Makeovers are so fun. I think I'll get one, too." She nudged Merilee. "We can pretend we're on *What Not to Wear.*"

Liz, of course, didn't need anything made over since she was already perfect, but she enjoyed playing with different shades of lipstick and adding comments as the makeup expert at the counter worked on transforming Merilee.

Transformation? That was an understatement. She was startled by the face in the mirror. Who was this woman with the arresting green eyes and full, coral-colored lips? She couldn't possibly look that good, could she?

"You look incredible," Gloria told her. To the clerk she said, "We'll take one of each," and whipped out her credit card.

"You just spent a fortune," Merilee said weakly.

"What, you think you're not worth it?" Gloria retorted.

Actually, that was exactly what she thought.

"I like giving to worthwhile causes," Gloria said. "And you're one of the worthiest causes I know," she added with a smile. "Anyway, think of it as payback for the time I convinced you to eat mud when we were kids."

"I remember hearing about that." Liz made a face. "I can't even imagine."

"She told me it was fudge," muttered Merilee. "You were such a bully."

"Still am," Gloria said, unrepentant. "And now that I can stand to look at you, let's go bully you into a new wardrobe.

Bully they did. Merilee watched in amazement as her sisters cruised past racks of clothes, selecting tops, jackets, and pants with unerring eyes. "You have to get this sweater. It will look great with your red hair," said Liz, stepping in front of a thirty-something woman and scooping a turquoise sweater off a sale rack.

The woman glared at Liz and Merilee felt her face heat. "I think she wanted that," she whispered.

"It's the holidays," said Gloria. "The race is to the swift."

There were certainly a lot of people out racing. The roads were slushy, but with Christmas only a few days away that wasn't stopping anyone. The store was packed with shoppers, mostly women, of all sizes and ages, browsing beneath festive faux-cedar swags and giant wine-colored ornaments. All that body heat was keeping the store warm and the collective perfume smell made Merilee feel like she was trapped inside a giant scented candle.

She eyed the loads of clothes in her sisters' arms and said, "I think we've got enough."

"It'll do for a start," Gloria decided. "Come on. Let's get you into a dressing room."

"Oh, boy," muttered Merilee.

"You just wait," Liz told her. "You're not going to believe how good you look."

And she didn't. "Oh, my gosh," she said, as she took in the sight of herself in jeans and the turquoise sweater Liz had found. "I look—"

"Incredible," Liz supplied, beaming. "Am I good or what?"

"I don't know," teased Gloria. "Let's ask that poor schlub you suckered into proposing."

"Go ahead. He'll tell you he's the luckiest man in the world," Liz bragged, polishing her engagement ring on her sweater.

"Well, right now I feel like the luckiest woman in the world," Merilee said, taking in her reflection. "I never thought I could look so . . . pretty." The word felt foreign, difficult to pronounce.

Gloria gave her a hug. "We did." She handed over a slinky black top with a plunging neckline.

"Oh, I don't think—" Merilee began.

"That's right. This time you don't. Let us do the thinking for you."

"Trust us," said Liz. "If you want to light a fire under that fireman you told us about, this will do it."

"Maybe," Merilee said as she pulled off the sweater. She sure hoped she hadn't imagined interest in his eyes when they stood at her door. Had it been been wishful thinking?

"That's no way to talk," scolded Liz. "You have to have a little confidence in yourself."

She did. Very little.

"I think he's already interested," said Gloria, dropping the black top over Merilee's head. "Cat whisperer, what a flimsy excuse to see a woman!"

"The cat really wasn't eating," said Merilee. Although he'd had no problem eating when she arrived.

"Trust me, this man is already on the edge," said Gloria. "He just needs a little push." She folded her arms and assessed the top and jeans. "This should do it."

"I'll say," added Liz. "Add some hot shoes and you won't need to push at all. He'll jump right over."

Merilee blinked to make sure she wasn't seeing things. She wasn't. The reflection of a pretty woman, now with some serious cleavage on display, gawked back at her.

"The boob fairy really blessed you, sis," said Liz, draping a casual arm over Merilee's shoulder. "And that great, new waistline sure shows 'em off."

Gloria crowded in on the other side and smiled. "Are we gorgeous or what?"

Merilee smiled. Her, gorgeous. Who knew?

An hour later and she had more new clothes than she'd ever had at any one time in her entire life. She looked from sister to sister with glistening eyes. "You guys, how can I ever thank you?"

"By going after this man," said Gloria.

"Don't be a fraidy-cat," added Liz. "Get out there and make something happen."

"In every area of your life," Gloria added, giving her a hug. "I meant what I said about having a pile of cash. I know you want to get back to school. If you need some money, it's yours."

"I think you've done enough," Merilee said, still feeling more than a little guilty over how much her sisters had spent on her.

"If the flip-flop was on the other foot, you'd be there for her," said Liz. "We're family. Family sticks together. Anyway, once you get through vet school we can have free care for our pets for the rest of our lives."

"If you ever get a pet," Merilee retorted.

"If you won't take it as a gift consider it a no-interest loan with no balloon payment," said Gloria, putting the conversation back on track. "I'm totally serious here. Don't give up on your dreams. Shoot for the moon, Mer."

Shoot for the moon. Merilee drove away from the mall in a daze. What was holding her back, really? Only herself. And what did she have to lose by taking a few chances? Some pride, perhaps. But how much more pride would she gain if she started really taking on life, and love, aggressively?

Before going to work the next day she would download the sample application for the College of Veterinary Medicine at Washington State University. This time she was going to finish no matter what it took.

On her way home she stopped by Little Angels Toys and picked up a game of Clue. Then she went home and changed into her new jeans and the slinky black top.

"How do I look?" she asked Queenie, who was perched on the bed watching her.

Queenie blinked.

"I know, you can't believe your eyes," said Merilee. "But it's really me. The new me."

She left the bedroom and Queenie jumped off the bed and followed behind to supervise while she wrapped the Clue game for Zach. She took extra care with the bow, making a big, fluffy one out of red curling ribbon. "There," she said at last, admiring her work. "That looks downright festive." And tempting. Just like her, she decided with a smile.

She picked up the cat and gave her a kiss on the head. "Wish me luck."

Queenie purred as if to say, "You go, girl."

The streets were slushy and slick but it wasn't the driving conditions that made Merilee's heart race as she drove across town. Would Zach think she was pushy? Would he ask her in? If he did, what could she say? Maybe: "Open your present and let's play." That definitely was pushy. Okay then: "I thought of you when I saw this." That sounded dorky. Well, she'd think of something, hopefully. She took a deep breath as she turned onto Lavender Lane, telling her heart to slow down.

A mechanical Santa waved a welcome as she drove past. She took it as a sign of encouragement.

But her heart started racing all over again when she pulled in behind Zach's SUV and got out of her car. This was probably a dumb idea. He would think she was pushy. He'd tell her he had plans. He probably wouldn't even let her in. Maybe she should go home, return the game to the toy store.

Maybe she shouldn't be such a wimp. That would be a total waste of new clothes. She clutched her package and started for the house.

She was halfway to the door when she heard the

shoosh of wheels on slushy pavement and turned to see a big truck driven by what looked like an equally big man pulling up to the curb.

Zach and this man obviously had plans and here she was descending like some man-hungry she-buzzard. This had been a stupid idea. She'd just leave the present on the porch and walk away, saying hello to this new arrival as she passed him. Yes, that was a good plan.

She propped the present on the door and started to leave.

The big man was coming up the walk now, carrying a Chihuahua clad in a Christmas red doggy sweater. "Hi there," he said.

"Hi," she said back. "I was just dropping off . . ." *Bait.* "Something."

"Zach's home. No need to run off." The big man looked her up and down appreciatively, taking in her tight jeans and the stiletto heel black boots Liz had insisted she get. The mint green parka Gloria had picked out for her showed off her new and improved slim middle.

She felt awkward and pleased all at once. And uncomfortable. "It looks like maybe you and he have plans."

"Nothin' much. Come on." He kept walking as if expecting her to turn around and follow him into the house. She would look really stupid if she kept running now, so she took a deep breath and turned around.

Zach met them at the door. "Hey, Merilee," he greeted her. His voice was casual but his eyes were big. He looked her up and down and blinked. "Is that a new coat?"

It's new everything, right down to my underwear. She clutched the collar of the green parka, pulling it tight around her throat. "I went shopping." Wouldn't her sisters have been impressed with that little bit of sparkling conversation? *Ugh.*

"You look good. Come on in. I guess you met Ray."

"Just now," Merilee said. "Hi, Ray."

"Hi," Ray said. He held up the little dog. "And this is Tacky."

Kind of like her showing up unannounced with a board game and new undies.

"Short for Taquito. He's my boy," Ray said, giving Tacky's head a pat with his big hand.

He set the dog down and it started trotting down the hallway. Halfway to the kitchen Tacky encountered Tom the cat. Tom arched his back, puffed out his fur, and hissed. Tacky yapped and took a step back. The cat let out another fierce hiss. That was all it took to send the Chihuahua running back to his owner.

"That cat of yours is a bully," Ray said, picking up his dog as the cat marched into the living room.

Zach just laughed. To Merilee he said, "As you can see Tom is doing a lot better."

"It looks like he's made a full recovery," she said, and then couldn't think of anything else. So she thrust the package at him. "I just stopped by to drop this off."

"Yeah?" Zach looked surprised.

Actually, he looked well beyond surprised. *Can you say deer-in-the-headlights?* She'd known it all along. She was being pushy. She could feel her cheeks warming. "I'd better get going."

"No. Come on in," he insisted, motioning in the direction of the living room.

She shook her head and started for the door. "You've got plans."

"Not really," said Ray. "We were just gonna hang and play some Halo." He motioned to the present in Zach's hand. "I told you that you needed a tree. Now you got no place to put your present."

"So I'll open it now," Zach said and ripped off the ribbon and wrapping paper.

Merilee's cheeks got hotter as the paper came off to reveal the Clue game.

"I haven't played that since I was nine," said Ray. "Forget Halo. Let's play Clue. Take off your coat and stay awhile," he said to Merilee.

She took off her coat and Zach's mouth dropped, right along with the game. "Uh, nice outfit," he managed as he bent to pick it up.

"Very nice," agreed Ray, his gaze drifting toward her chest. "So, Merilee, you live somewhere around here?" he asked, leading her into the living room and leaving Zach to follow.

She smiled. Gloria had been so right about the clothes.

The next thing she knew, she was seated next to Ray on Zach's leather couch with Zach sitting cross-legged on the floor opposite them, spreading out the board game on the coffee table. The guys each had a beer and she had the last can of Coke from the fridge. As for Tacky and the orange cat, they had settled into an uneasy truce, Tacky trembling in his owner's lap and Tom posted as an aloof sentinel atop the back of a chair.

"Hey, man, start a fire," suggested Ray. He grinned at Merilee. "Let's get cozy."

Zach frowned at his friend but he obliged, digging some kindling from an old bucket next to the fireplace. Another few minutes and a fire gently crackled in the fireplace while Mannheim Steamroller serenaded them courtesy of Zach's iPod speakers.

Merilee stopped feeling pushy. Her heart even settled down to a normal pace. Except for when she'd sneak a peak at Zach. The mere sight of that strong jaw was enough to make it do cartwheels.

Forty minutes later, Ray announced, "Okay, I'm ready to make my final guess. Miss Scarlet did it in the billiard room with the candlestick."

Did it. A picture of her and Zach falling onto a pool table in a fit of passion, sending balls flying in all directions, flashed into Merilee's mind.

Zach scowled. "You rat bastard. I'd have had it next turn." He pulled the correct cards from the little envelope and spread them out on the game board. "Did you know who did it?" he asked Merilee.

You and me on the billiard table. She willed herself not to blush. *Get your mind off of the pool table, girl.* "Of course," she lied. She had no idea, really. It had been impossible to concentrate.

"Okay, we're playing again," Zach commanded, collecting the cards.

"I'll still win," Ray gloated. He shot an assessing glance Merilee's direction. "So, what's the story behind this anyway? Did Zach ask Santa for it for Christmas?"

No, I was just being pushy.

Zach answered before Merilee had to. "We got to talking about games we played when we were kids. I was bragging."

"Ha! So you came over to whip his ass," said Ray. "How'd you two meet, anyway? And when were you going to introduce me?" he demanded of Zach.

"Merilee's the one who helped me with Tom."

Ray pointed a finger at her. "You're the cat whisperer. Awesome."

Zach had talked about her? Merilee felt pleased.

"I was telling him how you got Tom to cat," added Zach.

That was all? Well, it was a beginning, she supposed. She caught Zach doing a surreptitious scan of her curves. A very good beginning.

They played another game and this time Zach won. Merilee still couldn't concentrate. Miss Scarlet was at it again, this time in the kitchen with a rope. Miss Scarlet was a busy girl. Merilee had never been busy. How depressing. It was definitely time to change that.

Except she wasn't sure she was making much progress in the change department. Zach seemed to appreciate her new look, but the one doing all the flirting with her was Ray. So far he'd complimented her on her outfit, suggested they get together and play Risk, and had finished up by asking her if she could come over sometime and help him train Tacky.

"Train him to do what?" Zach demanded.

Ray shrugged. "I dunno. I'll think of something," he added, grinning at Merilee.

"Trust me," said Zach in disgust. "You don't want to go anywhere near this turkey."

True. Not that Ray was a turkey. He seemed like a nice man. But the person Merilee wanted to get near was Zach. If only he was the one making the offer.

With the second game over she decided to go home. There wouldn't be any doing anything tonight with Zach's friend around anyway. Probably there wouldn't have been any doing anything even if it were just the two of them. She sure hoped neither of her sisters asked how the new clothes were working out when she saw them at her parents' on Christmas. Her wardrobe obviously wasn't the problem.

Ray hovered while Zach helped her into her coat. When he offered to walk Merilee to her car, Zach said, "I'm on it."

So maybe he wanted a minute alone with her? This was encouraging.

He shrugged into his parka and walked out the door with her. Suddenly she couldn't think of a thing to say. "I hope I didn't mess up your plans for the night," she tried. *Wow, sparkling conversation, Merilee.*

"Nah," said Zach. "I can play Halo anytime. This was nice."

They were at her car now. She took her time getting out her car keys. Then she looked up at him and managed what she hoped was an encouraging smile. This would be the perfect time for a kiss.

Instead of kissing her, he simply said, "Thanks for the game. And for letting me win."

"How'd you know?"

He chuckled. "And thanks again for helping me with Tom. I owe you."

She didn't want him to owe her. She wanted him to want her. Her sister Liz would have come right out and said that, but Merilee simply nodded. Still, her eyes couldn't hide what she felt. If he looked into them, really looked, he'd see the longing in her heart.

He didn't. He skimmed the surface and then shoved his hands in his jeans pockets. "Looks like it's going to start snowing again. Think you'll be okay getting home?"

If you kiss me I will. She nodded. And hoped.

He nodded, too, and took a step back.

She was almost overwhelmed by the urge to grab him by the coat and close the distance between them, but his body language told her that would be a mistake. Still, she couldn't just give up and drive away. Not yet.

"You know, I think we need a Clue rematch," she said. "If you'd like to bring the game over to my place I could order that pizza we never got."

Zach's smile froze. "Uh, Merilee."

Oh, dear. She'd spooked him. "Or not," she said quickly, her whole face suddenly burning.

"Merilee, I'm not looking to start a serious relationship. If I gave you that idea, I'm sorry."

"Why is that?" she blurted. Oh, boy. What was she

thinking? Her face had to be beet red by now. Her skin felt hot enough to ignite her whole head like a matchstick. She should have gotten into her car like a good little fraidy-cat and gotten out of there. "I mean . . ." What did she mean? *Why don't you want me?* That was what she meant. And that was what she couldn't come out and ask. He might just tell her, and both the clothes and the attitude adjustment were too new to stand up to a self-esteem assault.

"I don't do well with commitment," he said simply.

"Maybe you've never been in a relationship with the right woman," she suggested, heart hammering. Why, oh, why couldn't she leave this alone and drive away?

He shook his head. "Believe me. You don't want a guy like me. My family's screwed up big time. My mom left when I was a kid, my dad's an alcoholic, and me, well, like I said, I just don't do commitment." The tears pooling in her eyes must have been too much for him because he cleared his throat and said, "Don't get me wrong. If you ever need anything . . ."

What she needed he wasn't willing to give. "I understand," she lied. *If I'd looked like your ex-girlfriend would you be making these excuses?*

There was really nothing more to say, nothing more to do but get in her car and drive away. It was time to go home to her cat.

TEN

Back home Merilee ripped off her sexy new clothes and pulled on her sweats.

"There's no point wearing them here," she informed Queenie, who perched on the bed, keeping her company. What a waste of her sisters' money!

The phone rang and caller ID told her it was Liz. Oh, boy. Maybe she'd just let it ring . . . forever. Hide out here in the apartment . . . forever.

But that wouldn't work with her sisters. They'd just come over and pound on the door . . . forever. She picked up.

"Oh," Liz said in surprise. "I didn't actually expect you to answer. I was just going to leave a message for you to call me and tell me if you've seen your fireman yet."

"I saw him."

"Well, how'd it go?"

"It didn't," Merilee said miserably.

"He got a look at you in those new clothes and let you get away?"

Merilee heaved a sigh. "He's screwed up."

"No kidding, and maybe just about the stupidest man

on the planet," Liz said in disgust. "Well, phooey on him then. There are more shoes in the store. Go shopping."

"Retail therapy?" asked Merilee confused.

"No, therapy's over. It's time to go man shopping. Open your laptop."

"What?"

"Just open your laptop," Liz instructed.

Merilee picked her computer off the coffee table and settled on her couch with the phone on speaker. "Okay."

"Now, go to Myotherhalf.com."

Merilee pulled her fingers back from the keyboard. "An internet dating site? Oh, no." That was for desperate people.

"Everyone is doing online dating these days," Liz insisted. "It's the best way to weed out the losers and find Mr. Right."

Merilee had already found Mr. Right. Oh, yeah. He didn't want to be found.

"Mer? Are you there yet?"

She didn't want to be there. She didn't want to go online and look for a man. She wanted the man who lived on Lavender Lane. "I don't think so," she decided.

"Come on, you owe it to yourself to just try this," said Liz. "Do you want to be alone all your life?"

Heavens no! She wanted what her parents had together. And she wanted kids of her own to haul to the family holiday celebrations. "Of course not."

"Then at least check this out. What have you got to lose?"

Nothing. She had nothing.

"So get on there already," said Liz. "If you don't, I'm calling Glorious and we're coming over and taking back the clothes."

She was teasing, but Gloria would probably do it. And make her eat mud. "Okay, okay. I'll check it out."

"Right now, while I'm on the phone with you," said Liz. "Otherwise I'm coming over."

"Okay already," said Merilee. She went to the Web site and was greeted by a home page plastered with pictures of couples who all looked like they'd been hired from modeling agencies. Insecurity landed on her, freezing her fingers. "Oh, I don't know about this."

"Come on," urged Liz. "What can it hurt to fill out the questionairre?"

She was right. What did Merilee have to lose?

A vision of Zach sporting firefighting britches and a bare chest popped into her mind. She reminded herself that she couldn't lose what she'd never had and started typing in her personal information: female seeking male, e-mail address, password. She got to credit card information and balked. "I don't know if I want to pay."

"You had money for clothes that you didn't use. You may as well spend it here," said Liz. "They have a two-week trial period, but you won't get to see all the men you're a match with, so just pay now."

"How do you know all this?" asked Merilee. Liz had met her fiancé at work.

"Glor's been using," said Liz. "She's tired of dating losers."

All right, if it was good enough for her glamorous older sister, it was good enough for Merilee. Resolved, she quickly clicked through the rest of the preliminary stages. Then she arrived at a very detailed questionnaire. "Oh, my."

"You must be on the questions page," said Liz. "Glor says it's a pain."

It probably would be, on many levels.

"Just do it, though, okay? If you get stuck, call me." With that Liz hung up, leaving her sister to bare her soul to a computer screen.

Oh, boy. Merilee took a deep breath and booted her fantasy image of Zach out of her brain. *He's not Mr. Right. Quit wasting your time on him.*

At least the questions were multiple choice. She went to work, trying to boil down her interests, needs, and insecurities into the short sentences listed under A, B, C, and D.

Your idea of a great date is:
A. Dinner for two at a nice restaurant
B. Watching a sporting event
C. Going dancing at a club
D. Doing something outdoors

Playing Clue with Zach. Merilee frowned and checked D.

How long has it been since you were in a relationship?
A. Less than a month
B. A month
C. Six months
D. Longer than six months

Did Queenie count? Merilee sighed and checked D.

When entertaining do you prefer to
A. Have a large party with simple refreshments
B. Host a small dinner party
C. Play games
D. Host a movie night

Have Zach over to play Clue. Oh, stop, Merilee told herself and selected B.

The questions seemed endless. Did she believe in love at first sight? How many books had she read in the last year? Did she shout or pout when she was angry? How important was it to her to have a pet?—very important; somewhat important; she'd be okay without one now but wanted one eventually; or wasn't fond of animals. At least that one was easy to answer.

She came to the final page which displayed a little box. *Add something personal.*

Personal? She'd just filled out four pages worth of "personal." She stared at the screen and gnawed her lower lip. Finally she typed, *I like cats.*

"Oh, real sexy, Merilee," she muttered. "At least add something else." *I'm going to be a veterinarian.* She smiled. Positive affirmation was good.

Finally, she was done. Then it was time to post a picture of herself. A picture? She didn't have one she wanted to look at, let alone show some stranger.

Oh, no, you're not going to let a little thing like a picture stop you from getting on with your life, she told herself sternly. She snagged her cell phone and snapped a head shot, then uploaded it. Not perfect, but then neither was she.

Finally she was done. *Congratulations,* read her computer screen. *You are now on your way to finding your other half.*

She'd thought that when she first met Zach in the grocery store. "We'll see," she said cynically.

While she was waiting she downloaded all the forms for veterinary college. At least she knew something positive would come out of filling out that form.

Hey, if you don't want her, I'll take her," Ray said, as the next level in their Halo game came up. "I'd do that little cutie in a heartbeat. Give me her phone number."

"I don't know it, and if I did I wouldn't give it to you. She's not some hook-up. She's . . ." *My hook-up.*

Except Merilee wasn't the kind of woman who would be out to just have a good time. She was the kind of girl a man gave his heart to. Zach had been there, done that. He didn't want to go there again. The songwriters had it right. Love hurt. Look at the mess it made of people's lives. Look at how his family had turned out.

"She's what?" prompted Ray.

"She's too good for you, numb nuts," said Zach, and started picking off Ray's guys.

"You know, you're falling for this chick."

"I am not," Zach insisted. "I just needed help with Tom."

"And a new Clue game?" Ray taunted.

Zach blew away another one of Ray's guys.

"If you don't want her for yourself you ought to quit leading her on and let somebody else have a chance. She's better off with someone like me anyway since, at the rate you're going, you're gonna turn out like old man Turner."

"The hell I am," growled Zach.

Hank Turner had been a grizzled, retired construction worker who lived alone in a ramshackle farmhouse at the edge of town. He had a penchant for muscle cars and Camel cigarettes, and practically every kid within a twenty-five-mile radius had bought his first car from Hank, including Zach. Hank also had been famous for his misogynistic lifestyle. "Women are trouble," he'd been known to say. "A man's better on his own."

Except Hank hadn't been better on his own. He was haggard and unkempt. He finally smoked in bed one too many times and burned to death. By the time someone had reported the fire, the house had been too far gone to save, and Hank had suffocated from the smoke long before the flames devoured his body. There'd been no funeral for Hank. He'd had no family around to organize one. Zach heard that his poker cronies got together at the the Fallen Angel Tavern to drink a beer in memory of him, but that was it.

Okay, so Zach didn't have a wife, but he had family, friends. He'd have people at his funeral. He didn't need to get married. So what did he care if Merilee ended up with Ray? Ray was a nice guy. And he was even willing to walk the plank into marital waters again, which was surely what Merilee wanted.

"So you think you're not gonna wind up like Turner? Look at you, man," said Ray. "You get a nice chick interested in you and what do you do? Nothin'. She'll get tired of waiting for you to come to your senses. And when she does, old Uncle Ray will be happy to show her what it's like to be with a real man."

"Yeah?"

"Yeah."

That ended the discussion. And the game. "I'm going home," Ray decided.

Zach didn't ask him to stick around.

Ambrose sat and regarded his human, who was sprawled on his big leather couch, frowning at the fire. Ambrose knew that mood. It was one humans referred to as grumpy.

Unless it directly affected dinnertime or getting petted, a human's mood wasn't of much interest to a cat. Humans had so many. Who could keep track? But this mood, well, Ambrose suspected it had something to do with Merilee. And if it had something to do with Merilee, that concerned Ambrose.

So, much as he disliked leaving the warmth of the fireplace, he made his way to the couch and then to Zach's lap to see if he could figure out what was going on. Well, okay, to get petted, also. That was the least Zach could do to show appreciation for Ambrose's concern.

Once on Zach's lap, he let out a questioning meow.

No response.

He tried again and butted Zach's hand with his head. Zach got the message and petted Ambrose, but he said nothing. This was hardly surprising. Human males weren't good at communicating—not like women, who told a cat more than he could ever want to hear. (Adelaide had been especially prone to that, confiding in Ambrose her every ache and pain. And he heard even more about her disappointment with her children, enough to confirm what he already knew: cats were a superior species.) Ambrose didn't need to know everything Zach was thinking. He just wanted to know what was going on with Merilee.

"Meow?" *What, in the name of catnip, are you doing?* Zach heaved a sigh.

"Meow?" *Why did you treat your friend like a rival and hiss at him if you're not going to mate with Merilee?* "Meow, meow?" *Would you hurry up and get it together, dude? Some of us are trying to do a good deed here and you're not making it easy.* "Meow." *And what the heck are 'numb nuts'?*

It wasn't long before Merilee had two messages waiting from the friendly folks at Myotherhalf.com. Both said the same thing. *Someone wants to chat with you. This could be your other half. Interested? Give him a nod.* Both of the men's profiles looked interesting. "Well, you've got nothing to lose," she told herself and logged on to the site to give Candidate Number One, Gary O, a nod.

Gary O lived one town over. Vocation: construction.

Favorite pastimes: hiking, watching movies, hanging out with friends. *Hey Merilee, I like cats, too,* Gary O messaged.

See? she told herself. *There are other men out there who like cats.*

My mother has three.

Oookay. What did that mean? Did he live with his mother? *That's nice,* she typed back diplomatically. Surely someone who was a construction worker didn't live with his mother.

Things are slow right now, Gary O continued, *and I've got lots of time. Want to meet at Hot Wing Heaven? Dutch treat.*

Dutch treat? Wait a minute, didn't that mean separate checks? Merilee frowned. Tacky.

She sent a message to Gary O thanking him for his invite and telling him she was busy. Then she checked out the next candidate, Chuck.

Chuck was a P.E. teacher who liked to be active. Good. She could be active. *Likes football,* said his profile. She liked Super Bowl Parties.

I've got a cockapoo and a cat, he wrote.

An animal lover. Perfect.

Unbidden, a vision of Zach holding his orange cat came to mind. She booted it out and began to message Chuck back. *You sound like a super guy . . .*

Super? Compared to a man who ran into burning buildings to save people?

She deleted the word "super" and typed in "nice."

Nice. She was settling for nice.

There's nothing wrong with nice, she lectured herself.

Chuck was back in less than a minute. *I'm free tomorrow night. Want to meet for dinner?*

No mention of separate checks. That was a good sign. *Sure.*

How about Angelina's? Do you like Mexican?

That would be great. And maybe Chuck would turn out to be great, too.

The following night she showed up at Angelina's wearing her new jeans and the black sweater she told Chuck she'd have on. The sweater was new, too, with a V-neck that made her mildly self-conscious. You've got to advertise, she'd reminded herself. Now she looked sexy and confident. False advertising.

She scanned the group of people waiting to be seated: an elderly couple, two thirty-something women, two men who were nicely dressed and good-looking. Chuck? One of the men gave the other an intimate smile. Okay, no Chuck. Now here came . . . oh, no. This middle-aged man with a beer belly jigging underneath a Seahawks football jersey couldn't be him. The Chuck in the picture had been lean and, well, younger.

He grinned at her and held out a hand the size of a ham. "You must be Merilee."

No, I must be insane. She smiled weakly and lifted her hand.

"Your picture doesn't do you justice," he said and squeezed it in his big, hairy paw, shutting off the blood supply to her fingers.

"You don't look anything like your picture, either," she said and tried not to whimper.

He let go of her hand just before it could wither and fall off. "It was the most recent one I had."

Uh-huh.

"Chuck, party of two," called the hostess.

"That's us." Chuck rubbed his hands together. "I'm starving."

Merilee wasn't. She'd lost her appetite.

"So," said Chuck when the waitress came to take their drink order, "I bet you like those fancy girlie drinks." And before she could say whether she did or not he was ordering a margarita for her. "And I'll have a Corona," he added. The waitress left and he didn't waste any time getting the conversation started. "So, you like cats, huh?" he continued before she could answer. "Did I tell you I've got a cat? It belonged to my ex. Man, I hate that animal."

Wait a minute, how had she gotten matched up with someone who didn't like cats?

It was all downhill from there. Merilee heard about Chuck's ex, the out-of-shape kids he had to teach, how he could have had a career playing pro ball if he hadn't blown out his knee his senior year in high school, why he'd lied about his age. ("Women my age, they're all overweight.") Meanwhile, Merilee smiled politely and asked herself what horrible thing she could possibly have done to deserve an evening with Chuck.

"So, how about dessert?" he offered after the waitress had removed their empty plates. (Chuck had emptied his and then cleaned up the last of her enchiladas.)

"You know, this has been nice," Merilee lied, "but I should probably get going." She started to scoot across the bench.

"Aw, don't go," Chuck begged, his voice slightly slurred from his fourth beer. He reached across the table to catch her arm and managed to knock over her untouched margarita, shooting it into her lap and dousing her new clothes.

"Now I really have to go," she said between clenched teeth.

"Oh, man, I'm sorry," he said, grabbing for an napkin. He leaned over to help her mop up and tipped her water glass, further drenching her. "Aw, shit."

Her thoughts exactly. If Chuck was her perfect match she preferred to stay matchless.

She'd barely gotten home and peeled off her soppy

clothes when someone knocked on her door. Who on earth could that be at eight at night?

She opened the door to find Mrs. Winnamucker standing there, wearing her favorite red coat, her gloved hands holding a copy of *Cat Fancy*. "Your magazine got put in my mailbox by mistake, dear," she began. "I know it's late, but I thought you might want . . ."

Her eyes got big and Merilee knew in a flash the woman had caught a glimpse of something she shouldn't have. She pushed away the furry, white form trying to slip past her, stepped outside and shut the door behind her. "Thanks, Mrs. Winnamucker. It was kind of you to drop by." She reached for the magazine.

Mrs. Winnamucker snatched it back. "You have a cat in your apartment. I knew it!"

There was no sense denying it. Mrs. Winnamucker wasn't likely to be convinced that she'd been hallucinating. The way she was looking at Merilee made her feel like a bad little girl about to get sent to stand in a corner.

"It's only temporary," said Merilee. "Just until I can find a home for her."

"I'm sorry, but that cat must go immediately."

"But this poor little cat—"

"Needs to live somewhere pets are allowed," Mrs. Winnamucker said sternly. "Really, Miss White. Pulling a stunt like this. It's grounds for breaking your lease, you know."

Merilee hung her head. "I know."

"I want that animal out of the apartment right now, before it can do further damage."

"She hasn't done any damage. She's a good cat. I change her litter box regularly and there's no cat odor anywhere in the apartment."

"Regularly?" Mrs. Winnamucker's eyes narrowed. "How long have you had the thing?"

"Not long," Merilee lied.

"Well, you can't have it a minute longer. The cat has to go, right now."

"But the animal shelter is closed and I don't have keys to get in. I can't do anything tonight," Merilee protested.

"Oh, you can do something. You can turn it loose," Mrs. Winnamucker waved expansively toward the great outdoors.

It was beginning to snow. It was cold and nasty out and, "Something will get her."

"Then take her somewhere," Mrs. Winnamucker snapped, her patience obviously at an end. "You know the rule. Pets are not allowed and I really can't make any exceptions."

Merilee blinked in shock. "It's a heartless rule."

"It's not my rule," Mrs. Winnamucker said primly. "It's Mr. Mook's. And if you have a problem with it, then you should talk to him."

"I think I will," Merilee decided.

"Meanwhile, I expect you to remove that cat from the premises," said Mrs. Winnamucker. "I'll wait."

This was wrong. Horrible! "I can't believe you would be so heartless."

"I am not being heartless, Miss White. I am being responsible, something you have not been."

"Please. It's Christmas."

Mrs. Winnamucker crossed her arms over her ample chest. "I am well aware of that, and believe me, it doesn't make me happy to have to do this. But you've brought it entirely on yourself. Now, I don't intend to stand out here in the cold arguing with you any longer. Are you or are you not going to get rid of that animal?"

"Fine," Merilee said through gritted teeth, and went back inside her apartment to fetch Queenie. Since Queenie was still hovering near the door, this wasn't difficult.

"You wanted to go out," she said as she scooped up Quee-nie and put the animal in its carrier. "It looks like you got your wish." If Queenie didn't have a fixation with that door, if she'd stayed in the living room like a sensible cat they wouldn't be in this mess now.

Queenie let out a pitiful mew.

Poor little kitty. What was Merilee going to do with her?

"I'll walk you to your car," Mrs. Winnamucker offered as Merilee stepped back out the door.

"That's nice of you, but I can manage," Merilee said, trying desperately to keep her grip on the cat, her purse, and her temper.

"It's no trouble," said Mrs. Winnamucker. "And I wouldn't try sneaking that animal back in again," she advised after Queenie had been loaded in the backseat. "Not if you want to remain here."

Merilee said nothing in reply. She got into her car and drove off, a little faster than necessary. Her departure sent up a spray of slush, dousing Mrs. Winnamucker and mak-ing her yelp. Merilee smiled grimly. *Merry Christmas to you, too.*

And now what?

ELEVEN

Zach was sitting in his living room, staring unseeingly at his TV screen and wondering if he was indeed going to turn into another old man Turner when the doorbell rang. Who the heck could that be?

He dumped Tom from his lap and went to open the door while Tom stalked off to the kitchen.

There on the front porch stood Merilee. The expression on her face told Zach that the world had just come to an end. Her eyes were red, her makeup was streaked, and she was sniffing. And she was holding a cat carrier. A little white face looked out at him and the animal let out a pitiful yowl.

"Could I come in for a minute?" she asked in a small voice.

"Yeah, get in before you freeze." He swung the door open wide and she stepped into the entry hall. "What's wrong?" Whatever it was, he was already determined to fix it.

She bit her lip and a fresh tear leaked from the corner of her eye. "I've got a problem. I've just been driving around

and calling people and I've run out of people and . . ."
That was as far as she got before she started to cry.

Zach gathered her in a hug. Her hair smelled like shampoo and fresh air and she fit in his arms like she'd been designed for him. *Don't go there.*

"I'm so sorry to bother you," she managed between sobs.

"It's no bother. Come on and sit down." He led her into the living room and settled her on the couch with a roll of toilet paper that he snagged from the downstairs bathroom. *Classy, Zach.* But it was the best he could offer. He sat down next to her. "Tell me what happened."

She did, in halting sentences, dabbing at her eyes with the toilet paper.

"That old woman has no heart," he said in disgust when she finished.

"I didn't mean to end up here, I really didn't," Merilee said miserably. "But you did say if I needed anything . . . I tried everyone else I could think of."

She'd come to him last. That was sad. Of course, after their conversation the other night it was a miracle she'd even come to him at all.

"My sisters aren't home," she continued. "Not that they'd take her anyway. Neither one is much of a pet person. My mom is allergic. My friends from the store all have dogs."

"What about the guy who works at the animal shelter?"

"Joel," she supplied, and blew her nose.

"I bet he likes cats."

"He does, but he has three already."

"Well, then, what's one more?" Zach said cheerfully. "Let's give him a call. I can run you and Queenie over."

She was shaking her head now. "I tried him. He said if he takes in one more cat Anders will leave him. They fought over the last cat he rescued." She turned big, green, tear-filled eyes to Zach. "Could you help me and keep her just for tonight?"

Zach rubbed the back of his neck. He never meant to keep Tom. Now here was another cat. But it was just for one night. He could take in a stray cat for one night.

"I can't turn her loose to get eaten by a coyote."

"Don't worry. I'll keep her." And what if she asked him to keep Queenie permanently? He probably would for Merilee's sake. Oh, man. What was happening in his head?

She dabbed at her eyes again. "Tomorrow I'm going to talk to the owner of the Angel Arms and convince him to let me keep Queenie."

Merilee the elfette was a determined little thing. For all he knew her landlord was a hard-ass and she'd be talking to the wind, but looking at those big eyes, that tear-stained face, Zach didn't have the heart to suggest the possibility of failure.

"I'll come by and get her first thing tomorrow morning, I promise."

"No problem," Zach assured her.

Letting this woman go on her mission alone felt a little like sending Dorothy off to go have tea with the great and terrible Oz. "I'm free tomorrow. I'll go with you," he offered. Just as a friend. They could be friends.

With benefits? No, no benefits!

"You don't have to," she said. "I'm already bothering you enough."

"It's no bother." He wanted to help Merilee. What was it about this woman?

"No," she said firmly. "You're doing enough keeping Queenie tonight." She laid a hand on his arm. "Thank you. So much." She looked at him like he was some kind of superhero.

"My pleasure," said Zach. Once upon a time the word

pleasure would have made him think of Blair. Tonight, a very different woman danced into his fantasy. His gaze strayed to Merilee's mouth. Those lips. He swallowed. Was it getting warm in here? Would she like to take off her coat? Would she like to take off something else? He stood suddenly, clearing his throat. "Well, then, is there anything I need to do to you, er, for her? The cat?"

Merilee's cheeks turned pink as she stood up. "No. Maybe keep her separate from Tom. You never know how a cat will act when a new cat comes into the house."

"She's pretty cute," said Zach. "I can imagine how he'd act." The same way he wanted to act right now. Merilee had nice legs. The top half of her was pretty damned nice, too. She had to be hot in that coat. He could just reach out and unzip . . . *Stop that!*

Zach ditched his four-legged houseguest in the laundry room just as Tom arrived on the scene, all curiosity. "She is not for you, dude," he informed the cat.

He said the same thing to himself as he returned to walk Merilee to the door.

They stopped in the hallway as if by mutual consent. She was wearing some kind of perfume that reminded him of flowers and bubble baths. Suddenly he pictured Merilee in a tub full of bubbles, wearing a Santa hat. Then, Merilee stepping out of a tub full of bubbles, wearing a Santa hat—better than visions of sugarplums. Joe Cocker's "You Can Leave Your Hat On," began to play in his head. It was definitely warm in here. Zach swallowed hard. *No more Santa hat visions,* he told himself firmly.

"Thanks again for helping me out," she said in that sweet, soft voice. "It's a relief to know Queenie will be okay for the night. I'll come by tomorrow around nine and get her, if that's all right."

He nodded. Then he said, "You know. I don't think you ever told me your last name." *You don't need to know her last name. What are you thinking?* Dumb question. He was thinking about Merilee in a Santa hat, of course.

"It's White."

Her lips puckered up so temptingly when she said her last name. Zach swallowed again. Then cleared his throat. Then nodded. "Okay. That's, uh, good to know." But it wasn't enough. "Maybe I'd better get your cell phone number. Just in case Queenie has a problem or something." Somebody here already had a problem and it wasn't Queenie.

"Good idea," she said, and gave it to him. "And maybe I should have yours. In case . . ."

"Yeah," he agreed. "Just in case," and gave it to her. She dug a piece of paper out of her purse and wrote it down.

Zach didn't need any paper. He already had Merilee's number committed to memory.

"I guess I'd better go," she said, standing right where she was.

"Yeah, I guess you'd better," he said, standing right where he was.

*O*h, *for the love of catnip, kiss her.* Ambrose watched from the end of the hallway. What was wrong with Zach anyway? He wanted this woman. It was so obvious even a dog could see it. Zach had scared off his rival and somehow lured Merilee back here, but instead of doing what he'd been made to do the stupid man was still acting like he'd been neutered.

He flicked his tail irritably as he watched Zach walk Merilee out of the house. Talk about a lost opportunity. At least a cat had nine lives to get things right. Humans got only one, and Zach was sure wasting his.

And that was not good, because someone else's life depended on Zach getting smart, someone's ninth and final life. Ambrose trotted anxiously back to the room where Zach had stowed their surprise visitor.

And what a wonderful surprise! That little white face peering out of the cage—he'd looked into those eyes and seen right into her soul.

He stood on his hind legs and scratched at the door. *Aphrodite, can you hear me?*

An indignant response drifted back to him. *Get lost, Blackie, you beast!*

Of course, what else would she think him? One moment they'd been mating and the next he'd been gone for good.

You left without so much as a meow good-bye.

He'd meant to come back. He'd planned to come back . . . until that horrible Blair Baby had taken him out with her car and her cell phone. That had been the end of both his sixth life and his first and only great love.

Aphrodite, I couldn't help it. I was hit by a car.

Silence.

I'll make it up to you.

More silence. Ambrose sat down and flicked his tail. Humans. Look how they messed things up for everyone else!

Merilee arrived to pick up Queenie promptly at nine the next morning.

"Oh, I didn't even think of bringing over her cat box," she said as she followed Zach into the laundry room where he'd outfitted Queenie with her own food, water bowl, and litter box. What a dork to forget something so basic. But with Mrs. Winnamucker breathing down her neck she hadn't thought much of anything except that she needed help and Zach was just the man to give her what she needed.

"I had one, so no big deal," he said. "I got it for Tom but he's been using his cat door and going outside." Queenie was enthroned on a pile of laundry sitting on top of the dryer. He picked her up and she draped herself over his shoulder and started purring. "She's a sweet cat," he said, stroking the animal's back.

Tom had slipped into the laundry room now and was looking up with interest at their guest. He meowed and, when Zach ignored him, stood on his hind legs and almost clawed at Zach's pants.

"I guess they would have gotten along fine," Merilee said with a smile.

"Sorry, dude," said Zach. "She's going to find a new home."

"I hope so," Merilee said. "I just can't stand to think of her being destroyed."

Tom jumped up onto the dryer and yowled.

"Looks like he can't either," Zach said. "Don't worry, dude. We'll save her."

He put Queenie's cat carrier on top of the washer. Merilee opened the carrier door and Zach gently put the cat inside. She meowed pitifully as the door shut behind her.

Merilee sighed.

"Are you sure you don't want some moral support?" he offered as he walked her to her car.

"I'm sure." Tempted as she was to simply hand over her problem to him, she'd already asked enough of him. Anyway, she could handle this. She opened the car door and Zach settled Queenie on the backseat.

"Tell the guy he'd better let you keep the cat or I'll come beat him with a fire hose."

She smiled. "I might just do that." Then she sobered. "Thank you for helping me out last night."

"I was glad to do it," he said. "You've got my cell number. Let me know how it turns out."

What if it didn't turn out well? Would he really want to know? She didn't even want to think about what she'd do if her plan didn't work. She nodded and slid in behind the wheel.

"Go get 'em," he said, and shut her door for her.

Go get 'em, her new mantra. She set her jaw and started the car.

Ten minutes later she was carrying Queenie into a small two-story office building on Angel Way. The bottom story housed a lawyer, a family therapist, and a yoga salon. The entire upper story belonged to Falls Property Management, which belonged to Mr. Richard Mook. She stepped inside the elevator and pushed the button for the second floor. Normally, she'd have simply walked up the stairs, but her heart was already beating so fast she was sure if she did she'd have a heart attack halfway up.

The elevator stopped with a bump and the door slid open to reveal a landing covered with new carpet. Directly in front of her was a door with a copper plate engraved with FALLS PROPERTY MANAGEMENT. She took a deep breath, tightened her grip on the cat carrier, and pushed open the door.

Inside the office she found a reception area holding a sleek leather couch and two matching chairs, a coffee table, a giant pot bearing some sort of palm, and a reception desk. At the desk sat a svelte, middle-aged woman with short salt-and-pepper hair wearing a stylish black suit and crisp white blouse. She smiled at Merilee and asked how she could help her.

"I need to see Mr. Mook," Merilee said.

"Do you have an appointment?" The woman eyed the cat carrier warily.

Merilee shook her head. "There wasn't time to make an appointment. It's an emergency. At one of his properties," she added.

The woman's eyebrows shot up. "What did you say your name was?"

"Merilee White."

The woman looked like she'd just swallowed vinegar. "I'm not sure he's available right now."

Obviously, Mrs. Winnamucker the tattletale had been busy this morning. "I'll wait until he is," Merilee said. She took a seat on the couch and set the cat carrier next to her. Queenie yowled.

Merilee wasn't sure whether it was her determined tone of voice or Queenie's crying that motivated the woman to vanish behind an oak door into the nether regions of the office but she didn't care. She sat back with a satisfied smile. "Maybe Mr. Mook is available after all," she told Queenie.

A moment later the woman was back. "I'm afraid Mr. Mook has a very full schedule."

Merilee's confidence vanished. Her heavy heart made it difficult to stand up and she got to her feet slowly. She'd lost the fight before she'd even gotten in the ring.

Queenie let out a yowl. *Help me!*

She couldn't give up. Queenie was depending on her. She raised her chin and drew back her shoulders. "I won't take more than five minutes of his time. Surely he could give five minutes to someone whose monthly rental check helps keep him in business. Or is he too big of a Scrooge?"

The woman blinked, then frowned.

Merilee sat back down. "I'll wait."

With a look of disgust the woman disappeared behind the door again.

Merilee's heart went into overdrive once more. *You can do this,* she told herself.

The woman returned, still looking disgusted, but she said, "Mr. Mook has a few minutes right now."

Merilee picked up Queenie and sailed past her through the door.

The inner sanctum held a large bookcase full of business tomes, another potted plant, a couple of lamps, a putting matt and golf club in one corner, a huge filing cabinet, and, dead ahead, a large mahogany desk sporting a laptop computer. Behind the desk sat a tall lean man as bald as Mr. Clean. He had sharp blue eyes, a pinched nose, and thin lips pressed together so tightly they looked more like a slash in a child's drawing than a real human mouth. He didn't exactly appear welcoming.

Merilee had thought her heart was beating fast before she came in here. That was nothing. Now it was banging around in her rib cage so hard she thought she might break a rib.

She swallowed. All her carefully rehearsed words fled from her mind and she clutched the cat carrier like a lifeline while casting about frantically for something to say.

Mr. Mook beat her to the punch. "Have a seat, Miss White. I understand from the apartment manager that you have a problem with our pet policy."

She nodded and slipped onto a big leather chair in front of the desk, setting Queenie's carrier on the floor. *Say something,* she told herself, but her mouth refused to cooperate.

"I hope you weren't coming here expecting us to change that," he continued.

It was now or never. "Actually, I was. It's unfair."

"Oh? To whom?"

"To your renters. And, I might add, that policy went into effect right after I signed my lease. I should be grandfathered in."

He raised an eyebrow. "And how long have you been a renter at the Angel Arms?"

"Ten months."

"Ten months. You didn't protest when you were told of the change in policy. You have, in fact, said nothing all along. In fact, I suspect the only reason you're saying something now is because you've been caught flagrantly disobeying the rules."

Merilee had never been the kind of child who got sent to the principal's office. Now she knew how it felt. She could feel her cheeks flaming and her tummy began juggling her breakfast, but she forced herself to speak calmly. "That was only temporary, until I could find a home for this cat." Wait until he saw Queenie. He'd understand. She started to open the cat carrier.

"Don't take the animal out, please," he said, holding up a hand.

So, he didn't want to see the victim of his callous policy. Would it make him uncomfortable? Hmmm. That meant he had a heart, probably one as thin as the rest of him, but a heart nonetheless. She took hope and her tummy stopped the juggling act.

He looked at his watch. "I'm afraid I have work to do, Miss White, so let's wrap up this visit, shall we? Mrs. Winnamucker tells me that, other than this one slip, you've been a reliable renter. So, if you would like to stay on at the Angel Arms—"

"I would, but I'd like you to consider changing your policy." Merilee's rehearsed speech came to her in a rush. "Mr. Mook, you're a businessman, so consider this from a business standpoint. Pet owners make good renters. They're responsible people who love their animals. They're willing to pay extra for the privilege of keeping their pets, so any damages could easily be covered. And, as a rule they stay longer since there are so few options for them."

"And do you know why there are so few options?" retorted Mr. Mook. "It's because most landlords have learned firsthand how much damage animals can do. Not all pet owners are responsible. I have rented to pet owners in the past, Miss White. I don't anymore for the simple reason that I got tired of cleaning up the messes they left behind. Dogs chew, cats ruin drapes. And although I've tried many products over the years I have learned that cat urine is close to impossible to get out of carpets. Dealing with that kind of destruction adds up to considerable expense and aggravation, so I have no intention of changing my policy."

"Not even to save a life?" In a bold move, Merilee set the cat carrier on Mr. Mook's desk. "Look at this sweet little kitty. She's litter box trained and well-behaved."

"Then I'm sure, if you take her to the animal shelter, she'll find a home," he said with a sickeningly pleasant smile.

This man did not get it. "People are too busy getting ready for the holidays. If I take her to the shelter she'll be destroyed."

He shrugged and made a what-can-I-do face. "I'm sorry for that, but in the end it's not my problem. My job is to provide housing. For people. Which is what I have done for you, and at a reasonable rate. I wish you the best of luck finding a home for the cat, but that is what you're going to have to do if you want to remain with us." Again, he looked at his watch. "Now, I'm afraid I must ask you to leave."

Inspiration came to Merilee like a gift from Santa. "Fine. I'll leave." She turned and started for the door.

"You forgot your cat," Mr. Mook said.

Merilee stopped and looked over her shoulder. "No, I didn't. I'm giving her to you. You can be responsible for taking this cat to the animal shelter just two days before Christmas."

She resumed her march for the door.

"Then I'll have my secretary deliver it today."

Merilee turned to see him removing the cat carrier from his desk. He set it on the floor with a careless thump.

He would. He actually would. Merilee dashed back and retrieved Queenie. "You have no heart."

He wasn't even remotely bothered by her scathing words. He merely shook his head. "And you have no common sense. But if you want to remain in your apartment I hope you'll find some and get rid of that animal. Otherwise, I'm afraid you'll have to find a new place to live."

"Don't worry," Merilee growled. "I won't be staying in your apartment any longer than necessary." She yanked the office door open. "Merry Christmas, Mr. Mook. If, after this, you can manage to have one."

"Merry Christmas to you, too, Miss White," he said as if they'd just met for a cup of coffee.

She managed to keep her head high as she left but by the time she reached her car she was crying. "Queenie, I'm so sorry."

A freezing rain began to pelt the windshield and Merilee could imagine the angels looking down from those fat gray clouds and weeping. A sweet kitty like Queenie going homeless or being destroyed—it wasn't right.

What now? No matter what Merilee decided one of them was going to be homeless.

"We're not going to give up," she told Queenie. "We'll get you all dolled up with a red ribbon and stand outside Safeway and show you off. Someone's bound to want you." Maybe. Hopefully.

Her favorite radio station was on holiday overload and Burl Ives was currently wishing her a holly jolly Christmas. She punched Burl into silence, switching instead to the local talk station.

The voice of Mandy Day greeted her. "Today we're talking about fabulous last-minute gift ideas. What's yours? Call us at 888-206-TALK."

Queenie let out a plaintive meow from her cat carrier. The message couldn't have been clearer if the cat had miraculously spoken English.

"I'm on it," Merilee said. She swerved onto the shoulder of the road and grabbed her cell phone from her purse.

TWELVE

Zach was just finishing painting his bathroom and wondering what was going on with Merilee when Mom called. Thank God for caller ID. He let it roll over to voicemail.

But by the time he'd stowed the paint can and cleaned his brush he was feeling guilty enough to check the message.

"I hope you can at least come by today, if even for a few minutes," said Mom. "The girls are going to be disappointed if you don't."

Yeah, use the Steps to lure me over, thought Zach in disgust as he started for the shower. For the Steps he'd come. Which meant he needed to do some Christmas shopping. He couldn't go over there the day before Christmas Eve with nothing for the girls.

What to get them? For a moment he considered gift cards to Heavenly Lattes since they were both caffeine addicts, but the idea of turning into his mother, the giftcard queen, made him reject the idea. Well, he'd think of something.

He was just pulling on his T-shirt when Ray called. "Hey, your friend Merilee's on the Mandy Day show."

"What?"

"AM 770. She's talking about pet adoption and she's got some white cat she's trying to give away."

Zach barely gave Ray a chance to finish talking. He ended the call, ran to his computer, and started streaming the program.

Merilee's voice danced out to him, reaching for his heart. "Yes, the shelter is open today, and you can still adopt an animal in time for Christmas."

"Well, this little white kitty you've been talking about sounds adorable," said Mandy.

"She is. She'd make a wonderful addition to some lucky family."

Suddenly, Zach knew just the lucky family. As soon as Merilee was off the air he called her. "Did anyone take your cat yet?"

"No, but I'm sure someone will," she said, forced cheer in her voice. "I'm on my way to the shelter with her right now."

"No need," Zach said. "I've got someone."

"You do? Really?"

"Yep. I'm going to give her to my stepsisters for Christmas. They'll spoil her to death."

"Oh, that's wonderful," said Merilee.

Hearing the relief in her voice made him feel like a superhero.

"Zach, I don't know how I can ever thank you," she said breathlessly.

A kiss would be good. No! No kisses.

"If you meet me at my place I can give you all of Queenie's things."

And a kiss.

No! No kisses, no . . . nothing.

He pulled into the parking lot of the Angel Arms just as Merilee was taking Queenie out of the back of her car. The way Merilee's eyes lit up at the sight of him made his heart swell with something he hadn't felt in a long time, something he refused to acknowledge.

"I'm so excited that you found a home for Queenie," she said as they loaded the cat into Zach's Land Rover.

"Glad to help," he said. No lie. He was genuinely glad to find a home for the cat. And come to Merilee's rescue. As a friend, a friend who wanted benefits. He gave himself a mental slap and put a civilized smile on his face as they walked together to her apartment.

Inside it was warm and cozy. He took in the little tree with its vintage ornaments and the tinsel garland she'd hung up. It made him think of old movies and women's magazines, in which everything looked perfect and enticing.

"This will just take me a minute," said Merilee. She bent and picked a cat toy off the floor, giving Zach a nice view of her curvy backside and making his mouth go dry. Then she was off to another part of the apartment, her voice echoing back to him, "I've got some extra cat litter left I can give you. And some cat food. Oh, and Queenie's toys."

How about a kiss? "Great," he called.

She had everything collected in a few minutes and soon Zach was standing in the doorway loaded up with cat litter, a cat box, and a bag filled with toys and cans of cat food, with nothing left to say. Well, he could think of things to say, none of them wise.

Good-bye. Say good-bye.

Merilee looked gratefully up at him. "I can't thank you enough," she said, and then she stood on tiptoe and kissed his cheek.

The next thing he knew the cat paraphernalia was

falling to the floor and he was drawing Merilee to him and making sure her lips connected with his this time around. She was soft and sexy and she smelled good and . . . what was he doing? He broke the kiss and put her firmly away from him.

She stood staring at him, her eyes wide.

"Sorry, that was out of line," he muttered.

"No, it wasn't." She grabbed his arms and pulled him back to her and latched onto his lips.

How could a man be rude and step away when a woman wanted him? Zach gave in to temptation and kissed her back and his greedy hands started a sneaky exploration of her curves. She moaned and the scouting party grew bolder.

And then, some rotten spoilsport voice at the back of his head demanded, "What do you think you're doing? This isn't some good-timing bimbo. This is a nice girl. If you're not going to go all the way to the altar back off."

Of course, the little voice was right. Zach pulled away.

She looked at him, confused. "Zach?"

"That was a bad idea."

"I didn't think so," she said softly.

"Well, it was," he assured her, and knelt to pick up the things he'd dropped.

She knelt, too. "Zach, what you said the other night, is that the only reason you don't want to be with me? I mean, it isn't . . . is there something wrong with me?" she finished in a small voice.

"No. Don't even go there." How could he explain heart failure to someone with a perfect family and a perfect life, someone who was loved and obviously had no trouble giving love? He stood up, fumbling with everything and grabbing for the door handle. "Look, I've got to go. Uh, Merry Christmas," he added stupidly, and backed out the door.

He left the apartment at a brisk pace and was practically running by the time he got to the parking lot. Once he reached the Land Rover he put the collection of cat goodies into the back and then fell in behind the steering wheel and let out a long breath.

Queenie meowed, reminding him that he had one more female to get rid of.

The sooner the better, he told himself.

Merilee collapsed on her couch and gave the cushion a furious slap. This wasn't right. How could a man kiss a woman with such passion and then run away? And not just any man, the perfect man. It wasn't right. It was so . . . un-Christmas.

A knock on the door brought her up and instantly off the couch. He'd come back. She knew he would! Dashing away her tears, she ran to the door and yanked it open.

There stood Mrs. Winnamucker, her lips pursed into a prim smile. "I just stopped by to see if you'd found . . ." She stopped mid-sentence, taking in Merilee's tear-stained face and unhappy expression. "Oh, my dear, are you all right?"

"Yes, I found a home for the cat," Merilee snapped. "And no, I'm not. Merry Christmas," she added, and shut the door in Mrs. Winnamucker's face.

The aroma of chocolate and cinnamon tickled Zach's taste buds the minute he walked through the front door of his mother's house. It smelled like Mom and the Steps had been busy baking. The aroma triggered memories from his early childhood, back when he'd had a mother and a father in the same house and his life had been cocooned inside a false sense of security. Mom had always made cookies for Santa and then let Zach and David consume most of them.

That was another woman, another time.

This woman still looked like a stranger to him. Her brown hair was salted with gray and she'd gained a few pounds over the years. She was still a good-looking woman, though. Today she looked put-together in a simple black sweater and jeans. Looking at her, Zach thought of Martha Stewart (only without the ankle monitor).

"Thanks for stopping by," she greeted him. "Now it finally feels like Christmas." She kissed him on the cheek and gave him a hug.

He gave her a shadow of a hug in return, then broke away. The disappointment in her eyes made him feel guilty.

Except he had nothing to feel guilty about. He hadn't abandoned anyone. Anyway, he was here. That should be enough for her. He held up the cat carrier. "I brought a present for the girls."

She followed his lead, stepping away from the awkward moment and peering into the carrier. "Well, aren't you cute," she cooed.

"Think they'll like her?"

"Absolutely." Mom went to the foot of the stairs and called, "Kendra, Natalie, your brother's here."

It was only a matter of seconds before he heard feet rushing along the upstairs hall. Then Natalie was running down the stairs, blond hair flying. "Zachie!"

Behind her came Kendra, the oldest, her pace a little slower, but her smile just as big. "About time you came by," she said when she took her turn to hug him.

"Just dropping off your Christmas present," he said.

"I guess that means you have to work tomorrow," said Kendra, her voice full of disapproval.

"Afraid so." He bent to take Queenie from her cat carrier.

"Oh, my gosh, a kitty!" squealed Natalie, taking the cat from him and snuggling her close. "I always wanted a cat. You are such a smart brother," she added, beaming up at him.

That was him, Mr. Smart. "Her name's Queenie."

"She's adorable," said Kendra, running a hand along Queenie's head. "Thanks."

"Queenie. That's so cute," said Natalie. "Queen of the house. Queen of our hearts."

Gag me, thought Zach. Still, he was pleased that his present was a hit. Merilee would be glad to hear it.

Never mind Merilee. She is out of the picture.

But not out of his thoughts, where she was firmly camped out wearing that Santa hat.

He dragged his mind back to the moment at hand. "You've got to keep an eye on this cat," he warned. "She likes to try and go outside."

"Well, then, maybe we should let her," said Mom, as the girls danced over to the living room couch with the new baby.

Zach watched as Natalie pulled out her cell phone to snap a picture. "No. She'd get hurt out there. Anyway, outside cats can pick up diseases."

His mother cocked an eyebrow. "You're becoming quite an animal expert these days. Where did you get all this information, anyway?"

"From a friend." The minute the words were out of his mouth he knew he'd made a mistake. His mother's radar had picked up something.

"What kind of friend?"

Zach shrugged. "Just a friend."

"As in nobody we get to ask about," Kendra translated with a cocked eyebrow of her own.

"As in, go play with your cat," he retorted and she stuck her tongue out at him.

"I've got your gift in the kitchen," said Mom, starting to lead the way through the living room.

Zach balked. "I should get going."

"Just stay a few minutes," she urged. "I'll make you a cup of coffee."

Zach gave up. She'd managed to give him a few good years. He could give her a few minutes.

In the kitchen he saw the plate of cookies wrapped in red cellophane sitting on the oak table and his mouth watered like he was one of Pavlov's dogs. There were the chocolate balls she used to make, the frosted Christmas trees, and the gingerbread boys.

She caught him looking at it and said, "Yes, those are for you."

He nodded, his neck stiff with embarrassment.

"Sit down," she said, and he perched on the edge of a chair. "I'm so glad you could come by."

He couldn't think of anything to say to that, at least nothing that would ring true, so he simply nodded again.

She poured him a mug of coffee and set it in front of him, then nudged the sugar bowl his direction. "Sugar?" She bit her lip and shook her head. "I don't even know what you take in your coffee. How pathetic is that?"

"Pretty pathetic," he informed her. Just like her mothering skills.

Amazingly, she seemed to have done okay by the Steps. He took a sip of coffee. Bitter.

She sat across the table from him now, picking at a perfectly manicured fingernail. "You know my biggest regret?"

"No, but I bet you're going to tell me." Now he sounded snotty, just like he had when she'd first asked him what he thought of Al, like he'd sounded after she'd informed him she was leaving and he and David were staying behind with Dad. He frowned.

She sighed deeply. "My biggest regret is that I didn't make you come with me when we moved."

"Make me? You never even gave me the option. Shit, Mom, are we doing revisionist history here?"

"Zach," she began.

He held up a hand. "Let's not go there."

"I think we need to."

"I don't need to," he said, pushing away from the table.

"Zach, wait," she pleaded. "I want you to know, I didn't want to leave you and David."

Okay, enough. "But you did." He stood up. He felt like he was towering over her.

Her eyes filled with tears. "I didn't want to uproot you and take you away from your friends."

So she'd just made his decision for him. "Well, that explains everything, like why we hardly heard from you all those years."

"I . . ." She hung her head.

Yeah. You. That about summed it up. Zach left the kitchen just as Kendra was coming in. "Are you leaving already?"

"I've got to go," he said. Before he really let Mom have it.

"But you just got here," Kendra protested, trailing after him.

"I'll catch up with you guys later."

They were in the living room again now. Natalie sprang from the couch, Queenie draped over her shoulder. "You can't leave yet, Zachie," she protested.

"Sorry," he said tersely.

"Where are your cookies? You forgot your cookies," Natalie said.

Zach shook his head and kept walking. "Thanks anyway. I'm not hungry." In fact, he felt like he was going to puke.

A visit to the gym didn't help him feel any better.

Neither did grabbing a burger on the way home. Once he was back inside his house, he pulled a Coke out of the fridge and then went into the living room, determined to leave behind all thoughts of his messed-up past. He flopped onto the couch and grabbed the TV remote. Tom appeared out of nowhere and jumped onto his lap. "Hey, buddy," he said, and patted the cat. "It's just us guys to-night. No women. Who needs 'em?"

The cat stopped purring and twitched his tail.

"Trust me. You're better off on your own," Zach said, and aimed the remote at the TV. But in all of Cable Land he found nothing to grab his attention. Nothing in his Net-flix queue interested him either. He switched off the TV and tossed the remote aside. He looked at Tom and Tom looked right back, his tail whipping back and forth.

"Yeah, I know. Can't live with 'em. Can't live without 'em. But we're going to, dude."

The determined affirmation sent him to the kitchen in search of beer. Then he returned to the living room and picked up the book he'd ordered from Amazon, *The Handyman Handbook,* and dove in.

CHAPTER ONE: TOOLS EVERY MAN NEEDS.

Never mind tools. What every man needs is a good woman's love.

Okay, that was enough sitting on the couch. He needed to do something, like take an inventory of what he had.

He already owned a lot of the basics: hammers and screwdrivers, wrenches, pliers, and a circular saw. But some of the items mentioned in the book, like a miter box, staple gun, grinder, and C-clamps, he still needed.

Wait a minute. Didn't he have C-clamps in that old toolbox Dad had given him when he moved out? What else was in there? He couldn't remember right off. Well, now was as good a time as any to find out.

He made his way to the second floor, Tom trotting up the stairs beside him. "What a man needs," he informed the cat, "is to stay busy." He pulled the chain that let down the ladder and climbed up into the attic with Tom still along for the ride.

Due to the steep pitch of the roof, Zach had to stoop until he got into the middle of the room. He looked around him and frowned. Chamber of Horrors II.

The attic of his childhood home, dubbed the Chamber of Horrors by his dad, had been a collection of everything imaginable, from birdcages that had outlasted the bird to childhood toys. One of the biggest messes in the attic had been the boxes of Christmas decorations which his mother had collected since the Mayflower landed. She would spend hours decorating the house each year, always in new colors and motifs. Every year Mom replenished her stock. Zach remembered Dad saying that he would sooner be dragged by the devil into hell than have to schlep any more Christmas stuff up to the attic. But the cache of holiday decorations continued to breed, right along with all the other household detritus—everything from winter boots to washers for the kitchen sink wound up in there, all in boxes, none of them labeled. It became a vortex, sucking in everything and anything.

Zach looked at the mess around him and shook his head. How did people manage to collect so much stuff so quickly? Over there by the far wall was the basketball hoop he'd taken when he moved out. He'd hauled that dumb thing from apartment to apartment. And now it was here even though he was planning on selling this place and moving to a condo. What did he think he was going to do with a basketball hoop in a condo?

That was just the beginning. He wove past the neglected markers of his life, wondering why he was keeping all this stuff. There were skis and poles and boots he hadn't used in the last two years, his lacrosse stick and gloves from high school, boxes of textbooks he'd never read again, and Gram's old rocking chair that he was going to get around to refinishing one of these years. There was the box of Christmas ornaments, souvenirs from happier times. Mom had left them behind for him along with a note that read, "For your first tree, when you have a family of your own."

Dad had insisted he take them. Why was he keeping them? God only knew.

He was halfway across the attic when he caught sight of the box with his Nintendo. He and David used to play that all the time. Now, that would be fun to haul down and . . .

He never finished his thought. Too distracted by the sight of the old game, he forgot to watch where he was walking and tripped over the runner on the rocking chair. Down he went, doing a face plant with a thud and a curse, raising enough dust to give himself a sneezing fit. What was he doing up here anyway?

"Forget this," he decided.

But just as he was getting to his feet, Tom jumped onto a pile of boxes. It had been stacked haphazardly and the landing wasn't a success. The top box tipped over and as Tom leaped for safety it broke open, spilling crap across the floor. *Lovely.*

Zach scowled at Tom, who was now crouching in a corner, ready to bolt if anything new toppled. "Thanks a lot, dude," he grumbled.

Tom flicked his tail, not happy with getting scolded.

"Yeah? Well, I'm not happy cleaning up after you. What do you think of that?"

The cat kept his thoughts to himself.

Zach had come up here to stay busy. He heaved a re-signed sigh and made his way over to the box, which held a collection of mementos: his first baseball mitt, a couple of Little League trophies, his high school diploma, senior prom picture, and some photo albums. He took one and plopped onto the floor cross-legged, all the while telling himself he was a fool. Going down memory lane was fun for some people, but his particular path was tangled with thorns.

Tom joined him now, and rubbed up against him as he opened it. "You're lucky you're a cat," he muttered. "No problems."

Tom meowed and rubbed again.

"And no, I'm not feeding you now. I'm busy." Wandering uselessly down that thorny memory lane, for no good reason. Except that he was already irritated and wanted to get good and pissed off? Maybe.

He thumbed through the album, seeing snapshots of himself in his Little League uniform, at Christmas with his first pocket knife (the one he managed to cut himself with less than two hours after opening the present), at the ocean with his dog Dexter, sitting on the deck, drinking lemonade and hamming it up for the camera with his brother, his best friend Henry, and Henry's sister Anna. In the background, lolling on a deck chair with a drink in her hand, sat Aunt Leslie.

Aunt Leslie. It had been the greatest day in Zach's young life when she and her two kids moved in next door. She'd been his mom's best friend and their two families did everything together. He still remembered how sad he felt when Aunt Leslie moved away and took his friends with her.

Now, searching through the mists of time, he re-membered another thing: his mother on the phone with his grandmother, saying, "She can't move soon enough for me."

Why?

What did it matter? That was just another relationship his mother decided wasn't worthy of her. He closed the album with a snap. Small wonder he didn't do relationships well, given the example he'd had.

Except Mom hadn't been the only one scrambling his psyche. There was another album in that box, the one he hadn't wanted to open, containing pictures of him with Ella, the last woman he'd ever been serious about, on the night they got engaged. They'd been crazy in love, or so he'd thought until she dropped him and broke his heart.

You were already pulling away.

"I was not!" Zach insisted forcefully enough to make Tom jump and dash to the other side of the attic.

He got up and tossed the album and the other useless junk back in the box. Then he picked up Tom and went downstairs to find a TV sitcom, where life was nothing but laughs and problems were solved in half an hour.

Ambrose was puzzled. Something in one of those picture books he'd helped Zach find when he tipped open that box had made Zach stop and do what humans seemed to need to do a lot: Think. Then he'd thrown things back in the box and he and Tom had left that interesting treasure room. Now Zach looked sad, always a bad condition for a human.

What happened? For the first time in his lives, Ambrose found himself feeling badly for someone else. Discouraged, too. He had tried his best to help Zach and obviously he'd failed. You can only do so much, he reminded himself. Ultimately, like every other creature, humans had to make their own choices and then live with the results.

Well, Zach would live with them. Ambrose, on the other hand, was on his ninth life and running on fumes. This wasn't good, not at all.

THIRTEEN

There was always plenty to do at the station, but Christmas Eve brought an extra duty. As soon as it turned dark it was time to take the truck, all decked out for the holidays, and visit the various neighborhoods, serenading residents with Christmas songs. This year it was Zach's turn to be Santa and toss mini candy canes to all the neighborhood kids.

"We need another pillow," Ray decided, eyeing Zach's costume. "Man, you just don't fill that thing out."

"Then let's put you in it. We won't need any pillows," Zach retorted.

"Amber thinks I'm just fine the way I am," said Ray, untouched by the barb.

"She's known you what, twenty-four hours? Give her time."

"We've known each other longer than that."

"E-mailing on HotHookUps.com," Zach said in disgust.

"You can learn a lot about a person that way," Ray insisted. "Anyway, we've had a date." He grinned. "She's really nice. And man, is she hot. Almost as hot as Merilee."

At least this new chick had distracted Ray from Merilee. That was a good thing.

"We should all go out," Ray said as he shoved another pillow at Zach.

"This isn't going to fit," Zach said with a frown.

Ray snatched back the pillow. "Never mind. Nobody's gonna climb in the truck to see how fat you are anyway. We need to get going."

And so off they went, armed with prerecorded music and the appropriate equipment to blast it loud enough to wake the dead, the truck decorated with lights and a huge Christmas wreath on its front, Ray driving and Zach hanging out the window, waving like some fool on a parade float. He much preferred the Fourth of July. Then they cruised down Angel Way with the siren at full tilt, looking buff in their uniforms. In this stupid red suit Zach looked like he'd escaped from the mall.

But this was a town tradition. When the truck rolled into a neighborhood playing "Here Comes Santa Claus" kids ran along the sidewalk, leaping for the candy Santa tossed. Senior citizens watched from their front windows, and moms and dads with little ones waved from their front porch.

As they drove through Falls View Estates one couple in particular held Zach's attention. They stood in the doorway of a modest house encrusted with lights, its yard sporting a manger scene. They were young, standing so close together they looked as though they were one person, and the dad held a baby in his arms.

That could be you.

Zach quickly pushed away the thought as the truck left the housing development and rumbled off down the road.

Yeah, the couple looked happy. They probably were, for now. But it wouldn't last.

His reasonable argument should have popped that little bubble of longing. It always had in the past. But not this time. Something inside him insisted, *Don't be stupid—do you want to end up bitter and alone like old man Turner?* End up that way? He was already there.

Next thing he knew, they'd turned and were circling the parking lot of the Angel Arms Apartments. Merilee's place. Except Merilee wasn't there. She'd be with her family by now, maybe getting ready to eat dinner. What did her parents look like? How did they look at each other across the table?

Ray gave him a shove. "Hey, turkey, smile!"

Zach forced the corners of his lips up. Why was he in a funk? His life wasn't so bad.

Maybe not so good, either. They had just returned to the station when the holiday fun began. Dad called to check in. Zach looked at the caller I.D. on his cell and was tempted to let it roll over to voicemail. He loved his father, but he didn't love hearing from Dad on Christmas Eve. It took three rings for the responsible half of his brain to override his reluctance. He picked up and said a wary hello.

"Hi, son," Dad began. "I was just thinking about you."

Dad was always thinking about him on Christmas Eve. And David. And Mom. Especially Mom. Especially after Dad had tossed back a couple of holiday drinks.

"How're you doing, Dad?" Zach asked and braced himself for an answer.

For a moment his father didn't speak and all Zach heard was the tinkling of ice. That would be Dad stirring his Scotch on the rocks with his finger. "Oh, fine. Got the cigars you sent. Thanks. Did you get my check?"

"Uh, yeah. Thanks." He should have called the week

before when it came, before Dad got feeling too sentimental.

"I thought maybe you could use it to buy a plane ticket to come see your old man this summer. It's been awhile."

"Yeah, it has." He should go see his dad. Except every visit somehow turned into a thinly disguised interrogation about Mom. Kind of like Dad's annual Christmas Eve call. Any minute now . . .

Sure enough. "How's your mother? Have you talked to her?"

"Yeah, she's good."

Another silence fell, broken only by the tinkling of ice. "Well, that's good. I'm glad she's happy." Dad heaved a big sigh. "You know, after all these years I still miss her. You kids grew up so fast. You know that? How're you doing, son? I miss you."

"We'll get together this summer," Zach promised.

"We had good times, you know."

"I know, Dad. How's Diane?" Zach asked in an attempt to steer the conversation in a less maudlin direction.

Now the silence went on for so long Zach wondered if the connection had been lost.

"Dad?"

"We're separated."

"I'm sorry," Zach said.

And he truly was. The old man couldn't seem to catch a break. Maybe the fact that he was making a habit of allowing Mom to haunt his life like the Ghost of Christmas Past had something to do with why wife number three had left him to ring in the holidays by himself.

It had been only three years ago that Zach had attended his father's wedding—a catered affair at the home of Dad's new in-laws, who were all of six years older than Dad. The champagne had flowed right along with the good wishes. The bride had looked at Dad like he was some kind of paperback hero, and Zach had hoped for the best. Apparently he'd hoped in vain.

Most people did. True love was myth.

"Oh, well. You know we really weren't right together," Dad said philosophically. "No one's ever been right for me but your mother."

Obviously Mom hadn't agreed. Zach frowned.

"When you find the right woman, son, hold on to her." The ice tinkled. "That's all I'm saying."

Zach sincerely hoped so. He didn't know how much more of this he could take. "Well, here's hoping the new year will be better for you."

"My life's in the toilet, son. How'd you say your mother is?"

"She's fine." *She's moved on. You should, too.*

"And how are you?"

Oh, boy. "I'm fine, Dad."

"Are you going to come see me this summer?"

Didn't they just have this conversation? "Sure."

"Maybe we should go to Australia and see your brother. Three bachelors living it up down under, eh?"

Picking up women in Australia with his father—there was a visual Zach was going to have trouble losing. "That's a thought," he said diplomatically. By morning Dad wouldn't even remember he'd called, let alone what they'd talked about. Thank God. "Listen, Dad. I'm on duty. I'd better go."

"Go? Oh, yeah. Sure. Well, Merry Christmas, son. Don't forget you're coming to see me this summer."

"I won't," Zach promised.

By summer Dad would probably be getting married again and Zach would find himself at another garden wedding. Poor Dad. Did Mom have any idea what she'd done to him?

Probably not. Maybe she never meant to hurt him.

Maybe they were drifting apart long before they split. Except they'd seemed fine. Everything had seemed fine . . . until it wasn't.

Who knew what happened to anyone? People started out madly in love and then just wound up hurting each other. To get serious with anyone was asking for trouble. There was always somebody in the equation who messed things up. That thought opened the door for more unpleasant thoughts and visions of a not-so-good Christmas future, so Zach gave himself a mental shake and went in search of distraction.

Ray had popped in the DVD of *National Lampoon's Christmas Vacation* and the guys were settled around the TV with store-bought Christmas cookies and popcorn. Some laughs, some downtime with his buddies—perfect. Just what he needed. He helped himself to some popcorn and settled in a chair for what he hoped would be a quiet night. After the conversation with his father he needed it.

The night was quiet until the call came in at ten.

The Klaxon went off, shooting everybody off the couch like human fireworks. Then the information from CenCom came in over the intercom and it went through Zach like a bolt of electricity.

Men grabbed their self-contained breathing apparatus and their personal protective equipment and raced for the truck. Meanwhile the printer spat out the information, proof in black-and-white that Zach hadn't imagined what he'd just heard.

In a matter of seconds they were on the truck and roaring down the street, battling the clock as well as the blaze, knowing it took only eight minutes for a house fire to spread from one room to another.

Adrenaline was not normally a factor. After a man had been doing this for a while, he concentrated on working with his team and getting the job done in the most efficient manner possible. Get the details, get the engine in place and the hose hooked up.

This time was different, though. Zach's adrenaline was flowing like a raging river as the truck roared across town, siren blasting. He knew the address where they were going. Still, he kept thinking, *Not my family. Dear God, not my family.* Suddenly it didn't matter that his mom had turned his childhood upside down and married someone new, that another man had moved into his life and then moved them all in different directions. All that mattered was to get everyone out alive.

By the time the truck arrived fire was chewing up the cast side of the house where the bedrooms were located. The neighborhood was all dressed up for Christmas, with lights on the houses and wreaths on the doors. A light snowfall was beginning to dust the ground. The blazing house made a mockery of the holiday scene. Flames licked the night sky and sparks flew dizzily from the smoke, arcing out like tiny demons.

A crowd of people had gathered on the street, many still in their holiday best, others with coats thrown on over bathrobes. Zach quickly spotted Mom and Kendra and Natalie. They were still dressed, wrapped in blankets and huddled together, holding each other and crying while a well-meaning neighbor attempted to console Mom by patting her shoulder.

But where was Al? Where the hell was Al?

FOURTEEN

At the sight of the truck, Zach's mother left the girls and raced up to him. Tears were making a crooked river down her soot-streaked face. Her hair was wild. So were her eyes. "Al's not here!"

Oh, no. Zach was going to be sick. *Do your job,* he told himself.

He let Daniel the company officer intercept her. It was Daniel's job to get that kind of information and form a plan of attack. "Where is he at?" Daniel asked Mom as Zach and the others donned their gear and covered their necks and ears with protective fluid to shield themselves from flash burns.

"I don't know. He went to get the cat."

Into the house? He went back in for the cat? What had he been thinking? Never run back inside when your house is on fire.

Daniel immediately began calling in vital information. "Single family dwelling, ten-zero-seven P.M. Two-story, wood frame. Fire on the first extending to the second. Possible rescue . . ."

A million thoughts banged at Zach's brain as he donned his gear and grabbed his ax and fire extinguisher.

What am I going to find when I get inside the house? Al dead in there? Unconscious? If only I'd traded with someone and gotten Christmas Eve off I could have prevented this.

The wild thoughts were counterproductive. Once more, he pushed them away and went to work. Ray, as engineer, was staying with the truck, taking care of the water supply, and Julio was already stretching a line. The medics were in place and the ladder truck had arrived. As Zach raced for the house he could see his pals Pete and Jason out of the corner of his eye, preparing to go up the roof and cut holes in it.

Zach had just reached the front porch when Al staggered around the side of the house, coughing and carrying Queenie. *Thank God,* he thought, as he helped his stepfather away from the blazing ruin that once was his home. Al would be spending Christmas in the hospital, the house would be unlivable for months and its contents ruined by smoke, but the family was alive. They'd be all right. Holding firmly to that belief, Zach entered the house, Daniel now right behind him.

The inside was an inferno, filled with angry flames bent on destruction. Within five minutes Zach was sweating inside his protective gear like a pig roasting over a spit. The stairs collapsed like a child's tower of blocks. He moved quickly and carefully, putting out the flame. Memory raced across his mind, showing Natalie and Kendra, a little first-grader and a preschooler, running eagerly downstairs ahead of him on Christmas morning. *Santa came! Come on, Zachie. Hurry!* Ancient history, but now important history.

He and Daniel finally stopped the last fiery tongues before they could devour the kitchen and family room. The rest of the house was toast.

It only took minutes to subdue the flames. It would take hours to do salvage and overhaul and investigate the area of origination. That wasn't Zach's job, but since his engine was the first on the scene, they'd still be the last ones out.

When the worst was over, he took a minute to check on his family. Al was long gone, whisked away by the ambulance, and Mom was trying to comfort the Steps, who were both crying.

"It's all my fault," wailed Natalie. "I forgot about my scented candle. It must have caught my curtains on fire."

"If we hadn't all been watching *Miracle on 34th Street* in the family room we'd have been dead," said Kendra. She shivered and rubbed her arms and Natalie sobbed harder.

Mom hugged them both close. "But we're not. We're all together and that's the main thing."

"You guys can stay at my place," Zach told his mom. "There's a spare key under that rock by the back porch."

"I'll get the girls settled and then go to the hospital," said Mom. Her voice was steady but she looked like she'd aged ten years.

Zach gave her a hug. "I'll be home day after tomorrow."

"Oh no, you won't," said his battalion chief. "You're off after we get done here. Spend some time with your family."

Amazingly, that sounded like a great idea.

No one got to bed before two A.M., so Zach had been sure Mom and the Steps would sleep the sleep of the dead. He hadn't figured on his mother prowling the house. He'd given her his bedroom and the Steps and Queenie were in Gram's old brass bed in the other room, while Zach sacked out on the couch in the living room with Tom curled up at his feet. But off and on he'd heard the faint creak of floorboards upstairs. At six he'd heard his mother slip downstairs and pad into the kitchen. The light didn't go on, though. Instead, she sat there in the dark. At six thirty he gave up and joined her.

She blinked and looked guilty when he walked into the room and flipped on the light. "Did I wake you?"

"Nah." She looked so forlorn. And alone. He leaned over and kissed her cheek, a gesture that felt both foreign and right. She smelled like his body wash. He made a mental note to pick up some girl stuff for her and the Steps. And some more body wash for himself. Between his mother and his stepsisters, they'd go through everything he had in a hurry. Natalie had taken two showers before she finally crashed, claiming she could still smell smoke. He'd heard her in there sobbing as the water ran.

Mom put a hand to his face, maybe to see if he was really there or if she'd imagined what just happened. "Thank you," she whispered.

"Hey, I wasn't going to leave you out on the street."

"No, for . . ." Her voice failed her and she looked at her hands, clenched tightly in her lap.

"You should try and get some more sleep," he said gently. He knew it was a futile suggestion. She wasn't going to be able to sleep any easier than Nat was going to be able to forgive herself.

She shook her head. "I can't. I . . ." She stopped, obviously choking on emotion, and shook her head.

Zach had seen the faces of stricken fire victims before, but they'd always been a sad blur on the sidelines as he raced to save what he could of their homes. This was different, a punch to the gut.

He sat down opposite her and reached across the table

to take her hand. "Al's going to be okay. You know that, right?"

She bit her lip and nodded. "I'm thankful we're alive, but it's all so hard to process. I don't even know where to start. I'm concerned about Natalie, that she won't be able to forgive herself."

"It was an accident," Zach said. "Accidents happen."

"That's easy to say when you're not the one responsible." Mom rubbed her forehead.

"I've got ibuprofin," Zach offered.

She shook her head. "I found it. I've already taken two. Zach." She bit her lip, watching him with teary eyes. "Can you ever forgive me?"

Five little words, but they flooded Zach with a tidal wave of emotions so strong he thought his chest would crack open—everything from anger to yearning, vindication to shame. "Oh, Mom." What was he supposed to say? What was he supposed to think?

"I don't blame you for not wanting anything to do with me. I wish I could redo the last fifteen years."

Fifteen? Longer than that. She needed to start the clock ticking from when she threw Dad out. Zach rubbed his aching head.

"Every time I called you were so angry. I just . . . stopped. I was a coward. And I was a rotten mother to you."

There it was, what he'd been waiting to hear for years. It should have made him feel better but it only made him want to bawl like a baby.

"Oh, Zach, I wish I could hit rewind. I'd do so many things different."

Now she was crying in earnest, her grief so strong it was an ocean that threatened to drown them both. Zach knelt beside her and wrapped his arms around her. "It's okay, Mom." Was it? He didn't even know at this point but it was all he could think to say. He, too, wished they could hit rewind, but the only way open to them was forward.

Maybe forward wasn't such a bad direction to go.

She got herself under control and managed a watery smile. "You grew into a wonderful man. I'm happy for that."

The observation didn't sit comfortably. "I think we need some breakfast," he decided.

She started to get up but he waved her back into her seat. "I can handle it. What do you want?"

"Just coffee."

"Coffee and eggs," Zach decided, and got to work. "It's going to be a long day."

She sighed. "I suspect it's going to be a succession of long days."

Breakfast was silent, a time of recovery from the emotional storm they'd just survived. Afterward his mother went upstairs to shower and dress.

Another hour crawled past, and Zach found himself feeling very much at loose ends. He loaded the dishes, he walked back to the couch and thumbed through a magazine, he paced. And as he paced he looked around his house. There was nothing here that said Christmas. Was that good or bad?

By nine, one of his mom's friends had swept her off to the hospital to see Al, and Kendra had surfaced. Zach knew as he watched his stepsister looking around with a trembling lip that the day was not starting well, but he had no idea how to make it better.

"Want some coffee?" he asked, trying to sound cheerful.

She nodded and followed him out to the kitchen and opened a cupboard in search of a mug. "Over here," he said, opening a door and grabbing one for her.

She thanked him and took it, poured herself some coffee. "Where's Angie?"

The Steps had never called his mother "Mom," just like he'd never called Al "Dad." They'd never been the Brady Bunch. Was it too late to try? "She went to see your dad at the hospital."

Kendra frowned. "She should have waited. I'd have gone with her." Now she was gnawing on a corner of her lower lip, and Zach knew exactly what she was thinking.

"He's going to be okay," he said.

She dropped onto a chair and scowled at him like it was somehow his fault her father was in the hospital. "How do you know? How do you know he's not going to get emphysema or something because of this?"

He would rather have been in a burning building than here in this kitchen trying to figure out what to say to his miserable stepsister. He took a deep breath. "You're right. I can't give you a money-back guarantee. But you know what, there are no guarantees. Meanwhile, he's getting the best care possible." Now Kendra's baby blues were turning into a sea of tears. *Oh, no.* "Hey, now, don't cry," Zach pleaded.

Too late. She burst into sobs. "Poor Daddy."

Zach found himself kneeling in front of that same kitchen chair once more, trying to make things right. He was trained to put out fires, not to offer grief counseling, and he felt his inadequacies like a boulder on his shoulders.

Half an hour later Natalie joined them and there were more tears. "It's all my fault," she wailed.

"Hey, now," Zach said sternly, "don't go saying stuff like that."

"But it is," Nat insisted.

Well, yeah, in a way. People got careless, especially at the holidays. But, he pointed out, "You're not an arsonist. It's not like you set out to start a fire. Shit happens, Nat."

"Our house is ruined," she sobbed. "And so is Christmas."

"No, it's not." Zach held her at arm's length and gave her his sternest big-brother look. "Everyone's alive and we're together and *that's* what matters. And it's still Christmas, so after breakfast we're going to go get a tree."

"We don't have any ornaments," said Natalie. "I burned them all up." With that she burst into fresh tears.

"I've got ornaments," said Zach.

Kendra looked dubious. "You do?"

He frowned at her. "What do I look like, the Grinch?"

"Your house looks like his headquarters," she retorted, softening the slam with a teasing smile.

"Well, we're going to change that." He marched to the kitchen cupboard and grabbed a box of pancake mix. Then he pulled out a big metal bowl. "We're going to fuel up with a good breakfast and then we're going out and getting a tree."

He put his sisters to work setting the table while he made pancakes. Of course, that turned out to be a waste. He set out a huge stack but neither girl ate more than one. In fact, Natalie only managed one bite, then spent the next ten minutes pushing what was left around her plate.

"Have another," he said to her, nudging the platter in her direction.

She just shook her head.

Like another pancake would make her feel better? What a dope he was.

What would Merilee of the perfect family do? And why on earth was he thinking about her at a time like this? Maybe it was because she seemed to have her act together. In fact, it sounded like her whole family did. How did people manage that, anyway? He didn't know but he hoped he'd learn.

"Okay, then," he tried, "let's go get us a tree."

Ten minutes later he had the girls bundled up in a couple of his cast-off jackets and gloves that swallowed their hands and they were in his Land Rover, all the necessary tree-toting ingredients in the back—ax, gloves, rope, tarp—and headed for Grandma's Christmas Tree Farm two miles outside of town, serenaded by Christmas songs on the radio. A few stray snowflakes drifted lazily toward the ground, framing gaily decorated houses with a touch of winter. Both the Steps were normally big talkers, but this morning they remained unnervingly quiet. Zach stole a look at them. Kendra was lost in dark thoughts and Natalie was surreptitiously wiping tears from her eyes as she looked out the window.

"Hey now, you two, everything's going to be okay." It would be. Somewhere down the road, it would be. They could rebuild the house. And while they were at it, maybe they could build a family.

Kendra reached out and took her sister's gloved hand and squeezed it. "He's right. We're alive and we're together."

"I know. But Daddy . . ." Natalie's voice broke.

"Will be okay," Zach assured her. "Who knows? They may even let him come home today."

"I doubt it," said Kendra, making Natalie's tears flow again.

Thank you, Kendra. He frowned at her.

"Sorry," she muttered.

"Well, he'll be home soon," Zach insisted. "So let's get the biggest kick-ass Christmas tree we can find to give him a good welcome. Okay?"

Both girls nodded and he breathed a little easier. Things were looking up.

Until they got to Grandma's Christmas Tree Farm and saw the gate across the road with the big CLOSED sign on it. Grandma was obviously too busy cooking Christmas dinner to bother with customers on Christmas day. Hardly surprising. People already had their trees.

Kendra cocked a mocking eyebrow at Zach as if it was somehow his fault that Grandma took the day off. "Now what?"

Failure was not acceptable. He couldn't change what had happened, but by damn he could at least get a tree. "We go get a bargain," he said and backed up the Land Rover.

They returned to town to the corner housing a now sparsely populated lot of live trees, circled with colored lights. The hand-painted sign at one end read UNCLE WALLY'S TREES. It seemed that everyone in the tree business was your long-lost family member.

Uncle Wally was right on hand to greet them as they approached. He looked like the kind of person you invited to your family Christmas dinner because you had to. He had a big belly, barely contained by a plaid flannel shirt and a parka, and was wearing baggy jeans and army boots. On the top of his head he sported a hunter's cap, on the bottom a couple of extra chins.

"Hello there, folks," he sang. "Got some great bargains for you today."

Zach looked around at what was left. Ten-foot giants and spindly messes losing their needles. *Bargains. Right.* "I can see," he said.

"You caught me just in time," said Uncle Wally. He nodded in the direction of a small trailer at the end of the lot. "Me and the missus are just about to have our turkey dinner."

Turkey dinner. Uh-oh. Zach hadn't even thought about dinner. Would the girls want turkey? Or would the sight of a holiday feast only make them wish they were back in their own house? It was a moot question. He knew enough about cooking to know there would be no thawing a turkey in time for dinner today. Heck, things weren't even looking good in the tree department.

"This is nice," said Kendra, drifting over to a small tree.

Natalie hung back but Zach joined her. He took the tree and gave it a shake. A million needles hit the ground. A nice, dry tree—that was what they needed.

"Hey," protested Uncle Wally. "Careful of the merchandise."

"This no longer qualifies as merchandise. It's kindling," Zach retorted. "Come on, girls, these trees are a fire hazard."

"Well, whaddya expect when you wait till the last minute?" Uncle Wally called after them as they trooped out of the lot. "It's Christmas Day, for crying out loud."

"Duh," said Kendra under her breath.

Zach ground his teeth.

She laid a hand on his arm. "It's okay. We don't need a tree."

"Yes, we do," he insisted.

"I think we're sort of out of options," said Kendra.

"No, we're not."

"Okaaaay," she said, humoring him. "So what now?"

"Now we do the manly man thing," he said. "We're going into the woods."

"The woods?" echoed Natalie, sounding anything but thrilled.

He turned and frowned at her. "What?"

She held up a foot shod in a black ballerina slipper. "No boots."

Oh, yeah. That. The girls didn't have a winter wardrobe anymore. The girls didn't have a wardrobe, period. "Well, then, you guys can wait in the car while I get the tree."

"By ourselves?" squeaked Natalie.

"I vote we go back to Uncle Wally," said Kendra.

Zach shook his head. "No. No fire hazard trees."

"Agreed," said Natalie fervently.

"Maybe Grandma will open up for us if we explain about the fire," Kendra suggested.

"That's a good idea," seconded Natalie.

Zach thought going into the woods was a better idea, but it was best to humor the Steps. "Okay. Back to Grandma's."

Over the river and through the woods to Grandma's place they went. And then it was over the fence for Zach and past the CLOSED sign and up the gravel road snugged in by rows and rows of cheery Christmas trees. He rounded a bend in the road and came on a clearing. There, in all its glory, sat a decrepit mobile home with an equally decrepit, rusted truck parked in front of it. An angry bark drew his attention to a pit bull chained to a scraggly fir tree.

This was Grandma's house?

FIFTEEN

A moment later, a thin sixty-something man in jeans and a sweatshirt appeared on the front porch. His hair was gray and thinning, and his chin was covered with gray stubble. A cigarette dangled from his mouth and he held a shotgun by his side. Grandpa.

"Can I help you?" he called in a tone of voice that added, *Off my property*.

Zach wasn't sure which looked more helpful, the pit bull or the shotgun. "I need a tree."

The man's lips turned down. "Are you blind? Didn't you see the sign? We're closed."

"I know, but I'm desperate," Zach called back. "This is for my family. Their house burned down last night and they're staying with me. And I don't have a tree," he added. Not having a tree hadn't bothered him before. Now he found himself embarrassed to have to confess it, even to old Father Christmas here.

The man shook his head in disgust and waved Zach away. "Well, then. Get one."

"How much?" Zach called.

"Just take one and get out of here," the guy said and then turned his back on Zach.

You didn't have to tell Zach twice. He trotted off down the road, the dog wishing him a Merry Christmas and good riddance.

"Can we get one?" asked Natalie when he returned.

"Absolutely."

"They were closed. How'd you do that?" Kendra asked, impressed.

"I've got connections," Zach joked. He went around to the back of the Land Rover and grabbed his ax. "Let's go."

"Uh, Zach, we're not exactly dressed for this, remember?" Kendra informed him.

"The ground's pretty much frozen." Zach stamped the gravel drive with his boot to prove it. "You should be okay for a few minutes. Come on. Help me pick one."

Kendra nodded and got out. Natalie remained in the backseat.

Kendra opened the door. "Come on, Nat."

Natalie shrugged. "You guys go on. I'll wait."

She looked like she was going to cry again.

"Come on, sis," Zach urged. "You're the one with the creative eye. Help us out here."

Natalie didn't smile but she did get out of the car. That was something. He gave her a hug and then led the way through the rows of manicured trees.

Natalie roused herself enough to help with the process but, once inside the car, her lips retreated from smile territory and she clammed up. Kendra and Zach exchanged glances. "It'll be okay," Zach repeated, both to himself and Kendra.

Back home they set up the tree and Zach hauled his ornaments out of the attic. Tom sat on the back of the couch, supervising, his tail switching back and forth as they worked. However, when Queenie made her appearance, the little guy lost all interest in the tree and hopped off the couch to sniff noses and give her sooty fur a lick.

Kendra stepped back to admire their handiwork. "Not bad," she said with an approving smile.

Natalie managed a nod. "How do you think Daddy's doing?" she asked in a small voice.

Probably better than she is, thought Zach. "Let's find out," he said. He opened the coat closet and tossed coats to the girls. "Come on. We'll go sing him some Christmas carols."

Christmas in the hospital wasn't what anyone had planned, but it sure beat sitting around looking at his half-decked tree. And right now the best present he could give Natalie would be to take her to see her dad.

Correction. Their dad.

"I win again," crowed Liz.

Christmas dinner was done, and Merilee and her sisters had been entertaining the younger generation with an old card game the family had been playing for years. Later in the evening would come the more adult games, such as Trivial Pursuit.

Gloria pointed a finger at Liz. "Either you cheated or you're a witch," she accused, making their little nieces giggle. "Nobody wins that much at Black Peter."

"That's for sure," said Merilee, grabbing for the makeup remover to take off the collection of black smudges she had on her nose that represented all the rounds she'd lost.

"She's just good," said Lance, Liz's adoring fiancé.

Gloria rolled her eyes. "Love is blind."

"Let's play Sorry next," said Annabelle, the oldest niece.

"Let's take a break first," said Gloria, taking the makeup remover from Merilee.

A break. That was code for the sisters slipping away to the sunroom with cups of cocoa and talking about their love lives. Her sisters would expect Merilee to have something to share. They'd been trying to worm details out of her ever since the night before, in between singing carols and attending Christmas Eve service. She'd managed to stall them so far but there'd be no more stalling once they settled in with their cocoa.

"I should probably go," she decided. The minute the words were out of her mouth she knew she'd made a tactical error.

Sure enough. Gloria's eyes narrowed. "You never leave this early."

"Got somewhere to go?" asked Liz, waggling her eyebrows.

Gloria grabbed Merilee's arm and hauled her away from the dining room table. "Not until she talks to us, she doesn't."

Five minutes later they had their mugs of cocoa and were in the sunroom with the door closed, cuddled under hand-crocheted afghans on comfy, overstuffed chairs while a winter sun pushed away the clouds and smiled in through the windows.

"Sooo, how's the man shopping going?" Liz asked. "We're all ears," she added, giving the new pink pearl earrings Lance had given her a flick.

Merilee couldn't look either of her sisters in the face. All that money they'd spent on her big makeover had been a complete waste. She gazed into her mug.

"Okay, I'm guessing not good," said Gloria.

Merilee sighed and looked up. "I'm not sure this is going to work for me."

"You have to give it a chance," said Liz. "You just signed up. And you know what they say. You've got to kiss a lot of frogs before you find your prince."

What did "they" say to do when you found your prince but he was a relationship-phobe who came complete with cold feet? Correction, make that frozen feet. "I already met my first frog," she said.

"I think there's a story here," Liz said, grinning and leaning forward. "Spill."

Merilee told them about Chuck and, empathetic sisters that they were, they laughed till they cried.

"You'll find someone," said Gloria, wiping her eyes. "Meanwhile just have fun. I am."

Fun. Was that what you called it? Bah, humbug.

Natalie actually smiled as they all stepped into the hospital elevator. "He's going to be all right." It was half statement, half question.

Mom hugged her. "Of course, he is. He'll be home tomorrow in time for dinner. We'll go out in the morning and get a ham and all the trimmings to go with it."

"And let's make another red velvet cake," suggested Kendra.

"Good idea. That's my favorite," said Zach.

Kendra grinned at him. "I know. That's why I suggested it."

He found himself smiling, too.

Kendra heaved a tired sigh as they made their way across the lobby. "I can hardly wait to hit the mall and get some new clothes. The jacket is great," she told Zach, "but not my size." She held up a floppy arm in which her hand was completely lost.

Both girls were swimming in his jackets. Mom had

refused the offer of a coat and was shivering in her sweater.

Natalie's blue eyes suddenly got saucer big. "How are we going to pay for anything?"

Of course, no purses, no credit cards. No nothing. "You can use my MasterCard," said Zach.

"I'm sure Mr. Gorton at the bank will be able to help us," said Mom. "I think you've already done enough."

"You're family," he said. "Since when is there a limit to how much a guy is supposed to do for his family?" Where had that come from? Someplace new, for sure.

"Thanks, sweetie," she murmured. "I don't know what we'd do without you."

He could feel his throat tightening, but he managed to say, "No problem."

"We've got a surprise for you," Natalie said to Mom once they were on their way home.

"I think I've had enough surprises," she said.

"No, you'll like this one," Natalie assured her.

Back at Zach's they ushered her into the house and Natalie ran over to turn on his crook-necked desk lamp, which they'd set up on the mantle and aimed at the tree. It was the best they could do given that he didn't own a string of lights.

The makeshift spotlight illuminated a rather pitiful tree, consisting of a couple of strings of gold beads and the ornaments from his early childhood. But Mom managed to feign awe and wonder. "It's lovely," she said. She smiled at Zach. "I knew a tree would look perfect in your bay window."

"I want a picture of this one for my Facebook page," teased Kendra. The words were barely out of her mouth when her smile collapsed.

"My pictures, all gone," Mom said, and tears began to leak from her eyes.

That got both the girls crying again, too, and suddenly they were all in a female huddle, sobbing, while Zach stood frozen next to his tacky tree, feeling awkward and useless. WWMD? What would Merilee do? He wished he knew because he suspected whatever she'd do it would be the right thing.

The loss of the family photo albums was the material possession people mourned the most after a fire. It was the one thing that would tempt a woman back inside a burning house. It was also one thing a firefighter couldn't help with.

Except this time. Suddenly he knew exactly how he could help.

SIXTEEN

Ambrose and Zach were back in the treasure room again, this time with Mom.

Why were they here? Not that Ambrose minded. He was just . . . curious. He watched with interest as Zach opened the box he had found when they were last up here.

Obviously, he had discovered something important to Zach. It was important to Mom, too. Ambrose could tell by the way she caught her breath and put a hand to her mouth.

He'd seen that human gesture before. Moms made it when they were moved by something. Zach was moved, too, judging from the way he was looking all pleased with himself. (As if he were the one who had knocked that box open and not Ambrose—humans loved to take credit for things they didn't do.)

Speaking of humans, Ambrose still wasn't sure why all these extra members of the species were in the house. He knew something bad had happened because they had arrived smelling like smoke and crying.

They hadn't arrived alone. They'd brought Aphrodite. She could stay as long as she wanted as far as Ambrose was concerned. They'd made up in the night while the humans slept and Ambrose took that as a sign that his nice, long ninth life was right around the corner.

But meanwhile, what was the significance of that book Zach had given Mom? And how did it affect Ambrose? He crept closer hoping to learn what was going on.

Mom opened the old photo album Zach had handed her and smiled. "Look how cute you were. And David— what an adorable pair!" Her smile faded.

Was she thinking of what could have been? He didn't ask. There was no point.

She turned the page. "And, speaking of cute."

He looked over her shoulder to see a skinny kid sitting at the kitchen table, his dorky smile displaying two missing front teeth. On the table in front of him sat a cake shaped like a robot. That had been a perfect Beaver Cleaver birthday. Dad had still been around. They'd still been a family. What would their lives have been like if Mom and Dad had stayed together?

"You loved that cake," said Mom.

"It was a cool cake."

She turned to a new page and there was the picture of Zach and David and Zach's buddy Henry and Henry's sister Anna, all on the front porch, right along with Aunt Leslie.

Mom quickly turned the page, but Zach reached out and turned it back. "What happened with Aunt Leslie?"

"She moved, honey," Mom said, her voice matter-of-fact.

"Why?"

"Zach, people move."

Zach frowned. *Way to state the obvious.* "You were best friends." And then they weren't. "You two had a fight, I remember. What did you fight about?"

Now Mom's face had turned to stone. "Nothing that concerns you," she said stiffly.

"Well, it concerned me at the time. I lost my best friend. One day we were all buddies and the next thing I knew they were moving." That had been the beginning of the end, when the ground under their feet first shifted and cracked. In a matter of months his perfect world crumbled. Mom stopped smiling. The fuse on her temper grew short. Four months later, Dad moved out.

Wait a minute.

No, don't go there. That thought was way off base. There couldn't be a connection between Aunt Leslie's sudden move and Dad's departure. Zach didn't want there to be a connection, and his brain shied away from the nasty thought.

But his gut couldn't let go. "I'm beginning to think it still concerns me. What really happened?" He didn't want to know. Why was he asking?

Except he needed to know. It probably wasn't what he thought it was anyway. If it was he'd have figured it out long before this.

Or not. Maybe he never wanted to solve the mystery of his father's sudden departure. That would have been too painful. It had been easier to blame Mom.

"Zach, this is ancient history," she said. She slapped the photo album shut and started to rise.

He caught her arm. "It may be ancient history, but it's our history. Mom—" He didn't want to say the words but now he had to. "Did Aunt Leslie and Dad . . ."

His mother bit her lip and dropped her gaze.

"Oh, no." Zach felt suddenly sick.

"Children don't need to know everything that happens between grown-ups," Mom said.

"I thought you left him. All these years you let me blame you, make you the bad guy." Why had she done that?

She managed a small shrug. "In a way it was my fault."

"Your fault!"

"Your father felt terrible afterward. He wanted to try and put it behind us, start again. So did I. I tried, but I just couldn't get past it." Tom crept over to her and she scratched behind his ear. "I didn't see the point in telling you boys. You didn't need to hear bad things about your father from me. Our relationship was ruined but I didn't want to poison yours."

Zach ran a hand through his hair. "All this time . . . Mom, I'm sorry." He was going to cry. He was a grown man and he was going to cry, just like he did after Dad moved out. So many nights he'd buried his face in his pillow and shed angry tears about the unfairness of the whole thing, racking his brain to figure out what he or David could have done to make Dad want to leave.

Mom put her arms around him and kissed his cheek. "It's okay."

"No, it's not," he said, the words coming out in an angry rush. "God, Mom. He cheated on you with your best friend."

"He made a mistake, one he's regretted all his life. We all make mistakes, Zach. I wish we didn't, but we do. Your father and I have both paid dearly for ours."

Zach shook his head. "It was such a shock when he left. We had a good life before. You seemed happy."

"We were. Once."

"It never lasts for anyone," Zach muttered.

"Yes, it does." Now she sounded angry. "Zach, look at me."

He felt like he was eight years old again, about to get a lecture. He had to force himself to meet her gaze.

Her expression turned earnest. "It can and does last. Yes, things went sour between your father and me. But then I found Al and he's been a wonderful husband and we've been happy together. Love isn't always the most stable emotion, but when you find the right person it's the best of life's prizes. You have to take a chance."

"It's a big chance."

She smiled. "Yes, it is, but when it pays off you win big. I took a chance moving back," she added softly. "And I'm so glad I did."

This was all too much to process. His head was going to explode.

"Honey, a person really only has two choices. You can wander through life safe and alone or you can take a risk."

"I think I'll wander."

"Then I'm afraid you'll miss out," she said simply.

A certain sweet face with big green eyes and kissable lips came to mind. He shook his head in an effort to dislodge it but it remained like a psychic burr.

"It's cold up here," he decided. He rose and held out a hand to his mother. "Come on. Let's go downstairs and I'll make a fire."

The rest of the day was filled with good Christmas experiences. The chief stopped by with an envelope full of cash courtesy of the guys at the station so Mom and the Steps could get new clothes. Mom's friends from the old neighborhood tracked her down and came to the front porch caroling and delivering a holiday feast as well as money and presents. One family had put together a basket of DVDs for the Steps.

As Zach stood looking at happy couples and their kids singing "Joy to the World," the little face with the big green eyes whispered, "That could be us."

Wishful thinking, he replied.

"That was awesome," said Natalie after the last batch of visitors left.

"Let's eat this turkey while it's still warm," suggested Mom.

"And watch a movie," added Kendra.

Zach tried not to cringe when she plucked *Mamma Mia* from the basket, in his opinion, one of the dumbest flicks ever made. "I should probably run by the station," he said.

"Oh, no," said Kendra, grabbing him by the shirt. "The chief gave you the day off to spend with your family. That's us, in case you didn't notice."

He was beginning to.

They made themselves at home in the living room with plates loaded with turkey and dressing and cranberry sauce and watched Pierce Brosnan singing "S.O.S." People not knowing what they were doing, falling in and out of love, chasing each other around—what a dumb movie. It was enough to make a guy toss his Christmas cookies.

And then, just when Zach thought the flick couldn't get any dumber, one of the women in it started singing "Take a Chance on Me."

The little green-eyed face at the back of his mind started singing, too. *Take a chance. Take a chance. Come on. You run into burning buildings for a living. Get some guts. Take a chance.*

The little voice kept singing long after the movie was over.

And when Tom managed to knock the Clue game from the window seat and Natalie picked it up saying, "Hey, this might be fun," it started screaming. *TAKE A CHANCE, BOZO!*

Zach jumped off the couch like his pants were on fire. "I've got to go."

SEVENTEEN

Merilee had shed her fancy clothes and changed into her cozy jammies: pink flannel with a candy cane print. She'd turned on her tree lights and served herself some light eggnog along with the small plate of Christmas cookies her mother had sent home with her (comfort food), and now she was snuggled under an afghan (more comfort) with *It's a Wonderful Life* playing on her TV (which should have been comforting). A perfect ending to a perfect day.

Not. She was by herself. She didn't even have a cat now. What was so wonderful about that?

It will be a new year, she told herself. You'll go to school. You'll find the right man on Myotherhalf.com. And you'll move and get a cat. There. The new year was looking better already.

She took a big slug of light eggnog. This stuff sucked. Tomorrow she was going to the store and get some good eggnog. And meanwhile she was going to . . . ? Quit obsessing over Zach!

She opened her laptop. She'd check and see if Myotherhalf.com had sent any new frog princes hopping her way.

George Bailey was begging to live again and Merilee was checking out a new potential other half when someone started pounding on her door. What on earth? She wrapped her afghan around her and padded over to the door and peered through the peephole.

Zach? Was she hallucinating? Under the influence of too much eggnog?

"Merilee, open up."

She looked down in horror at her flannel jammies. Great. Where was her slinky black top when she needed it? She pulled the afghan around her shoulders and opened the door, sure her cheeks were as red as her hair, to find him standing there, filling the doorway.

"Zach," she said stupidly.

He didn't give her time to say anything else. He pulled her to him and kissed her. And what a kiss it was! The only thing that kept her from going up in smoke was her flame-retardant jammies.

Was she dreaming? No. Her eyes were still wide open in shock, and there was that handsome face, up close and personal. Right along with other parts of him. *Ooh.*

But . . . "What are you doing here?" she asked when he finally set her mouth free. And why was she asking? Whatever Christmas spell he was under, did she want to break it?

"I'm taking a chance," he said, and kissed her again.

Those potential princes were immediately forgotten and the afghan fell to the floor.

From the TV, Mary Bailey cried, "It's a miracle!"

And she was right.

EPILOGUE

One year later

This was the life, thought Ambrose as he stretched by the fire. It looked like it was going to be a nice, long one.

He had sure earned it. It hadn't been easy getting Merilee and Zach together, but he'd managed. He still looked back on some of his lives and couldn't make sense of them. One thing he knew for sure, though: this last one had been his most important. He had used it well.

And it had paid off. It was snowing outside, fat flakes laying a freezing carpet on the lawn, but in Zach's living room everything was cozy. Christmas music came from the funny little contraption on Zach's coffee table, and in the bay window, the lights on the Christmas tree twinkled temptingly. However, Ambrose was too smart to get fooled into going anywhere near the thing. He'd had enough tree encounters to last a ninth lifetime. Still, it was pretty to admire from a distance.

His evening stretch finished, he relocated to the couch where Zach and Merilee were snuggled with Zach's computer looking at pictures of brides, making himself at home on Merilee's lap. She had been off to something called veterinary school but she had come back for the holidays, and to welcome her home Zach had given her a diamond ring.

Ambrose knew about that. Cats didn't bother with such fol-de-rol, but humans seemed to need things like rings and ceremonies before they could take mating seriously.

Come summer, there would be a big ceremony and then probably, somewhere down the road, children. *Ugh*. But into every cat's life a little rain must fall.

A new song started and a chorus of humans began to sing, "We wish you a Merry Christmas."

It had been a Merry Christmas, with all of Zach's family over, and lots of women to pet Ambrose. They hadn't brought Aphrodite but that was okay. It meant more attention for him. He and Aphrodite had managed to keep in touch and probably later tonight he'd be slipping out his cat door for a rendezvous. Ah, life was good.

"We wish you a Merry Christmas," crooned the singers, "and a Happy New Year."

A log shifted on the fire and settled with a little whoosh, adding "And a happy ninth life."

Thank you, thought Ambrose, and he closed his eyes and purred.